Illinois Central College
Learning Resources Center

WITH A TANGLED SKEIN

By Piers Anthony
Published by Ballantine Books

THE MAGIC OF XANTH
  A Spell for Chameleon
  The Source of Magic
  Castle Roogna
  Centaur Aisle
  Ogre, Ogre
  Night Mare
  Dragon on a Pedestal
  Crewel Lye: A Caustic Yarn

THE APPRENTICE ADEPT
  Book One: Split Infinity
  Book Two: Blue Adept
  Book Three: Juxtaposition

INCARNATIONS OF IMMORTALITY
  Book One: On a Pale Horse
  Book Two: Bearing an Hourglass
  Book Three: With a Tangled Skein

Book Three

INCARNATIONS
OF IMMORTALITY

With a Tangled Skein

PIERS ANTHONY

A DEL REY BOOK
BALLANTINE BOOKS • NEW YORK

A Del Rey Book
Published by Ballantine Books

Copyright © 1985 by Piers Anthony Jacob

The song "The Wetlands Waltz," is used by permission of the author
Jill Jarboe of Pine Jog Environmental Sciences Center, 6301 Summit
Boulevard, West Palm Beach, Florida 33415.

Library of Congress Cataloging in Publication Data

Anthony, Piers.
  With a tangled skein.

  (Book three of Incarnations of immortality.)
  "A Del Rey book."
  I. Title. II. Series: Anthony, Piers. Incarnations
of immortality; bk. 3.
PS3551.N73W5   1985   13'.54   85-6179
ISBN 0-345-31884-6

Manufactured in the United States of America

First Edition: October 1985

10 9 8 7 6 5 4 3 2 1

CONTENTS

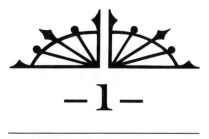

−1−

THE BONNIE BOY

Niobe was the most beautiful young woman of her generation, with hair like buckwheat honey and eyes like the sky on a misty summer morning and a figure that was better imagined than described. But she had her trifling faults, such as an imperious nature fostered by the ability to use her beauty to get her own way, and she was of only average intellect. Also, though she did not know it, she had been marked for a more difficult destiny than she had any right to dream of.

"But, Father!" Niobe protested prettily. "Cedric Kaftan is but sixteen years old, while I am twenty-one! I couldn't possibly marry him!"

Old Sean raised a pacifying hand. "Some rivers are harder to cross than others, and some boats smaller. These are not easy times, my daughter, for Ireland or the world. He belongs to an excellent family, farmers and scholars, and they take care of their own. His age is immaterial."

"Immaterial!" she snorted. "He is but a child! Father, you do me wrong to marry me to one who is so young!"

The man's jaw tightened. He had the power of the patriarch, but he preferred to have harmony. "Daughter, I did not do you wrong. It is true he is young, but he's growing. He will be a match for you when I am dead and gone."

"Let him be a match for some little snippet his own age! I absolutely refuse to put up with this indignity!" Her eyes seemed to brighten with her anger, becoming as intense as the midday welkin.

Sean shook his head ruefully, not immune to the luster of his child. "Niobe, you are the bonniest lass in the county, and nicely talented on the loom, but perhaps the most headstrong, too! Twice you have balked at excellent matches, and I was weak enough to let you. Now you are becoming embarrassingly old for a maiden."

That shook her, but she fought back. "Oh, pooh! A fat old moneybags and an ugly aristocrat! You call those matches?"

"Wealth is not to be sneered at, and neither is aristocracy. You could have had a very easy life, or a very noble one. Such marriages are not easy to come by."

"Why can't I have a handsome, virile man of twenty-five or so?" Niobe demanded. "Why burden me with a child who probably doesn't know his nose from his—"

Her father's glance stopped her before she went too far. She could only balk him to a certain extent, however softly he might speak. "Because the war has drawn away such men, so that none remain here who are worthy of you. I will not give you to a peasant! You will not marry beneath your station. Cedric is qualified and financially comfortable, thanks to an inheritance, and—"

"And he's growing," Niobe finished with disgust. "And *I'm* growing—sick of the very notion! I won't marry such a child, and that's all there is to it."

But that wasn't all there was to it. This time Sean's foot was firm. Niobe raged and pleaded and cried, to no avail. She was very good at crying, for her name meant "tears," but her father was impervious. He was determined that this match be consummated.

And so it was. The banns were duly published, and the wedding was held in early summer, when the groom got out of school. Everything was accomplished according to form, but Niobe hardly noticed; she was too chagrined at being married to such a youth. She wouldn't even look directly at him. As the ceremony concluded, he at least had the wit not to try to kiss her.

Thus they found themselves alone in a cottage, which was his inheritance. It was in a glade near a swamp—pleasant enough by day for those who liked that sort of thing, but sinister by night. That was perhaps part of the idea: a couple was supposed to be bolted inside during darkness, huddled together for warmth and comfort. There were great romantic possibilities; the locale was conducive.

Niobe had no trouble resisting conduction. She wrapped her lovely self up in a voluminous quilt—a wedding gift—and slept on the bed. Young Cedric lay beside the hearth, where there was dwindling radiation from the embers. As the quiet chill of the night intensified, neither stirred.

So they spent their nuptial night, the woman and the boy, in silent isolation. In the morning Cedric got up, stoked the ashes in the fireplace, and went out to relieve himself and fetch more wood. Niobe woke to the sound of an axe splitting billets of wood. It was a good sound, for the morning air was chill indeed; soon there would be physical warmth.

Or would there? She remembered that a fireplace was an ineffective way to heat a house. A good stove put six times as much heat into the surrounding air for the same amount of wood burned. There was a stove here; she would see to it. She might not be a genius, but she was practical when it suited her purpose. For one thing, she needed warm hands to operate her loom properly.

She wrapped her coat about her nightrobe and went out to use the outhouse. There was an old catalog beside the wooden seat, half-used, and a bucket of ashes. It was an efficient system, she reflected, for this was the classic place for reflection; one could read each page of the catalog before using it, or simply stare at the pictures. The mind was edified while the body was cleaned. The ashes were to sprinkle over the refuse, cutting down on the smell, and of course there was a ready supply of them at the house. The refuse was periodically toted to the garden for compost. It was an old-fashioned system, but a good one; nothing, really, was wasted. Still, she would have preferred a modern city toilet.

She emerged in due course, shivering in the cold, but she paused to watch Cedric at work. He was not cold at all; the effort of splitting heated him. She had to admit he was good at it; he set each billet of wood on the chopping block and halved it cleanly with a single blow of the axe, so that the pieces toppled to either side. He was a boy—but a big boy, with a fine ripple of muscle as he swung the axe. His blond hair jumped as the axe struck, and a muscle in his cheek tightened momentarily. A bonnie boy, indeed!

He saw her and paused. "You're cold, Miss Niobe," he said with a rich backwoods accent that, like Niobe's form, is better imagined than rendered. "Here, take my jacket till I get the wood in. I'm too hot anyway."

"Don't call me miss," she protested. "I am, after all, your wife." It grieved her to say it, but it was a truth she could not deny, and honesty required that she not attempt to. A marriage, however ill-conceived, was a marriage.

He paused, half-startled. "Uh, sure, I guess so. But you know, ma'am, it was none o' my notion to get married like this; I'm not even through school."

She might have guessed! "It wasn't my idea either," she said. "At least not—"

"Not to an ignorant kid!" he finished with a rueful grin, "Come on, now, take the jacket before you freeze your toes off, miss—uh, ma'am." He approached her, jacket extended.

"Just a moment," she said, constrained to assert her independence even from this. "You look a lot more comfortable than I am. Give me that axe."

"Oh, that's not no woman's work, ma'am! I'll do it."

"That *isn't* woman's work," she said, annoyed by the double negative.

"That's what I said!" Then he paused, embarrassed. "Oh—you mean the way I said it. I'm sorry. I'm just a backwoods boy, ma'am, and sorry you had to get stuck with—"

"What's done is done, Cedric," she said firmly. She wrested the axe from his grip, knowing he could offer no effective resistance to her because she was an adult. She set up a billet and swung at it—and caught the very edge of it. The blade caromed off and plunged into the ground beside her right foot.

"Uh, ma'am, please—" Cedric said, worried.

"No, I can do it!" she said, hauling the axe up again in a wobbly trajectory.

He jumped to intercept her. "Let me help you, ma'am, no offense."

"You're afraid I'll break the axe!" she accused him.

"No ma'am! I'm afraid you'll chop off a toe, and I'd sure hate to have anything like that happen to a foot as dainty as that."

She relaxed. His diplomacy was effective because it was unschooled. "So would I! I did come close, didn't I? All my incidental studies about trees, and I never split a single blivet of—"

"Billet, ma'am," he said quickly.

She had to laugh. "Of course! I don't use the language as well as I supposed!"

"Oh, no, you talk real fine, ma'am," he said. "Now you take the handle like this, see, and—" He reached around her to put his hands over hers, setting hers properly on the handle. His hands were larger than hers, callused and strong, seeming too big for his body. She wondered whether boys, like puppies, had outsized paws if they were still growing into them. If so, Cedric would in due course be a young giant.

"How is it your hands are so rough, when your family is scholarly?" she asked thoughtlessly.

He snatched his hands away. "Oh, you know, fighting," he said, embarrassed.

Fighting. Well, boys would be boys. "There shouldn't be cause for that here," she informed him gently.

"No, 'course not," he muttered, scuffling his feet.

"You were showing me how to chop," she said, taking pity on him.

He got her grip right and her stance right, then guided her through a swing at the billet. She felt the strength in his arms and body as he moved in contact with her; it was amazing how strong he was for his age. This time the blade came down cleanly, perfectly centered, and cleaved the wood asunder. The halves did not fly apart, as this had not been a fully powered blow, but they offered no further resistance.

Niobe tried the next one alone, following the procedure he had shown her. Her strike was not sufficient to split the billet, but it was remarkably close to the center. It was a victory of sorts. She owed that, perhaps, to her coordination with the loom; she could generally place an object where she wanted to, when not struggling with too much weight.

But now the axe was stuck in the wood. She tried to draw it free, but it wouldn't budge. "Just turn it over, heave it up, and hit it back-side, ma'am," Cedric advised.

She did so, struggling to haul up the heavy billet, and brought the head of the axe down on the block. The wood split itself on the blade and fell apart. "Oh, it worked!" she exclaimed, pleased.

"Sure thing, ma'am," Cedric agreed. "You got a knack for it."

"I *have* a knack—" But she realized that she did not want to be lecturing him about language; it was not the wifely way. "No I don't, either! I'm just a duffer. But it *is* fun!"

She split wood for several minutes, and soon was warm enough to remove her coat. "If I had known how satisfying it is to split wood, I would have done it long ago," she gasped.

"You sure look good doin' it," Cedric said.

"No I don't!" she protested, pleased.

"Yes you do, ma'am. You're one pretty woman."

"And you're one bonnie boy. But I'm getting tired; let's go in and get some breakfast."

"No, I mean it, ma'am. You're the prettiest woman I've ever seen, specially when you move like that."

She looked down at herself. She was glowing from the exertion, breathing hard, and her nightwear was plastered to her bosom. This was not her notion of feminine beauty, but she was flattered all the same. "And I mean it too, Cedric. You're a young Adonis. When you get your growth, you'll be attracting all the girls." Then she paused, flustered, realizing what she had said. Attract girls? He was already married—to her. She felt the flush climbing her face.

He did not reply. He stopped to gather an armful of wood, then carried it into the cabin. But she could tell by the flush on his neck that he felt just as embarrassed as she did. He was young and socially inexperienced, but he was a good young man, meaning well. It was as awkward for him as it was for her.

"Cedric, I—" But what could she say that would not exacerbate the situation? Better to let it drop.

Inside, she explained about the stove. "Sure, ma'am," he said agreeably. "We use a stove in winter." He showed his expertise in getting it going, making sure the ashes were not clogging the air vents, adjusting the damper in the stovepipe, and carefully building a structure of paper, kindling and wood in the firebox. "Got to start a cold stove slow," he explained. "Don't want it to crack." But soon enough it was producing comforting heat, and Niobe was making pancakes on its surface.

"You sure know how to cook, ma'am!" Cedric said as he wolfed down his share. He had a huge appetite, as befitted a growing boy.

"I'm a woman," Niobe said wryly.

"You sure are!" he agreed enthusiastically.

She changed the subject. "I gather that you did not want to—to get married?"

"Pshaw, ma'am, I'm not ready for nothing like that!" he agreed. "I don't know nothing about women. And I wanted to finish school, and get into the track program, so I could maybe make something of myself, you know. But you know how it is when the family decides."

"I know," she agreed. "I suppose it's no secret that I objected to this—I mean, I didn't even know you, Cedric, just your name and age and that you came from a good family. It's nothing personal—"

"It's a good family, all right," he agreed. "And so's yours, which is why—you know." He shrugged. "I just wasn't, well, quite ready."

She found herself liking this honest, unassuming boy. She had an idea. "Look, Cedric—why don't you go to school anyway? We can afford it, and if you really want to get an education—"

His face brightened. "Say, you mean it, ma'am? You'd let me go?"

"I would encourage it, Cedric."

"But you'd be alone here, ma'am, and—"

"I'll be safe enough. There are no dragons in these forests." She smiled.

He paused, as if slightly stunned. Her smile had been known to have that effect on men. Then he frowned. "There is magic, though," he said darkly. "Those trees cast spells—"

"Not against those who understand them," Niobe said. "I have been studying the magic of the wetlands forest. Those trees and plants only want to live and let live. But when you come marching in with an axe—"

He was startled. "Say, I never thought of that! If I was a tree, I wouldn't like it none neither!" Then he paused. "Say—I know I didn't say that right. Ma'am, would you—"

"If I were a tree, I would not like it any, either," Niobe said carefully. "Eliminate the double negative."

"Were, ma'am?"

"That's the subjunctive mood, used to show supposition. I'm not a tree and never could be, but I'm trying to put myself in the tree's place, so I signal this by saying 'If I *were* a tree.' To say 'If I *was* a tree' would be to suggest I might have been a tree in the past, and that would be a misrepresentation."

"It sure would!" He caught himself. "Certainly would. It certainly makes sense the way you tell it, ma'am."

"Cedric, you really don't need to call me 'ma'am,'" she said gently.

"Well, it's a term of respect for an older—" He broke off.

Niobe smiled again. "Now we're even, Cedric. I misspoke myself outside, and perhaps you did the same, now. We are in a difficult situation, but we must make the best of it. In time we shall not notice the five-year difference in our ages; it is little enough, really. Were it reversed—"

"Yeah, the men figure sixteen is prime for a girl," he agreed. "Funny, isn't it!"

"Perhaps it *is* a prime age—if a person is not interested in getting a genuine education."

He turned serious again. "You know, all my family have been smart in—you sure about the school?"

"I am if you are, Cedric."

"I certainly am! I want to get smart."

"Lots of luck," she murmured.

He winked at her, and she realized he had caught the irony. She blushed, suddenly and hard; he was smart enough to know what she thought of him. "I did it again," she said through her burning face. "I owe you one."

"No, you already paid me when you told me the subjunctive, ma'am. Oops!"

She started to laugh, halfway hysterically. He joined her. They both knew it wasn't funny, but it cleared the air somewhat. They finished their breakfast in silence.

The day warmed rapidly. Niobe dressed and finished with the dishes and straightened up the cabin, for she believed in order. Cedric carried more split wood inside so that there would be no problem the following morning. Then it became awkward again, for they had nothing else to do. This was not normally a problem for the newly married, Niobe knew, so no provision had been made.

"I can set up my loom," she said. But it didn't seem appropriate, this first day.

"I can go scout a trail to run on," he said.

That was right; he had mentioned being interested in track. If he returned to school, he would have the opportunity, so training would be in order. But he, too, was doubtful, knowing that this was not what honeymooners were supposed to be doing.

"Let me help you," she said. "We can take a walk through the forest, exploring it. I'm eager to verify the local magic."

He smiled. To take a walk together: *that* was a suitable occupation. "And leave the axe behind," he said.

"So as not to frighten the trees," she agreed.

They walked, and it was beautiful. The foliage had not yet been jaded by the heat of summer, and the bright sunlight kept the mosquitoes at bay. They discovered a path that led down into the swamp, where the bases of the trees became swollen and the green moss climbed high. Now Niobe's expertise in wild magic came into play. She showed him how the huge water oaks of the swamp extended protective spells for the little fish who lived among their roots and helped fertilize them with their droppings, and how the hamadryad, or tree nymph, could be glimpsed if one had the patience to be still and really look for her. "She dies when her tree dies," she explained. "That's why she's so sensitive to the sight of an—" She paused, then spelled it, "A–X–E."

"She's real pretty," he agreed. "Almost as pretty as you. From now on, I'm not cutting no—not cutting any live wood."

Niobe felt a warm wash of pleasure. It was foolish, she knew, but she liked being reminded she was beautiful, and nymphs were the standard against which mortals were measured. Nymphs were eternally youthful and supple—as long as their trees were healthy. A woodlands specialist could diagnose the ills of a tree merely by looking at its nymph.

They went on, getting their feet muddy in the slushy sections of the path. "Maybe we could drain this bog and farm this rich soil," Cedric said.

"Drain the bog!" Niobe repeated, shocked. "But it's vital to the forest! It's a recharge region for water. It stores excess rainfall and sustains the plants when there's a drought. Without the wetlands, the land would lose many of its best trees, and not just those that grow in it. The water table extends everywhere, and the roots find it—but the wetlands keep the level right."

Then, in her enthusiasm for the wetlands, Niobe burst into song:

"I want to waltz in the wetlands,
    The swamps, the marshes and bogs (oh, the bogs).

Yes, I want to waltz in the wetlands
With the birds and the fish and the frogs."

Cedric watched and listened, openmouthed, until her conclusion:

"I want to waltz in the wetlands, a place where nature gets
by
And I . . . will cry . . . will cry when the wetlands are
dry.
Yes I . . . will cry . . . will cry when the wetlands are
dry."

She was so moved herself that the tears were streaming down her face.

Cedric seemed awed. "Niobe, I don't want you to cry! I'll never drain the wetlands. Never!"

She smiled at him, then accepted his handkerchief to wipe away her tears. "It's only a song, Cedric."

"It's only a song," he agreed. "But you—*you're* special."

"Thank you," she said, touched. She knew she was not any great singer. The fit had come on her unexpectedly, and she had half expected him to laugh. Obviously he was impressed, and that was very flattering.

They completed their survey of the region and returned to the cabin. It occurred to her in retrospect that for the first time he had called her by her unadorned name. She wasn't certain how she felt about that, but she had after all made an issue of his calling her "miss" or "ma'am" and certainly he had a right to use her name. He was after all her husband—in name.

"I'm going to study the wetlands!" he declared abruptly.

Ah, the impetuosity of youth! "They are worth studying," she agreed carefully. "But of course you shouldn't restrict your interests."

He just looked at her. She had seen that look in the eyes of the family dog when he had been praised and patted. It was going to take time to adjust completely to this situation.

Nevertheless, they felt more comfortable with each other now. Niobe fixed their meals from the stores in the cabin, and when these were depleted, Cedric hiked into town to buy more and haul them back in his knapsack. He liked to hike; he was a very physical person, with the burgeoning energy of youth. But they also played games together, including a contest of riddles. She quickly discovered that he had a remarkably agile mind and could best her readily at this sort of thing. She fed him the riddle that had stymied her family for years:

it concerned six men trying to cross a river using a boat for two, with certain conditions. He solved it immediately, as if it wasn't even a challenge. He also caught on to the nuances of correct speaking so rapidly that he was soon perfect. She could understand, now, why his family had a scholarly tradition.

Meanwhile, he showed her how to manage the physical things, such as stacking wood for the winter so that it wouldn't rot and emptying the base of the outhouse. But she continued to sleep on the bed, and he on the hearth; there was no physical romance between them.

In two weeks Niobe came to know Cedric very well and continued to be impressed by his superior qualities. He was a strong and smart youth, with an amiable disposition and good potential—but he *was* a youth. He was also her husband. Niobe knew she could not send him away to college without consummating the marriage. But how was she to go about it? She had no experience in this aspect, and no great inclination. Still, it was evident that Cedric was not going to initiate the matter; he treated her with a respect bordering on worship. So it was up to her.

"Cedric," she said one pleasant afternoon.

He met her gaze, then looked away shyly. "Ah, Niobe, and has it come to that now?" At times he seemed almost to read her mind.

"When the honeymoon is over, my mother will ask me, and your father will ask you. For the news."

He sighed. "That they will. But I am not so naïve as to think I could force my attention on a woman who doesn't love me."

He had an excellent grasp of the fundamentals and he expressed them well. "Oh? You have been loved before?"

He shook his head, embarrassed. "Never. I lack experience."

"So do I," she admitted.

"But you are *supposed* to lack it!"

She had to laugh. "Cedric, I am sure that had you been permitted to wait until you could marry at my age, you would have had it. But I hardly condemn you for this particular lack. It means you come to me—pristine."

"I'm only sixteen," he reminded her defensively. "Aye, there's talk among boys, but I'll wager I'm not the only one who never—" He shrugged.

"Of course," she agreed quickly. "A double standard is hypocrisy. It is best that a man and a woman come to—" She hesitated. "To learn together."

"It is hard to—" He, too, hesitated. "If you loved me as I love you, it would be—" He faltered as he saw her react, then blushed.

"What did you say, Cedric?"

"'Twas a slip o' th' tongue," he said, slipping back into his idiom as he reddened further. "I apologize."

"You apologize—for loving your wife?"

"But you know," he said miserably. "It isn't real!"

"The marriage, or your love?"

He scuffed his foot. "Oh, you know. You're such a fine woman, so lovely I get lightheaded just from looking at you, and you know so much, you're so poised, you deserve so much better, and you certainly didn't ask for this. I don't want to make it worse for you. I'm just a kid."

Niobe, her pulse racing, focused on the single thing. "When? When did you know you loved me?"

He shrugged, as if passing it off as something beneath notice. "That first day—when you sang in the swamp. When you cried for the wetlands. I never heard anything so—" He spread his hands, lacking a word.

"But I'm not even a good singer!"

"You *believe!*" he said seriously. "You really *do* love the wetlands—and I do too, now, because of you. What you love, *I* love."

"Cedric, you never said—"

"And make another fool of myself?" he asked with mild bitterness. "And maybe drive you away? Because here's this gangling boy mooning over you? I'm not that stupid."

"Cedric, you aren't stupid at all! You're a fine lad—a fine young man! I'm sure that—"

"Please, can't we just forget it?"

"No, we can't! Cedric, I can't claim I love you—that sort of thing is more gradual with a woman, and—"

"And there has to be a man."

"Cedric!"

He just looked at her, and looked away. She knew there was no way to make him lose sight of the truth: that she didn't see him as a man.

Niobe had generally gotten her way, in life. This time her beauty acted against her. It was, she realized, time that she herself grew up. She would do what had to be done.

"Cedric, we've been over this matter of age before. It's a chimaera. It really doesn't matter. *Love* doesn't matter. We're married."

"Love doesn't matter?"

"I didn't really mean that. Of course it matters! I meant that I'm ready to do what I have to do, without waiting for something that may never—I mean hasn't yet—"

"I understand what you mean," he said gravely.

"I do respect you, Cedric, and I am your wife. There are many women married to men of mature age who don't—who do what is required regardless of their personal feelings. It is time we made our marriage—real."

"No! Not with one who doesn't love me. It just isn't right!"

She agreed with him, but had to argue. "Why isn't it?"

"It would be r—" He stalled on the word.

She flushed. "Rape?"

He nodded.

She felt as if she were in a pit that kept getting deeper the more she tried to scramble out. Where were the euphemisms, the handy oblique references that sugar-coated the unfortunate reality? Cedric wouldn't lie, and neither would she, and on that jagged stone of integrity their marriage was foundering before it began. Where was the way to make it right? They were each trying to do the right thing, and the irony was that they agreed on what the right thing was, yet had to go counter to it. Of course there should be mutual love!

And there was not. She could give him her body and her best wishes, but not her heart. Not yet. She felt the tears starting again.

"Oh, don't do that, please!" he pleaded. "I can't stand to see you sad."

"Cedric, it's not your fault. You're right, you know. You need a woman to love you, and I wish I—" Now the tears overflowed, choking her off.

"Oh, miss—" he started.

"Missus," she corrected him, forcing a smile.

"I'd do anything to make you happy! But I don't know how!"

"Then make me love you!" she flared.

There was a silence as they both realized what she had said.

He shook his head, baffled. "Niobe, how—?"

"The same way any other man does. Court me!"

He looked at her sidelong. "You would sit still for that?"

"Do you think you're some monster, Cedric? If you love me, prove it!"

"And that I will!" he exclaimed. "Come to the water oak where you sang to me, and I will sing to you."

"Yes!" she cried, as if it were a phenomenal breakthrough. And, in a way, it was. The realization that he loved her excited and flattered her; she had never been loved that way before.

They went to the water oak, and she sat on one of its projecting roots, clear of the water, and leaned back against its massive trunk. The hamadryad peered nervously down from the high foliage, wondering what they were up to.

Cedric stood before her, then dropped to one knee and struck a pose. Niobe kept a straight face, determined not to spoil his effort. He took a breath and sang:

"Come live with me and be my love,
And we will all the pleasures prove
That hills and valleys, dales and fields,
And all the craggy mountains yields."

His voice was untrained but strong, and he had good pitch and control, and a great deal of feeling. It was a nice song, with an evocative melody, and she was impressed.

"And we will sit upon the rocks,
Seeing the shepherds feed their flocks."

As he sang, he reached forth to take her hand.

"By shallow rivers, to whose falls
Melodious birds sing madrigals."

At his touch, something happened. Suddenly there was music, as of a mighty orchestra, filling the forest with the power of its sound. His voice seemed to become amplified, magnificent, evocative, compelling, beautiful. She sat stunned, mesmerized by his amazing presence, by the phenomenal music, and she only came out of it when the song ended.

". . . If these delights thy mind may move,
Then live with me, and be my love."

As he stopped singing, the grand music also died away.
"What's that?" Niobe asked, awed, still holding his hand.
He looked concerned. "Is something wrong?"
"That—that *music!* Where did it come from?"
"Oh—that. I thought you knew. It's my magic. It runs in our family, off and on. I'm sorry if I—"
"Sorry!" she exclaimed. "It's absolutely beautiful! How do you do it?"
He shrugged, letting go of her hand. "It just comes when I sing, when I touch. See." He put his hand on the trunk of the tree, and sang:

"Come live with me and be my love."

Niobe heard nothing special—but the tree shuddered as if reverberating to some potent sound, and the dryad almost fell off her branch.

Niobe put her own hand on the bark, and the orchestra returned.

"And we will all the pleasures prove."

"Cedric—it's terrific! It's—an experience!" She was unable to define it further.

"It's just—the way it is." He seemed nonplused by her reaction.

"Sing to me again," she urged him.

"But the song's finished. All that follows is the maiden's response."

Niobe took his hand. "Then sing that, Cedric!"

He sang, and the orchestra was with him, buttressing his voice and elevating it to the transcendence manifested before. It was not mere sound or mere music; it seemed to be more than three dimensions, as if pure emotion had been harnessed into melody. Could love, she asked herself, be more than this?

> "If all the world and love were young,
>   And truth in every shepherd's tongue,
>   These pretty pleasures might me move
>   To live with thee, and be thy love."

These were words of negation, but it didn't matter; the evocative power remained. Niobe realized that anything Cedric sang would have similar effect. She remained entranced until the last verse.

> "But could youth last and love still breed,
>   Had joys no date nor age no need,
>   Then those delights my mind might move
>   To live with thee, and be thy love."

The song finished, and with it the magic. But now Niobe gazed at Cedric with a new appreciation. He did indeed have magic, and love was possible. "Take me home, Cedric," she told him.

By the time they reached the cabin, however, Niobe had had a chance to restabilize. It was, after all, only magic; Cedric was no different than he had been, and their situation had not really changed. It made no sense to do anything she might be sorry for later. So she did not push the matter, and Cedric did not, and their marriage remained unconsummated.

After another week of this, Niobe realized that time was running short. They had been give a full month to themselves; thereafter the relatives would be visiting. Niobe realized this as she was about to sleep.

—14—

"They'll *know*," she said, abruptly sitting up in bed.

"Yeah," Cedric agreed from the hearth.

"Cedric, come over here," she said in peremptory fashion. "We must get this done. We can't face them, otherwise."

He got up and perched on the foot of the bed. He seemed to be afraid of her. "Cedric, it's really not all that complicated," she said. "We've both been told about the birds and the bees and we've seen animals."

"You are no animal!" he said, horrified.

That set her back. This remained awkward. If he had come on like a bull in the mating pen, she would have been appalled, but would have tolerated it; that, her mother had warned her privately, was the way men were. At least the ice, so to speak, would have been broken. She didn't feel quite comfortable with that metaphor, but it seemed to apply. As it was, they were in trouble. "Forget the animals," she said. "Come into bed with me. It's ridiculous sleeping apart like this."

He moved up, and stretched timorously beside her on the bed.

"Not in your clothes!" she exclaimed.

"Oh, ma'am, I couldn't—"

She reached across and took his hand. It was cold and stiff. "Cedric, are you afraid of me?"

"Oh, no, ma'am!" he protested. But he was shivering.

"Of—what we have to do?"

"Terrified," he agreed.

"Cedric, this is ridiculous. You know I like you, and if you sing to me—"

"That's the magic, not me."

And he wanted her to love him, not his magic. He had a point. But she suspected this was mainly an excuse to justify his fear. "Cedric, I know you're no coward. What's really bothering you?"

"I couldn't—just couldn't do that to you, ma'am."

That "ma'am" again! She was trying to bring them closer to each other, but was only succeeding in increasing their separation. "Why not?"

"Because you're so—so beautiful and wonderful and—" He shrugged, unable to express himself properly.

"But Cedric, I'm your wife!"

"Not by your choice!"

This ground was too familiar; she had to get away from it. "But not by yours either, Cedric. We are two people thrown together by circumstance and the will of our families, and they really have tried to do what was best for us, and now we—"

"A woman and a boy," he said.

There it was again. He felt inadequate—and she couldn't argue with this assessment, privately. But she knew she had to change that. "But you're growing," she said.

"I don't think I'll ever be grown enough for you."

"Oh, Cedric, that's not true!" she protested. But she knew she sounded like a mother encouraging a child. This dialogue was going nowhere. Like all the others.

She considered, while he lay in uncomfortable silence. After a bit, she said: "Cedric, maybe we're trying to do things too abruptly. Let's start in stages. Take off your clothes, lie beside me under the quilt, and sleep, tonight. Nothing else."

"You promise?"

She laughed. "I promise, Cedric. What do you think I could do to you?"

He had to laugh too, but it was strained. "What if it gets cold?"

"Then we move together, to share our warmth under the covers. That's the idea, isn't it?"

"But you—you aren't wearing much."

She sat up and unbuttoned her nightie, pleased at her own daring. "I'll wear nothing at all."

He actually rolled over and fell off the bed with an awful thunk. Alarmed, Niobe jumped out, ran around, and bent to help him up. "Oh, Cedric, I'm so sorry! Are you hurt?"

"Please, ma'am—your shirt—" He turned his face away.

She glanced down. In the faint light of the dying fire, she saw that her partially unbuttoned nightie had fallen open, exposing part of her bosom. "For God's sake, Cedric, you can look at me! I'm your *wife!*"

"It's not right," he said, face still averted.

"Cedric, *look at me!*" she ordered. But he would not.

Anger flared in her exposed bosom. She got up and stalked back around the bed and plumped back down. What was she to do with this boy?

Then, through her cooling fury, she became aware of something. She listened.

He was leaning against the bed and sobbing, trying desperately to muffle it so that she would not know.

Her emotion spun about in a full turn. "Oh, Cedric!" she breathed, and started across the bed to comfort him. Then she stopped, realizing that that might be the worst thing she could do. She was no mother, and he no child, and these roles had to be avoided like plague. She had thought originally only of her own chagrin at being married to a boy; now she realized that the problem was far more acute for him. She had to find some way to free them both from these perceptions, so that she would be a woman and he a man.

Tonight was a loss. She would just have to let it grind itself out and try to do better on the morrow.

She did try on the morrow. "Cedric, let's get drunk."

He was taken aback. "I never touch the stuff, ma'am."

"Niobe," she said firmly. "Call me by name."

"Niobe," he agreed reluctantly. "I don't drink, Niobe."

"Neither do I. But there's a bottle of white wine on the shelf."

"I don't know. Some folks get wild when they drink."

"Yes, don't they!"

He smiled. He seemed recovered from his distress of the prior night, and she knew she had been right to leave him alone. Tonight she would get him in that bed!

They opened the bottle after the evening meal. They sat out on the slope of the knoll beyond the cabin and watched the sunset. Each took a small glass of the golden fluid and drank it down. "Oh, it burns!" Niobe gasped.

"Sure does!" Cedric agreed. "Say, that's good stuff!" He refilled his glass, and she refilled hers, but she sipped her second more cautiously than he did. She was not, she found, all that partial to burns, and anyway *she* didn't need to get drunk, just him.

It did not take long for the wine to reach their minds. "Hey, my head feels light!" he exclaimed happily.

"So does mine," she agreed. "Maybe we'd better go slow."

"Slow? Why? This is fun!" He refilled his glass, not noticing that she had not yet finished hers, and downed it at a gulp.

Niobe was getting worried; it was evident that the alcohol was carrying him away, and she wasn't quite sure where it would take him. "Cedric, let's sing!" she suggested, taking his hand so that he couldn't use it to take any more wine, yet.

"Sure, Niobe," he agreed cheerfully. Without preamble, he sang:

"Drink to me only with thine eyes, and I will pledge with mine."

The orchestra manifested, because she was touching him. It added its grandeur to the simple song. Again she was entranced. When she had first heard the magic, she had realized that there was more to Cedric than she had supposed. This time she realized that she had developed a definite fondness for him. She could love this bonnie boy, in due course. It was easy to believe that, as the music encompassed her.

After that he sang a straight drinking song, *Three Jolly Coachmen*, about a trio that was merry for the evening, knowing that they would be sober and therefore less jolly in the morning. They pontificated on the man who drank light ale—

"He falls as the leaves do fall, so early in October!"

And on the one who drank stout ale—a jolly fellow! The background music was becoming somewhat uneven, as his mind was dulled by the wine, as if the players of the orchestra were getting tipsy too. Niobe found that excruciatingly funny.

As it happened, she knew that song, and had a couple of verses to contribute:

"Here's to the girl who steals a kiss, and runs to tell her
     mother.
She does a very foolish thing; she'll never get another!"

Cedric, high as he was, laughed with agreement.

Then she leaned over and kissed him on the mouth. He looked started. He glanced around, leaned forward, and vomited on the ground.

Oh, no! He had had too much, and gotten sick. He was in no particular distress at the moment, but Niobe knew that this evening, too, was finished.

She managed to get him inside, and cleaned up, and onto the bed to sleep it off. This time she slept by the hearth.

In the morning, grim with hangover, Cedric picked up the bottle and stared at the remaining wine. "It looks exactly like urine!" he said savagely, and went to the door and flung it outside. He simply wasn't cut out to be a jolly coachman.

That evening Niobe tried again. She sat him on the bed beside her, took his hand, and asked him to sing again. She sang with him, and the magic surrounded them, and it was very like love. But when it was time to complete the act of love, Cedric could not. The magnitude of the task rendered him impotent. He was chagrined, but she was in her secret heart relieved; she had tried her very best, and failed. It just did not seem to be time.

"But Cedric," she said. "You must sleep without clothing in this bed from now on, and I will too."

He stared at her with dismay. "But—"

"So we can honestly say we slept together," she explained. "Would anyone believe that was all there was to it?"

Slowly he smiled, as relieved as she. He joined her, naked, in the bed. It was a cheap compromise, but it would have to do.

– 2 –

COLLEGE

In the fall Cedric went to the local college. It was not far distant, but inconvenient to commute to by foot, and it would have been complex to arrange for a horse. A magic carpet would have been ideal, but reliable ones were still so expensive that it wasn't expedient for this situation. It was best, all things considered, for him to board—and romantic incompatibility did not even enter the picture.

Niobe sent him off with a kiss and a tear and watched him march away with his knapsack full of clothing. He would buy his books there and pay tuition and board; they had budgeted for it and had a comfortable margin.

She was depressed when he departed and sorry they had not been able to make their marriage work. Cedric was certainly a fine boy with wonderful magic, and she had become quite fond of him. Of course no one knew about the failure of the marriage—or at least the relatives were too discreet to mention any suspicions. With luck, things would work out better after Cedric had matured a year or two in college, and no one would ever know. As a last resort, she could buy a love potion and take it herself; but if Cedric caught on, he would react negatively, and she really didn't want to deceive him anyway. Love was not really the problem.

Meanwhile, she was lonely. She could have gone home to her parents for the term, but knew that, if she did, her mother would worm the truth out of her, and she couldn't stand the mortification.

She made do alone. Running the house was simple enough, and she did a great deal of reading and weaving in the days and cultivated the acquaintance of the dryad of the water oak in the swamp. It was an acceptable existence, for the time being.

She arranged the cabin to suit herself precisely, and it was very comfortable. She worked on the yard, and that was comfortable too. When she had the near portion of the swamp nicely policed, she decided it was time to visit Cedric.

She rented a horseless carriage for the occasion. This was considerably cheaper than a carpet, but slower, and the wheels bumped over the rutted track, jolting her uncomfortably. Nevertheless she arrived after a day, reaching the college in fair order, though her prim traveling dress was dusted with grime.

She spied Cedric walking along a pathway between the dormitory and a classroom building. Only two months had passed, but he did seem to have grown. He was the tallest of the youths there, though he was a freshman, and two college girls flirted outrageously with him as they passed.

Then he spied Niobe and smiled. He had grown more handsome, too! He seemed to be in his element here. But he became diffident and awkward as he approached her. The problem between them still existed.

She visited his dormitory room and met his roommate—a pudgy, scholarly type. Cedric showed her his work so far: projects relating to wetlands reclamation and natural magic. It was evident that he took it seriously and was learning a great deal. She was sure he was a joy to his professors.

First she had a little chore to do. "Give me your cap," she said.

"My cap?" he asked blankly.

"Your college cap—the one you wear to show you're a student. I believe you'll find it on your head."

Perplexed, he removed it and handed it to her. She brought out her needle and thread and sewed a bright band of silk around it. "That's to show the college girls that you're married," she said firmly, returning it to him.

"Oh. Sure. Of course." He seemed nonplused.

She kissed him chastely, then returned to her carriage. She found herself both reassured and disquieted as she rode home, and it took time to ferret out the sources of her feelings. But at length she realized that she was pleased to see Cedric properly established in college and doing well, pleasantly surprised to see him so tall and handsome and confident, and jealous of the attention he received from the girls of his own age. A married man, after all, had no business attracting such interest. So she had done what was necessary, but still was bothered. After all, what had she done with him all summer, when she had had him all to herself? There was the nagging suspicion of failure on her part; or, if not exactly that, of imperfection. Would they have succeeded in consummating the marriage if she had been more alert to the problem? If she had been sensitive to his side of it? If she had refrained from correcting his errors, from being the perfect lady, and just concentrated on being a person he could relate to as he could to a college girl? Naturally he had been diffident!

Having resolved the mixture of her emotions and gotten them suitably shelved in her mind, she resumed her ordinary life and produced some truly fine tapestries depicting forest and wetlands scenes. One showed the water oak in the swamp, with the hamadryad perched on its lowest branch, posing. It had taken time and patience to befriend the nymph enough to get her to do this, and Niobe knew that not many human people could have accomplished this at all; she was quite pleased. If only she could have done that with Cedric!

Near the end of the semester she visited Cedric again. He had been dutifully sending her letters about his life and progress at the college, and his writing showed increasing perception and literacy. He was gaining mentally and socially as well as physically; the college experience was indeed good for him. He was majoring in Wetlands Magic and already was learning things they hadn't taught in Niobe's day. He knew how to test trees for their specific forms of magic and all about the ecological cycle. Next term he would take a course in Wetlands Fauna and their relationship to the vegetation. He was excited by the enormous store of information available and determined to master it all. But Niobe wanted to see for herself, just to be sure he wasn't exaggerating. The impetuous young were prone to exaggeration, after all.

Cedric was taller yet and marvelously handsome in the sunlight, and his ready smile charmed her. He had one class to attend before he could give her his full attention. "I'm sorry," he apologized, but his grin was one of accommodation rather than chagrin. "I must attend; I have a report to give. Then I'll be with you. But my Water Magic Prof wants to talk to you anyway, so you won't be bored."

How his confidence had grown! Niobe was almost dismayed to see that her husband was prospering just as well without her as she was without him. But she went to see the Prof, who was expecting her.

The Prof was typical of his breed: aging, stooped, with a shock of white hair and a deeply serrated face from which the eyes fairly gleamed with intelligence. "Ah, Mrs. Kaftan!" he exclaimed. "I recognize you at once by your extraordinary beauty!"

"Oh, come on!" she demurred, foolishly flattered.

"No, indeed!" he persisted loudly. All teachers had voices that carried to the farthest recesses of the mind. "I asked Cedric how I would know you, and he said when I saw the loveliest mortal woman of this world, that would be Niobe. Lo, it is so! He is much in awe of you, and it is not difficult to perceive the reason. You are indeed outstanding!"

"Enough, Professor! I'm an old married woman! Why did you wish to talk with me? Is something wrong with Cedric's program?"

"Quite the opposite, my dear!" he protested enthusiastically. "Cedric is the most brilliant and conscientious student I have had in a decade. His work is outstanding for a student! Do you know, Mrs. Kaftan, a mind like his is seldom brought to these, if you will pardon the pun, backwaters of scholarship like Wetlands Ecology. I wanted to compliment you on the good work you have done for our discipline by motivating him to enter it. I know that when he matures he will carry our research forward to new heights, as it were."

Niobe was taken aback. Evidently the Prof was a creature of superlatives! "I only showed him the local—I do have some interest in—"

"Indeed you do, Mrs. Kaftan!" he agreed. "He tells me that he owes it all to you. He says you took an ignorant hick and showed him the wetlands in a way he had never seen, and it changed his life. Mrs. Kaftan, you are a wonderful woman, and I salute you!"

She found herself halfway overwhelmed by the Prof's enthusiasm. He was not bad at motivation himself! "Then Cedric is—doing well?" It sounded inane, but she couldn't think of an adequate remark at the moment.

"Straight A's," he agreed. "And we do not issue those lightly! But that does not begin to suggest his potential. Do you know, Mrs. Kaftan, if I may be so candid, at first I wondered why a woman as lovely as you have been confirmed to be would marry such a youngster, as obviously you could pick and choose among the best the War has left us, but as I came to know him, I understood that you *had* picked the best. There is only one like him in each generation. You will never regret that decision, I am sure!"

"Uh, yes," Niobe agreed faintly.

"Cedric worships the ground you tread, and I am not certain I mean that figuratively. If you had sent him to business school, he would have become in due course a tycoon. What a loss that would have been for science and magic! You turned him instead to the wetlands—" He shook his head, then impulsively reached out to take her hand, lift it to his lips, and kiss it. "My most abiding gratitude, Mrs. Kaftan. If there is ever any favor you require of me, do not hesitate to ask."

She found herself back outside in the sun, dazed. No wonder Cedric was doing well; the Prof was an amazing catalyst. Probably he treated everyone like that, turning each student on. Still, he had had no need to call Cedric brilliant unless it was true. She had known Cedric was smart; apparently she had underestimated him. The college environment had evidently brought out the best in him.

Cedric finished his class and rejoined her. He was still a tousle-headed youngster under his banded cap, but now she fancied she could see the smartness in him, radiating out from his head. She remembered the magic of his music. Yes, there was definitely more to him than youth!

But again, in her private presence, he became shy and awkward. "I—it's great to see you, Niobe," he said. "What do you want to do?"

"Well, I will need to check your wardrobe," she said. "I'm sure your clothing is wearing out and will need attention." Which was not at all what she wanted to say and, indeed, fell comfortably into the major category of Things Never to Be Said, because she was being motherly. But she couldn't even conceive of, let alone formulate, what she might have intended to say. The Prof's remarks had colored her perspective, and she had not yet completed her readjustment. She liked to keep things orderly, like threads in a tapestry, and hated it when a thread broke. But mending a thread was a special process, requiring time and consideration.

"Uh, sure," he agreed somewhat lamely. "You always take good care of me."

Damn it! she thought furiously. She had definitely done it again, putting him in the junior role. How could he ever become a true husband this way?

So she wended her way home, bearing a burden of tangled feelings greater than before. She might be an expert weaver of ornamental tapestries, but she was plainly inadequate in marriage. She had expected to marry a more experienced man and just wasn't competent to educate a younger one in the necessary way. If only there were a college course in—

She halted that thought in place. No, she certainly didn't want Cedric taking that kind of course! Not with those colleens! Marriage was a private thing.

The winter passed somewhat bleakly, and when the ice melted from the surface of the swamp, she proceeded again to the college. This time the students were out in force, enjoying the first genuinely nice day in some time. Some of the more voluptuous girls were in very brief outfits for sunning, and the youths were in shorts. Niobe, conscious of the flattery of the Prof last time, and not wishing to be taken for a college girl, had garbed herself this time in very conservative fashion. She wore an old-fashioned long skirt her mother had outgrown, and a figure-de-emphasizing jacket. Her hair was severely bound back in a bun, she wore no makeup, and she had button-down boots. She felt quite dowdy.

She checked Cedric's room, but he was not there, and she wasn't sure what class he might be in at the moment. So she sat on a bench near the dormitory and waited for his return, taking advantage of the time to do some knitting. She was good at that too; in fact she was adept at any type of yarn manipulation. It really was pleasant enough here, and of course she had arrived early; he wouldn't be expecting her for perhaps another hour.

Several college youths came walking along the path. They had evidently been drinking; in fact one still carried a bottle of red wine, half-finished. Niobe's nose wrinkled; she detested wine of every type, ever since the disaster during the courtship. She was surprised and not pleased that its use was permitted on the campus. Was Cedric being subjected to bad influences?

One of the youths paused as they passed her bench. "Say, who's the old lady?" he demanded half-facetiously, staring at Niobe. She knew she looked older than the college girls, as was her intent, but he was exaggerating. He was the one with the bottle, showing signals of intoxication; as he paused, he lifted the bottle and took another swig. A driblet of pale red fluid ran down the side of his chin; then he lowered the bottle and burped.

"Somebody's mother," another youth joked. Oh, that stung, for a private reason she would never let them know.

"Hey, whose mother are you?" the first demanded.

"No one's," Niobe replied primly. "I am Cedric's wife."

"His wife!" the youth exclaimed. "He never let on he was robbing the retirement home! He always claimed his woman was beautiful!" And all four of them laughed coarsely.

Niobe tried to ignore their gibes, hoping they would go away, but the wine gave them persistent insolence. They closed about her, their wine-soaked breaths fouling the air. "Please go away," she said at last.

"But we just got here!" the bottle-holder said. "And it's our dorm! Come on, old lady, you gonna show us a good time?" He reached for her jacket and grabbed the lapel, yanking the front open so that a button popped off. "I'll bet you got some good stuff hidden away in there!"

Niobe jerked away and slapped his hand.

"Hey!" he exclaimed as the others laughed. Then his mouth turned mean. "Hit *me*, will you? Well, how do you like *this*?" And he poured the red wine on her head.

Niobe gave a cry of surprise and dismay and jumped up, trying to get away from the stream. But he caught her arm. "Beautiful woman, hell!" he said breathily. "You're just a damned slut!"

She kicked him in the shin and spun away, knowing it was not possible to reason with drunkenness. But one of the other youths caught her about the shoulders from behind and heaved her off the ground. A third grabbed her legs. "Come on, let's see what she's made of!" he cried. "Pull her skirt off!"

Niobe struggled valiantly, drawing up her legs and then shoving, but the youths were too strong for her. They held her at shoulders and feet, and the bottle-wielder dropped the spent container and groped for her skirt, hauling it down over her legs so that her undergarments were exposed. "Say, she's not so old!" he said, pausing to squeeze her left thigh.

Niobe screamed, but it did no good. The youth jerked her skirt down to her ankles, and the one holding her feet let go of one so that the wadded skirt could pass around it. She tried to kick him, but he caught her ankle again and pushed it away, forcing her legs to spread. "Look at those legs!" he exclaimed.

"Get her down on the ground," the bottle-youth directed. "Hold her still, and we'll take turns." He licked his lips and loosened his belt.

"Turns at what?" a new voice demanded.

Niobe recognized it. "Cedric!" she cried.

Indeed it was he, standing tall and dynamic as he flung away his jacket. "That is my wife," he said, and it was as if a cloud crossed his face, turning his normally sunny expression pale and grim.

No pretense was possible, at this stage. "Get him!" the bottle-youth cried.

They dropped Niobe and turned as one to face Cedric. They closed on him from four sides, not so drunk as to give him any fair chance singly.

"No!" she cried, knowing that Cedric could not possibly prevail against four. She tried to get up, but her feet got tangled in her skirt and she had to pause to get it on again. As she did, she watched with dread while the four attacked her husband.

Two took hold of Cedric's arms while a third drew back his fist and struck Cedric in the stomach. Niobe winced—but Cedric just grinned. "God, he's like a damn rock!" the youth exclaimed, amazed.

"Now you have had the first blow," Cedric said. "I'll have the last."

Suddenly Cedric brought his arms together in front of him, hauling the two in from the sides as if they were puppets. They stumbled along, colliding with each other. Then he flung his arms out again, and they fell away on either side. Cedric was free.

He stepped forward, his two fists swinging like sledgehammers. One connected to the gut of the youth who had struck him, and *his* stomach was more like mush than rock. He folded forward, the wind gushing out of him—just as Cedric's other fist slammed into the side of his head. The youth's hair flew wide and he staggered and fell, semiconscious.

Cedric whirled and struck the bottle-youth on the chest. The air whooshed out of him, too, and he sank to his knees. But the remaining two had regained their feet and were charging in again.

Cedric ducked down, caught one of them by arm and leg, lifted him on his shoulders, and hurled him into the other.

As suddenly as it had begun, the fight was over. Cedric stood, his chest heaving, the muscles of his upper arms bulging; the four youths were spread in various ignominious attitudes about the lawn. Niobe was virtually spellbound, looking at him. Suddenly he seemed twice the size he had been before.

Then he stepped across to help her up. "You all right, Niobe? I heard your scream and I got out of that class—"

"Cedric—you never told me you could fight like that!"

He shrugged. "You told me I'd be through with that."

Now she remembered. He had liked to fight. She had presumed it to be mere mischief. She looked around at the four. Some mischief! "Perhaps I spoke prematurely. Just what kind of fighting did you do?"

"Well, I was bare-knucks champ of my district, junior division. But you were right; I had to put aside childish things when I got married."

"Childish things!" she echoed, shaking her head. In her spot memory she saw him again, shrugging off a solid blow to the stomach; saw the two youths almost jerked off their feet as he drew his arms together, then flung like rag dolls to the ground. Now she felt the amazing power of those arms, as he held her steady. She should have gotten the hint when he had shown her how to split wood, for his strength had been there then. "And I called you a bonnie boy!"

Now a crowd was gathering, and the Prof she had talked to before appeared. "What happened here?"

The bottle-youth struggled to his feet. "He set upon us!" he cried, pointing at Cedric. "For no reason!"

Niobe's mouth dropped open at the audacity of this lie. But she realized that there had been no witnesses to the initial part of this incident—just her and the four youths. The word of four against the word of one.

"Shall we see?" the Prof inquired, as if unconcerned. He spied the bottle and picked it up, frowning. "Good—a drop remains. We shall invoke the water magic."

He brought out a little dish containing a film of mold, set it carefully on the ground, and upended the bottle over it. A driblet of wine descended into the dish.

There was a pause. Then a reddish glow developed at the dish. It expanded rapidly, and there were roils of vapor in it, as the wine was vaporized in the magic pattern stimulated by the potent mold. An enchantment of water, certainly; Niobe was fascinated. She had known of such magic, but had never before actually observed it.

"Move back, give room," the Prof warned. "We do not want to interfere with the re-creation."

They all moved back, even the youths, who seemed to be completely intimidated by the Prof's presence. The vapor diffused into the entire area, and stabilized, lending a reddish cast to the air. Then it swirled and coalesced into a ghostly image: a woman seated on the bench. "This is a ten-minute spell," the Prof explained. "It should be enough."

"But I don't think the wine was here yet," Cedric said. "It had to have come with *them*."

"That is why the picture is fuzzy," the Prof agreed. "You did not suppose my magic was vague, did you, lad? The wine was distant, but the magic is here; it is re-creating a still scene until further definition is possible."

Several minutes passed. No one moved. All were absorbed by the promise of the water magic.

Then, abruptly, the image brightened. The woman became Niobe, in color, though tinged with the red of the wine's eye. The four youths barged into the scene, ghostly yet clear. The early stages of the molestation were reenacted. Niobe felt Cedric wince as the wine was poured over her figure's head; he had the same bad associations that she did.

"So this is your 'no reason,'" the Prof murmured, glancing at the youths.

At the height of the struggle, Cedric entered the picture. Now, seeing him more objectively, Niobe was even more impressed with his demeanor. He had indeed been growing; he seemed inches taller than he had been the day of his marriage, and was now a young giant of a man. He was so handsome in his righteous anger that a nimbus seemed to surround him. Or was that the wine-haze?

Niobe saw now that Cedric had actually invited them to grab his arms, and had deliberately accepted the first blow. She saw the youth who had struck him pull back, shaking his right hand as if it had been hurt. Then Cedric started to fight, and in moments it was over. Bareknucks champ? Surely so!

The scene ended and the vapor dissipated into invisibility. But the evidence was in. "Clean out your rooms," the Prof directed the youths. "You will be discharged from this institution with prejudice; your illicit wine has condemned you." They scrambled up and sheepishly departed.

The Prof turned to Cedric. "You were intelligent to provide them the initiation of the combat; now there will be no question of abuse of your power. You were aware that folk of your prowess are enjoined from abusing it?"

Cedric nodded soberly. "I knew I had cause, but if I killed anyone—"

"You had cause, and you did not kill anyone," the Prof agreed. "I commend you on your discretion. Now take your wife to the guest house; she is in need of cleaning and comfort."

Indeed, now that the threat was over, Niobe was suffering a reaction. She had almost been raped—and Cedric had been set upon by four men! Never before in her life had she been exposed to violence like this. She put her face in her hands, and discovered it wet with tears, reddened by wine. She tried to wipe them away, but they just got worse, and soon she was openly sobbing.

Cedric picked her up and carried her to the guest house. She felt his arms like flexible steel, and his chest and stomach like iron; he was seventeen now, coming into the flush of his physical potential. Growing . . .

She had locked in the image of a boy, and never observed the emerging man.

He set her carefully down on the bed of the guest house. "I will fetch the nurse," he said, concerned. "You are hurt."

But she clung to him. "Cedric, I need you!" she cried. "I love you!"

He paused. "You're upset, Niobe, with reason. A bath and some rest—"

She drew him down, desperately. "I've been such a fool, and I reek of wine! Forgive me, Cedric!"

"There is nothing to forgive," he said gently. But he allowed himself to be brought down to her until he was lying beside her on the bed. "You have always been perfect, Niobe," he added, murmuring into her ear.

She rolled onto him, hugging him close. Her tear-wet lips found his and she kissed him with a passion that astonished her. Her breast was suffused with reaction and emotion; she could not get enough of him. He responded, as he had to, to the fire of her desire, kissing her in return.

Suddenly she laughed. Startled, he lifted his head to look at her questioningly.

She sat up, reached for his shirt, and unbuttoned it. "There!" she said, smiling. "I have had the first blow."

Slowly he smiled. "But this is no fight."

"Isn't it? We have been trying to do this for most of a year, and have always been defeated by our own reticence. Cedric, you have fought for me, most valiantly and effectively, and now you have won me. Take your spoils!"

"Spoils!" he muttered wryly. "You are the woman I love."

"And you are the man I love!" she replied gladly. "I want to be yours—completely."

He kissed her. Then he undressed her. Her blouse was sticky with drying wine, and her hair was matted with it, but she knew better than to pause for even a minute to clean up. Now was the time to strike!

Now Cedric looked at her body. She smiled and reached up to him. She knew that her reaction was no more important than his and that their physical interaction was only a portion of their emotional one. For the first time she truly desired him, and for the first time he believed he deserved her.

Still, he was inexperienced, as was she. She helped him as much as she could without seeming aggressive and, when he hesitated, she held him and kissed him passionately; when he sought to come into her and found the way obscure and paused in confusion, she thrust herself at him and abated the obscurity herself. It hurt—but with the pain came an unutterable pleasure and a closeness she had never before known. "Cedric . . . Cedric . . ." she whispered, and gently bit his bare shoulder.

Yet simultaneously she found herself in the bog, by the water oak, seeing it from three sides. From one side she viewed it with the freshness of youth and innocence, as if seeing it for the very first time. From another side she viewed it with the cynical eye of experience, understanding its nature and appreciating it for what it was. From the third side she viewed it with the significance of age. She had an endless memory of it in all its seasons, spun out into an eternal thread and wound about her distaff, the small staff on which her yarn was wound for spinning. She was aware of its entire history. Yet the three views were one, faceted, neither merged nor separated; all three views comprised the impression of the whole, like colors or contrasts. She *understood* that tree!

Somehow, too, there was a fourth view, but shrouded, and she knew that it was one she never wanted to see, for it was completely horrible. Yet it, too, was part of the whole, the painful aspect of a generally positive reality.

Then the moment of ultimate rapture passed, fading into a more general but pleasant awareness. She remained locked in Cedric's embrace as the great tide ebbed. Impulsively, she kissed him again.

"Now I am possessed," she whispered. The word had a triple or quadruple layer of meaning, relating to property, sexual expression, and diabolical awareness. Her vision of the water oak seemed to have fragmented her consciousness, so that what had seemed simple now seemed marvelously complex.

In due course Cedric, fulfilled, fell asleep. Now Niobe became aware of her discomfort. She got up, carefully cleaned herself, washed her hair, and applied some healing salve. She did not want Cedric to think he had hurt her, though it was a pain that changed her life. Then she checked the bed and spied the stain of blood on the sheet; how was she to conceal that? Certainly she did not want that going through the college laundry, betraying to the staff not only what they had been up to, but that it had been the first time. So she fetched a sponge, dampened it, and worked on the stain until it had faded to the point of unidentifiability. Now, at last, she could relax.

She lay down—and Cedric stirred. She took his hand, kissed it, and murmured a soothing word to him, and he drifted off again. She was relieved; she loved him, but right now she wanted to sleep.

In the morning she returned home, leaving Cedric to his studies and his phenomenal new memories. But she did not allow much time to elapse before she visited him again. It was not that she had suddenly become a sexual creature—she had been advised by her mother that no woman could match the appetite of any man in this respect— but that she missed him and wanted to be with him as much as possible. Her tidy house no longer satisfied her. She wanted it to be animated again by Cedric's presence. She was indeed in love.

They made love again in the guest house, and this time it was easier because they were slightly experienced. Also, as she thought wryly, she was broken in. Again she responded almost as rapidly and emphatically as he, despite her mother's cautions, for love propelled her. Again, at the climactic moment, she had a vision.

This time, as she stood before the water oak, she saw a spider climbing an invisible strand. *I can do that*, she thought. She reached up and caught hold of her own invisible strand and climbed it, for she had four hands and four feet. In fact she was a spider, the ultimate spinner and weaver. What a web she would make! But then the ecstasy abated, and she was human again, relaxing in the embrace of her beloved.

She thought to ask him whether he, too, had visions in that moment, but she desisted, fearing that it would seem that she was bored with lovemaking. She wasn't; in fact it seemed more likely that her visions represented a transcendent overflow of pleasure. When a system was stimulated beyond its rated capacity, it could short out or blow off; could this be why the images were so far removed from the present experience?

She had no decent answer—but she would be glad to explore the matter further. She liked making love to Cedric, and she liked the visions, even if the thematic connection between the two was tenuous. "Oh, Cedric!" she exclaimed, hugging him again. "I'm so glad we found each other at last!"

"You're still the perfect woman," he said, and fell asleep.

"You foolish man," she murmured fondly, and nibbled on his ear.

Cedric completed his first year of college with outstanding grades and came home for the summer. He now knew more than Niobe did about the wetlands, and she was fascinated by the lore he had acquired. He would squat by a stagnant pool and scoop out a handful of glop and show her how the algae in it emitted little spells of nausea to discourage such interference. It was true; when she came close to the handful, she felt like retching, but when she stepped back she felt all right. Of course the smell might account for it—but it didn't help to hold her nose, so she was satisfied that it was, as he said, magic. He was able to identify the exact species of water oak near their cabin, and the variety of hamadryad too. He knew where the timid forest deer hid and what their preferred forage was. "I owe it all to you, Niobe," he said generously. "You showed me the wetlands!"

"I'll cry, I'll cry when the wetlands are dry," she agreed, smiling. How little had she realized what her innocent song would start!

And of course they made love again, for the first time at home, erasing their prior failures here. Once more she launched into vision—but this time it was sinister. She saw the face of a saturnine man—and that man's mouth curled into a sneer, and he winked at her. She screamed and snapped from the vision to find Cedric frozen in midmotion, horrified that he had somehow hurt her.

"No, no," she reassured him immediately. "It wasn't you! I had a bad dream."

"You were asleep?" he asked incredulously.

Then she had to tell him of the visions, for the misunderstanding would be worse than the reality. He admitted that he did not have such visions, but had heard of those who did. "Mostly women," he concluded.

"Oh? How do you know about women?" she asked archly.

"My text in human biology," he said. "It's one of the freshman required courses."

So she was, after all, typical. "But the awful face—why would I see that, when I'm having such joy of you?"

He shrugged. "Maybe we should stop those visions."

"Oh, Cedric, I don't want to stop—"

—31—

"I said visions, not love!" he said, laughing. He was no longer shy about sex; once he had gotten into it, he liked it. "I'll try to sing to you, next time."

The notion appealed to her. The rapture of his magic superimposed on that of the loveplay—the ultimate experience!

They tried it, and it worked. He did not even have to sing aloud; if he ran the song through in his mind, the orchestra played for her, and no visions came, no matter how transported she was by the experience.

So it went through the summer. In the fall it was time for college again, and she packed him off with genuine regret. But he had a real future, once he completed his education, and she refused to deny him that. She would suffer through the separation and visit him often.

But it was harder on her than she had anticipated. She felt chronically out of sorts, and sometimes ill. Then she got nauseous in the mornings. What was wrong with her?

Suddenly she realized: she wasn't ill—she was with child.

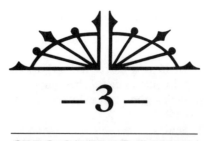

– 3 –

SHOOTING DEER

She had to tell him, of course. She did so on the next visit. Cedric was amazed at what he had wrought, and pleased. "I'll be a father!" he exclaimed, as if this were a completely unique experience.

"Well, it isn't as if you didn't try for it," she reminded him.

"I guess that will have to stop now," he said regretfully.

"No, not yet. Just—carefully."

They were careful. The winter passed, and the baby expanded within her. When Niobe reached the eighth month, her mother came to stay with her and midwife the birth if it occurred early, for there was no convenient hospital. Cedric was ready to quit college and come home, but Niobe made him remain to complete his courses; he had gone too far to throw it away now. So it was that, before he turned eighteen and just before he made it home for the summer, Cedric became the father of a healthy son.

He was pleased—but he knew there was a price. Niobe had been able to make do alone, but she would no longer be able to do that. Cedric had to retire from college and become a full-time family man. He was ready—but she knew he also regretted it. It had been clear that if he had continued his program at the college, he could have become a professional, perhaps even a professor in due course. He could still be one—but now there would be a delay, and by the time he could return, years hence, the situation could have changed. So it was a calculated risk for Cedric's career. Almost, she wished she had not conceived so quickly.

"It doesn't matter," Cedric said. "A man's got to do what he's got to do in the time he has, and I want to be with you."

"That's sweet," she said, and rewarded him with a kiss. Still, she felt guilty.

"Prof told me that if he'd had a wife who looked like you, she would have had a baby just as fast," he added.

"Still, you have such a good career awaiting you; you must return to it as soon as possible."

"We'll see," he said.

But when she thought of the baby, her mood swung the other way. Junior was an absolute joy! She knew from the first hour that he would be a genius like his father—and *he* would have proper schooling from the outset. Oh, she had such dreams for Junior!

Cedric took care of things, pretty well running the household until she was back on her feet. Then, as time opened up, he began spending time in the swamp. He was making a chart of the local ecology—the trees, the smaller vegetation, the animals, the insects, the algae, the waterflows, and the observable interactions between them.

Hunters roamed the forest, in and out of hunting season, poaching game. Cedric came across the remains and grew angry. "If the deer shot back, the hunters would be less bold!" he exclaimed. Then he paused in realization. "Maybe I can arrange for the deer to shoot back!"

Niobe laughed—but he was serious. He was a wetlands major, not a magic major, but he got a tome of spells and searched through it, trying to find one that could be adapted to his purpose. If magic could bounce an arrow or a bullet back on its origin, so that the hunter in effect shot himself—

But magic was no subject for amateurs, any more than science was. It required years of study to master the basic precepts and stern discipline; even then it had its special hazards. Cedric was smart, but more than intelligence was needed. "I just don't have the *time!*" he exclaimed, frustrated.

"You're welcome to take all the time you want, dear," Niobe said. She was nursing Junior and hated to see Cedric upset. When he was annoyed, she tended to echo the feeling involuntarily, and it seemed to change the milk and make Junior colicky, and if there was one thing worse than an upset husband, it was a colicky baby.

Cedric paused as if weighing something momentous. "Of course," he agreed, and went outside. Had she somehow offended him? Her husband seemed more nervous, irritable, and generally tense than he had been. Maybe she should try to hire a maid for the chores so that Cedric could, after all, return to college. She knew what a sacrifice he was making and she wanted to set things right. Their love was so wonderful that she hated to have any strains put on it.

But when she broached the matter, later in the day, Cedric would have none of it. "I'm through with college!" he declared. "My destiny is here."

"But the Prof said you have such potential! I think he wants you to become a—"

He put his big hand on hers. She felt a stirring of the music in him, but this time it was a strange, discordant, disturbing sound. "It would not be worth the cost," he said. "Prof understands."

She experienced a kind of dread, but could not fathom its cause. The flickering image of a demonic face came to her, and one of the water oak, three of whose views were positive, the fourth an unglimpsed horror. What cost? Separation from her? Yet Cedric had endured that before and prospered. Why had he changed his mind?

"Cedric—is something wrong?"

"Of course not," he said quickly.

She didn't believe him, but realized that he would not tell her the truth. That disturbed her further, and she had to stop nursing Junior. She was sure it wasn't any fault in Cedric's love for her; that was unfailing. He was a father now, a proven man, yet sometimes even now she would be working at the loom, and would look up to discover him watching her with a touching expression of adoration. No, he loved her and wanted to be with her. Still—

She laid Junior in the crib. "Cedric, we could move closer to the college so you could commute—"

He took her in his arms and kissed her. "This is our home. I love you—and the wetlands. My life is here."

So it seemed. She did not try to argue further, and indeed their life together was good. They resumed making love as she recovered from childbearing, and Cedric was enormously gentle and he sang to her, and in those moments it seemed that nothing else mattered.

As Niobe grew stronger, she started taking Junior for walks outdoors, for fresh air was good for babies. He seemed to like the wetlands, especially the huge water oak. Niobe would sit at the foot of the tree and sing, and Junior would listen. The hamadryad got used to the new arrival and came to like Junior. She didn't quite trust Niobe, for adults had a long and bad history of cynicism toward wild magic, but when Niobe set the baby in his carrier by the tree and retreated a reasonable distance, the dryad would come down and play with him. Niobe was thrilled; very few mortals could approach any of the wilderness creatures, either natural or supernatural, and it was a mark of special favor when one could. Maybe Junior would grow up to be a world-famous naturalist! Certainly there was no threat from the dryad; Cedric had assured her of that, and she believed it. In the dryad's presence Junior was always alert and smiling.

Events elsewhere were not as sanguine. A developer bought a large tract of land that included their swamp. It was theirs in proximity and spirit, not in the eyes of geographic law. The company planned to drain the swamp, cut down the trees, and build a number of identical houses there.

Cedric exploded. He trekked to all the residents for miles around and so impressed them with the need to preserve the wetlands that they formed a citizen's committee to oppose the development. They wrote letters to newspapers and the county authorities; when these failed to halt the project, they set about constructing deadfalls for bulldozers. They filed suit in court to stop it. When the company lawyer tried to suggest the swamp was nothing more than a murky waste that posed a public health threat as a breeding ground for disease-carrying mosquitoes, Cedric argued persuasively that those mosquitoes carried no diseases in this region, being the wrong species for that, served as food for pretty birds, and wouldn't even bite people who were sensibly protected by repellent or a spell. Then he spoke of the other aspects of the wetlands—the fish and amphibians, the foxes and deer, the trees that could grow nowhere else, the special interactive magic these living things had developed to get along. "There is no bad water coming from this region," he concluded, and he had documentation to prove it: studies the college had made. "No erosion, no bad flooding. The wetlands keep the water pure and contained, so that we who live near it can live at peace with nature. Too little of this kind of natural paradise remains; how can we pave it over with another foul city!" And such was the nature of his eloquence that the spectators in the courtrooms applauded. Few had really cared about the wetlands before; now they all did.

But man's law remained on the side of the developer, and the judge, with open regret, ruled in favor of the company. The bulldozers would be allowed to forage in the swamp.

"I'm so sorry," Niobe told him, but Cedric only shrugged. "They will be stopped," he said grimly. But he didn't say how.

One foggy morning Cedric kissed her with special tenderness and lifted Junior out of his crib. "I'm taking him for a walk down to the oak," he said.

She was pleased—but somehow alarmed too. There seemed to be an edge to his final words: "We'll be there." Yet they were innocent words, and the water oak was the safest kind of place for the baby; the hamadryad was virtually a babysitter now. In fact, the nymph had begun to teach the baby some wild magic—and if there was one thing rarer than the company of a dryad, it was the sharing of the magic of a dryad. Junior, too young to walk or talk, nevertheless did seem to understand and almost seemed to be able to do a spell. So why should there be any concern? Niobe knew she was being foolish. There was, she reminded herself firmly, absolutely no threat to Junior.

She labored at the loom, forming a fine picture of that very tree, and as her hands moved, largely of their own volition, she daydreamed. The image of the tree fogged out and was replaced by that of the saturnine face. "Today I come for you!" it said, grinning evilly. "My emissary is on its way and cannot be stopped. You are doomed, mistress of the skein!"

Niobe screamed. The image vanished, and there was only the forming tapestry. She was shuddering with reaction. This was the vision of her lovemaking rapture, but it was quite foreign to love. Cedric had banished it by his music, but now it was terrorizing her directly! What did it mean?

Then she heard a shot. She jumped. That was the sound of a gun— and it was from the direction of the swamp—and Cedric was there with Junior. He had no gun!

Horribly alarmed, she rushed outside and ran headlong down the winding path to the oak. As she approached, she heard a thin screaming from the tree. It was the dryad, hanging by a branch, shrieking with all her frail strength. Below her was the carrier, overturned.

"Junior!" Niobe cried, her horror magnifying. She scrambled to the tree and took hold of the carrier.

Junior was in it, his body smudged with dirt, and now he bawled lustily. But he seemed to be unhurt. He had overturned and that had alarmed him; that was all.

She glanced up at the dryad. No, of course she wouldn't have tried to hurt the baby! In fact the nymph was still screaming, one little hand pointing away from the tree, to the dark lower side where the gloom of the swamp was strong.

Niobe looked in that direction—and saw Cedric's body sprawled in the bushes. Suddenly her premonition of dread had a sharp new focus. Not her baby—her husband!

She ran to him. He was face down, and blood welled from the wound in his belly. He had been shot! He was unconscious, but his heart still beat.

She looked up—and the dryad was there, for the moment away from her tree. "What—who—?" Niobe asked, forgetting that dryads do not talk.

The nymph took a stick and held it like a rifle, then shook it to suggest its firing. But Niobe already knew he had been shot. "Have you any magic—for his wound?" she demanded.

The dryad ran back to her tree, ran up it as a squirrel might, and disappeared into the foliage. She returned in a moment with a small branch.

Niobe took this and touched it to the wound. The flow of blood abated. The nymph's magic was helping! "Thank you," Niobe said.

But how was she to get Cedric back to the cabin—and what was she to do with him there? He weighed far more than she and would be almost impossible to drag, and the movement could kill him. And there was the baby!

The dryad pointed to the tree. "You'll help?" Niobe asked. "He'll be safe, there, for a while?"

The nymph nodded yes. So Niobe struggled to drag Cedric the short distance to the tree and there she propped him against its healing trunk. "I'll bring help!" she told the dryad as she picked Junior up and hurried away.

Some hours later, that phase of the nightmare was done. Cedric was in the distant hospital, receiving the best care, and his family and hers had been notified. Both were quick to respond. But that was as far as the good news extended.

Cedric was on the critical list and sinking. The bullet had damaged his spinal nerve, paralyzing him, and it had evidently carried an unidentified infection that was now spreading through his weakened system. "We can keep him alive for perhaps a week," the doctor said grimly. "He has a fine constitution; otherwise he would be dead already. Even if we could save him, he would be crippled below the waist and in constant pain, and there is a chance of brain damage. It would, I regret to say, be kinder to let him die."

"No!" Niobe cried. "I love him!"

"We all love him," the doctor said. "He was doing a great thing for the land. But we cannot save him."

"But we may be able to avenge him," the wetlands lawyer said. "Obviously the developer arranged to have him assassinated so he could no longer rally the people against the building project."

"But they had already won!" Niobe protested. "Why should they do this now?"

"They must have been afraid he was planning something new."

Niobe remembered Cedric's confidence that the developer would be stopped. Indeed, he must have been planning something! But that was no comfort to her now; she wanted him alive and whole.

"How can I save him?" she asked, clinging to that hope.

The doctor and the lawyer looked at each other. "You must appeal to a higher court," the lawyer said.

"What court is that?"

"The Incarnation of Death," the doctor said. "If Thanatos will agree to spare him, he will live."

She was ready to grasp at any straw. "Then I will appeal to Death! Where can I find him?"

Both men spread their hands. They did not know. "We do not go to Death," the doctor said. "Death comes to us, at the moment of his choosing, not ours."

Niobe took Junior and traveled hastily to the college. There she sought the old Prof. "How can I find Death?" she pleaded.

The Prof gazed at her unhappily. "Lovely woman, you do not want to do this."

"Don't tell me that!" she blazed at him. "I love him!"

He did not misunderstand. It was Cedric she loved, not Death. "And do you also love your baby?"

She froze. "You mean—I must choose between them?"

"In a manner. You, perhaps, might reach Thanatos—but your baby is beneath the age of discretion. He would die. If you insist on making this terrible journey, you must in fairness leave him behind."

She looked at Junior, horrified. "But—I can recover him, after—?"

"If you are successful," he said. "But, Mrs. Kaftan, you have no guarantee of success. This is no ordinary person you seek; he is a supernatural entity. You may never return from such a journey."

"Suppose—I place my baby with a good family?" she asked with difficulty. "So that if I don't—don't return—he will be well cared for?"

"That would be an expedient course," he agreed. "Of course you would have to take a lactation-abatement spell, and arrange to have him fed from a bottle while—"

"Then you will tell me how to reach Death?"

"Then I will do that," he agreed reluctantly. "I did, after all, make you a promise to help you when you asked."

She drove her carriage hastily to the farm of Cedric's cousin, Pacian. Pacian himself was twelve years old, six years younger than Cedric, but his parents were kindly folk with a strong sense of family loyalty. Yes, they would board Junior; he was, after all, their kin, a Kaftan. Pacian, a pleasant-faced lad who reminded her eerily of Cedric, welcomed Junior as a little brother.

Then, with confused emotion and more than a tear or two, she returned to the college, where the Prof would show her the way to Death.

There was a small lake beside the college, and they had taken an old, unseaworthy sailboat and spruced it up for the event. Its leaks had been temporarily caulked, and its sail was lashed in position. This craft could proceed only one way: directly before the wind. But physical direction didn't matter; spiritual impulse was what counted.

The small deck was piled with kerosene-soaked brush. A single spark would render the boat into a bonfire in an instant. The sail was charcoal black and painted with a picture of a bleached skull and crossbones: not the symbol of piracy, in this case, but that of Death. Indeed, this was a deathboat.

Niobe stepped onto the pier. She wore her most elegant black evening gown, with black gloves and slippers, and her flowing honey hair was bound by a black ribbon. There was a murmur of awe from the assembled college students, male and female, as she appeared, and she knew that she had never been more beautiful. The anti-lac spell had halted her production of mother's milk, but her breasts remained quite well developed.

The Prof stood at the end of the pier by the boat. He looked old and hunched, and his face was as pale as bone. "Ah, lovely woman, it is a horror you face!" he murmured. "Are you quite, quite sure—?"

"If Cedric dies, what life is there for me?" she asked rhetorically. She braced herself against his arm and stepped onto the boat. It wobbled in the water, and she hastily sat down.

"Perhaps we shall meet again," the Prof said.

"Of course we shall," she said and blew him a kiss. She knew he had done his best and she trusted his magic. But her expression of confidence papered over a monstrous dread within her, akin to that of the fourth face of the water oak tree. She felt like a deer stepping out before the rifle of the hunter. It was in this sense a season for the shooting of deer, and the huntsman was Death himself.

"Remember," the Prof cautioned her, "you can jump off, and a swimmer will rescue you." He gestured to three husky young men in swimsuits standing alertly at the shore.

"And forfeit my love?" she asked disdainfully. "I shall not jump."

"Then God be with you," he said, and it was no casual expression. He closed his hands together in an attitude of prayer and lifted them toward the cloudy sky.

Where was God when Cedric was shot? she wondered. But she smiled. "Cast off, please."

The Prof bent down and lifted the rope from its mooring. The breeze caught the sail and the craft moved out into the lake. Left to its own devices, it would in due course bump into the far shore— but she had a different plan for it.

She turned and waved to the folk on the shore behind. Then she reached into her purse, brought out a big wooden match, and struck it against the hard surface of the deck. It burst into life.

For a moment she held the little flame before her. Then she clamped her lower lip between her teeth, closed her eyes, and flung the match forward into the brush. If it did not ignite this tinder, would she have the courage to try it again?

But it caught, and in a moment there was the crackle of spreading fire. She opened her eyes, and saw the flame and smoke pouring up. The fire did not spread instantly; it took several seconds to infuse the full pile. Then it intensified, and the sudden heat of it smote her body. The sail caught, and became a bright column.

Now was the time to jump, before fire surrounded her. She was tempted. Then she thought of Cedric, lying critically ill on the hospital bed, and her resolve solidified. She stood, held her breath, and walked directly into the conflagration.

Cedric! Cedric! she thought as the flame engulfed her. *I love you!*

Her dress caught fire, and her hair shriveled, but she took one more step, bracing herself against the pain she knew was coming.

It came indeed. All her world became fire. She inhaled, and the fire was inside her, searing her lungs and heart. The agony was exquisite, but she endured it, refusing to collapse or even to scream. *Death, I am coming for you!*

The boat was formed of flame, now. The caulking popped out and water spurted in, drenching her feet. But the flame danced above it, and the smoke roiled about, as if fighting the water for this living prize. Niobe stood amidst it, her flesh burning, waiting for Death.

A figure came. It was a great stallion, galloping across the surface of the water, bearing a cloaked and hooded man. The horse came to the boat and stopped, standing on the lake. The man dismounted and brought forth a scythe. He scythed the flames as he would a field of tall grass, and the flames were cut off at their bases, their tops falling to one side. A path was cleared through the conflagration, leading to Niobe. Death had arrived.

Thanatos paused beside her and extended his skeletal hand. Niobe took it in her own, feeling the cold bones of his fingers.

Abruptly the pain of the fire abated. Thanatos led her along the scythed path to the pale horse and boosted her up into the saddle, then mounted behind her. The horse leaped into the remaining column of smoke—and through it, up into the sky.

Soon the stallion was galloping through the clouds above, his hooves sending little divots of fog flying back. Then they emerged to a scene above, where the grass was green and the sun shone warmly. Ahead was a mansion. They came to it, dismounted, and Thanatos guided her inside.

A motherly maid hurried up. "You brought a mortal!" she exclaimed with surprise and perhaps indignation.

"See to her restoration," Thanatos ordered gruffly. "She is not one of mine."

The pain returned when Niobe lost contact with Thanatos, but the maid hastened to bring salve. Niobe's skin was charred black, but where the salve touched, the normal flesh was instantly restored. The maid applied it to Niobe's entire body and made her inhale its fumes, and then no pain remained. Niobe stood naked and whole.

"My dear, you are beautiful!" the maid exclaimed, spraying something on the frizzled hair. The hair grew rapidly until it too had been restored to its former golden splendor. "Why should a creature like you try to suicide?"

"I love him," Niobe repeated.

"Ah, love," the maid breathed, understanding. She brought a bathrobe and new slippers. It seemed that the salve could not heal Niobe's incinerated clothing. "Thanatos awaits you," she said and showed Niobe to a sitting room.

Death—Thanatos—did indeed await her. He was like a stern father in his manner, despite his skull-face and skeletal hands. "You have done a very brave and foolish thing, young woman," he informed her disapprovingly. "You were not on my list. I had to make an emergency call for you."

"It—it was the only way to get your attention," she said, taking the seat indicated. "Thank you for coming." And she smiled.

The skull itself seemed to heighten its color, showing that Death himself was not immune to beauty. "It had to be done," he said gruffly. "When an unscheduled death occurs, the threads of Fate tangle."

That was what the Prof had told her. There was a certain order in the universe, and the Incarnations saw to its preservation. "I—where am I? In Heaven?"

Thanatos made a derisive snort, despite having no flesh in his nose. "Purgatory," he said. "The place of indecision—and of decision. All the Incarnations are here."

"Oh. I—haven't been beyond life before." She was somewhat intimidated by all this.

"And what brought you, ravishing mortal maiden?"

"Oh, I am no maiden! I—my husband Cedric—I have come to beg for his life. I love him!"

"Without doubt," Thanatos agreed. He snapped his bone-fingers, and a servant hurried in with a file box. Thanatos opened the box and riffled through the cards. "Cedric Kaftan, age eighteen, to go to Heaven five days hence," he remarked. "A good man, not requiring my personal attention." His square eye-sockets seemed to squint at the card. "A *very* good man! He loves you well indeed."

"Yes. I must save him. You must—"

Thanatos gazed at her through the midnight frames of his eyes, and suddenly she felt a chill not of death. It had not occurred to her before that the Incarnation might require a price for the favor she asked—and what did she have to offer?

Then she thought again of Cedric, lying in the hospital, and knew that there was no price she would not pay to have him whole again.

But when Thanatos spoke again, he surprised her. "Good and lovely mortal, I cannot do the thing you request. I do not cause folk to die; I merely see to the proper routing of the souls of those who are fated to die. It is true that I have some discretion; on occasion I will postpone a particular demise. But your husband is beyond postponement; to extend his life would be only to extend his pain. He will neither walk nor talk again."

"No!" Niobe cried. It was literal; her tears wet her robe. "He's so young, so bonnie! I love him!"

Even Death softened before that beauteous plea. "I would help you if I could," Thanatos said. "To be Incarnated is not to be without conscience. But the remedy you seek is not within my province."

"Then whose province is it in?" she demanded brokenly.

"At this point, I suspect only Chronos can help him."

"Who?"

"The Incarnation of Time. He can travel in time, when he chooses, and change mortal events by acting before they occur. Therefore if he—"

"Before the shot was fired!" she exclaimed. "So that Cedric is never hurt!"

The cowled skull nodded. "That is what Chronos can do."

The strangeness of talking to the Incarnation of Death was fading. The renewed chance to save Cedric recharged her. "Where—how—can I find Chronos?"

"You could search all Purgatory and not find him," Thanatos said. "He travels in time. But if he cares to meet you, he will do so."

"But I *must* meet with him! I have so little time—"

There was a chime that sounded like a funeral gong. "That will be Chronos now," Thanatos said.

"Now? But how—?"

"He knows our future. He is surely responding to the notice I will send him shortly."

A servant ushered Chronos in. He was a tall, thin man in a white cloak, bearing an Hourglass. "Ah, Clotho," he said.

"Who?" she asked, confused.

Chronos looked at her again. "Oh, has it come to that? My apology; it is happening sooner than I hoped. In that case, you must introduce yourself."

He had evidently mistaken her for someone else. "I—I am Niobe Kaftan—a, a mortal woman," she said.

"Niobe," Chronos repeated as if getting it straight. "Yes, of course. And you are here to—?"

"Here to save my husband, Cedric."

He nodded. "That, too. But that really is not wise."

"Not wise!" she exclaimed indignantly. "I love him!"

It was almost as if she had struck the Incarnation. He blanched, but then recovered. "Love is mortal," Chronos said sadly. "It passes, in the course of time."

"I don't care, so long as it passes naturally! Cedric is dying and he's not yet nineteen!"

Chronos shook his head. "I could travel to the moment before his problem commenced and change the event—but I hesitate. The interactions can extend far, and we interfere at peril to the larger fabric."

"But I *love* him!" she cried. "I *must* save him!"

Chronos glanced at Thanatos, who shrugged. They might be Incarnations, but they seemed very much like mortal men, baffled by the hysteria of a mortal woman.

"But you see," Chronos said reasonably, "to change an event, especially this one, could lead to consequences that none of us would wish."

Niobe began to cry. She put her face in her hands, and the tears streamed in little rivulets through her spread fingers.

"Perhaps a female Incarnation would handle this better," Thanatos said, evidently feeling awkward. Men tended to, in such situations; they didn't understand about crying. Niobe didn't like this situation much herself, but she couldn't help her reaction.

"I will take her to Fate," Chronos agreed quickly.

He came to Niobe and drew diffidently on her elbow. "Please come with me, ma'am."

At the sound of "ma'am," the term Cedric had used early in their relationship, Niobe burst into a fresh surge of tears. She was hardly aware of Chronos taking firm hold of her with his left hand and raising his glowing Hourglass with his right. But suddenly the two of them were zooming through the air and substance of the mansion as if they had become phantoms. That so startled her that her tears ceased.

They phased across a variegated landscape that was not the world she had known. Then they homed in on the most monstrous web Niobe could have imagined, its pattern of silken strands extending out for hundreds of feet in a spherical array. In the center the web thickened, forming a level mat, and on this they came to rest. "How—what?" she said, amazed and daunted.

"My Hourglass selectively nullifies aspects of the chronological counterspell," Chronos explained. "Enabling me to travel—oh, you refer to the web? Do not be concerned; this is the Abode of Fate."

"Fate!" she exclaimed, realizing how this might relate to her. "It was Fate who determined that Cedric—"

"Indeed," he agreed as they walked to the huge cocoon in the middle of this resilient plane. "She should be more competent to satisfy you than I am."

"But—this is a gigantic spider's nest!" she said.

He smiled. "I assure you, good and lovely woman, that Fate will not consume you in that manner. She is—much like you."

Now they were at the entrance. Chronos reached up, took hold of a dangling thread, and pulled on it. A bell sounded in the silk-shrouded interior, and in a moment a middle-aged woman clambered out of the hole, very spry for her age. "Why, Chronos!" she exclaimed. "How nice to see you, my backward associate!" Her gaze turned on Niobe. "And a mortal woman who shines like the moon!" She glanced slyly back at Chronos. "What are you up to, sir?"

"Lachesis, this is Niobe," he said. "She comes to plead for the life of her husband, who suffered a recent accident. I—am unable to assist her in this."

Lachesis' eyes narrowed as if he had said something of special significance. Then she studied Niobe with a certain surmise. "Come in, child," she said at last. "We shall examine your thread." She glanced once more at Chronos. "You, too, honored associate."

They followed her through the hole, which was a finely woven mesh-tunnel that opened into a comfortable interior. Everything was made of web, but it was so thick and cleverly crafted that it was solid. In fact, it was the ultimate in web—silk. The walls were woven in a tapestry that was a mural, showing scenes of the world, and the floor was a rug so smooth a person could have slept on it without a mattress.

Niobe took a seat on a plush web couch, while Lachesis stood before her, set her hands together, drew them apart, and looked at the lines of web that had appeared magically between her fingers. "Oh, my!" she exclaimed. "That is a strange one!"

Niobe's brow furrowed. "Do you mean—me?"

"In a moment, dear," Lachesis said, preoccupied. She looked at Chronos. "Tell me, friend, is this—?" she asked. Then she shimmered—and in her place was a woman of perhaps twenty, quite pretty, with a nimbus of black hair, and cleavage showing. Her dress was yellow, and very short. Then she changed again, and was the middle-aged woman in brown.

Chronos nodded slowly, affirmatively.

Lachesis seemed dizzy. She plumped into another couch. "Oh, my dear!" she exclaimed. "This *is* a pretty snarl!"

"I don't understand," Niobe said.

"Of course you don't, dear," Lachesis agreed. "Neither did I. But Chronos knew, of course." She mopped her forehead with a bright silk handkerchief. "What am I to tell her, sir?"

"I suppose the truth, to the present," he said.

Niobe was increasingly bothered by their attitude. "Of course the truth!" she exclaimed.

Lachesis came to join her on the couch, taking her hand. "My dear, truth can be a complex skein, and often painful. I have looked at your thread, and—"

"Look at my husband's thread!" Niobe exclaimed. "I must save him!"

Lachesis disengaged, put her hands together, and stretched another gossamer thread between them. "Cedric Kaftan," she said as if reading from a text. "His thread—" She clapped her hands together, causing the thread to disappear. "Oh, my dear, my dear!"

"You really are Fate? You can save him?"

Lachesis shook her head. "I am Fate—an Aspect thereof. I determine the length and placement of the threads of human lives. I arrange for what befalls each person, in a general way. But this is a special case—a very special case. I cannot do what you ask."

Now Niobe's sorrow turned to anger. "Why not?" she demanded. "You—you arranged his death, didn't you?"

"I arranged his death; I did not decree it," Lachesis agreed sadly. "I remember the case now. I did not want to do it, but I had to. Now, thanks to Chronos, I begin to understand why."

"Then tell me why!" Niobe cried. "I love him!"

"And he loves you," the woman returned. "More than you can know. My dear, it would only bring you further grief to know more. Some deer must die, that the herd prosper."

Some deer! That hurt her anew, for Cedric had tried to protect the deer. "You refuse to tell me?"

Lachesis sighed. "I know how difficult it is for you to understand, Niobe. You are a brave and good woman, and your love is great, but you are mortal. I would help you if I could, but I cannot." She raised a hand to forestall Niobe's objection. "To a child, life seems a series of arbitrary constraints; the child longs for the freedom of adult existence. But when the child becomes adult, she finds that the constraints remain; they only change their nature, becoming more complex and subtle. Even so, we Incarnations appear to have greater freedom of action than do mortals—but our constraints exist also, of a nature few mortals are equipped to comprehend. I can only assure you that a situation beyond your control and mine decrees that your husband must die. I can only say I'm sorry."

"Sorry!" Niobe flared. "*Sorry!* What possible justification can you have for arranging the death of a man as noble as Cedric?"

"I have two," Lachesis said. "One I may not tell you, and the other I will not."

"Then send me to someone who *will* tell me!"

Lachesis shrugged. "Perhaps Mars; he is aggressive—"

"I will take her to him," Chronos said.

Lachesis glanced at him sidelong again. "You have a special interest, Chronos?"

"I owe—Clotho," he said.

Lachesis nodded, knowingly. "It is a tangled skein we work from," she said. "A tangled tapestry we weave. Thank you for informing me, Chronos."

Chronos nodded and stood, and Lachesis stood, and they kissed briefly. This startled Niobe, but she was too distracted by the frustration of her own situation to ponder theirs.

Chronos took her elbow again, lifted his Hourglass, tilted it—and they were moving again, in their immaterial fashion.

They came to a mighty stone fortress, with armored turrets and embrasures and battlements and massive walls. It stood on a mountaintop in Purgatory and looked impregnable—but Chronos landed lightly before its main gate. "Ho, Mars!" he called.

A tiny window opened. "He's at work," a helmeted head said. "Down in France, you know."

"Oh, yes, the war," Chronos agreed. He tilted his Hourglass again, and they slanted down through the ground and the cloud and the air beneath. Looking down, Niobe saw lands and waters passing by at supernatural velocity; she felt dizzy, and had to close her eyes. Chronos might be a man, but he had astonishing power!

As did Thanatos, she reflected. That business with the scything of the flames, and that magnificent horse, and a body made of bones without flesh that nevertheless had voice and strength. Lachesis, too—that business with the threads, and the way she had changed momentarily to another woman—no mortal talent, that! They were all phenomenal beings—yet strangely helpless to aid her. She sensed that all three of them really wanted to help her, but were unable—and could not tell her why.

They slowed as they approached the landscape of France. At last they landed at the edge of a great trench, part of a messy series of fortifications that seemed to extend endlessly. This was the frontline of the war, she knew—the war that had drawn away most of the eligible young men and left her to marry a sixteen-year-old youth. She had cursed that war; now, perversely, she blessed it, for without it she would not have known Cedric.

A man in Greek or Roman armor—she was not enough of a military scholar to distinguish between them—stood between the trenches. This was evidently Mars.

"Ah, Chronos," Mars said, waving his red sword in greeting. "What brings you here—with such a lovely creature?"

"This is Niobe, a mortal. She came to see Thanatos, to plead for her husband's life, but the matter is complex and we are able neither to help her nor to explain it to her."

"Naturally not," Mars agreed as a shell detonated nearby. Shrapnel shot through the area, but none of them were hit. Niobe realized that there was a spell to protect them from such incidental mischief. Power, indeed! "Mortals are not equipped to understand."

"Of course I don't understand!" Niobe said hotly. "Fate pulled her string to seal my husband's doom, and Death will come to take him, and Time refuses to change it! I can't say I expect anything better from you!"

If she had thought to shame him into some favorable action, she failed. Mars merely smiled. "A woman after my own heart!" he said, pleased. "A fighter. All right, Chronos, I'm curious too. I obliterate thousands in a single battle, and there is scant justice in their passing, and often great irony, and you other Incarnations tend to glance askance at my work. So why are you killing in seemingly arbitrary fashion now? That is not normally your way. I should think that if this woman had the courage to brace Thanatos himself, she deserves some consideration. Where is your chivalry?"

Suddenly Niobe liked this gruff man better.

Chronos touched his Hourglass—and the world blinked. Now he and Mars were standing in different positions, and the sun shone from farther along in the sky.

"You did something!" she accused Chronos. "You changed time! Why?"

"I had to explain to Mars," he said. "I merely set you forward half an hour, while we talked."

"Why not explain to *me*?"

"Do not blame him," Mars told her. "He has reason, as has Lachesis. It turns out to be an unusual case."

"Then you won't tell me either, Mars?" she demanded. "You Incarnations must feel pretty big, teasing mortals—" She was overtaken by tears of frustration, a sudden torrent.

"She does that," Chronos murmured, embarrassed.

"Oh, come on, woman," Mars said. "I have delivered similar tears to tens of thousands of women, though none as pretty as you. What are you made of?"

A blind fury took her then. "And tens of thousands of similar griefs to *you*, you unfeeling ilk!" she cried. "I hope you choke on your own sword!"

Mars smiled. "Lovely!" Then he sighed. "I will try to clarify it for you, in a general manner. You see, God and Satan are at war, and there are countless skirmishes, occasional major engagements, and some devious nexuses. We Incarnations favor God, who is the Incarnation of Good. At times it is necessary to make small sacrifices in the pursuit of eventual victory, and it seems that your husband is such a case. Therefore, in the larger picture—"

"A small sacrifice? *Cedric?*" she demanded. "I *love* him!" She had said that many times, and would say it many more, if it could get him back.

"And he loves you," Mars agreed. "Indeed, he has proved it. And it may be that because of this sacrifice, our side will win the war. You should be proud."

Suddenly she remembered how Cedric had been before the shooting. Almost as if he had anticipated what was to come. "He—*knew?*"

"He knew," Mars agreed. "He went voluntarily to that mission, and great glory accrues to him therefore. I salute him!" And he raised his red sword.

Cedric had known he was going to die! Stunned by this realization, she hardly knew what to do next. Then she stabilized. "Then I will take his place!" she said.

"You cannot," Mars and Chronos said together.

"Can't I? What do you care? One way or another I will save my husband, despite all of you!"

Mars shook his head. "You had better take her to Ge," he told Chronos. "She will know what to do."

Chronos took her elbow. Niobe jerked it away, but he caught it on the second try. Then they were flying again, leaving the trenches of France below.

"I think you're all a bunch of—" she started, but couldn't think of a suitable conclusion. These Incarnations seemed to be in a conspiracy of silence! Yet she remained shaken by what she had learned about Cedric, confirmed by her memory. He had known, or suspected. But why should he have gone, then? It didn't make sense!

They came to a dense copse of small trees. They passed through it in immaterial fashion and came to rest in a pleasant interior glade.

An ample woman sat on a chair shaped like a toadstool. No, it *was* a toadstool, huge and sturdy. There were flowers in the woman's hair and they too were alive, their little leaves and roots showing. The woman's dress was green, formed of overlapping leaves, and her shoes were formed of earth that somehow flexed with her feet without crumbling. This was surely the Incarnation of Nature!

"So you bring her at last to me, you nefarious time-traveler," Nature said to Chronos. "Begone, you callous male; I will do what you could not."

"As you wish, Gaea," Chronos said, seeming relieved. He tilted his Hourglass and disappeared.

"You—you knew I was coming here?" Niobe asked.

"Mortal woman, you have generated quite a stir in Purgatory," Gaea said. "I suspected those men would muff it."

"But Fate—Lachesis—"

"Lachesis knows—but cannot tell. And I will not tell either; trust the Green Mother to have some discretion! In time you will understand. But I will explain to you what you need to know at this time, and with that you will have to be satisfied."

"Gaea, I want to take my husband's place!" Niobe exclaimed. "Let him survive, healthy, so he can have his career, and I will die!"

The Green Mother gazed at her with understanding. "Yes, of course you feel that way, Niobe. You are a woman in love. But that cannot be."

"It must be! I would do anything to save him!"

Gaea shook her head. "Niobe, you cannot—because he has already sacrificed himself for you."

"He—what?"

"*You* were the one Satan slated for early demise, Niobe. Your husband asked the Professor about your bad visions, and the Prof, who is a pretty fair magician, investigated. He was grooming the young man to assume a chair at the college and wanted to be sure the background was stable. He discovered the plot and informed your husband. Cedric never hesitated; he went in your place."

Again, Niobe was stunned. She remembered her visions of dread. "He went—for me?"

"It seems that you are destined to be a real thorn in Satan's side. None of us can know the details, of course, not even Satan, but he moved to eliminate you. Satan has terrible power, and he is subtle and methodical; we other Incarnations did not realize. Almost before we knew, it was done. The envoy of Hell was loosed—but Cedric took the shot intended for you."

"How—?"

"The assassin was a hunter possessed temporarily by a demon spirit. The demon's orders were to shoot the mortal who was singing at a particular oak tree, with a baby. Satan presumed that would be you. That was the loophole."

"It *would* have been!" Niobe agreed faintly. "If Cedric had not—"

"He loved you," Gaea agreed. "And he knew that Satan wanted you dead. So he saved you and balked Satan at one stroke. Seldom has a nobler deed been done."

"But if I—"

"You cannot make a mockery of your husband's gallant sacrifice," Gaea said. "You must accept the gift he gave you, and do what he has enabled you to do."

"I—but I don't know what—"

"That is what we may not tell you, though it is little enough we know ourselves. But it is enough for you to know, now, that Satan himself regards you as a dangerous enemy, and surely he is correct. Live—and you will discover your destiny in due course."

Niobe realized that her quest had come to nothing. Cedric had already done for her what she had thought to do for him. She had no choice, now, but to accept.

She stumbled out of the glade, through the thickly growing saplings, and emerged—beside the water oak near her home. The hamadryad recognized her and waved.

"Oh, Cedric!" Niobe exclaimed. "*I* was the deer to be shot—and how great was your love for me! Now I must let you die!"

Then she lifted her tear-streaked face to the sky. "But I will avenge you, Cedric!" she swore. "Somehow I will make Satan pay!"

She sank down beside the tree, and cried against its trunk, while the dryad wrung her hands. *O Cedric!*

– 4 –

CLOTHO

The following days were unpleasant, despite the grief-abatement spells she was using. They merely dulled the cutting edge of her sorrow, but did not—could not—*should* not!—provide happiness in its stead. They enabled her to function in a superficially normal manner, but below, in a cavernous depth of despair, the agony remained. There was only so much that magic could do.

Niobe went to the Prof and asked why he had not told her what Cedric had done. "Because he forbade me," the man replied sadly. "I hoped—by interceding with Death, you might—but—"

"The murder was willed by Satan," she said. "It was too late. One of us was doomed."

"He insisted that you be saved," the Prof said. "I, selfish as I am, wanted him for the college. He had so much potential! But he—and evidently Satan!—believed that you were more important, and I could not refute that case."

"He *was* the one with all the promise," she agreed. "Cedric was worth two of me. I have no idea what I can do to justify my survival. But for his sake I will carry on, raise our son, and seek my retribution against Satan. If the Prince of Evil suspected that I would cause him trouble, he has surely guaranteed that I will do so now!" But once more she was overtaken by tears. She felt so desolate! Her marriage to Cedric had been, to a large extent, promise—the promise of his maturity. The promise of the life they would have together as two adults. They had just begun to taste that joy—and now it was gone.

She went to the hospital in the city, where the doctor still labored to hold life in Cedric. "Let him go," she said. "I love him. I will

not let him suffer longer." And she kissed her husband's unrespon-
sive lips, and wet his face with her tears, and turned away. "May
you have joy in Heaven, my bonnie boy," she whispered. "May I
join you there—when my business here is done."

She went to Cousin Pacian's parents' farm, where Junior had been
boarded for several days. Junior saw her—and burst into tears. She
picked him up, in tears again herself, and held him close.

"But he was doing so well!" Pacian protested. "He was having a
good time here, honest!"

"Of course he was," Niobe agreed. "It's just that once he saw
me, he realized how he missed me. It's a natural reaction." But what,
she wondered bleakly, would be his reaction to the permanent loss
of his father?

Indeed, once reassured, Junior returned to his play with Pace, and
it was obvious that the two liked each other, the baby and the boy,
though about twelve years separated them. It was more than kinship.
"You are a truly wonderful family," she told them as she departed
with Junior. "I can never thank you enough."

"Bring him back to visit soon," Pace said, hiding a tear of his own.

Niobe nullified the anti-lac spell and nursed Junior—but he quickly
turned colicky and screamed in pain, and she realized that her grief
for Cedric was in her blood and in her milk, poisoning her baby. She
had to restore the spell and prepare a formula and return him to the
bottle. She felt guilty doing it and less a mother, but perhaps it was
for the best. Certainly she had no right to inflict her pain on him.

And I—will cry—she sang to herself. *I'll cry when the wetlands
are dry.* It had new meaning now; it was as if her own drying-up was
an echo of the suffering of the forest wetlands when man interfered.

She attended Cedric's wake, and Niobe smiled dutifully, but she
had no taste for festivity. The ghost did hover near the corpse, reluctant to depart before the burial, despite the burning candle and
ritual eating of bread. No one could make it depart until Niobe herself
faced it and tearfully demanded an accounting. Then the ghost floated
to her, touched her wet cheeks, shook its head, kissed her with the
touch of gossamer but also of music, and faded away. It seemed to
be a message of reassurance, ironic in this circumstance.

Now it was over, and her life loomed bleak before her. *Come live
with me and be my love*, she sang to herself, trying to remember the
feeling of being with Cedric, but she could not. She knew, too well,
that he was gone.

She set about fulfilling as much of Cedric's ambition as she could.
She talked again with the Prof to see whether it was feasible to develop a spell to enable the deer to shoot back, but he said that such
magic was beyond his ability. "The magician who accomplishes that
will be a master," he said.

With a Tangled Skein

Cedric's death did accomplish something useful: the suspicion that the developer had done the deed turned out to be unfounded, but local sentiment was now so solidly against the project that all such plans were canceled. Perhaps Cedric had known that this would be a side effect of his sacrifice.

There was a death settlement on Cedric which left her economically comfortable for the time being, but she also returned to her weaving, producing fine tapestries for sale. She kept herself busy—but though she had lived mostly alone for two years while Cedric was in college, this wasn't the same. That had been temporary; this was permanent. Now she knew he wasn't coming home, and that hurt constantly. It was a tunnel with no light at the end.

Increasingly she thought about her trip to Purgatory. She had met five Incarnations—entities she had hardly believed in before. She had seen some of their powers and realized that there had to be more that she had not seen. They had pleaded inability to do what she asked—but they had enormous abilities nevertheless. What did they do when they weren't talking with visiting mortals?

She had no life here on Earth, really. Even Junior would be better off with his cousin's family; she knew that. He was her baby; she loved him. But she had no illusions about the long-term life she could provide for him, alone.

She went to the water oak, set Junior down to play with the hamadryad, and explored the region near it where she had emerged from Gaea's home. As she had expected, it was now merely brush. The magic was from the other end. She could not get to Purgatory this way.

Neither could she use the route she had used before. When she had had a living love to salvage, she had been able to face the prospect of incineration in a burning boat—but she had no love to salvage now. She needed to find another way.

But what did she have in mind to do there, once she got to Purgatory? Ride Death's pale horse? Zoom about the cosmos behind Chronos' traveling Hourglass? The fact was, Cedric was not in Purgatory, either; it would be just as lonely there as here on Earth.

She glanced at her baby, now asleep, lulled by the dryad's soundless lullaby. Of course she wasn't entirely lonely; she did have Junior. He was of Cedric's blood, and that was an enormous comfort. But— he was only a baby.

Increasingly, as the days passed, another emotion rose in her— her need to be avenged on the true perpetrator of this outrage: Satan. She wanted to find some specific way to implement her vow. The Incarnation of Evil had sought to kill her, and instead had destroyed her happiness. She knew that if she had been the one to die, Cedric's fists would have sought the hide of the one responsible, though Hell barred the way. Instead he had chosen to save her. Could she do less for her husband than he would have done for her?

But how could she do it? She was only a mortal woman, caring for her baby, while Satan was the ultimate bastion of evil. She had no way to reach him, and no way to prevail if she *could* reach him. It was ludicrous to believe she could punish Satan—yet that was her vow and her need. Mars would have understood!

She continued to ponder, for this need was restoring some purpose to her existence. Obviously Satan was neither all-knowing nor all-powerful, for he had muffed the job on her. Also, she must have some power he feared, for otherwise he would not have tried to snuff her out.

What could Satan have feared about her? Surely he did not try to kill a person without reason. He had to be a very busy entity, seeing to all the wrongdoing in the world, constantly waging his war against God and the other Incarnations. She had not thought of interfering in Satan's designs before and was hardly a threat to him. She was not smart like Cedric or magical like the Prof; she had no great muscles, only her beauty and skill with tapestries. Yet he had sought her demise—now she knew her visions had been the first suggestion of that evil—and the other Incarnations seemed to agree that Satan had reason.

So she did have some power—if only she could ascertain what it was. Power enough to make Satan notice! What could it be? And why should the Incarnations refuse to tell her of it? She knew they were not in league with the Prince of Evil! It seemed to make no sense.

And Cedric—why had he not simply saved her from death? Surely he had not been required to go in her stead! He could have told her of the plot against her, and they could have gone far away until the danger was past. Cedric had had free will and had loved life; it just didn't make sense for him to seek death.

But it *had* to make sense! Cedric had been an extraordinarily intelligent young man, with a clear notion of his destiny. He had talked with the Prof and, instead of telling her, he had sworn the Prof to secrecy.

The Prof! He had to know why! But she knew he would not tell her. Why?

For days she mulled it over, debating with herself. She knew she was not nearly as smart as Cedric had been, but she was sure she could solve this riddle if she kept at it. It was like a code puzzle, with the letters of a sentence changed to other letters so that it seemed to be gibberish. But the underlying pattern remained, and bit by bit the letters could be corrected until the original sentence was restored. She had a number of hints, if only she could understand their application.

Bit by bit, she pieced it together. Satan feared her—so she must be more than mortal. The Incarnations knew of her, and Chronos knew her personally; he had called her Clotho. She had almost forgotten that, but now in her deliberations it came back. Chronos had also seemed to have a personal interest in her welfare; Lachesis had remarked on it, and certainly he had gone out of his way to help her. He had jumped her ahead half an hour so that he could explain things to Mars, who had then agreed. Yes, Chronos had known her—but the others had not. How could that be? Didn't the Incarnations work together? Well, presumably each focused mostly on his-her speciality; Chronos might know people the others didn't. Yet Lachesis had acted as if it were more than that. She had shimmered and changed into a young, lovely form, then back, and Chronos had nodded. He had confirmed—what?

Also, Lachesis had called Chronos "my backward friend." That had obviously not been an insult. What did it mean? Chronos was not backward, either physically or magically; his power had been as great as any. In fact, Gaea had called him a nefarious time-traveler.

But backward also meant to travel in reverse, as in a person walking backward. Yet Chronos was not fixed on the past; he seemed rather to know something of the future.

And then it came to her: Chronos, the Incarnation of Time, could travel backward in time! He could know the future, having been there and back. In fact he could have come originally from the future!

He could have seen Niobe there first—then recognized her here in the present. He had known her as Clotho. But who was Clotho? The name did have a certain familiarity.

She concentrated, focusing on it—and placed it. The Incarnation of Fate had three aspects: Clotho, who spun the threads of life; Lachesis, who measured them; and Atropos, who cut them.

Chronos had remembered her *as an Aspect of Fate!*

She sat perfectly still, shocked at the implication. Herself—Niobe—as Fate? How was it possible? Yet it explained so much: the diffidence of the Incarnations and Satan's effort to eliminate her. As Fate she could indeed interfere with Satan! She wasn't sure how, but was sure she could. Those Incarnations had their special abilities!

Yet if that were so—if it could be so—why hadn't they told her? The question brought the answer: they *hadn't* known, except for Chronos—and they didn't want Satan to know. It might be that if they had told her, that would have changed it so that it wouldn't come true. A paradox.

But Satan *had* known! Or *had* he? Could Satan see the future? He was the Incarnation of Evil, not of Time; his foresight had to be relatively limited. More likely he had some crude divination, some indication that she was going to cause trouble for him, or at least had the potential. So he had struck at her. And the Prof, reading the same divination, or interpreting her visions—which suddenly fell into place in this connection!—had told Cedric, and Cedric had done what he had done.

But, again—why hadn't Cedric simply told her, so she could avoid it? Why had he died, then come to her as a ghost with his gesture of encouragement?

She wrestled that about and finally concluded that probably Satan's minion had been told to go out and kill and, if balked, would continue to try, again and again, until at last successful. Who could avoid a demon-spirit forever? Distance would not have balked it; it would have flown wherever they could have gone, taken over the body of someone there, and stalked them. That would have been a sustained horror, with only one ending. But once it completed its mission by making the kill, it was done and would be no more threat. Satan's minions did not survive beyond their missions. So Cedric had saved her by interposing himself, by abating the demon's imperative—with his life. Cedric had not told her, so that neither Satan nor the demon would know of the ruse. And so she would not scream and carry on and cry, forcing him to desist from his sacrifice. Now it was done, and it seemed that Satan was unable to attack her again. That one demon must have been all that the Prince of Evil could spare. Or perhaps he simply hadn't checked and didn't realize that she hadn't died.

It did seem to fit together. It did account for Cedric's action—and that was a perverse but considerable comfort to her. Cedric had acted to abate once and for all the threat to her so that she could fulfill her destiny—which was, apparently, to become an Aspect of Fate.

But how was she to do that? Again, she knew what the answer had to be. *She* would do it; Fate would do it—when the time was right. When, perhaps, she needed the skill of a mistress of weaving. Fate—the ultimate worker of thread! The ultimate weaver of tapestries.

All Niobe had to do was wait. She was probably safe as long as she did nothing to attract Satan's attention to her. Of *course* the Incarnations weren't talking; the fewer who knew a secret, the better it was kept.

But now she had some hope. She could not bring Cedric back, but she could tackle Satan. When she became Fate.

But what about Junior? Surely she couldn't take him to Purgatory! She would have to give him up.

If Cedric had lived, she realized, none of this would have been possible. Had he known that, too?

Perhaps he had tried to tell her at the wake: that he wanted her to do this, to assume the office, that this was part of his motive. *O Cedric!*

She could not turn it down, now.

She continued about her routine, her grief slowly easing. She took Junior daily to play with the hamadryad, for he really looked forward to it and seemed to be learning something, though she was uncertain what. She worked hard to complete her current tapestry, lest it be forever unfinished if she were called suddenly away. She took Junior to visit Cousin Pace, because now she knew that one day he would have to go there to stay. She did not want to part with him, but knew this would be necessary—and that it had better be done sooner rather than later, to make his emotional transition easier. She quietly put her finances in order, arranging for a trust fund that would pay a stipend to his guardian, so that he would be no financial burden on others.

Weeks went by. Almost, she began to doubt. Then a fat letter arrived. It was addressed to her—but inside was a ticket to a city on another continent, with another woman's name on it. One Daphne Morgan.

Niobe looked again at the envelope. It was definitely addressed to her. She looked for the return address and found none. The postmark was indecipherable. Evidently the wrong ticket had been inserted, but there was no way she could send this letter back.

Wrong ticket? Why should she receive a ticket at all?

Who was Daphne Morgan? Had she received something intended for Niobe? From whom? Why? This seemed like total confusion.

Yet someone had prepared the envelope, and mailed it. It could not be a complete mistake.

She thought about it. She nodded. "Of course!"

She bid farewell to the hamadryad, explaining that she would be going away for a while and would not be able to bring Junior to the tree. The dryad didn't answer, but looked so sad that Niobe felt terrible. But this was a thing she had to do. "Maybe the family who will be keeping him—maybe they will bring him here," she said. "I'll ask them to."

The dryad smiled, and Niobe felt better.

She turned Junior over to Cedric's cousin's family. She had taken a null-grief spell, but still it hurt. "Once before," she told them, "I boarded my baby with you, uncertain whether I would return. I am uncertain again. I have arranged for regular money to cover his expenses—'' She could not continue.

"He is kin," Pacian's father said gravely as his wife took Junior. That said it all for these good folk. The Kaftans would do anything for kin and do it generously, without asking any return. Niobe could tell by Junior's reaction to them that he had had loving care here. Wise indeed had Niobe's parents been when they had her marry into such a family.

Niobe felt her tears starting again. She kissed her baby farewell and kissed the good man and good woman, too, and Cousin Pace, who seemed stunned. At age twelve, he had never been kissed by a truly beautiful woman before. "There is a tree, a water oak near our cabin," she said. "If—well, Junior has befriended the hamadryad there, and—''

"We will take him there," Pacian said eagerly, and the others nodded.

Then Niobe turned quickly away and returned to her carriage.

She rode directly to the train station, bought a ticket, waited for the train's arrival, boarded, and settled into her seat. She was on her way. She sobbed silently into her hanky.

In due course she was at the port city of Dublin. She presented the ticket she had been sent, the one made out to Daphne Morgan, and it was honored without question. She was provided a first-class cabin, and her meals were covered. As Miss Morgan, she traveled in style. But what would happen when she arrived at Miss Morgan's destination?

The ship got up steam and set sail. As it got out on the larger swells of the open sea, the captain invoked the proper spells and the wind manifested and filled the sails. Some of the passengers turned greenish as the continual sway got to them and lost their appetite, but Niobe had sensibly brought along a spell against motion sickness and had no trouble.

There were men aboard, of several generations, who seemed to view her as approachable; she declined politely. "I am a recent widow," she explained—and then had to retreat to her cabin as the tears welled up again. *O Cedric!*

Thus it was that, five days into the voyage, she had not made any genuine acquaintances. She spent much of her time alone, reading. She missed her loom and her baby and she tried not to think about Cedric, without success.

She looked up from her book to discover a spider descending by its thread. It reached the floor, then shimmered and became a human woman. "Lachesis!" Niobe cried.

"Niobe, do you understand what we ask of you?" Lachesis asked.

"To become—part of you," she replied. "To be an Aspect of Fate. I am ready."

"But we must be sure you understand completely, for this is no simple thing. We are three, but we have only one body. If you join us, you will never be alone."

"I have lived too long alone!" Niobe exclaimed.

"Because we are three in one, there is no privacy or separate identity," Lachesis continued. "No individual rights. Each must do what is needful for the whole, without exception. If, for instance, it is needful to dally with a man—"

"Oh. You mean—my body might have to—"

"To indulge with my man," Lachesis finished. "The most youthful Aspect generally bears the onus of such endeavors, because of the nature of men, just as the middle Aspect bears the onus of household chores, and the oldest performs grandmotherly functions."

This set Niobe back. She had never imagined having physical relations with any man other than Cedric and hesitated even to commence such imagination. "But what of the spinning of the threads of life?"

"That, too," Lachesis said. "But you will have no trouble there. A woman is not a single-purpose creature, and most purposes you are already prepared for. Our use of the distaff is merely more sophisticated than what you have known before." And in her hand appeared a glowing distaff, the short staff on which thread or yarn was wrapped. "We have only to keep the skein orderly; it is the social aspect that can be difficult."

Difficult indeed. The idea of being with another man—another woman's man—appalled her. Yet she could see that it did have to be a consequence of joining with other women, when there were not enough bodies to go around. "Suppose—I decline?"

"My dear, we do not force anyone to join us! It may be different with a couple of the male Incarnations—though of course there is no law about that, only custom—but we women are more accommodating. If you elect to remain mortal, you will return to your prior life, and we will select another woman for the exchange. But I confess that we do like you, and not merely for your beauty; seldom does a mortal person have the courage to approach Thanatos as you did."

"I have no courage!" Niobe protested. "I *had* to do it!"

"Oh? Why?"

"To save my husband, the man I love!"

"And for love you went literally into the fire. If that is not courage, it remains a quality we deeply respect."

"And it was all for nothing!"

"Yes, it is an irony. We could not give you what you desired, then, and we offer you some of what you do not desire now. Yet there are compensations."

Niobe knew she would burst into tears again if they remained longer on the subject of what she had desired; she had to focus on new things. "Compensations?"

"Immortality—as long as you choose. Power—as much as you can manage. Purpose—for you will spin the ultimate threads of man's existence. We are Fate."

Niobe thought about returning to her former life—without Cedric. Then she thought of immortality, power, and purpose—and the opportunity to seek to settle her score with Satan. She would rather have had Cedric, but she really had no choice—as Chronos had known. She was destined to accept this role. "How do I join?"

"Take my hand," Lachesis said, extending it.

Niobe took her hand. There was an odd sensation of flux. She felt simultaneous loss and gain. Then she saw that Lachesis had changed to the form of the young, pretty woman who had appeared momentarily in her Purgatory Abode.

Their hands separated. "Farewell, Daphne," Lachesis said. "And welcome, Niobe."

What? Niobe looked down at herself—and discovered she looked like Lachesis.

Yes—you are with us now, Lachesis said silently to her. *Your body has gone to Daphne—the former Clotho. Be silent; your day is coming, while hers is done.*

Niobe was silent. She watched and listened and felt, while Daphne turned about, verifying her new separateness, then faced them. "Farewell, old friends," Daphne said, and her own eyes were bright with tears. "And thank you, Niobe. You have given me back my life." She opened her arms, and Lachesis embraced her; this time there was no transfer of personality.

Tell her she is welcome, Niobe thought, feeling an almost overwhelming surge of nostalgia. Her body—changed to that other form—gone forever!

You tell her, Lachesis replied. Something shifted—and Niobe was back in her own form. Except that two other minds were with her.

She glanced in the cabin's mirror—and there she was, as lovely as ever, standing beside Daphne. Fate had assumed her likeness!

"You are welcome, Daphne," Niobe said.

Then, suddenly, she was crying uncontrollably. Daphne opened her arms to her, and they hugged each other, the tears streaming down both their faces.

At last they pulled apart, looked at each other, two comely young women, smiled—and burst into tears again. *For pity's sake!* the third mind in her body grumbled. That was, Niobe realized, Atropos, the oldest Aspect.

Eventually Niobe and Daphne ran dry. "I can see you resemble me," Niobe said tearfully. "I hope you have the very best of lives ahead of you."

"I surely do," Daphne replied. "Fate pulled a thread."

They had to laugh at that. Then Niobe turned the body back to Lachesis, who turned it into the spider, and they climbed nimbly up the thread to the cabin ceiling, on through the ceiling, and up out of the steamship and into the sky, suddenly cruising with great velocity along a cable extending across the world. In a moment they slid into their web-home in Purgatory and resumed human form.

"You will not need to learn the way things are by yourself," Lachesis said. "We will guide you when you need it—and routine homelife is mostly my department anyway. But you will need to spin the threads."

First Lachesis introduced her to Atropos. The body assumed the form, and the old woman went to stand before the mirror so that Niobe could see her clearly through their eyes. Atropos was in her sixties physically, with iron-gray hair, deep wrinkles, and an overlarge nose; she looked like anybody's grandmother. "I lived a routine life on a goat farm," she said. "I helped my husband milk the goats and I cooked and washed and bore four children—one of them died of smallpox when he was eight—but my two girls and remaining son grew up and married and moved away. I felt put out when they made it on their own; I had, I confess, enjoyed running their lives. So I concentrated on my husband and made him sell the farm—the market for goat's milk was declining as the big cow-dairies got established, though of course their milk could not compare in quality to what we produced—and invest the proceeds in a furniture factory. But we had been deceived about its prospects; it went bankrupt, and we lost our life savings. My husband took sick, got consumption, got pneumonia, and died broken-hearted, and I knew it was my fault; I should have left well enough alone. But meddling in other people's lives was always my predilection, and when Fate came to me and asked whether I wanted a *real* chance to meddle—well, here I am! I've been at it fifteen years, and I'm satisfied. And, I trust, I am not ending people's lives frivolously."

But doesn't Death—Thanatos—end people's lives? Niobe asked in thought. She couldn't talk aloud when she didn't have the body.

"Thanatos sees to it that the souls of those who die go to their proper appointments—Heaven, Hell, or Purgatory. He must judge the balance of good and evil in each soul, and tend to the difficult cases personally. But *I* determine when each life shall end; I cut the threads."

You cut the thread of Cedric's life?

"I had to. He had arranged to take the place of the thread I was supposed to cut short, so I had no choice. I do not have complete autonomy, especially when there are changes in the existing tapestry. I do not act capriciously. I must operate within parameters so that no thread extends beyond its proper position, or ends too soon. Otherwise the tapestry would be distorted."

But why any *thread?* Niobe demanded. *Why not let good folk live?*

Atropos formed a weary smile. "Child, that is a common fallacy of mortals. They assume that Death is the enemy and that everything would be all right if only they could live forever. It's just not true; the old must pass that the young may come into being. None of us would exist today if our elders had not made place for us. So each thread of life is given its appropriate term, some being longer than others, and each must end as it begins, according to the pattern of the tapestry. I simply tailor the individual threads for the good of the whole tapestry, facilitating the greatest good. It is not for any single thread to decide its own place in the tapestry! It would be disaster to live forever!"

What about the Incarnations? Niobe still felt guilty that she should have such a future reserved for her, while Cedric, the one with the most promise, had been cut short.

"The Incarnations are immortal, but not forever," Atropos explained patiently. "We maintain our lives without aging, as long as we hold our offices—but we do not hold them for all time. We have variable terms. Your predecessor, Daphne, served for twenty-six years, doubling her mortal life—until she spied a situation that was too tempting to resist. She found a good man—there's much to be said for a good man!—and he needed a good woman he would not otherwise obtain—and she simply had to have him. So she has left the office. Now she will age normally, until I or my successor cuts her thread, and she will move on to the Afterlife. Similarly, the other Incarnations change office, all in their own fashions. Thanatos dies when he becomes careless and is slain by his successor; Chronos assumes office as an adult and lives backward until the hour of his birth or conception—I have never quite been certain which—"

Backward? This was confirmation of what she had suspected. *How can he associate with others?*

"When you want to talk, here in the Abode, just take over the mouth," Atropos advised. "When we are in the company of others, we maintain separation of identities, but we can relax here at home. But to address your question: Chronos controls time. He can reverse himself in order to converse with others, or he can reverse them to align with him, for brief periods. At any rate, immortality is not perfection, and we Incarnations do eventually become bored or tired, and so we leave office. Only in mortality can the true guts of existence be experienced. Theoretically one of us might continue forever, but it has never happened, except in the case of God and Satan, and I'm not entirely sure about Satan.''

The old woman seemed to have the answers. Things did seem to make sense—but still Niobe could not accept the necessity of her husband's death. ''Would it have hurt the Tapestry so much,'' she asked, discovering that she could indeed assume control of the mouth without the rest of the body, when Atropos permitted, ''if Cedric had lived?''

Atropos shifted to Lachesis. ''That is my department, Niobe,'' she said. ''I measure the threads of life, which means I determine their approximate length and placement. I don't actually weave the tapestry—it is far too complex for any individual mind to compass—but I set the threads according to the pattern and see that they are properly integrated. Mortals tend to blame Fate for their failings and fail to credit Fate for their successes, which is annoying, but actually my options are limited. The overall pattern is determined by the interactive compromise between God and Satan—the macrocosmic balance between Good and Evil—and we other Incarnations simply implement it to the best of our ability. Certainly there would have been no harm if your beloved man had lived; he was *supposed* to live. Then we were forced to substitute your thread for his—and then to eliminate that too, for you are no longer listed among the mortals, though they are not aware of your departure. Let me show you.''

Lachesis gestured, and the mirror clouded, then opened onto an awesome scene. It was a phenomenal pattern in glowing colors, a Tapestry as wide as the world, with threads in their myriads like stars in the nocturnal welkin, forming a pattern of such marvelous intricacy as to baffle the mind of the beholder. Niobe had never seen a tapestry as magnificent as this; she simply stared, entranced.

''Your thread, and Cedric's, are approximately here,'' Lachesis said, using the distaff to point to one section, which expanded obligingly to show a better definition. It was like descending to Earth from Purgatory, watching the continents expand until they lost their cohesion, only this was not land but the enormous and splendid Tapestry of human existence. The line of color that Lachesis indicated became a mighty river of threads, and these continued to be magnified until at last the individual threads showed like cables, each in its separate region. ''To this side is the future, and to this side the past,'' Lachesis continued. ''The present is the precise center of the image; as you can see, it is moving.''

Indeed, the cables seemed to be traveling toward the ''Past'' side, so that the center drifted steadily toward the future without actually moving. The Tapestry was like a river flowing by. Niobe had to blink and blink again to avoid being mesmerized—but this was futile because at this moment Lachesis had the body and control of the eyes.

Lachesis indicated two cables in the near past. They converged from different parts of the Tapestry and linked, twining about each other. "Your marriage to Cedric," Lachesis said. The two continued on, separating a little to show when he went to college, and touching again when she visited him there. There was a sparkle at one point, and Niobe blushed in her mind when she realized that was their first lovemaking, a significant point in their relationship. Then, after a bit, a new thread started, tied in to theirs: Junior's conception or birth. Then the two major threads exchanged places, and Cedric's ended. There was his death—in lieu of hers.

Finally her thread separated from Junior's and faded out. It was not cut off; it just became obscure. Her assumption of the Aspect of Clotho. Its texture changed: Daphne. Niobe's mortal flesh had not left the world, only her spirit.

"So you see, the Tapestry now has one thread where there were two," Lachesis concluded. "And that one differs. We have tied it in in such a way that no one who does not inspect this region closely will realize that any change occurred. But the Tapestry as a whole is basically unchanged, no cohesion lost."

"But Cedric—"

"Incarnations do not make policy. We conjecture that Satan anticipated your assumption of the Aspect and sought to prevent it. In that he failed—but there generally is a cost when one foils the Prince of Evil."

"Then Satan can force mortals out before their time?"

Lachesis sighed. "Niobe, our firmament is not perfect. God and Satan made a Covenant of old that neither would interfere with the operations of mortal humanity. The idea is that each soul is given its chance in life, to make of it what it will, and those who prove they deserve to be in Heaven then go there, and those who deserve to be in Hell go there. All of mortal existence is merely the proving ground for the classification of souls, which is one reason why eternal mortal life cannot be permitted: it would clog the Tapestry and interfere with its function. But there was one loophole."

Lachesis turned away from the mirror and went to the Abode's kitchen to fix a meal. Niobe was half afraid that the larder of this spider's den would contain some huge, juicy fly for consumption, but the food was normal. She realized that Fate, unlike some of the Incarnations, did not have a household staff. As a woman—or three women—Fate preferred to do for herself. Niobe approved.

"God, as the Incarnation of Good, naturally does what is right; He honors the Covenant," Lachesis continued as she worked.

"Satan, being the Incarnation of Evil, naturally does what is wrong; he cheats. So Satan is constantly interfering in the affairs of mortals, yanking the threads about, generating no end of mischief. We other Incarnations, who are supposed to be neutral, must thus oppose Satan, just to get our jobs done. So the answer to your question is: Satan *shouldn't* take out mortals before their time, but he *does*. We try to prevent this—but your own case is an example of the problems we encounter. It is no easy thing to deal with determined evil, as we all know to our cost. I am sorry; we would have saved you and your husband if we could, but Satan has agents in the Purgatory Administration office, and he has absolutely no scruples. Your husband's death is a miscarriage of what was supposed to be—but it happened."

And with that Niobe had to be grudgingly satisfied. It strengthened her resolve to make Satan pay. Somehow.

— 5 —

VOID

It took a few days for Niobe to get into the routine. She learned how to travel on threads she flung out magically at will so that she could slide quickly to any portion of the globe. These were travel-threads, not the same as the threads of life; they appeared when needed and vanished when done. She learned how to generate the "Read Only" threads between her fingers for spot checks on individual lives, though she could obtain only a fraction of the definition that Lachesis could; it was a skill that went with the Aspect and experience. She learned how to change into spider form for special occasions. As Fate, she had an affinity for the web weavers, and no spider would protest her presence in its web or her intrusion onto its hunting ground. In fact, spiderwebs were convenient landing places when she traveled; she could slip to one much faster as an arachnid, then change to human form for whatever task required her attention.

She gained confidence: she might appear to be a weak woman, but an invisible net of web surrounded her, making her invulnerable to any mortal attack. She learned where the Purgatory Administration Building was, and who the key personnel were. These were not Incarnations, but lost souls—people whose balance between good and evil was so exactly even that they could not be relegated to either supernatural realm. They seemed like ordinary folk, which of course they were, and quite solid, which they were not. They were really ghosts, able to act only here in Purgatory. And she learned to spin souls.

But first she had to fetch the raw stuff of souls, and that was no easy task. "It's in the Void," Lachesis explained.

"The Void?"

"In the beginning, the earth was without form and void. God created the world from the stuff of the Void, and reality as we know it came into being. But not all of the Void was used. What remains of it occurs at the edge of Purgatory, and no one can go there except you."

"Me?"

"As Clotho. Not even we two other Aspects of Fate can go there; we become tuned out. This is the one journey you must make alone."

"But I'm so new here! I know so little about any of this! I can't—"

"There is no one else," Lachesis said. "Do not be unduly concerned; it is not a dangerous trip. It is merely a unique one."

She had to do it; it was a duty of the office. But she dreaded it. Her nightmare visions of what was to happen at the water oak had proved to be well-founded; now she hesitated to go into any truly challenging situation alone.

Lachesis took her to the edge of Purgatory. It looked quite normal and it was—but it was the boundary beyond which it was unsafe for any other person to go.

"And you and Atropos won't be with me, even in my mind?" Niobe asked uncertainly. She had found she liked their company; it abated the grief in her memory.

We will be with you—but unconscious, Lachesis replied in thought, for they were no longer at the Abode. It would have seemed strange if any other person overheard her talking to herself. *Our minds cannot face the Void. But we know yours can, for Daphne went many times. She told us it became easier each time.*

"The first, the worst," Niobe agreed wanly. "And I must seek the heart of it?"

Yes. Only there is the essence pure. Don't forget to play out the skein.

So she could find her way back. This time a temporary, vanishing travel-thread would not do; she had to be guided by the Thread of Life itself. She certainly would not ignore that detail!

She walked on along the road. If no one could go beyond this point, for whom was the road?

Some do go beyond, Lachesis replied, more faintly. *Tolerances differ. But you must go where no other goes.*

"Oh? Who else uses this road?"

Some of the other Incarnations. Now Niobe had to strain to pick up the fading thought. *Mars, Gaea. . . .* It was gone.

Niobe walked on, and the road dwindled into a footpath through a dense forest. Evidently the vegetable kingdom did not feel limited!

"The Incarnation of War," she murmured. "And of Nature. I wonder what business they have here?" But there was of course no answer. She was on her own.

The forest darkened and the path narrowed until it was a vague ribbon through the gloom. The trees became oppressively large and close, as if seeking to encroach on the path and squeeze whatever was on it. She did not recognize their types; they were simply walls of rough bark, extending up until the branching foliage closed overhead, sealing off the light. But her eyes adjusted, and she could still see. It was mostly her apprehension that was affected.

Nervously, she looked back. Her thread glowed behind, marking the way she had come. She was surprised to see that it soon curved out of sight; she had thought she was going straight. But it was a comfort to know she could not get lost, and she continued to hold the distaff so as to let the thread unwind. It was a thin thread, and she worried about its breaking. But she reminded herself that no one except Atropos could sever the Thread of Life and that there was no one else out here to interfere with it anyway.

The path ended ahead. She stopped, dismayed, then realized that, though a sullen tree blocked the way, it was possible to go around it. She squeezed on by—and found another tree blocking her off. It was just as if they were stepping in front of her, like aggressive men. A false impression, surely! She squeezed around that one, too. Because the trees took up more volume of space above, they could not stand trunk-to-trunk at ground level.

They tried, however. Their roots spread out of the ground and interlocked, and their lower branches reached down. But there was always a way through, however tortuous. The trees might try to balk Fate, but could not succeed. Probably this path was so devious because it fitted through the avenue of least resistance, no straighter or broader than it had to be.

Then the trees seemed to lose cohesion. They became misshapen, with trunks either swollen or shrunken, and their foliage—

She paused to blink and stare. The foliage was wrong! It was no longer green, but purple, and the individual leaves were formed into the shapes of stars or squares or triangles. How could that be?

Obviously it could be, because it was. She moved on. The forest retreated from the path, the trees becoming stranger yet. Now they were multicolored blobs of wood and brush, and some were floating. Apparently the laws of reality were weakening.

The path led her to a slope, and the slope became steep. She walked along the contour, and on her left a mountain stretched until the peak was lost in the brightness of the sun, and on her right the slope continued down into a valley so deep as to give her vertigo. As she proceeded, the slope increased until it was almost vertical—but her feet held the path, which was a level niche cut into the slope. Then the slope above actually passed the vertical, and overhung the path, while that below became undercut, so that the path was no more than a ledge cut into a horrendously leaning cliff. One misstep would send her hurtling down!

Niobe had never been timid about heights or depths, but this daunted her. Still, she saw no reasonable alternative other than to continue on. It was, after all, supposed to be safe, and Lachesis and Atropos, her better two-thirds, would not have sent her to her doom. Their own identities were in similar peril.

But what did they really know? Apparently Daphne had never told them exactly what she had faced here. Maybe it wasn't possible to convey the full effect—or maybe the attempt would cause needless alarm. After all, the soul substance had to be gathered, and this was where it was, so there was no choice.

She walked on. The slope became more extreme, until the upper wall curved down over the path and the lower wall seemed to curve up under it; she was walking in a notch or groove cut in the roof of a cave. There was no floor, just cloudy vagueness.

Then the upper wall curved down until it was below the path, and the lower seemed to curve above. She was walking in the eye of a pinwheel! Who could believe geography like this?

At length she emerged from the strange configuration. Ahead was a river—no, it was the path, but—

She stopped and looked back. Behind her was the vertical pinwheel, its walls spiraling outward from the center, which was her path, and expanding in ever-greater sweeps, until she was unable to trace them with her eye. To the sides was open space, with a few faint stars winking. Before her was—well, it started like a path, but continued like a stream. She kept trying to focus on it, but kept not succeeding.

One way to find out. She resumed her walk—and the path softened. Soon she was sloughing through muck. So she removed her yellow cloak—there was no mandatory color-coding, but it seemed that Clotho traditionally wore yellow, Lachesis brown, and Atropos gray—and laid it on the path. Then she stepped into it, trying to bring as little mud along as possible. There was no problem; the mud did not adhere to her shoes at all. It was like soft plastic, slimy and flexible but cohesive, sticking only to itself.

She settled down cross-legged, feeling exposed in her underclothing, though there really wasn't anyone to see. She set the distaff in her lap, stretched her hands out to either side, and set her fingers in the stuff. She pushed off—and the cloak moved slightly forward.

She pushed again, and it slid farther forward. After several pushes, the cloak was sliding along well enough.

Then the current caught it, and she was floating on down the stream. Her cloak formed into a saucer-shape; it made a decent if somewhat clumsy boat. She wasn't sure why it didn't collapse in on her, but she wasn't sure about much else in this region, either. She took hold of her distaff before it could spin out of her lap, and played out the lifeline of thread.

The stream carried her by a floating tree, which now seemed more like an island, and on through the starry sky. Perhaps it was a reflection in the water—except that the only water was the stream that the path had become.

Then the islands became big puffs of nondescript matter, which fell apart into lesser blobs that in turn sundered, until she was in a great cloud of pebbles, and then motes, and then smoke. The smoke dissolved, and she found herself drifting in nothingness.

She glanced at her distaff, and discovered that her thread had almost run out. But the stream had not yet run its course; it was carrying her somewhere, which meant that she had not yet gotten where she was going. She couldn't stop now, but if she didn't, she would leave her thread behind, and she was pretty certain that would not be expedient. She had to have more thread!

She considered a moment, then dipped her hand over the side and scooped up a handful of substance. It was like thin jelly or thick water. She stretched it between her hands, and it thinned into a taffylike strand. Could she fashion a thread of this? Why not; it was part of the stuff of the Void. It might not be pure, but it might do for this temporary purpose.

It was awkward doing it barehanded; she really needed a spinning wheel. Most yarn or thread was spun into fibers, ranging from the half-inch long cotton to the infinitely long silk; each type required its own special technique. The object was to render the fibers into a continuous thread that could then be worked into whatever fabric was required. The essential process in this conversion was spinning—which, very simply, was the winding of fibers together so that they became the thread. It could be done by hand, and she knew how to do it. She was, after all, a woman.

She had her distaff and spindle, but nothing to card or comb out the fibers. But this stuff of the Void didn't seem to be fiber; it was more akin to taffy. Presumably she could stretch it out into whatever diameter and length she wanted, and fix it in that form by spinning.

She experimented. She stretched some out between her hands, then used the distaff to take up a crude skein. When she had what she wanted, she used the spindle to twist the line, and she wound it fairly tightly on the spindle. The trick was to stretch and twist and coil in just the right manner to produce an even, strong, and fine thread. This stuff was unlike any she had worked before, but Niobe had excellent coordination and experience. If anyone could do it, she could.

Indeed she could. Her body looked and felt exactly like the mortal one she had left behind, but she was Clotho now, and had magic. Under her will and guidance the stuff of the void spun into crude thread, and this she spun onto the end of the thread she had brought with her, extending it. Now she could safely continue.

At last the cloak drifted to a halt. At least, so she judged; she had no external reference points, but she no longer had to play out the thread. This, evidently, was the heart of the Void, where she had to collect her month's supply of soul substance.

She had no container, so she used her skill again. She took a handful of the stuff she floated in, and processed it in the way she had the river. This was almost intangible, so she seemed to be going through the motions, spinning in a vacuum. But she felt a slight resistance and had faith she was suceeding. Soon she had some crude substance on her distaff: her skein of soul. She didn't know how much she needed, but knew she could come back for more when she ran out. This had not been as bad as it might have been.

Now she had to get back. She had drifted to this region, as it was the natural direction; things always drifted toward entropy. Now she had to go against the current—and how was she to do that?

First she tried the obvious—and it worked. She hauled on her life-line thread. She and her makeshift boat moved readily forward as she hauled; she seemed to have no inertia, no resistance. And she realized now that in the Void inertia was as baseless as matter; the rules of matter were unformed, here. Her thread was now her only connection to the material frame—if it was fair to call Purgatory that—so she was actually hauling herself in to her anchor. She hadn't needed the thread for finding her way, but for *making* her way.

The floating blobs reappeared, and the river became more evident; it was a runoff from organized matter, flowing from the organized to the disorganized. She had had to get beyond it, because the river was polluted by some aspects of organization. For new souls, the substance had to be as pure as she could make it; Lachesis had stressed that.

She reached the mucky portion of the stream, and finally had to get out and slough to the solid path. She was reentering contemporary reality.

"Hi, babe."

Niobe jumped. Someone was there, standing in the path, where no person could be!

"I see you are surprised, sweets," the figure said. He was hazy in outline, but seemed familiar.

"No one—can be here," she faltered. "Except Mars, or Gaea, or—"

"Or Satan," the figure concluded. "Where God can go, so can His Nemesis."

Her whole body stiffened. This was the Prince of Evil—the one who had arranged for her death! The one she intended to punish—somehow. "I hate you!" she exclaimed.

The figure laughed. "Of course, you phenomenally lovely creature! I am the Incarnation of all Evil, and hate is far from the least of evils! Did you realize they have issued a postage stamp in My name? It says HATE–HATE–HATE–HATE–HATE! Already you are coming into My bailiwick!"

This gave her pause. It was true; when she indulged herself in hate, she drew closer to Satan, even though it was Satan she hated. A treacherous situation indeed! She really couldn't afford to hate him.

She realized ruefully that Satan had scored against her at the outset. It was his advantage. "What are you doing here?"

"I need to clarify certain matters, sugar, as we shall doubtless be interacting henceforth."

She couldn't help herself. "Why don't you clarify why you killed my husband!"

"That is precisely why I have come here, luscious plum," Satan said. "It is known to Me that you have some misunderstanding about that matter, and it is not meet for confusion to exist between Incarnations."

"I have no misunderstanding! You interfered in my life!"

"Not so, sweet rose! I specialize in evil; I understand its workings better than any other entity does. Evil is everywhere, to greater or lesser degree, except perhaps in God, who is, frankly, naive in this matter. Let me show you the evil that is in the other Incarnations."

Niobe hurried along the path, poking her distaff forward to move Satan out of the way, but he floated back without moving his legs. He was simply fixed in place in relation to her, like a mirage. She could not escape his attention. "I—won't listen to this!" she exclaimed. "The other Incarnations aren't evil!"

"Evil is as evil does, love," Satan said. "From your contaminated thread on, evil lurks in every mortal creature, and it is not necessarily expunged by Incarnation."

"Contaminated thread!" Niobe exclaimed. "I just fetched it from the purest essence of the Void!"

"Purity does not exist in the Void, delicious thing," Satan said. "Only chaos. What you have is virtually pure entropy—that is, complete disorder. When you spin it, you are imposing order—your brand of order—on the purest chaos you can obtain. That is because you want to define its order completely, with no contamination by order from any other source. But because chaos *is* complete, it excludes nothing, not even a smidgeon of order. You are necessarily working with imperfect substance, O heart's desire; in fact it is that contamination of order that enables you to spin it. Without that, you would not be able to get a grip on it. But that is only part of it. That substance is a mixture of good, neutral, and evil, and it is impossible to tell which will prevail in the end. Therefore we run it through the ultimate test for its bias: animated free will."

Niobe was trying not to listen, but not succeeding. The voice of Evil was insidiously compelling. "I'm making this thread for life!"

"Exactly, darling. Animated free will—otherwise known as life. By the time each modicum of this soul substance runs its course, the nature of its individual balance between good and evil is known, and final order can be achieved. Eventually the last of the Void will have been processed, and the entropy of the universe will have been reduced to zero. All good will be in Heaven, and all evil in Hell. The job will done, and the system will be shut down."

Niobe was appalled. "All—life—just a—a laboratory to classify the substance of the Void?"

"Indeed. Beautiful, isn't it? Just like you, cutie. On that day of final reckoning we shall at last know which is dominant: God or Satan. The score will tell."

"Then what am I doing here?" she demanded, feeling dizzy.

"You are initiating the sequence, honey," satan said. "You are taking another spoonful of chaos out of the Void. It is a good and necessary task. But evil is in your thread of life; were it not so, we would not need life at all."

"Well, the Incarnations aren't evil!" she said stoutly. "You said yourself that this task I'm doing is good."

"The task is good, to be sure, doll. But the Incarnations are human—which is to say, imperfect. They have human ambitions, weaknesses, and lusts."

"Lusts!" she exclaimed indignantly. "What are you talking about?"

"I'm so glad you asked, precious." They were passing through the pinwheel now, the Incarnation of Evil still drifting before her like a specter, unavoidable. He was becoming clearer, and more eerily familiar. "Indeed the Incarnations do have lusts! They indulge them on occasion with mortals, but this is problematical. You see, ravishing one, the Incarnations do not age, physically—but mortals do. It is difficult for an Incarnation to maintain a relationship with one who constantly ages, particularly a romantic connection. So it is better to do it with another of his kind."

It had not occurred to Niobe that that sort of thing existed in Purgatory. Still, Lachesis had mentioned the possible use of the body; perhaps that was not merely an extreme occasion. She herself retained her grief for Cedric and her anger at Satan for his connivance in that. She knew from her personal experience already that much of what Satan told her was true: Incarnations did retain human passions.

"Unfortunately, scrumptious," Satan continued relentlessly, "there are relatively few Incarnations, and most are male."

"Chronos, Thanatos, and Mars," Niobe said shortly. "And you."

"Those are the major ones. Some would consider God to be male too, though that really doesn't matter. God is indifferent to mortal passions other than power."

"The major Incarnations? There are others?" She was still trying to ignore him, but he kept intriguing her curiosity.

"Didn't you know, sweet-buns? There's Hypnos, who is in charge of sleep, and Eros, in charge of—"

"Never mind. What's your point?"

"My point, fair creature, is that there is a severe scarcity of Incarnate young flesh. Gaea can of course assume any form she wishes, and she can be a lusty wench indeed, but she lacks one quality that most males prize in a female."

He paused, as if inviting her query—and Niobe was hooked. She had to ask. "What quality is that?"

"Innocence," he replied succinctly.

Niobe mulled that over. She could think of only one relatively innocent female in Purgatory: the newest one. Herself. "Surely you don't mean—"

"Consider Chronos, beautiful," Satan said. "He lives backward. He remembers the future, and doesn't know the past. Association with a mortal woman is, if you will excuse the expression, hellish for him. They just don't understand."

"But he can change time to coincide—"

"For short periods, cutie. Not for long-term. Which means that if he wishes to have a liaison once a week without a hassle, he must find a woman who understands his situation and is willing to accommodate him. That means another Incarnation. Gaea, or—" Again he paused, artfully.

"Are you implying that *I*—?" she demanded indignantly. Again she remembered how solicitous Chronos had been, and how understanding the other Incarnations had been during her first visit. And how closemouthed. That gave her an abiding disquiet.

With a Tangled Skein

"Chronos surely remembers," Satan said. "What is to be, has been, for him."

She was becoming outraged. "And you claim he—I—we—that I'm here because Chronos wants—"

"And the other Incarnative males," Satan agreed. "Fate is known as an accommodating woman. But of course those males prefer her youngest and firmest Aspect, as perhaps your better two-thirds have already explained to you."

Niobe could not answer. She *had* been told. Now that notion was becoming much less theoretical.

"You see, honeypot," Satan continued inexorably, "we Incarnations have to get along with each other. We are too small a group, and our duties overlap; if we do not cooperate, the world will revert to chaos and all will be lost. We are not antagonists; we are the several Aspects of the job. Fate cannot operate without Time—so it behooves her to keep him satisfied, and she has one exceedingly potent mechanism therefor."

"I can't believe that!" she cried, beginning to believe.

"You may verify it very simply, roundheels. Ask Chronos. He remembers."

"No!" she said. "I love Cedric! I will never—" But she had already agreed when she assumed the office. What had she thoughtlessly gotten herself into?

"Ah, yes, Cedric. Your sacrificial husband, the boy wonder. Allow me to clarify the story on that."

"No!" she said, turning her face away. But she continued to listen.

"The Incarnations—and not just Chronos—wanted a new face and body and innocence in Purgatory," he said. "I mean, even the sexiest and most accommodating young woman—and Daphne was certainly that!—palls after a few years or decades, especially when her body doesn't change at all. Especially when her mind gets too knowing. She's a good one to visit—don't I know!—but not to stay with. The novelty is gone, and novelty is chronically in short supply in Purgatory. So when Clotho found a compatible situation among the mortals, she took it. She was bored out of her gourd, as the saying will one day go, and—"

"How can you know what a future saying will be?"

"Chronos uses expressions he remembers from the future, and some of them are apt. At any rate, trixie, the Incarnations did an informal survey of mortal flesh, and you were the prettiest innocence they found, and your ability with loom and distaff made it even better. The perfect unliberated, docile sex object! So they arranged to bring you in. That meant eliminating your man."

This was appalling. She had to deny it—yet could not. Satan might be the personification of evil, but he was making sense. Still, she tried to fight, weakly. "But it was *me* they—you tried to kill, not Cedric."

"So they told you, cheesecake. But that was a ruse, to shift the blame to Me. After all, they could hardly have found a better surrogate for blame! So that you would agree to join. It does, in that limited sense, have to be voluntary; you have to think you want it. They have to remove the one you love, to leave you no further reason to remain mortal. They conveyed to your innocent bonnie boy that *you* were the target, thus very cleverly tricking him into doing exactly what they wanted—"

"No!" Niobe cried like a drowning woman.

"And it worked perfectly, as you know, trophy-piece. Now the most desirable and innocent morsel of a young woman on Earth is in Purgatory and available for duty. The Incarnations are already champing at the nether bit. I could hardly have done it better Myself—but of course such evil is Mine anyway, by definition. I suggest you relax and enjoy it, toots."

"Relax, hell!" she screamed.

Satan smiled. "Exactly."

She peered at him more closely. His image had been slowly clarifying as they progressed, and now at the verge of the forest he was at last recognizable. He had assumed Cedric's form.

"You utter cad!" she screamed, trying to push him into a tree. "You have no right to—to—"

He caught her hand. "Shall I kiss you, sweetlips?" he asked in Cedric's voice. "I, too, find you desirable, and I can make you forget—"

She struck at him with the distaff she had been rewinding. He ducked, and the thread sprang out and settled about him in a tangle. "Get out! Get out!" she screamed.

Satan resumed his normal form, and sighed. "Another time, perhaps, when you have been suitably broken in." He faded away, leaving her with the tangle.

Niobe stood and cried in rage and grief for some time. *Damn* Satan! He had changed her promising new existence into a torment of savage emotion.

But after a while she reasserted such cynicism as she could muster. She detached the tangled mass of threads, as they were from the borrowed section of the river, spun the ends together, and resumed her walk. She was not a plaything of Fate; she had free will, and she could leave this position if she wanted to. They had explained that each Incarnation, except perhaps Chronos, had a trial period in office, after which he or she was granted indefinite tenure if suitable. She would simply declare herself to be unsuitable and return to mortality. Certainly she would not serve in the—the capacity they wanted!

She wended her way through the trees, her tears drying on her face. What a monstrous conspiracy she had fallen into! To think that Cedric had died in order to make her available for—

She was still furious as the forest retreated and thinned, and the path straightened and became a road. She was back in structured reality, now—and not one bit pleased.

What's the matter, Clotho?

They were back! "You should know, you hypocrites!" she flared.

She was met by a thought of amazement. *Why do you say that?*

Niobe let loose a torrent of why.

Wait! Wait! We can't assimilate all that! We can feel your anger, but you will have to vocalize to clarify the reason.

"Cedric!" Niobe shouted. "You conspired to kill Cedric, so I would—would—" Her tears started up again, and her emotion was a confusion of love, sorrow, and fury reminiscent of the chaos of the Void she had just departed. Perhaps, she thought in an isolated flash of humor, she had brought the Void with her—in her head.

Cedric? We explained about him!

"Well, Satan explained it better! I'll not stay in this job! You had no right to—"

Satan! Lachesis' thought came.

That explains it! Atropos agreed.

"Yes, Satan!" Niobe agreed. "He really understands evil! He was there in the Void, and he—"

And he told you an intricate lie, Lachesis continued.

And you believed him, Atropos concluded.

"Yes, I believe him!" Niobe cried. "And I want to go back to mortality! At least there my body is my own!"

You believed the Father of Lies, Atropos thought.

It is your right to return, Lachesis agreed. *But first we must hash this out. You must know the truth before you act, lest Satan lead you to tragedy.*

"Why should he do that?"

He does not want you in the office. He knows that somehow you will cause him great trouble. That is why he tried to kill you before you could become Clotho.

Niobe suffered doubt. Satan had been persuasive—but he *was* the Incarnation of Evil, and certainly he would lie to suit his purposes. She should not believe him without establishing the case thoroughly. "How can I verify this?"

Perhaps Chronos knows.

"Chronos!" Niobe exclaimed indignantly. "All he wants is—"

That is a half-truth.

"You admit to half of it?" Niobe demanded.

Lachesis made a mental sigh. *Satan has poisoned your mind. You must cleanse it yourself. Go to Chronos, challenge him. We will be silent until you address us.*

That, of course, was the answer. Chronos was at the heart of this. She would give him a jagged fragment of her mind!

She returned to the Abode, deposited her new batch of yarn—she would reprocess that into much finer thread later, as she spun out the lives of new mortals—assuming she remained in office that long—and set off along the line that connected to Chronos' mansion. She was awkward in her use of the travel-thread; it would have been faster and smoother if one of the other Aspects had handled it, but she needed to master the techniques herself in order to—

To what? Be a good Clotho? When she had no intention of retaining the position? Unlikely chance!

She made it to the mansion. She had learned that time reversed when a person entered Chronos' residence, so that she would actually depart before she arrived. She found that aspect of it intriguing. It existed so that others could converse comfortably with Chronos; otherwise each would be talking backward at the other.

She knocked on the door, and was admitted immediately. Chronos met her, wearing a pure white robe; he stepped right up, smiling, and took her in his arms and kissed her.

Niobe was so surprised that she simply froze for a moment. Then she recovered, jerked back her head, brought up her arm, and slapped him smartly across the cheek. "What kind of nerve do you have, trying a thing like that?" she cried.

He turned her loose, a look of astonishment on his face. "Why, Clotho—what happened?"

"What happened?" she repeated furiously. "You just grabbed me and kissed me!"

"But of course! As I have always done, here at home."

"Always done!" she screamed. "Then it's true!"

Now a look of realization spread across his countenance. "The time—are you just beginning your cycle?"

"My what?"

"Have you just begun your office? As Clotho?"

"Of course I have, as you well know! And if you think I—"

"But I *don't* know!" he protested. "That's in my future, and you have never said exactly when—"

Because he lived backward. Now she understood. "You—you couldn't have conspired to—because it hasn't happened yet, for you!"

"I would never conspire against you, Clotho," he said. "I love you."

She felt as if a demonic hand had squeezed her heart. She reeled, and sank onto a couch. It was true—they were going to have an affair! This man she didn't know, and certainly didn't love!

"Ah, Clotho," he said. "I didn't realize. You have not done this before. You don't—remember. Had I realized—I'm sorry. I should have known. Long ago you told me the date of your origin. I had forgotten. I apologize for—"

"What do you remember?" Niobe asked dully.

He took a seat opposite her. "When I assumed my office, thirty-five years hence in your view, I was bewildered by everything. I did not know what to do, or how to do it—even the Hourglass was a mystery to me. But you, in your three guises, came to me, and took me in hand, and set me straight. It was as if you had known me all along, though we had never before met. You did so much for me, and I was grateful, and then you—"

He broke off, putting his face in his hands. "Oh, Clotho! It's over at last, and so abruptly! I owe you so much and I will miss you so much!"

Suddenly he reminded her of Cedric, as he had been at the outset of their marriage. So forlorn and lost and unable to come to grips with what he knew had to be. She, in her naiveté and insensitivity, had only exacerbated his problem. How much she regretted that now!

And the magnitude of Satan's lie was manifest: Chronos had never, *could* never conspire. *She* had initiated their romance—thirty-five years hence. And now she was blaming *him*!

If she had known, at the outset of her marriage to Cedric, what was to be, she would have been far more understanding and careful. Now she faced a roughly similar situation. She did not love this man—but neither had she loved Cedric, at first. The lesson was there.

Did she really want to return to mortality? Cedric still would not be there. If she had to live without him, wouldn't it be better to do it with the power of the Incarnation of Fate, rather than as a simple mortal? Chances were that this job would offer her many distractions. She could keep herself busy—and she could leave whenever she chose to. She didn't have to make a decision yet. Yet—

Satan had tried to talk her into leaving. He wouldn't have bothered if she were not destined to cause him some grief.

Chronos remembered three and a half decades' association with her. That showed her decision and her future. What point to rail against it? Better to take herself in hand and do what had to be done. Cedric was dead; he would never live again. She had to face reality, and the sooner the better. This was her moment of commitment. She did not relish the prospect, but she had to put the past firmly behind her.

She dried her face, arranged her hair, and stood. Chronos sat with his face covered. He was not pretending; he was a decent, vulnerable man, and he was mourning a relationship he knew was past. Indeed it was, for him. It was an emotion she understood.

She crossed over to him and put one hand on his shoulder. "Chronos, I understand. But this—is the last time."

He looked up. "The first—for you."

"For me. I do not—love you, but—" She shrugged. "I misjudged you, Chronos, and I'm sorry. I—I give you this. There is only now, for us. Such as it is."

"Such as it is," he agreed, lifting his hand to her.

She took it. "When next we meet, it will be different. I will not remember—this. Or know of it."

"I will not speak of it." He drew her down to him.

She tried to conceal her aversion to being handled by any man not Cedric. She felt guilty and unclean—but, perversely, she was sure she was doing right. She was no longer married, no longer mortal, and she had a job to do here and a role to fill. It turned out that Chronos' long experience with her future self gave him a special touch, and it became easier to cooperate.

When it was done, she dressed and departed, using an exit opposite to the entrance she had used so that there was no chance of encountering her arriving self. She did not want to try to explain or justify what she had done to that self!

Then, because she also did not wish to return to her web Abode before she had left it, she elected to spend an hour elsewhere. That would allow for the half hour she had spent in Chronos' mansion, and carry her another half hour beyond. The net effect would be the same as if her half hour within had been composed of normal, forward time.

Where would she go in that period? Where else! She went to Earth. She slid down a thread—this was good practice!—to the farm where Junior was. She walked up to the door and knocked.

They were surprised and pleased to see her, with masked concern. "I am only visiting. My other business is not yet done; I must still leave Junior with you."

She saw relief in them, and it gratified her. They really wanted to keep Junior, and she knew it wasn't for the support stipend. This was certainly the place for him.

She picked him up and held him and kissed him, then set him down. In a moment he was back playing with Cousin Pace.

"That's a very nice water oak," the woman remarked. "The dryad came right down to join him when we retreated.'

They were doing it! At least the dryad was not being deprived. "She is teaching him magic," she said with a wink.

"If he can learn it, he'll be some magician!" the man said.

Yes—she had done right here. The loss of her baby hurt her, but she could adapt to this, just as she could adapt to the affair with Chronos. She was a different person, now, with new and different commitments. Even her body wasn't her own, but a construct from the flesh of Fate, as if formed from the substance of the Void.

But she was no creature of the Void! She had a new kind of life to live. She hoped it would turn out better than the old one.

– 6 –

GENEALOGY

Niobe's life as Clotho settled in comfortably enough, now that she had made the necessary emotional decisions. Each Aspect slept for six or eight hours, and they generally staggered these, so that at any given moment one Aspect would be dominant—would have the body—and another would be keeping her conscious company, while the third would be tuned out or asleep. For convenience they generally proceeded from sleep, to company, to dominant, so that an Aspect could be fully alert and ready the moment she took over the body. Thus Niobe, as Clotho, would sleep, then keep Atropos company for her shift, then assume the office while Atropos slept and Lachesis kept her company. Sometimes they varied it, and special circumstances caused them all to wake or sleep together, but normally the routine held.

Niobe liked the other two. They talked with each other a lot, comparing notes on experiences and feelings. The other two had eavesdropped on Niobe's first engagement with Chronos, for this was as novel to them as to her. They had indeed not conspired to put her in that position; they had not been having an affair with Chronos. Evidently he, in the progress of his life toward their past, had not been interested in the to-him new Clotho. "But the body is only the body," Lachesis said philosophically, as Niobe spun her Thread of Life from the supply of yarn she had fetched from the Void. "You are young, you like to think that there is only one man for each woman and one woman for each man, but any combination can occur, and couple, and love. In this office we are forced to be less romantic and more pragmatic."

"Yes," Niobe agreed sadly. "And Chronos is a good person. But I'll always love Cedric."

"There is no love like the first," Lachesis agreed, taking over the lips again. "I remember mine . . ." And she recounted her own first romance. It was not as immediate as Niobe's experience, but it had its own poignancy, and it did show that the older woman understood. Men tended to think in terms of the physical, while woman related to the social; men focused on bodies and action, while women focused on character and feeling. They agreed that woman's way was more sensible, but on occasion man's way had merit, and it was possible for the two to relate.

They learned each other's jobs, to a certain extent. Niobe normally slept while Lachesis measured the threads, but not always, and of course she was alert while Atropos cut them. The cutting was not merely at the terminal end; the threads had to be started, too. So after Lachesis had analyzed, measured, and marked each potential life, on the endless thread Clotho spun, Atropos would cut and place it. The beginning of a cut thread was the conception of a baby; it had to be tied in to the threads of its parents before moving out onto its own course in the Tapestry. The physical, mental, and emotional qualities of a life were determined by heredity, provided by the parental tie-in, and its development was influenced considerably by environment. But its circumstance—the odd coincidences that governed every life—was arranged by Fate. Some excellently endowed lives were doomed to disappointment and failure, while some seemingly weak strands were destined for greatness. Lachesis planned these threads with an eye to the esthetics of the larger picture. Some she regretted, as when a thread had to be measured short, meaning that a child would die. But it had to be done, for stresses in the fabric of the Tapestry could distort the whole, and lead to the damage of many more innocent threads unless the correction was made in the key region. It would not have been easy to explain to the average mortal why he should suffer, as the stresses were cumulative and subtle; indeed, there were generally several ways in which a given stress could be alleviated. But it was Lachesis' job to select a course and implement it, and this she did.

Cedric's early death had not really been Lachesis' doing. Satan had stretched the fabric in such a way that only the truncation of a specific thread would alleviate it—and Niobe had been that thread until Cedric abruptly switched places with her. Lachesis had had to mark it for elimination, and Atropos had had to cut it—but that had been in the nature of emergency surgery. They were still adjusting for the distortion in the fabric caused by that unscheduled removal; it tended to buckle, and several more distant threads had had to be cut short, and new ones added elsewhere. Now Niobe, tracing the pattern and grasping the stresses on it, understood how complex the matter of Fate was. Fate was not all-powerful or capricious; she merely had to accomplish a purpose that mortal man was not properly equipped to appreciate. It would make as much sense for an individual soldier in battle to break ranks and demand of the general why he should be subjected to this danger.

But Niobe was no longer a foot soldier. She had become an Aspect of an Incarnation. She was now in a position to grasp the larger picture—and to understand just what Satan had done to her. She still had a score to settle with him!

The problem was, she didn't see how. Satan had no Tapestry; she could not mess up his threads. She concluded that whatever it was that made Satan object to her presence as Clotho had not yet manifested and that she was on the way to gaining her satisfaction merely by retaining her office. Eventually her chance would come—and then she would take it with a will. Meanwhile, she just had to be patient.

In due course the routine became dull. Then the interactions with the other Incarnations, including Satan, became more interesting. Niobe did not love Chronos, but he was so grateful for the particular favors she rendered that it became a kind of pleasure for her. She did have to work with him quite a bit, or rather Lachesis did, for only Chronos could accurately locate the timing of the key events in each life—the kinks in each thread. The Tapestry would not be right if the threads were too loose or tight, or crossed each other in the wrong places. It was especially important that Atropos inform Chronos of the precise end of each thread, for Chronos programmed the watch that Thanatos carried. If Thanatos was not present for particular terminations—the souls in close balance between good and evil—those souls could escape and drift back to the Void, causing the whole effort to be wasted. No one approved of wasted lives.

But this, too, became dull. Therefore the Aspects of Fate were wont to visit the mortals directly when slack-time was available. They would merge anonymously with the throngs of people, and pretend to be going home from work, or taking a vacation, or performing some business. People tended not to perceive the Incarnations as such, and to forget them, so it was simple enough to do. Each Aspect had her favorite region of the mortal world to visit. It was a kind of holiday.

Lachesis liked to go to special restaurants and enjoy good meals. The Incarnations did have natural functions, including the need to eat. If they did not eat, they would not starve, because of their immortality, but they would become increasingly uncomfortable. They had everything provided in Purgatory, but there was something special about doing it among the mortals. The male Incarnations, Lachesis confided wickedly, sometimes indulged other appetites with mortal women, though they had to be careful not to change the lie of any particular thread. An Incarnation could not sire a baby, because of the freeze on aging—a baby would never develop beyond the single-cell stage—but that was not the only way to affect a mortal. Once Mars had formed a relationship with a mortal Amazon—he had a weakness for violent women—and her thread had changed its course. This affair superseded one she would otherwise have had with a mortal man that would have generated offspring. Lachesis had had to bail him out; she had measured that thread but found no way to attach it to start the baby. The necessary interaction had not taken place. She has spoken sharply to Mars about that, requiring him to break off the affair so that the natural order could reassert itself; then she had tied in the new thread a little farther down the line. Clotho had had to sweeten the pot for Mars until he found a new mortal to dally with. It was a private scandal.

Atropos preferred to go to orchestral recitals, operas, and plays. Indeed, she had a reserved box at one prominent playhouse. Niobe got to watch these too, and learned to enjoy them. In this manner she was able to acquire some culture. Once, however, a gentleman had challenged Atropos' credentials; it seemed they had not been able to verify her social credentials and suspected she was a commoner in disguise. At this point Niobe had taken over the body, smiled, and asked the man what he meant. He blinked, for she was young and beautiful instead of old and homely; he had apologized for the confusion and departed. Atropos resumed form and watched the opera in peace.

Niobe herself went to visit her son. At first she went as she was, but she soon realized that this could not continue. For one thing, she did not age; she was locked at the physical age of twenty-three, and before long this would be noticed. Also, she did not want Junior to be accustomed to her presence; it was better that he forget her and orient entirely on his new family. It would be easier on him, in the long run. And—it was evident that young Cousin Pacian was smitten by her. This sort of thing happened with adolescents; it was a liability of beauty. She deemed it best simply to absent herself.

Still, she wanted some personal interaction with her son. So she asked Atropos to pose as a grandmotherly friend who visited relatives in the area and liked children. Atropos, with Niobe's silent advice, cultivated the lad's acquaintance, and in time Pace, ever on guard for any threat to his little friend's welfare, came to accept her also. As the years passed, and Junior became an active child and Pace a tall and surprisingly handsome teenager, Atropos took them to light operas and plays of interest to all ages. Because Atropos had a wide knowledge of the form, she knew which ones were appropriate, and it worked nicely. Both boys enjoyed it, and Pace's parents looked with favor on it. Atropos herself found this to be a rewarding experience, so it was good all around.

But there was one experience that shook them all. It happened when Junior was six years old and Pace eighteen. It was the day of the annual fair, and everyone went—but the old folks soon got separated from the young folks in the press of the throng. Atropos counted as a young folk; Pace hardly needed supervision, but little Junior did, and anyway they had long been a threesome for such jaunts. They cruised the fair, trying the games of psuedo-skill, eating candy, and riding the small captive sphinx. They watched a magic show that was somewhat faked up to make the magic appear more impressive that it was, and sat through two choruses of the Nymph-vs.-Satyr dance. But though it was suggestive, it wasn't potent; the participants were authentic, but in the course of a dozen shows a day they lost their ardor. Nevertheless, little Junior's eyes almost bugged; he wasn't supposed to be in here, but enforcement was lax and he had promised not to tell the folks. Niobe herself had grave reservations, but Atropos had pooh-poohed them: "The lad's interested in magic, and this is an aspect of magic. It isn't as if he's never seen a nymph before." Of course that was true, because of the hamadryad of the water oak.

Then they passed a prophecy booth. "Hey, tell my fortune!" Junior cried. This was magic, so he liked it.

"Ah, it's probably fake," Pace protested.

"I can verify that, if you wish," Atropos said.

What are you doing? Niobe thought at her. *The fortune-teller will recognize you!*

"Very well, let's test her," Pace agreed, as he liked to expose humbugs. Junior clapped his hands.

So they stopped there, and Atropos paid the seer. The woman looked at her, then proffered the return of the money. "You seek to fool me, immortal one?" she demanded. "You know I cannot read your like!"

"She's authentic," Atropos reported, and pushed the money back. "Do it for the two boys; they are mortal."

"You're immortal?" Pace asked, looking at Atropos.

"I'm old, but I won't actually live forever."

He wasn't quite satisfied with that explanation, but let it pass. "Very well. Do us together, me and my little brother here." He hefted Junior up to sit on the counter. "Who are we going to marry, and will our children be famous?"

With a Tangled Skein

Junior giggled at the audacity of the question, not believing that the present order would ever change, but the seer took it seriously. "Give me your hands," she said.

She took Junior's right hand and Pace's left, and closed her eyes. In a moment they opened again. "Hooh!" she exclaimed, as if letting off a head of steam. "A most remarkable pair!"

Niobe became more interested. What did the seer see?

"Each to possess the most beautiful woman of her generation, who will bear him the most talented daughter of her type," the seer intoned. "Both daughters to stand athwart the tangled skein, and one may marry Death and the other Evil." She cast loose their hands, seeming shaken. "More I dare not say."

Pace lifted Junior down, and they moved away from the booth. "That was a true telling?" he asked, awed.

"So it seems," Atropos said. "Of course interpretation changes things, so it may not mean what it seems."

"That prophecy is loaded!" he exclaimed. "The most beautiful daughter?"

The tangled skein? Niobe asked. *That's our business!*

"And one may marry Death, the other Evil," Atropos said thoughtfully. "I'm not sure I like the smell of that."

Niobe had similar doubts. *Death is Thanatos, and Evil is Satan. Their daughters will marry Incarnations?*

"What's a tangled skein?" Junior asked.

"Trouble!" Atropos said.

Trouble, Niobe agreed.

They settled down under a tree and talked it out. "This is not a bad prophecy," Atropos told the boys. "It is no disaster for a man to possess—that is, to marry—the most beautiful of women, and to have talented offspring. If they stand athwart the skein, that probably means they are to be very important figures. As for marrying Death and Evil—well, remember the prophecy says *may.* Any person may get into trouble if careless! You have your warning; you must educate your children to beware of such things as Death and Evil, and there should be no problem."

"Say, yes!" Pace agreed, brightening. "We have been given warning. We can make it come out all right."

But little Junior, oddly, was more pensive. "Aren't prophecies un—un—"

"Unavoidable," Atropos finished for him. "Yes, a true prophecy will be fulfilled, and this seems to be a true one. But it does provide leeway."

"I want another," Junior decided. "A corr—corr—"

"A corroborative opinion," Pace finished.

Atropos shrugged. "I suppose it can't hurt."

Asking for a corroborative opinion? Niobe thought. *My son is smart!*

So they went to another seer. Again Atropos proffered the money, and again the seer did a double take. "What do you do here, you sinister trio?" she demanded.

"It is for the boys," Atropos said, knowing it had not been the physical three the seer referred to. This was another qualified one! "Do them together. What is to become of them and their children?"

The seer took the boys' hands, as had the first one—and her eyes also widened. "One to be savior of deer, his child savior of man; other to love an Incarnation, his child to *be* one. But the skein is tangled—oh!" The seer tore her hands away. "I cannot finish; it is too much for me." Indeed, she was shaking.

They retreated and discussed this one. "Deer?" Junior asked.

His father sought to enable the deer to shoot back at the hunters, Niobe clarified. So Atropos explained about that, and the boy was satisfied.

"I'm going to do it!" he exclaimed. "Hama will show me how! I'll make the deer shoot back!"

But Pace looked narrowly at Atropos. "How do you know about that? My cousin Cedric died before you met us."

"I know his wife, Junior's mother," Atropos said. "I told you I was a friend of the family."

"Oh? Where is she now? She hasn't visited us in a long time."

"She is locked into a very special project," Atropos said. "A secret one. That is why she couldn't have Junior with her."

"She's the most beautiful woman I ever saw," Pace said dreamily.

"What's an Incarnation?" Junior asked.

"The Incarnations are human personifications of the important aspects of existence," Atropos said carefully. "Love, War, Time—"

"Death, Evil," Pace put in. "That other prophecy—"

"I think," Atropos said, "your daughters are going to associate with some remarkable figures, and perhaps become—"

"An Incarnation," Pace said. "Is that possible?"

"Mortals do become Incarnations on occasion," Atropos said. "But it is a very rare thing."

"Which one?" Junior asked.

Atropos spread her hands. "As both seers said, it is a tangled skein. I doubt we can unravel it before the event—and it may not be wise to try."

"Yes, I think we should stay away from prophecies after this," Pace said. But Junior didn't seem convinced.

They went on to other distractions of the fair, but the boys were pensive, and so was Niobe. As Aspects of Fate, she and Atropos could trace the threads of life—but not far into the future, for the vision of the Tapestry soon fuzzed. This wasn't because of hostile magic, but because the Tapestry itself was so immensely complex that only direct inspection of its present portion could unravel any of it. But Niobe knew that the threads for both Pace and Junior were of normal length; neither would die young. After Cedric, she had made sure of that! But she could not see their precise interactions in the coming Tapestry. These prophecies seemed to confirm that the boys, who were already associating with an Incarnation, would continue to do so. In that sense the outlook wasn't as remarkable as it seemed. But obviously there was a great deal destined to occur!

Time moved on, and none of them discussed the prophecies further, but Niobe knew that the boys had not forgotten. From that point on, Junior focused increasingly on magic. He bought a magic kit, and practiced simple conjurations and transformations. He wasn't really good at them, but no other boy his age even attempted genuine magic; it was easier to hire a professional magician, or to buy packaged spells. Junior did seem to have a special talent for imprinting stones; it seemed the hamadryad had shown him that. He could take a pebble from the shore of a lake and cause it to glow or make a sound. Stone-magic was a specialty that few did well, and his ability was remarkable in one so young. Niobe bought an intermediate gemstone, a green aquamarine, and had Atropos give it to him for his eighth birthday. He was thrilled, and indeed the quality stone was much more responsive to his spells than the crude pebbles were. He fashioned it into a homing stone that showed by its glow which way home was, so that he could never get lost. "That boy is going to be a major magician, mark my word," Atropos said.

Pace progressed to other interests, as well as taking over most of the management of the family farm. When he was twenty-two he married Blanche, a schoolmate with hair so fair it was almost white. Blanche was a fine person, warm and generous and competent about the farm, but by no stretch could she be termed the most beautiful woman of her generation. Pace gave Atropos a significant glance at the wedding, showing that he remembered the prophecy—and had deliberately avoided it.

Niobe was uneasy. The prophecy had said "possess" rather than "marry"; if he did not marry the most beautiful woman, how would he associate with her? But she kept her misgivings to herself.

The following year, when Junior was eleven, Blanche gave birth to a baby girl. From the start, Blenda was dazzling, certainly the prettiest baby in the vicinity. She grew into a stunning child. If Pace hadn't married the prettiest woman, he seemed to have fathered her, and in that sense possessed her. Blenda was the talk of the county.

Junior was now an only child, for Pacian and Blanche lived separately. It was a considerable adjustment for him at first, for his cousin/brother had been much of his family. He knew that his natural father was dead, and his natural mother absent, but his identity was with his cousin's family. He turned inward, focusing even more on his pursuit of magic. Niobe hated to see him lonely, but could do nothing; she had given him up, and, anyway, it was the sort of adjustment a person had to make in life. But Atropos seemed to take it harder than Niobe herself did. The old woman had really come to like the boy and missed the threesome adventures. Perhaps by no coincidence, Atropos decided to retire from her Aspect. "I've had enough of immortality," she said.

Lachesis searched the Tapestry, and located a widowed grandmother who would do. They went to visit her, in the form of Atropos. The woman listened gravely while Atropos explained her nature and her desire. "But if what you say is true, I will become immortal and you will die of old age!" the woman pointed out. "Why would you seek such a bargain?"

"It is true that I will not survive long as a mortal," Atropos agreed. "But I have lived fifteen years beyond my time, and I have no fear of the Afterlife. I know I have done well enough and will see Heaven and I am ready for it."

They showed the woman their other two forms, and she was duly impressed. "Do you mean that I can be young again, and be like that? I have never seen a woman as beautiful!"

Niobe had the body now. "You can share with me," she explained. "But I will govern; you will be an observer, just as I will be an observer when you govern. But after a while we seem to overlap; we become in effect a single person with alternate forms. In that sense you can become me, if you wish."

The woman shook her head. "I am astonished. Let me think about it."

She thought about it for a week, then put her affairs in order and joined Fate. No complexities of meeting were necessary, as this was not a person Satan opposed; Niobe had been a special case. This time Niobe watched from inside as Lachesis took the woman's hand, and her essence entered them, while the old Atropos departed. In a moment the Atropos they had known stood before them, a separate person, molded from the flesh of the mortal woman. Again there were tears; however voluntary the transition was, there was sorrow in it too. They separated.

It took time to break in the new Atropos, and to get to know her well. Now Niobe knew what the others had gone through when she had joined. It wasn't good or bad, it was mainly a lot of work and adjustment, for the personality of the total entity of Fate had made a significant shift. The fascination with opera was gone; new interests took its place. It was months before they were really comfortable as a group. But the process did serve to distract Niobe's attention from Junior for a while, for she was too busy to visit the mortals on any but a strictly business basis.

When Niobe did go to visit Junior again, she had to do it in her own form, for the new Atropos had no interest in this matter. Lachesis would have helped, but they decided it was better to save her as a reserve, in case it should be necessary to change identity quickly. So Niobe donned a wig and applied makeup to make herself look older.

She discovered that the prior Atropos, the one she had known in office, had settled in Ireland, and was now visiting Junior as a mortal. They still enjoyed attending plays together, and she was able to provide magical materials for him that he could not otherwise obtain. They went regularly to visit the hamadryad of the water oak.

Niobe considered that situation, and decided to let well enough alone. Atropos really did like the boy, and would see that no harm came to him. "Bless you," Niobe murmured to herself. Then she reconsidered, and visited the old woman privately to repeat the sentiment aloud.

"Well, you know my own kin wouldn't know me anymore," Atropos said. "They think I died fifteen years ago. I'm a grandmother; I need to practice my art."

Evidently so. But Niobe kissed her anyway.

Time passed. Junior grew to adulthood. He specialized in magic when he attended the same college Cedric had, and showed similar brilliance. He progressed beyond the level of his professors. For his Ph.D. project he developed the spell that enabled the deer to shoot back: any missile discharged, whether from bow, gun, or hand, swung around to score in the hunter. Suddenly hunting lost its appeal, not only in the local wetlands, but in *all* wetlands and most of the remaining wilderness of the world. Similarly developers were balked; their bulldozers tended to crash back on their starting points, unable to penetrate far into the living wilderness. Junior made an A for the project, and the construction industry filed a lawsuit against the college. In the end they had to compromise: the deer-magic would be applied only to those regions officially designated as parks. But the closest one was so designated immediately. Junior had fulfilled his father's ambition. The hamadryad was so thrilled she gave him a kiss, then hid in the deepest foliage for three days, blushing.

Junior became Magician Kaftan, a professional enchanter of stones. His business increased; soon he was filling orders from all over the world. He did not become famous because he maintained a low profile; the lawsuit against the college had taught him caution. The stones were merely a business to support his continuing researches into magic. He was fast becoming the most formidable magician in the world. Magic was all he cared about, especially after Grandma Atropos passed away. He would disappear into his laboratory and not reappear for days.

Concerned, Niobe went to visit him. She wore her wig and makeup, but he recognized her instantly. "Hello, Mother! How is Fate treating you?"

She sighed. Her son the Magician was now thirty-four years old, eleven years older than she, physically, and he was a genius in his trade. Perhaps she should not have been surprised; his father had been brilliant, and Junior had had unique schooling along the way, beginning with the hamadryad. Naturally he had researched his own lineage, and discovered exactly what had happened to his mother.

"I am doing well," she said. "But you, Junior—I wish you would not seal yourself off from the world so much. It's not healthy."

He smiled, prepared to indulge her in small matters. "What would you have me do, Mother?"

"Socialize a little, at least with your friends and relatives! How long has it been since you visited the water oak?"

"Five years," he confessed.

"And how long since you've seen Pacian?"

He counted off on his fingers. "A decade. It wasn't the same, after he married."

"Well, go see them," she urged. "You owe a lot to the hamadryad, and Pacian is a good man, with a nice family." She studied him with motherly solicitude. "Speaking of which—when are you going to marry?"

"When I encounter the most beautiful woman of her generation," he said, smiling. "According to the prophecy." It was evident that he no longer credited the prophecies. Possibly he had researched them, too, using his superior magic, but she doubted it. That wasn't his *type* of magic, and it was difficult for any person to research his own destiny; paradox closed in rapidly.

"Well, all in good time. I want you to visit your cousin, at least," she said firmly. "He was very good to you."

He nodded, remembering. "He was, indeed. Very well, Mother, I will visit the water oak and Pacian."

"Promise?"

"Promise."

"And soon," she said, and changed into arachnid form and slid up her thread to Purgatory. There was no point in concealing her magic from him anymore.

The Magician was as good as his word. The following day he phoned Pace, and later that week they had a reunion. In the interim he visited the water oak. The hamadryad was glad to see him, though the passage of years made her diffident. "Mother tells me I should get married," he said, and she nodded agreement. "But where on Earth will I find a mortal woman as beautiful as you?" She shrugged and blushed, forgiving him his five years neglect; even immortals were subject to flattery.

At the reunion he met Blenda. He had seen her as a baby and occasionally as a child. Now she was twenty-three, the same age as Niobe's body, and she was so beautiful she seemed to light the room she entered. It would have taken an expert to judge between her and the hamadryad—but she was mortal. She smiled shyly at the visiting Magician—and worked on him a magic more fundamental than any he had studied.

They were married the following year. Niobe attended the wedding, at her son's request, doing it in her own guise, as no one would recognize her now. After all, she was fifty-eight years old, chronologically; who would ever believe she could be the mother of the groom? But Pacian, the father of the bride, gave her a single piercing look, then shrugged, not able to believe the wild thought that had touched his mind.

It was a lovely wedding. Niobe sat alone in the crowd, in the section reserved for the groom's relatives, and cried. When the two exchanged vows, she could hardly contain herself. "I am losing my son!" she sobbed. More than one head turned to face her, perplexed.

Between the wedding and the reception, they posed for pictures. The groom could not present any proud parents for this; the family he had known belonged to his cousin, the father of the bride. "Indulge me, dear," he murmured to Blenda, and beckoned to Niobe. She approached uncertainly, stifling tears.

"This is a blood relative; she can pose in lieu."

So Niobe stood beside Blenda and smiled, and Blenda smiled— and there was a murmur of awe through the assemblage. "Look at them!" a woman exclaimed. "Like twins in beauty!"

Niobe realized it was true. She had been said to be the loveliest of her generation, and Blenda of hers. Niobe's hair was dark amber, like buckwheat honey, while Blenda's was light amber, like clover honey; with both, it flowed loose to the slender waist, and both sets of eyes were bright blue. They were a match of feature and figure, like two scintillating gems. It was a remarkable coincidence.

The photographers went on to other subjects, and Niobe and Blenda had a moment together. "Please," the girl begged. "Tell me who you are! Kaf said he had a beautiful relative, but I never suspected—"

Niobe had of course checked Blenda's thread of life, and knew she was a fine person all around, as her mother was. She could be trusted, and she deserved to know. "You will find this hard to believe—"

"After seeing Kaf's magic, I can believe much!"

"I am his mother."

Blenda's perfect mouth dropped open. She looked across the room at her new husband, who nodded gravely, though he could not have overheard their dialogue. Then she recovered. "Oh—a youth spell! Of course! He said his mother was the most—but you know that, of course!"

"And his father was as handsome and intelligent as any," Niobe said, feeling the tears begin again. "Like yours. It is not a youth spell, precisely. I never aged. I became an Incarnation. That's why I had to give up my baby."

"An—?"

"Fate."

"Fate!" Blenda's eyes widened in realization. "Did you arrange—?"

"For my son to marry you? Not in that manner! I simply told him to get back in touch with his closest friend, his cousin Pace, and the rest happened. I confess I wasn't even thinking of you, but I'm glad it happened. You are worthy of him, dear, and it does fill the prophecy."

"Prophecy?"

"That my son would possess the most beautiful woman of her generation, and have a daughter who would be the most talented of her type and love an Incarnation."

"My father mentioned a prophecy," Blenda said. "But he said he foiled it."

"Prophecies are hard to foil," Niobe said. "Certainly it seems to be coming true for my son, and if the rest follows, your daughter will consort with the Incarnation of Death or Evil. That is not necessarily bad, horrendous as it may sound. But she is also to be the savior of man and to stand athwart a tangled skein. Since there is an entity who objects to the salvation of man, she could be in danger."

Blenda made a soundless whistle. "I shall do my best to protect her! In fact, I will consider carefully before I bear her. I thank you for telling me of this prophecy. I had not known the full nature of it."

"No one ever knows the full nature of a prophecy—until it is too late."

They kissed, then moved on to the reception chamber, where Blenda had to rejoin her husband and cut the monstrous cake. She picked up the knife, and the groom put his hand on hers, and they brought it to the outer layer.

"Hold!" the Magician exclaimed. "There is evil here!" He drew his bride back and brought out a stone.

There was a hush. The Magician held the stone high and moved it in a circle. When it approached the cake, it glowed brilliantly. He nodded; there was the focus of evil.

"Go to your parents," the Magician said tersely. "This may be messy."

"I knew cake was fattening, but . . . " Blenda murmured. She went to join Pacian and Blanche, and the three watched anxiously from one side, while Niobe and other guests watched from the front. What was wrong with that cake?

The Magician brought out another stone and held it carefully before him. Suddenly a beam of light speared out from the stone, into the center of the cake.

There was a crackle of scorching frosting. Then the cake exploded. Splotches of icing sprayed out, plastering ceiling, Magician, and guests. Someone screamed. From the cake leaped a demon. The thing had red skin, a barbed tail, and a horrendously horned head. With an inchoate roar it leaped at the Magician—and bounced away from an invisible shield. Naturally the adept had seen to his own protection.

"So you refuse to die, Kaftan!" the demon cried, its voice so guttural that it was barely comprehensible. "But it takes two to make a child!" It whirled on Blenda, making a prodigious leap.

The Magician threw a stone at his bride. "Catch it!" he cried.

Blenda, almost frozen in terror, moved automatically to catch the stone just before the demon landed. The demon bounced again, for now she had the protection stone. The monster rolled off the side of the invisible sphere—and came down on Blanche. Its outsized mouth opened, and its terrible fangs closed on the woman's throat. Blood spurted.

"Mother!" Blenda shrieked in absolute horror.

Then the Magician brought another stone into play. Blue radiance spread from it to encompass the demon—and the demon screamed and melted into a bubbling puddle.

But it was too late. The bride's mother was dead. The demon had gotten neither its primary nor its secondary target, but had wrought terrible mischief in its failure.

— 7 —

CHANGES

Niobe was an Incarnation, but she could not do anything about the tragedy. She had not thought to check Blanche's thread. Satan had scored a partial evil again. As it had been when he tried to strike at Niobe herself, he had been balked, but an innocent party had suffered. "I should have seen it coming," Lachesis said with deep regret. "Perhaps I could have rearranged the threads in that part of the Tapestry—"

"But I'm the one who cuts the threads," Atropos said. "I've been with you long enough to know—"

"That thread was cut by your predecessor," Niobe said. "But I'm sure I checked it when Pacian married her, and it was of normal length. When Satan strikes, we all make mistakes. No one was supposed to die at that wedding; Satan interfered by sending his demon to—" She shrugged and swallowed, then continued. "And now we simply have to patch the Tapestry on a makeshift basis, as we have done before."

"Still, it could not have happened if I hadn't become careless," Lachesis said. "When Thanatos gets careless, he gets killed by his successor; when I get careless, innocent mortals suffer. It is time for me to retire."

Naturally Niobe protested. But they all knew it was true: Lachesis, as the measurer of the threads, should have been alert to Satan's interference in her measurement. No Incarnation could successfully interfere with another, if the other was on the job. Satan prospered by deceit—and Lachesis had been deceived. She had erred.

They located a suitable prospect, a woman of middling age who had no close family and had a talent for managing things, and approached her. She agreed, and the change was made. This time Niobe, as the senior remaining Aspect, handled it. She took the woman's hand, and the woman's essence entered while Lachesis' essence departed. Again it was done—and they had a new Aspect to break in.

Unfortunately, the change of Lachesis-identities did not make Fate's job easier. Satan took this opportunity to yank the threads about to his benefit. Once again it was a struggle to stave off disaster, and once again the staving was not complete.

The political scene was constantly in flux across the world, whatever nominal form of government a country had, and Satan was adept at the corruption of politicians. At any given moment, the representation of good and evil in politics was about even, worldwide. Every time an evil power-wielder was ousted, another developed. It was evident that Satan was really trying to gain a clear political advantage that he could use to gain a social advantage. Nowhere was the war between good and evil shown to better advantage than in politics.

Quite a number of Niobe's countrymen had emigrated to America, and now they were achieving political representation there. Whether this was good or bad depended on the particular men, but she tended to favor her own. Thus when, in trying to clarify the nature of the job for the new Lachesis, she discovered a Satanistic tangle of threads in the Tapestry, involving one of this lineage in America, she investigated. Satan was certainly up to something; tangles never occurred naturally. But she could not make it out clearly, and Lachesis was as yet too inexperienced to do so.

"Someone's thread is to be prematurely cut," Atropos said.

They zeroed in on it. Sure enough, the thread of a potential future candidate for the American presidency was to be artificially cut. That would seriously distort the Tapestry. But they weren't sure how bad it would be.

Niobe consulted with Chronos, who remembered the future. Her affair with him had proceeded intermittently for thirty-five years, and she was really quite fond of him; he was a decent man. Because the two of them moved temporally opposite, there was always a certain novelty in it, and it was a relationship they found mutually convenient. It was true: it took one Incarnation to truly understand another.

But Chronos was unable to help her in this. "As you know, I have only been in office a year, and I have no knowledge of the world's future beyond that."

"I *didn't* know!" she said, startled. "I—I suppose I thought you were eternal, though I'm sure you told me at the outset." Indeed, now she remembered the reverse situation, when he had forgotten that her beginning-end was near. It was easy to do, over such a timespan! "Why, that means we'll have to be breaking you in, soon!"

He smiled. "You have done that very competently, Clotho; I will always be in your debt. I hope someday I can repay the favor."

"You did, Chronos," she reassured him.

Lacking the perspective of the future, they could obtain more specific information only by going to Earth to check the living threads. There they discovered that a demon had been dispatched from Hell. It would drive a car to intercept the senator on a back road at night and crash into him. Rather, the demon-spirit was to take over the body of a Satanist—a Satan worshiper—for this mission; naturally the mortal had not been told that he would probably lose his own life. He merely understood that, in return for assisting Satan, he would be richly rewarded.

The old, experienced Lachesis could have twitched the threads expertly to clear the tangle and prevent Satan from interfering. But what would have been simple for her was complex for the new one. It did take time to gain proficiency. They had to take the direct route: a visit to the senator himself.

The night the "accident" was scheduled, Niobe took the body and slid a thread to the spiderweb nearest the country house where the senator was having a private party with his workers, volunteers, and friends. There was a lot of liquor going around, and many of the attendees were comely young women. Niobe didn't approve; if this was one of the good politicians, what were the bad ones like? But of course a man could not be judged by his private entertainments; it was his performance in office that counted. Women could not be blamed for being attracted to the focal points of power like bees to flowers; that was their nature. She herself had not loved Cedric until he had shown his power. At least this made it easy for her to infiltrate; she was assumed to be a professional of another type.

She filled a wineglass with water and carried it about so that no one realized she was not imbibing. She had never imbibed since that night Cedric got sick. She fended off the approaches of interested young men and worked her way to the senator himself. "Senator, your life is in peril," she murmured as she danced with him.

He smiled in that vote-getting way he had. "You are a Russian agent?"

"Just a friend of the status quo. There is a car ready to crash yours. Do not go driving tonight, Senator."

He smiled again, but this time there was a certain masked malice behind it; he did not like to have anyone tell him what not to do. Politically he stood for the right things, and more often than not did

With a Tangled Skein

the right things, but that did not make him a perfect man. There was, she had long since learned, a mixture of good and evil in every thread of life—which was the point of life, if Satan was to be believed. She had never been satisfied that that was the whole of it, but it was at least a half-truth. So he was annoyed at her warning—but she was physically the type of woman the senator did not openly affront. That was why she had approached him in her own form, in a revealing gown. In a moment he would make a pass at her.

"You have something better to offer?" he asked.

"Your life," she replied evenly. "This house is protected; the assassin will not enter. It must catch you on the road, tonight. Remain here; by morning the threat will abate." For they had ascertained that this particular demon-spirit could not survive away from Hell for more than a few hours.

"Remain here—with you?"

"No, Senator. I am here merely to warn you, not to entertain you. Heed my warning, and all will be well." She turned and walked away.

When she was out of his sight, she changed to Lachesis, so that the senator could not recognize her, and moved on out of the house. Outside, she shifted to spider form and sat on the branch of a tree, watching.

Sure enough, her warning had not sufficed. Once a thread was positioned, it was hard to reposition, and this one was locked in a tangle. The senator emerged with a young woman; he was going to take her for a ride. He was married, but such men did not take such things too seriously.

Niobe, uncertain what to do, slid down a line to land on the senator's shoulder. She would just have to go along and hope she could enable him to avoid the assassination. Maybe if he saw the assassin-car approaching, he would take heed and get off the road in time. Of course, then the demon might come after him afoot, but perhaps she could balk it. Certainly she had to try. How she wished that this tangle hadn't occurred just now, when Lachesis was inexperienced— but of course that was *why* it had occurred. Satan never passed up a chance!

The senator got into a small car, and the girl took the passenger seat. He drove out the back way, avoiding the guard at the front; he evidently didn't care to be recognized and have news of this tryst relayed to his wife. The fool!

Niobe knew the assassin was lurking out there, waiting to spy the senator's car. There would be little chance to escape once that happened.

It was difficult to talk while in spider form, but possible. "Senator!" Niobe said near his left ear.

—100—

He glanced at the girl to his right. "Yes?"

"What?" the girl asked.

"She didn't speak," Niobe said. "*I* spoke. I'm the spider on your shoulder."

The senator looked left, startled. "What sorcery is this?"

"Just a little shape-changing. I'm the woman who warned you before."

"The lovely one!" he said. "I didn't know you were magical!"

"What *is* this?" the girl on the other side demanded.

"There is a spider talking to me," the senator explained.

"A lovely *spider*? I don't believe it!"

"Take warning!" Niobe cried. "Get off the road before the assassin spies you!"

Now the senator was doubtful. "I thought it was a ploy for attention. But you disappeared. Now I learn you're a shape-changer. But why should you care about me?"

"I don't care much about you personally," Niobe said. "If I did, I'd probably tell your wife what you're up to tonight. But you are one of the better men in the bad mess that politics is today and you may have a considerable future, so I don't want an evil force to take you out. Please, Senator—turn about, get back to your party. Save your little dalliance for some other night."

"Now *I* hear it!" the girl exclaimed. "How can a spider talk?"

"I'm not sure," the senator said, and Niobe knew he meant about the situation, not about talking spiders. That was one of his weaknesses: the inability to make a firm decision on short notice. Normally he had advisers and scriptwriters to put words in his mouth; perhaps he depended on them too much. When caught unprepared, he could seem positively tongue-tied.

"Then play it safe!" Niobe urged. "The most you can lose is one tryst! The alternative will cost you your life!"

Still he hedged. "You may be magical, but I don't really know your motive. There may be danger at the party."

"Then go somewhere else!" Niobe cried in her tinny spider-voice. "Take a walk through the forest! Anything but a drive along this road tonight!"

He ground to a decision. "All right—I'll check this out. Emjay, you take the wheel. I'll get out and watch. If there's an assassin looking for me, he won't bother you—and I'll know him if I see him." He brought out a pair of tinted glasses and put them on as he brought the car to a halt.

"But I don't know the way!" the girl protested.

"Just follow the road; it dead-ends at the beach. It's not far; I'll catch up with you there, once I've verified Miss Spider's story. I want to see what else is on this road."

"Well, if you say—" the girl said doubtfully. She moved over and took the wheel. She moved slowly on while the senator hid behind the bushes at the side of the road.

As the car's headlights retreated, the senator addressed Niobe. "All right, spider-woman—change back to your human form! You got my attention, all right!"

"I didn't come here to—" Niobe protested.

"Change—or I'll squish you where you sit!" He brought up his open hand and made as if to slap his shoulder.

Niobe hastily changed. It wasn't that she was vulnerable in arachnid form; she was protected by the same web-ambiance that kept her safe when in human form, no matter how exposed she might seem. Thanatos and Chronos had their cloaks; she had her web. But she didn't want to tell the senator her true nature, so she obeyed his demand. She leaped off his shoulder and landed in her own form before him.

"Now that's better," he said, reaching for her.

She skipped away. "Senator, if you think this was all a device to get you alone out here—shouldn't you be afraid it's a trap?"

"Nope." He tapped his glasses. "These show evil. There's hardly any evil in you; you're just as lovely through these lenses as you are without them."

"Well, I'm not evil, but also not—" She broke off, hearing something.

He heard it too. He crouched behind the bushes, peering down the road.

The car came slowly from the direction the girl had gone. Its glass was reflective in the night, but the motor had an ugly sound. The senator stared—and gave a stifled gasp. Niobe put a hand on his shoulder, cautioning him to silence.

The car passed. The senator faced her, removing the glasses, his eyes round in the moonlight. "That thing in the car—it was a demon!"

"It was a man possessed by an evil spirit," Niobe agreed. "Now you know."

"If I'd been out there—"

"It would have spotted you, accelerated, and deliberately rammed you. It doesn't care if it dies; it's already dead, though the living man it possesses isn't."

He glanced down the road. "Will it go after Emjay?" he asked, worried.

"It shouldn't. It's targeted for just one person: you."

"I'll go after her anyway," he decided. "I don't want her out here while that thing's on the road!" He started down the road at a lumbering run.

Niobe paced him. "It's not safe for you afoot either, Senator! That demon will be back, and—"

"I'll hide when it comes!" he puffed, slowing to a walk; he was in no condition to run the whole way.

The assassin car did return, and the senator did hide in the bushes. Demon-possessed people were not very alert or observant because it took most of the demon's energy to operate the host's body, so the thing never even looked to the sides. It would have worked better if the demon-spirit merely rode along in the body, letting the living person follow instructions—but when the instructions included a suicide collision, that was not feasible. The demon had to retain complete control so that there would be no last-moment balking. That was probably why it wasn't destined to survive long; it took a great deal of spiritual energy to translate into physical energy.

Why hadn't Satan sent a full physical demon, as he had to the Magician's wedding? Probably because that was very awkward to do. True demons were confined to Hell, and only on very rare occasions could they be sprung loose. The mortal plane was a hostile environment for demons, as it was for angels. It was easier to spring demon-spirits, as in this case—but they were less reliable. Probably Satan had not expected Fate to come to the scene personally; he had forgotten the score Niobe had to settle with him.

They reached a bridge that crossed a minor inlet of the sea, and stopped, appalled. The wooden guardrail had been smashed. Obviously the car had gone off the bridge and into the water.

"She didn't know the road!" the senator exclaimed. "See—the bridge curves, and she was going straight—"

He ripped off his jacket and kicked off his shoes. He dived into the water, searching for the car. In a moment he surfaced, gasping. "It's down there!"

He dived again, and surfaced again. "I can't get it open!"

Niobe sent a magic thread down and slid along it, impervious to the water. But in this mode she could only observe, not act on anything physical. She saw the car, and the girl inside.

She returned to the shore. "She's dead," she reported. "There's nothing you can do. Get on back to the house." Then, sick at heart, she retreated to Purgatory.

Satan himself awaited her there. "So you sought to interfere, sugarplum," he said. "Well, you did not succeed."

"I saved his life!" Niobe retorted angrily.

"And exchanged it for that of an innocent girl," he countered. "And My purpose has been served. I don't care whether that man lives or dies; I just want him finished politically. That has been accomplished."

Niobe brushed on by, refusing to speak to him again. But the following events proved Satan correct. The senator put out the story that he had been driving the girl back to town, and had taken a wrong turn and blundered into the bay; he had fought free of the car but she hadn't. Some believed that; some did not; after all, his bulk was twice that of the girl. How could he have been more agile in escape than she? There were too many questions. The senator had been perhaps the leading candidate of his party for president; after the scandal of the girl's strange death, he could not come close to nomination. He continued as senator, but he would never be president. His career had been capped. All because he had let the girl drive an unfamiliar road alone.

"If I hadn't been inept with the threads . . . " Lachesis said.

"It takes many years of experience to foil Satan," Niobe said grimly. "He is an infinitely wily and indefatigable opponent. We thought it was the senator's life Satan wanted, not merely his career. It was probably too late to undo the damage when we became aware of the tangle." But her rage at Satan was renewed. So many times she had tried to foil him and had taken her losses, as it had been with Cedric, with Blanche, and now with the senator. She wished she could skunk Satan completely. But the person of goodwill seemed always to be at a disadvantage before the completely unscrupulous power that was Evil Incarnate.

Chronos' time was growing short. He became less confident as he approached the moment of his changeover. For him it was the assumption of his office; for the others, it was the termination of it. Each Chronos officeholder took the Hourglass, the single most potent magical instrument in existence, after a mortal existence. In this respect that office was similar to the others. But from that moment Chronos lived backward until the moment of his origin, when he had to pass the Glass on to his predecessor. It was an exceedingly awkward adjustment.

Niobe had always been—would always be—closest to Chronos, and now it was especially important. Physically he was twice her age, but in other respects he was much younger. There was now a kind of desperation in their lovemaking, as if he needed reassurance that some things remained as they had been in his mortal life. He could change time itself, but lacked experience, and that made him highly insecure.

Finally it came to the first time. Niobe knew it, because she had had the foresight to ask him, as if playfully, how many times they had done it, and then she had kept count. Now he was obviously smitten by her, but afraid to confess it, and unable to get a proper grip on his job while this impasse remained. She seduced him gently, letting him know it was all right, that she understood. Indeed she did! In her mortal life, so long ago, she would have been appalled to see herself now. But she was thirty-six years wiser now, and she knew Chronos better than he could believe at this stage. He was an old friend, and though she never had loved him, she regretted no part of their relationship. Satan, of course, called her a call girl, but it was a calling that had its self-respect. The understanding she brought to Chronos was important, yet she missed the true love she had once had, so briefly, as a mortal.

The affair was over, or had not yet begun. It came at last to Chronos' last/first day in his office. He was so bewildered she knew she had to take him literally in hand, leading him to his mansion where she could explain things more comfortably. Away from the mansion their times were reversed, making communication difficult, for now he had not yet learned how to use the Hourglass to control time. She had to use printed signboards to tell him how to reverse himself long enough for her to take him in hand, for the print was comprehensible whether a person was traveling forward or backward in time.

The place was near an amusement park, where he was standing, bewildered. She knew, from what he had told her before, that this was an hour after his assumption of the office; he had blundered out of the park by himself, and wished she had found him earlier. But now she understood why she had not (would not): she needed that hour to orient him. So her printed sign told him how to use the Hourglass to reverse himself. When he did that, he was suddenly moving forward in time again, and they could talk. Once they were in his mansion they were still together—but now *she* was reversed, not he. The half hour of his reversal canceled the half hour of hers, so that she emerged at the same time as she had started the dialogue—a convenience she had carefully arranged. Chronos now understood enough to continue, and was in the hands of the loyal staff of the mansion; she knew it would work out, however haltingly, because she remembered that it had.

Now she had to get on with the other part of it: seeing the new Chronos in. Chronos was too important to her job to be left to chance, as it were; she had to know exactly what she had to deal with. She returned to the amusement park and explored the situation.

She picked up a few minutes after she had intercepted Chronos with her printed signs, before. This time she concealed herself from him. She retained her body, because Lachesis was too inexperienced to handle this, and it was Atropos' off-shift. She concealed her face somewhat with a kerchief, so that Chronos wouldn't recognize her if he saw her—not that he had any notion of her identity or nature at this point. He hadn't met her yet. She followed him as he meandered backward into the park. No one else paid him attention; mortals seldom noticed Incarnations, and the backward-living Chronos was difficult to relate to. So though they were in a crowd, it was in effect just the two of them, playing a kind of hide-and-seek.

She felt sorry for him, seeing him so confused and ill at ease. She knew what he was feeling, because he had told her about it. She knew him better than any other person did, now, and better than any other person would. Thirty-six years as associates and lovers did make for mutual understanding. Perhaps it would have been better if she had loved him, for certainly he had loved her. But, she decided, it had been necessary for one of them to be objective; that had enabled her to cope with the backward nature of their association, and not to take misunderstandings too seriously. She remembered when they had agreed to try the act of love in their natural states, moving in opposite temporal directions. They had had to coordinate it carefully, before and after. It had turned out to be possible and intriguing as a novelty—but, for her, not really much different from the normal act, because she had been only slightly aroused. She had simply been there for him, and for her own curiosity. So it had been a disappointment—but now she remembered it clearly, for what reason she was not sure, as she watched him wandering backward through the crowd. Perhaps, she thought, this was an analogy of the human condition: each person blundering along in his own course, trying to relate to others, and succeeding only fractionally. Because each person, mortal and immortal, was traveling along his own unique timeline, unable to tie in with others perfectly, however much they all tried.

Finally he backed into the horror house. She followed. Neither of them bought tickets, as the park proprietors were no more aware of them than the other mortals were. It was not a matter of invisibility, just of not being noticed. There, too, she thought, was an analogy of mortality: the key forces that governed the lives of people were generally unobserved by those who were most concerned.

The horror house was stocked with ghosts who floated out periodically, made faces, and yelled "Boooo!" supposedly scaring the paying customers. Only the smallest children were actually frightened; the others knew that ghosts were insubstantial and therefore harmless. Still, it was fun, in the sense that playing the rigged gambling games was fun. The illusion of fear and potential riches was what this sort of park was all about.

Niobe paused beside a ghost. "But what do *you* get out of it?" she asked. "Don't you feel pretty stupid, play-acting like this?"

"Well, it does get dull, and it *is* stupid, and it contributes to the prejudice people have against ghosts, but the pay is good," the ghost replied. "A ghost can't get a job just anywhere, you know."

"But what use do you have for money?"

"Well, it's like this," the ghost said, clarifying into the semblance of a woman. "I was on my way to work, when I was alive, and I was late, so I cut through this alley. I knew I shouldn't have, but I'd been late twice before that month, and I was on notice; I just had to get there on time. Suddenly a masked man jumped out at me. I screamed and ran, but he chased me down, held a knife to my face, and raped me. I was screaming all the time, but no one came to help me—and there were others in the alley, too, who could have helped. Finally—too late—I got mad, and I grabbed his hand and bit it. The last thing I remember is his knife coming down at my neck."

"Ah, yes," Niobe said. This was much more of an answer than she had sought.

"By the time I recovered consciousness, I was dead," the ghost continued. "I guess it took me a few minutes to die, while I was unconscious. There was my body, naked from the waist down, and my throat was a mass of blood, and the rapist was gone. Well, I didn't exactly take kindly to that. So I stayed around, determined to find out who had done it and make him pay. But that takes money, because private eyes don't work for nothing, so here I am, earning money. Pretty soon I'll have enough to hire one for a day, and if that doesn't do it, I'll keep working until it does get done." She shrugged. "When you get down to it, geeking isn't so bad." She paused to jump out at another child, screaming "Booo!" The child eeked and giggled, pleased, and went on.

"I wish you luck and fortune," Niobe said.

"Say—how is it you see me as a person?" the ghost asked. "I mean, most of the living folk don't—"

"You *are* a person," Niobe said. "I spun your thread myself. I'm sorry it was cut short."

"Oh—you're Fate! I didn't recognize you!"

"Few do," Niobe said, and proceeded on after Chronos, who had backed up the passage.

Why, she wondered, had Chronos chosen to make the change here? It was the next Chronos who had done it, the one coming from the future. He had not been bound to the site of birth, just to his moment of origin. He picked the place he wanted, and his successor had to come to it and take the Hourglass. Exactly how the successor knew where to come she was not sure; apparently there was a guidance in these things, and not the normal guidance of Fate. Lachesis had, of course, measured his mortal thread, but when that person became

Chronos, that deleted the thread from the Tapestry as if it were an unscheduled demise. Chronos—the one she had known so long— had remarked that his mortal existence had seemed pointless and dull—jejune was the actual term he had used—so that when the opportunity came to become an Incarnation, he had taken it. But he hadn't realized that it meant living backward, or battling Satan.

Well, she was about to learn about the future Chronos. She watched from a cranny of the horror house as the Chronos she knew backed to a dark chamber illuminated only by the glow of the Hourglass. From the far side another figure came, walking forward. The other Chronos!

No—it was the one she knew! She could tell by the way he moved. He walked forward, and the other walked backward, and they met in the center of the chamber. The Hourglass flared.

Suddenly, in the glow of the Glass, there were three: two young women and a child! Of all times for horror-house customers to pass through!

But the women looked oddly familiar. Niobe saw one in silhouette as she turned: wasp-waisted, hair flowing—

She stifled an exclamation. It was her double!

The double walked right toward her. "Come with me, Niobe," she said. "I'll explain." She took Niobe's hand.

Bemused, Niobe suffered herself to be led out of the dark chamber, leaving the other women and the child behind. What was happening?

Out in the light of day, her double turned to her with a smile. "I am yourself, two hours later," she explained. "You remember how you double up when you spend an hour in Chronos' mansion?"

Oh. "Yes. But—"

"There are three of you then," the other continued. "Self One is the one approaching the mansion; Self Two is the one within it, living temporarily backward; and Self Three is the one living forward again, after emerging. You have always avoided each other before."

"Um, yes. But—"

"Right now you are Self One. I am Self Three. Self Two is with Chronos, living backward."

"But this is not his mansion!"

"He reversed us for an hour. He wanted company to see him out. He's only a child, after all."

"The—child I just saw?"

"Chronos can be any age or sex, as can any Incarnation," Self Three reminded her. "He'll tell you about it, as he told me. I'm just making sure you understand the situation."

Niobe took a deep breath. "I—think so. But who—who explained things to you when you were Self One? I mean, if we are all parts of the same person—"

Piers Anthony

"Self Three explained then, of course."

"But you *are* Self Three!"

"I am *now*. Then I wasn't. I was you."

"But—"

The other laughed. "Don't try to analyze it, self-sister! You'll lose your mind. There really aren't three of us, just one in three consecutive roles. Remember, Chronos is immune from paradox, and so are we when we interact with him."

Niobe nodded, though she felt dizzy. "Now I know how Chronos felt when he started in office, just a few minutes ago. It's almost too much to grasp!"

"I know. But it's hard for the other Chronos, too. He's afraid. So be kind to him; it won't hurt you. I'm in a position to know."

Then they both laughed; they were by no coincidence very similar people.

The two of them reminisced for the rest of the hour, finding themselves compatible. "We'll have to do this again some time!" Self Three said, and Niobe agreed. "Next time we spend time in Chronos' mansion—which I don't think will be for lovemaking—you come early, and I'll wait for you."

"Agreed." They shook hands.

Then, as the moment drew near, they returned to the chamber. "We must part," Self Three said, hugging her. She was a very huggable person. "It's been nice talking with you."

"Yes," Niobe agreed. She saw tears on the other's cheeks. In all the years she had been Clotho, shd had never done this before. Now she realized what she had been missing.

Niobe entered the chamber, hesitated, turned—and Self Three waved her on. So she walked to the center, where the child stood with the other woman. "Hello," she said.

",olleH" Self Two replied.

Then Self Two suddenly stepped backward into Niobe. There was a mild jolt, and Niobe stumbled forward.

"Hello," Niobe said.

",olleH" the other replied. But the other was backing away.

"I guess you know I reversed you, Obe," the child said.

Startled, she looked at him. He was about eight years old, with tousled sunbleached hair and eyes as blue as her own. He was indeed Chronos, for he carried the glowing Hourglass.

"Yes," she agreed. "You—want company. For—the change."

"I've never died before," he confided. "I just didn't want to do it alone."

Niobe glanced about, seeing Self Three escorting Self One out— or rather *in,* as they were moving backward. She was Self Two, now.

—109—

With a Tangled Skein

She had exchanged greetings with her other self, coming and going. To each, it had seemed that the other had spoken second, because of the reversed perspective. Now she had another job to do. "It's not death," she said reassuringly.

"It's the same thing, for me," he said. "I'll be in Heaven—or Hell."

Niobe shifted to Lachesis, who checked her threads. His was obscurely looped back on itself, but seemed otherwise unsullied. "Heaven, I'm sure." She changed back.

There were two chairs by the wall. "I hope," he said as they sat. "I know I shouldn't worry, but I'm just a kid. I'm scared!" Then his eyes brimmed over, and he was crying.

Niobe reached across and pulled him in to her bosom. She had never in her life been able to resist a person who required comforting, and she understood tears about as well as anyone could. "Of course you are, dear, of course you are!" she said soothingly. "Not one of us is sanguine about—that."

Soon his tears abated, but she continued to hold him, much as she had held his successor. There were times when men of any age needed the special favor of a woman's embrace. It was too bad that people of either sex tended to confuse this with sex.

"You know, Obe," he said, "when you came in, three years ago I guess it was, maybe two, I was mad; I liked Lisa. But when I got to know you, I liked you even better. You're prettier."

Lisa, evidently, was her successor—two or three years hence. Niobe stifled her shock. She had had no idea her own term was ending. "Beauty is no indication of merit," she said. "I'm sure Lisa was a fine woman."

"Oh, sure. And when she got mad at me, she'd tease me with that gibberish language of hers. But you—"

Niobe changed the subject. "How did you come to be Chronos?" she asked, glancing at the glowing Hourglass which floated before them. He had set it there when he started crying, and it remained.

"Oh, you know." He straightened up, shrugging.

"I *don't* know," she reminded him. "I wasn't there, remember? Lisa was."

"Oh, yeah. Well, the Glass was going to be changed, but the guy coming for it chickened out." He smiled toothily. "He saw it, and he ran! He just got the hoorah out of there. I was playing in the park, and I just knew someone had to take it, so I just stepped up and grabbed. I was too young to know any better. And here I am, eight years after. Before, I mean."

"I'm surprised you were able to handle the job," she murmured.

"Aw, Maw Cheese showed me how. I got the hang."

"Maw Cheese?"

"You know, Obe. Your middle third."

Oh. Lachesis. The accent was properly on the first syllable, and the *ch* was hard: LAK-e-sis. But obviously the child didn't take names seriously. *Maw Cheese!* Lachesis snorted mentally. *This whippersnapper—*

"But I always liked you best, Obe, after Lisa went, though Attapose is okay too. If I coulda growed up, I'da married you."

"Immortality does have its liabilities," Niobe said, smiling.

And so they talked, and Chronos was comforted, and as the hour ended he was ready for the Afterlife. In the final minute he lifted the Hourglass, and Niobe bent to kiss him, and backed off. As the Hourglass was taken by the shadowy other Chronos, the spell of reversal left her, and she moved foward again.

Quickly she intercepted the confused Self One. "Come with me, Niobe, I'll explain." She led the woman out before their presence could interfere with the backward dialogue of Self Two and the juvenile Chronos. "I am yourself, two hours later," she explained, and went on to clarify the situation. Her prior self was duly impressed. It was fun, now that she knew what she was doing.

In due course she guided her other self back into the chamber, and waved her on when she hesitated. She watched as Self One and Self Two merged—and suddenly they were both gone. There was only the child Chronos, waiting nervously for his company.

How had he known she would come to him and agree to be reversed for that hour? Obviously she had told him she would do it when the time came. Nevertheless, it was a good thing that Chronos was immune to paradox!

She departed quietly. She had had enough of this scene; it was time to get back to her regular business.

One thing stayed in her mind, though. Three years—or two—until she left her office! To be replaced by Lisa.

— 8 —

SECOND LOVE

From time to time Niobe checked on her mortal family. The rawness of the tragedy of the wedding eased. Her son the Magician seemed to be quite happy with his bride Blenda. She was a schoolteacher, disdaining to exploit her beauty by going into show business. Blenda visited her father, Pacian, often, making sure he took care of himself during his bereavement. It was her bereavement too, but she used a spellstone her husband provided to damp its misery. This was not, Niobe knew, from any selfishness. It was simply that, with a husband and a father to attend to, and a class to teach, she could not afford to be incapacitated at this time. This was one of the benefits of modern magic; it did make it easier for people to survive such crises. Perhaps it was for similar reasons Blenda postponed starting her own family.

But Pacian was not doing as well. He refused to use magic to ameliorate his misery, and his suffering did not appear to ease with time. He maintained himself with solemn dignity, meeting his commitments, keeping up his health, but he seemed to be aging too rapidly.

Niobe was concerned. As the mother of the Magician whom Satan had sought to strike down, she felt a guilty responsibility for the tragedy of the wedding. Also, as an Aspect of Fate, she knew she should have been able to balk Satan more effectively than she had. So it was at least in part her fault. Pacian had been her son's best friend in youth, virtually his brother; it was not right to let him suffer.

She visited him in her own form and apologized. At first he hardly listened, but then he remembered. "You—you are the Magician's relative! The one who posed with my daughter."

−112−

Niobe wrestled briefly with her sense of propriety and decided it didn't matter. "I am related to the Magician," she reminded him. "Closely."

"He has no little sister," he said. "I am his only cousin, once-removed, so you cannot be related that way. Yet you are strangely familiar. Exactly how are you related?"

She delayed a moment more, hesitating before the plunge. "You have met me before."

"I'm sure I have—or someone like you. It nags me every time I see you! But I can't place the connection."

"Certainly you can. I am the Magician's mother."

He laughed. "Sure, and you're sixty years old!"

"Closer to sixty-two."

"I knew his mother when I was a boy. She was the prettiest woman extant! But after she left Junior with us, she visited for a while, then disappeared. She had some kind of important job that took all her time. I think she just couldn't stand to stay around where cousin Cedric had died." Suddenly his animation deflated. "I know the feeling."

"I am Niobe Kaftan," she said firmly. "What you say is true; I could not remain. I loved my baby son, but I knew I could not raise him as well as your family could, so I gave him up. I have never truly regretted that decision; your folks did a fine job with him—and with you."

"He was always a good boy," he agreed. "I was so pleased when he took an interest in my daughter. Of course they are second cousins, but it reunified a family that had been drifting apart." Then he refocused on her. "The irony is that you *do* resemble her. But you are no older than my daughter."

"I never aged, physically," Niobe explained. "I am still the physical age I was when you were twelve. When I kissed you and departed."

"That kiss . . . " he murmured, remembering.

But he was still unable to accept it. Blenda, being younger, had readily acclimatized to the truth and kept her mouth shut, but Pacian at age fifty was too adult to swallow the impossible readily. "The Magician, perhaps, has a spell for eternal youth—but he has never used it, and certainly he did not have it in time for his mother's use."

"I became an Aspect of Fate," she said. "An Incarnation. They are physically frozen; they are Incarnations of Immortality—for a while. So, as Clotho, I never aged."

He looked at her again. "You *are* beautiful," he said as if yielding a point. "Probably as lovely as she was. I had a crush on her—"

"I know."

He sighed. "Very well. I will entertain the notion that you are she, unaged. I'm sure the matter can be verified readily enough; the Magician will know."

"He does."

"But I require proof of my own. As I recall, Fate has three Aspects—"

"Yes. I assumed the Aspect of Atropos to continue visiting Junior—and you."

"Atropos?"

"The oldest Aspect of Fate. She—"

"You can change—just like that?"

"Yes."

"Do so."

She gave the body to Atropos.

Pacian shook his head. "No, you are not she."

"Of course I'm not," Atropos said. "The Atropos you knew retired to be with you and the boy until she died; I am her successor." She gave the body back to Niobe.

"And you were there, too, in the body—all the time?"

"Yes," Niobe said.

"There is something that happened—"

"The prophecy."

"Which I voided. I married Blanche. She was the finest woman—"

"But not the loveliest of her generation," Niobe finished.

"Correct. *You* were that."

She laughed. "So I have been told. And Blenda is the one of *her* generation. She honored the prophecy by marrying—"

She broke off, suddenly making a connection. She stared at Pacian. He stared back with similar astonishment.

Then he turned away. Niobe got up quickly and departed.

Back in her Purgatory Abode, Niobe tried to concentrate on her spinning, but the others wouldn't let her. "I wasn't there," Atropos said. "But what's wrong with Pacian?"

"He's my husband's cousin!" Niobe retorted.

"Your husband died almost forty years ago, didn't he?" Lachesis asked. "And Pacian's wife four years ago. You are both free, now."

"But we never thought of each other in that way!"

"But he had a crush—" Lachesis said.

"And you *are* the most beautiful—" Atropos put in.

"To Hell with the prophecy!" Niobe cried.

"That is what Satan would like," Lachesis said snidely.

"To Hell with Satan!"

"Exactly how did that prophecy go?"

"Each boy would possess the most beautiful woman of her gen-eration," Niobe said, concentrating to remember it accurately. "Each would bear a most talented daughter. One girl would love an Incarnation, and the other would become one. No, wait—there were two prophecies; I've got them mixed."

"That's all right," Lachesis said. "Remember all you can."

"Both would stand athwart the tangled skein," Niobe said.

"That's us!" Atropos said.

"One may marry Death, the other Evil," Niobe said, fishing an-other fillip from her memory. "One to be the savior of man—the daughter of the savior of deer. I think that's all of it."

"Then it's the Magician's daughter who will save man," Lachesis said.

"But he has no daughter," Atropos pointed out.

"And Pacian's daughter certainly didn't marry Thanatos or Satan!" Niobe said. "So it remains a mishmash; it doesn't—"

"Unless you marry Pacian," Lachesis said. "And give him another daughter."

"That's preposterous!"

"You are leaving us within a year," Atropos said. "That would be a fine way to do it."

"You damned matchmaker! I don't love Pacian!"

"Yet," both other Aspects said together with her mouth.

It was a month before Niobe could bring herself to face Pacian again. He looked at her with a certain resignation. "Prophecies are difficult to void," he said.

"And often not understood until too late," Niobe answered. It was a familiar dialogue.

"I want you to understand that I never—"

"Of course. I'm over sixty years old."

"And you look younger than my daughter. In addition, your love was Cedric, mine Blanche. I am sure you would not wish to be untrue to your love any more than I would to mine. So we really should dispense with this foolishness—"

Untrue to her love. Niobe sighed. She had been physically untrue to Cedric a thousand times! Yet that had provided her with a better perspective. She had entered a new life, a new role, after Cedric's death, and it would have been wrong not to fulfill that life and that role in the requisite manner. Her private love had remained sacred, and that was what counted.

"Pace, I'm not sure it *is* foolishness. Those prophecies have not been voided after all. When you married Blanche—"

"I generated the most beautiful woman my cousin was destined to marry," he finished. "The skein was more tangled than I realized. But that doesn't necessarily mean—"

"There have been other signals. It seems I am to leave my office soon. I think I must at least explore the possibility that it is to marry you." There—she had said it.

"Niobe, you owe nothing to me! That prophecy dates from when I was a teenager!"

"But you see, Satan has evil plans for the world. I suspect that if the prophecy can be voided, that means that the child of my son and your daughter will not be the savior of man. Maybe she will never be born—unless the full prophecy is honored."

"That's ridiculous! Prophecies don't hold parts of themselves hostage for the performance of the rest."

"I am Fate," she said slowly. "A prophecy is a signal of Fate. The threads of our lives run true, and we try to interfere with them at our peril—and perhaps the peril of man. I'm not sure we have the right to toy with such destiny. Pace—I must know!"

He shrugged. "It is not that I have any aversion to you, Niobe. Far from it! I loved you in my secret heart until I came to know Blanche, and I think that feeling remains. But I always knew you were never to be mine. I simply would not tread upon my cousin's grave."

"Nor I on your wife's! But if the prophecy is voided, and there is no savior of man—" She spread her hands. "Pace, I married once because it was destined to be, not for love. Love came after. I would do it again—if I were sure."

"How can anyone ever be sure about a thing like this?"

"I would like to consult with—an acquaintance. Perhaps she will know."

"And who is that?"

"Gaea. You would call her the Incarnation of Nature."

"Nature." He nodded. "Yes—such an entity might know."

"I want you to be with me, so she can see us both."

He laughed tensely. "Niobe, I can't enter your realm!"

"Yes, you can—if I take you. Will you do it?"

He pondered, then shrugged. "I agree that this should be settled, one way or another. If you can take me, I will go."

She held out her hand. "Then we shall do it."

He was startled. "Now?"

"I have time available now. Don't you?"

"It's the weekend."

She took his hand. "This will be a trip to remember."

"That is my fear." But he smiled.

She flung a strand to Purgatory and slid along it, bringing him with her. They passed through the walls and the foliage of a tree, then up into the sky. Pace watched with the wonder only a mortal could have, and that restored some of the wonder for her, too. She had become jaded in thirty-eight years, as was natural enough, and it was good to be reminded of the phenomenal nature of her powers. She was not eager to give them up!

They slid through the cloudbank underlying Purgatory and stopped before Fate's Abode. "This is where I live, now."

"A giant spiderweb?"

She shifted to her arachnid form, and back to human. "I am no longer an ordinary woman."

"You were never that," he said.

"Now I will take you to Gaea's green mansion." She flung another strand, took his hand again, and slid the two of them across the pleasant landscape of Purgatory. She remembered how Chronos had taken her from Incarnation to Incarnation, so long ago—his parting favor for her, laying the basis for her eventual understanding. In the interim since then, a significant segment of the Tapestry had moved by!

They arrived at the edge of the Green Mother's demesne. Before them a hillside slope dropped into a broad valley covered with waving grain. On the far slope of the valley stood Gaea's vegetable palace. All they had to do was cross.

They started down. "You can't fling a web across?" Pacian inquired.

"Not here. Ge protects her environment, so it can be a challenge to reach her."

"You have not been here before?"

"Oh, yes, many times. We often consult. But this time I'm bringing you along, so her defense system has been activated. It's just her way."

"Nature does have her way," he agreed.

"All the Incarnations do."

He shook his head with mock wonder. "All this—up in the clouds!"

"This is not in the clouds; it just seems that way. Purgatory is between Heaven and Hell, but it is impossible to define their locations. For convenience, we think of Heaven as above, Hell below, and Purgatory between."

"And I suppose this isn't really physical, either."

"It's indeterminate. You and I are alive and solid, but many of the others who seem that way are neither."

He paused and turned to her. "Niobe, I am glad after all these years to learn where you have been. I can appreciate now why you had so little time for mortal matters."

"I had time for mortal matters!" she said defensively. "I was spinning the threads of life!"

"Of course," he agreed, and she felt guilty for her sharp comment. He was a good and decent man, not looking for any quarrel. It was hardly his fault that she still thought of him, in a sense, as a twelve-year-old boy. She had not changed, physically, but he had.

They reached the level floor of the valley and waded into the grass. At the first step it was knee-high; at the second, waist-high; at the third, chest-high.

They stopped. "Oh-oh," Niobe said. "I forgot about the challenge. It's not a matter of just walking across. There's no telling how deep this valley really is."

"It could be a V-shaped valley—concealed by level grass?"

"It could be. Ge can do anything she wants with plants."

"Then we can walk under the grass," he said. "It's not far."

"We'll have to," she agreed uncertainly.

They proceeded. The slope continued, while the height of the grass rose until it was taller than they were. Soon it was twice their height, the long, thin stems giving way elastically before them so that the broader blades at the top were undisturbed. The light dimmed as they went deeper; it was like descending into an ocean, toward the utter dark at the bottom.

Niobe put her foot down—and found nothing. "Oh!" she exclaimed as she lost her balance.

Pacian's strong hand caught her windmilling arm, and he drew her back. Then he squatted to check the ground. "There is a dropoff," he reported. "About a yard, here—but I suspect that is only the beginning. We need a light."

Niobe extended a glowing strand of web. Its light was not great, but it was enough. It showed that the even slope was converting to a treacherous pattern of rocks and crevices.

They moved on down, now holding hands for safety. When they reached a dropoff of more than six feet, Niobe spun a strong thread and looped it about Pacian's waist. Then he braced himself to support her weight while she lowered herself down. After that, he knotted the web to the stout base of a grass-stem and let himself down. She was unable to dematerialize, here.

Now the gloom was Stygian indeed! She had to extend several glowing strands to illuminate the ground clearly, for even a small hole could trap a foot and break an ankle. Even so, it was no fun.

Then the ground shuddered.

They paused. "What's that?" Niobe whispered nervously.

"The tread of a monster," he whispered back. "Now I believe in live and let live; I value the wilderness as my cousin did, as the

Magician does now. But the denizens do not necessarily feel the same way."

"No, they don't!" she agreed. "And we are in some kind of channel or ledge, here in the gloom, without defensive means. Pace, let's get out of here!"

"Agreed!"

They hastened up the slope the way they had come. Pacian gave her a boost up the line they had left, though she didn't need it; she climbed her threads magically. But he was being unconsciously chivalrous, and she appreciated the gesture. In a moment he followed, climbing up hand over hand. The thread, so thin it was almost invisible, was spelled not to cut flesh, and he was in good condition for his age. He had no trouble.

The ground shuddered again; the monster was coming closer.

They rejoined hands and hurried up the slope, following the line she had left. There was no way to tell how close the monster was; the shuddering was everywhere. Panting, they scrambled out of the grass and into the sunshine.

"Oh!" Niobe gasped. "I was so frightened!"

"Aren't you invulnerable, as an Incarnation?"

She laughed. "Of course I am! How silly of me to forget!" Then she frowned. "But *you* aren't."

He smiled, reminding her fleetingly of Cedric. They were, of course blood kin; if Cedric had lived to this age . . . "Just as well we hurried, then," he said. Somehow they both knew that they were safe in the bright light; the monster would not leave the shelter of the deep grass.

She looked across at Gaea's treehouse, so near and yet so far away. "But we still need to get across."

Pacian considered. "You know, that looks like a roving ocean. The surface ripples in waves under the wind."

"Too bad we can't sail across it," she joked.

"Can't we? If this is a magic challenge—"

Her mouth dropped open. "It could be!"

He looked about. "Perhaps a raft. I see some driftwood." He walked over to the bonelike branches of a dead tree and began collecting them. "This wood is strong and light. If we lash pieces together—"

"I have threads," she said. "They'll work for that. Do you really think it will float—on grass?"

"With magic, anything is possible," he said cheerfully. It was evident that he liked a challenge. He was more animated now than she had seen him in the past two years.

As Pacian worked, he commented on a river-crossing riddle that this effort brought to mind. Niobe remembered that one from her days with Cedric. "All right," Pacian said, smiling. "Then try this one: A coin dealer has twelve coins, one of which is counterfeit . . . " He defined the problem for her, and she struggled without success until he explained the key step in the solution. He had the same joy in such puzzles that Cedric had had.

As they talked, he arranged the larger branches to make a framework, which she bound together with lengths of her thread. Then they tied smaller branches on until they had a raft about six feet square. They saved two long, thin branches to use as poles, and several more for paddles. "But a sail would be better," he said.

That reminded her of her voyage across the college lake, on the patched-up sailboat. She was not reassured.

There was no suitable material for a sail. With time and a loom she could have woven one from her threads, but of course she had no loom here. They heaved the raft onto the surface of the thick grass—and it floated. "That's it!" Pacian exclaimed. "It would never work without magic; this isn't real water. But your friend Nature has enchanted it as a challenge, and we have found the key."

Had they? Niobe hoped so. Pacian helped her aboard, and they shoved off. The raft floated somewhat uncertainly, and the feel was not the same as for water, but they were on their way.

Poling got them well into it, but then they went beyond the depth the poles could reach. Pacian sat down, hooked his feet into the twisted planking, and set up the two longest paddles as oars. "Um, we need to anchor them," he said.

Niobe saw the problem. She knelt and tied the oars to the edges with more loops of thread, so that they swung on crude fulcrums. Then Pacian started rowing—and the raft moved. The oars tended to slide past the leaves of grass, but there was enough friction to make it work. They were on their way, again.

There was a jet of vapor down the valley. "There she blows!" Niobe exclaimed. Then she had a second thought. What kind of whale would swim in grass?

Pacian had the same thought. He accelerated his rowing, but the clumsy raft moved slowly, while a second plume erupted, closer. The whale was coming toward them!

"Is that coincidence?" Niobe asked worriedly.

"Here? I doubt it," he puffed.

"I don't think we can outrun it." She was alarmed.

Pacian ceased rowing. His face was red from his effort. "Another challenge?" he gasped.

"I'm—afraid so. And this time we can't retreat. It would catch us in a moment."

He hefted a paddle, pondering. "I suppose I could try to fend it off," he said. "If it's big enough to take a bite of us, it's big enough to get a paddle or a pole wedged edgewise in its mouth. But I don't like molesting wildlife. After all, we are intruders on its preserve."

"You're a soft-hearted fool!" she chided him.

"It runs in the family," he agreed without rancor.

She was stricken. He was right. Once Cedric had taken to the wilderness, he had refused to harm any of it. And Junior's long association with the hamadryad of the water oak had left him with a profound appreciation of the magic of the wetlands. She herself felt the same. Pacian was very much in that mold.

The leviathan drew near. Its huge snout broke the surface of the grass. The thing was big enough to swallow them whole, raft and all!

"They say that music has charms to soothe the savage breast," Pacian said. "That is most often misquoted as 'savage beast.' It just may be worth a try, rather than futile force."

Niobe liked the way his mind worked, but the leviathan terrified her. Already its ponderous jaws were cranking open. "You mean— sing it a song?"

"Sounds silly, I know—but it's harmless, at least. I have sung to the animals on the farm with some success. We can always try to fight, as a last resort. Have you any idea what it might like?"

Doing requests, for a monster? Niobe found her mind largely blank. "I—maybe a round—"

He nodded agreement. He faced the leviathan as if about to deliver a speech. He sang, crudely but adequately:

"Have you seen the ghost of Tom?
Round white bones with the flesh all gone!
O - O - O - O - O - O - O!
Wouldn't it be chilly with no skin on!"

Niobe started to laugh, hysterically. To sing a Halloween song to a monster!

The leviathan paused in place. The jaws stopped opening. It was listening, and like some animals, it could not focus its attention on two things at once.

"Have you seen the ghost of Tom?" Pacian sang, with greater volume and confidence. This time Niobe picked up on it, repeating the first line as Pacian continued with the second line, for it was indeed a round. It worked out rather prettily, despite the macabre and foolish words.

They went through it three times, and the leviathan did not move. Whether it liked the song was uncertain; perhaps mere curiosity held it. But that was certainly preferable to an attack.

When they stopped, the jaws slowly resumed motion. Quickly Pacian started another song, one long beloved in his culture:

"O Danny-Boy, the pipes, the pipes are calling,
From glen to glen and down the mountainside . . . "

Niobe joined in, making the harmony. She had not sung like this since her mortal days, and had almost forgotten how grand it was.

"The summer's gone, and all the leaves are falling . . . "

Pacian turned while singing, and reached to take her hand.

" 'Tis you, 'tis you must go and I must bide."

And Niobe was transfixed as the song abruptly expanded to magnificent sound. *He had the magic!* The same phantom orchestra that Cedric had had when he sang. The same phenomenal magnification of the music!

Of course! This, too, ran in the family! Not in every member, for her son did not have it. But here and there. She had never guessed! No wonder Pace could pacify animals!

The leviathan was aware of it too. Slowly, now, its jaws subsided, no longer menacing the raft. They had indeed found a way to soothe the beast.

But Niobe's attention was only partly on that. She had thought she would never love again, after Cedric. Now, suddenly, amazingly, she knew it was possible. The prophecy had not been based on what she knew, but on what she would discover.

They finished the song, and the internal music faded. The leviathan did not resume its aggression, but Niobe now had need of more music. She clung to Pacian's hand, and started a song.

"In the gloaming, O my darling, when the lights are dim
and low . . . "

He joined the song and the music rose in them and surrounded them.

"Will you think of me, and love me, as you did once long
ago?"

Even as she sang, Niobe felt the love expanding from her long-isolated heart, encompassing her being. The beginning of her love for

Cedric had come with the magic music. She had not seized upon it, then, and so had wasted much of the scant time they had had together. She was much older, and perhaps wiser now—and she found herself entering into it as into a primeval sea, gladly giving herself to its tide. *O my darling . . .*

When the song ended and the music faded again, the leviathan was satisfied. It backed off slowly and turned about, and swam away.

"It sems we have navigated the crisis," Pacian said. "Now we can go to meet Mother Nature." He reached for the oars.

Niobe put her hand on his arm again. "Pace—do we need to?"

He considered, then laughed. Then he drew her in to him, and they kissed. The grand music encompassed them.

They reversed course and returned to her Abode, and then to the realm of the mortals. As they landed back in his house, he said: "I don't think I'm going to be lonely anymore. But let's not act precipitously."

"This is very sudden," she agreed. "We can afford time to be sure it's real." But she already knew it was.

He nodded. "And if it is—"

"Then I will retire on schedule, to become mortal—and be your wife."

"Fulfilling the prophecy," he agreed.

She left him without further comment. The moment she was alone, a babble broke out among her Aspects. *Did you feel that music? He's a rare one! If that's what your first love was like, no wonder you waited for his like! We'll have to locate your successor, whatshername, Lisa. When's the wedding?*

"Enough, you hens!" Niobe exploded. "It's tentative!"

Lachesis snorted. *As tentative as a pregnancy, girl!*

Indeed, all that developed over the course of the following months was certainty. Niobe visited Pacian several times, and each time it was as if another layer of love was added. "I *do* love you, Pace," she said. "I must marry you."

"I thought I would never be whole again, after I lost Blanche," he said. "But it is no denigration of her to confess that now I love you as I did her. When I was a child I adored you hopelessly; now I am a man I have reason to live again. It is as if you were saved for the time in my life when I would most need you." He paused. "*Is* that coincidence?"

She shook her head. "I am an Aspect of Fate—but my power is limited. Lachesis handles the disposition of the threads of life I spin— but her power too is limited. It was Satan's interference that caused me to lose my spouse, and you yours. Fate never planned those horrors, and now the Tapestry is healing."

"Yet the prophecy—"

She sighed. "Yes, there must be a deeper current of Fate, beyond our awareness, that the seers drew from. Maybe our manipulations of the Threads of Life are only to restore the pattern Satan sought to disrupt. It has made for a tangled skein!"

"Which our daughter—and granddaughter—will stand athwart," he agreed. "But for the moment, there is only our love."

They kissed, and there was music. He was right; their offspring might be destined for horrendous adventures, but at the moment love made all that beside the point.

In due course, as the time of her departure from office neared, Niobe made it a point to bid adieu to her friends, the other Incarnations. First she went to the Green Mother. This time she had no trouble reaching the domicile of Nature. "You knew, didn't you?" she charged the woman. "You arranged that challenge course!"

"Love is one of my Aspects," Gaea admitted. "I knew your heart and his. I only facilitated what was inevitable."

"So we never even consulted you!"

"Not overtly."

"You are devious, Ge."

"Coming from Fate, that is indeed a compliment."

They embraced, and Niobe cried a little, and they parted. Gaea's face was serene—but when Niobe stepped outside the domicile, she discovered a gentle rain falling, and knew that Ge was crying too.

A few days later, in the course of routine business, she visited Thanatos. Fate worked most intimately with Chronos, but she also had considerable interaction with Thanatos, for the threads had to be terminated as well as started. "I am soon to return to mortality," she said. "I pray you do not come too soon for me or the man I love."

The death's-head smiled. "I will postpone it as long as your successor permits. Who is she to be?"

"I don't know. We are conducting a search, but no suitable prospect named Lisa has shown up."

"Will Lisa be as pretty as you?"

"Not quite. But you are sure to like her."

"I envy you, Clotho. You are able to step down voluntarily, returning to life. I will be assassinated by my successor, even as I assassinated my predecessor."

"Yet it was to Heaven you sent your predecessor, and to Heaven you will go."

"That is a comfort," he agreed.

She embraced him, not repulsed by his skeletal hands, and she kissed his grinning skull-face. His business was grim, but he was a decent person. He was not the same one she had first met, but the office had made him similar.

Her supply of yarn ran low, and she made her monthly trip to the Void for more. She wondered, as she often did, whether this monthly cycle stood in lieu of the feminine cycle that had abated when she became immortal. There were, indeed, patterns she did not understand.

"So you are quitting, cutie," Satan said, appearing before her.

"Go to Hell," she told him shortly.

"You have been a delectable thorn in My side for too long," he continued blithely. "It will be an excellent riddance."

"Go damn yourself."

"I really will enjoy working over your successor, scrumptious."

She paused. "Why so positive, Lord of Flies? Can it be that you don't want me to go?"

He puffed smoke. "Of course I want you to go!" he said.

She nodded. "Because I am fated to produce a mortal child who will be a real pain in the tail for you."

He did not respond with the derogatory or cynical exclamation she expected. Instead he was oddly pensive. "There are currents of destiny that perhaps only God comprehends," he said. "Our glimpses of the future are fleeting and imperfect. I have taken a reading on your daughter and I see only a terrible storm perhaps forty years hence, and she is caught up in it—and so am I. I do not know the outcome."

Niobe suffered a chill. "And one may marry Death, the other Evil," she said, again recalling the prophecy.

"I am the Incarnation of Evil!" he said. "Why should I ever bind Myself to a mortal woman?"

"She is to be an Incarnation."

Satan turned and paced in air, his gaze downcast. He was almost handsome in that moment of reflection. "And what woman, whether mortal or Incarnation, would ever bind herself to Me?"

It was a serious question. "Only an evil one," Niobe said.

"Are you about to birth and raise an evil woman?"

"Of course not!"

"Of course not," he agreed. "For you are indeed a good woman, as well as a lovely one. She can only oppose Me. Yet the prophecy—"

He was genuinely disturbed! "Satan, what are you getting at?"

He faced her without any sign of cruelty or mockery. "Simply this: there is a tangle coming in your skein that neither of us understands. Never would I bind Myself to a good woman, nor would she to Me. Something very strange is brewing. Let us avoid the whole issue, and oppose each other on conventional grounds. Keep your present office, O lovely woman! Do not generate that child.''

Niobe was astonished. "You are pleading with me to do you a favor—by abrogating the fulfillment of my love?"

"I suppose I am, Clotho. I can proffer inducement if you prefer. I could assume the likeness and manner of your—"

"You're crazy!"

Satan sighed. "No, I am evil, not crazy. I have merely confirmed that no decent woman would accept Me if she knew My nature, however I might clothe Myself. You know Me, therefore you will not do for Me what you did for Chronos."

Niobe stared at him. "You—desire my favor?"

"I do desire it."

Almost, she felt sorry for him. Then the memory of Cedric surged back, and the emotion became anger. "Well, you will never have it!"

"That I know. Still I would have you remain in office."

"You should know better!"

"You will not do it?"

"I will not do it!"

Now he flared brightly with his abrupt fury. "I *tried* to be reasonable! To be honest, though it pains Me! I'm not good at it, I know, but I did try. Now you will feel the brunt of My wrath!"

"Go to Hell, Satan," she repeated mildly.

"And your child will suffer too!" he cried as he faded out. "You and yours will rue this hour!"

He was gone—and Niobe found herself shivering with reaction. *Had* she made a mistake by refusing to deal with Satan? He had seemed oddly pensive, and his expression of desire for her had seemed honest. Satan, of course, had all the women he wanted, in all the forms he wanted, in Hell—yet none of them were good, by definition. Did he have a hankering for the opposite type? Was there some good even in the Prince of Evil?

Surely not! Satan's designs were always evil, also by definition. If she opposed him, she was probably correct. If he was angry, she should be pleased. She was fulfilling the vengeance she had so long sought against him.

Yet Satan was also devious. The Father of Lies knew how to deceive by indirection as well as by direction. Why had he come to her to make his plea and why had he shown such obvious anger when she declined it? That suggested that it was an act, and that she was in fact doing exactly what he wanted.

She shook her head. Her safest course was to pursue her course as she intended, not allowing herself to be influenced *in any way* by

Satan. Still, it bothered her. She brooded on it throughout her business in the Void. Would she—and her daughter—be vulnerable to Satan's wrath, as mortals?

She visited Chronos next. Mindful of his reversed timeline, she phrased her farewell carefully. "Hello, Chronos. I thought I would introduce myself, as we shall be working together for the next two or three years. I am Clotho, an Aspect of Fate."

"Oh, go on!" the child snapped. "You aren't Lisa!"

"Of course I'm not. Lisa has gone mortal. I am Niobe." She smiled.

Chronos was eight years old, physically and emotionally. He melted like ice cream in the radiance of that smile. "Gee, you sure are pretty, Obe! I guess you're okay!"

"I guess I am," she agreed. "I know you and I will get along well." She tousled his hair.

"Hey, wait a minute!" he protested. "You live forward, not backward like me! You've already been through it!"

She smiled again, daunting him. "Smart lad! Yes, I know you a good deal better than you know me, though that will change as you advance into my past. But when your tenure comes to a close, and you are afraid, I will come to you and hold your hand. So don't annoy me, okay?"

"Geez, it's weird having you come in like this, knowing so much! Lisa was sorta timid and sweet, specially at the end when she forgot my language. I'll sure miss her."

Forgot his language? How could that be? But Niobe preferred not to discuss it with him. "Just remember, sport—I chose her."

"Yeah, I know. Yesterday. Funny thing, you coming up with her."

"What's so funny about bringing in a woman who can do the job?"

He stared at her a moment, then laughed teasingly. "That's right! You don't know her yet. You'll find out, Obe!"

"I'll find out," she agreed, kissed him on the forehead, shifted to spider form, and climbed out of his sight. He always enjoyed that trick.

This was getting stranger. First Satan's pointless offer and threat, then Chronos' reaction. Chronos knew something she didn't, of course. They had been searching diligently for Lisa, and still had not found her, one day before the event.

What would happen if they failed to find her? Would there be another snarl in the threads, pinching the Tapestry, and could Niobe find herself stranded in office, unable to turn mortal and marry Pacian? Was that the mischief Satan contemplated?

No, it couldn't be, for the change to Lisa *had* occurred tomorrow; Chronos remembered it, and Chronos was no tool of Satan's. She really didn't need to worry about it; what would be would be—and she would be mortal, tomorrow.

But tomorrow came with no further illumination. There was no sign of Lisa even as the hour approached. Niobe's better two-thirds were as mystified as she was. "The thread has to be here in the Tapestry," Lachesis said. "But nothing distinguishes it. So it is lost until we find it. There simply is no signal that Lisa is to step out of life and into Fate."

"I'll bid farewell to Mars," Niobe decided. "Then it will be time, and we'll see."

She sailed down a thread to the spot on Earth where Mars was working. This was the great double city of Budapest, at the moment torn by strife. Huge Soviet tanks were moving in the streets, and buildings were burning.

She landed on a street beside him. Mars, too, was different from the one who had been in office when she first came to Purgatory. She wasn't certain what the mechanism for his changing was, but it seemed to occur irregularly and without warning. But this one had been in office for several years, and she liked him well enough, considering the differences in their philosophies. "Mars, I came to say good-bye."

He glanced at her. "Ah, so soon, lass? There'll never be a sweeter or prettier Clotho than you! Give me a buss!"

She submittted to his embrace and hugged him back. She had had liaisons with him on occasion, as appropriate, and so had Lachesis. "How's it going, Warrior?"

He released her. "Always a novelty! See that line of refugees?"

She looked where he pointed. A seemingly endless line of bedraggled civilians were walking along the side of the street, going north. Obviously they had been bombed out of their homes and were fleeing to whatever safety they could find.

Now he took her by the shoulders and turned her to face the other way. "And those?"

She looked dutifully. Another line of refugees was traveling south. "But they're each going where the other's coming from!" she exclaimed.

"True. What do you make of that?"

"It has to be a tragedy! No hope for either group!"

"Now you have it, lass," he agreed gruffly. "War is hell."

She knew better, but she couldn't help herself. She challenged his rationale: "How can you encourage such an appalling situation, Mars? Those are living, feeling *people* there, surely innocent of the causes of this war!"

Mars, always ready for combat, answered without hesitation. "Aye, lass, that they are, by your definition. But not by mine! They sought freedom, so brought this consequence on their heads!"

"Freedom?"

He nodded. "Freedom to speak, to assemble, to read, to choose their own work. They forgot they were a satellite nation. Those tanks are here to remind them."

"And you approve of this?" she demanded incredulously.

"To be sure! Freedom is the most precious thing man can grasp, and its price is commensurate. These people suffer to prove that they are worthy of what they seek, and I'm proud of them!"

"And what of the tanks?"

"I am proud of them, too."

"Oh, Mars, you're impossible! I wish I could save even one of those poor souls!"

Mars made a gesture that included both lines of refugees. "Take your pick, Clotho."

"What?"

"If you are exchanging your office in a few minutes, you can do it with one of these. She, at least, can be spared."

The incredible boor! Lachesis thought.

But it may be true, Atropos replied.

"All right, I will!" Niobe walked out to the line going north and stopped the first young woman she spied who seemed to be traveling alone. She was a dark-haired, pretty girl of perhaps twenty, toting a large suitcase. She stared at Niobe.

"Would you like to become Fate?" Niobe asked.

The woman's large eyes looked at her blankly.

"To exchange places with me and be forever free of this?"

The woman spoke unintelligibly.

Of course! Atropos thought. *She's Hungarian!*

Doesn't Mars speak all tongues? Lachesis thought.

"Yes!" Niobe said. She took the woman by the hand and tugged her across the street toward the Incarnation of War. The woman seemed to have been stunned by the horror of the violence around her. Perhaps she thought Niobe was offering her a place to stay in safety for the night.

"Mars, tell her," Niobe ordered. "Ask her to exchange."

Mars spoke to the woman in her language, gesturing to Niobe. The woman shook her head, not believing it. Then a shell landed nearby, blowing out part of a building, and the woman changed her mind. She nodded affirmation.

"Any port in a storm," Mars translated.

It was Atropos' turn to handle the change. She assumed the body. "Farewell, Niobe," she said. "It has been a pleasure working with you."

Good-by, sister Aspect, Lachesis thought, giving her a mental kiss.

Atropos took the woman's hand—and Niobe found herself standing separately, in her own body, facing Atropos. "Farewell, sister Aspects!" she cried—and as always, tears flowed.

Mars touched one of his pockets and brought out a fragment of reddish stone. "Take this, Niobe," he said gruffly. "It is from my planet. It will guard you from harm until you can reach your destination."

Niobe took the stone. She opened her mouth to thank him.

Another shell burst, close by, momentarily blinding her and causing her to cower. When she straightened up, both Mars and Fate were gone. She was on her own. Deprived of her two alternate Aspects, she felt abruptly naked. They—and immortality—were no longer part of her. Her tears continued.

But she could not remain here, crying in the street of the war-torn city. She knew where she was going. She hefted the suitcase and started walking.

– 9 –

TWIN MOONS

Thanks to the Mars fragment, she made her way safely from Budapest, across the Iron Curtain, and to Ireland, where Pacian was waiting for her. She was tired and bedraggled and felt exceedingly mortal, but she was ready to marry him.

But first she consulted with her son the Magician. "Satan swore to harass me and mine," she said. "Is it possible to be secure from this?"

"Satan is constrained to operate somewhat through channels," he replied. "My power does not approach his, but I can protect us all from his mischief." He gave her a bright green garnet, mounted on a silver chain. "Wear this always, Mother, and you will be secure. I will see to the daughters in their turn."

"Thank you, son," she said, smiling. He was now forty, she twenty-four, physically.

"And one for Pace," he said, handing her another.

The wedding was in spring, and by summer Niobe was pregnant. The Magician's wife, Pacian's daughter Blenda, turned up pregnant that same summer, after five years of marriage, by what coincidence or design only Lachesis might know. Niobe and Blenda took walks together and compared notes, still seeming like sisters though Blenda was now five years older physically.

When spring came again, both women gave birth to daughters within a week of each other. Niobe named hers Orb and Blenda named hers Luna, for they were like twin moons. The Magician presented each baby with a polished moonstone, to protect her from misfortune.

The two girls were raised together and were amazingly similar even after allowing for the fact that they were closely related. Niobe and Pacian were the ancestors of both; strangers assumed that Orb and Luna were twins. The Magician still tended to bury himself in his studies, and Blenda had retired from teaching in order to assist him, so that Luna would spend days at a time at Niobe's house. Pacian, always a farmer, was now going into tree farming, gradually remaking the wetlands without destroying it; this took long hours. Thus most of the child care fell to Niobe. She loved it. She had given up her first child, Junior, and now was glad to make up for it by raising two. It was her fulfillment as a mother, forty years delayed.

She put them together in a double pram for walks through the countryside and, when they grew old enough to do their own walking, she took them through the wetlands to admire the fine magical trees Pacian was cultivating. Sometimes they would ride their family carpet to the place where she and Cedric had lived. The old cabin had been replaced by a modern bungalow, complete with electricity and central heating, but the old water oak remained. The hamadryad was now a middle-aged nymph, showing it more by manner than by form, but she remembered Niobe, once she introduced herself, and came down cautiously to play with the little girls. Niobe was as happy as she had ever been, despite the nostalgia. But she always made sure both girls were wearing their protective moonstones, for Satan could be lurking, awaiting his chance for mischief.

The children reached school age, and Niobe took them there together and got them enrolled. She had to wrestle verbally with the clerks who assumed that two similar children whose surname was Kaftan *had* to be sisters if not twins. "Orb is mine, Luna is my son's child." They stared at her, for she was physically thirty.

Both girls were bright as well as pretty. Niobe's side of the family accounted for the beauty, and the Kaftan side accounted for the brilliance. It was genetics more than merit, but still she was inordinately proud.

As school progressed, the girls became more differentiated. They adopted different clothing and hairstyles; one would wear pink, the other green, and then they would switch. One would grow her hair long, while the other cut it short—and again they would switch. Luna's hair was clover-honey, like her mother's, and her eyes were pearl-gray; Orb's hair was buckwheat-honey, like Niobe's, and her eyes pale blue. But they could still be very similar when they chose.

Luna became interested in art, while Orb liked music. Luna showed real talent with pictures, proceeding from crayons to pastel chalk to watercolors and finally to oil; her efforts were always prominently represented in class shows. Orb started with the guitar and gravitated to the piano, then centered on the harp. She had genuine talent for it, and when she was ten, she gave a recital of *The Shepherd's Song* that sounded so like the magic music her father and grandfather had had that Niobe was stunned. *She had the magic*—and it reached a short way out beyond physical contact to touch those who listened closely. The audience, though it heard only the physical music, was still entranced, and applauded her enthusiastically.

By the time they were twelve, both girls were almost as pretty as their mothers had been, and their talents were solidly established. "It's time they had better equipment," Pacian said and he took Niobe to see the Magician.

"The instruments exist," the Magician said. "But they have to be won. They are in an annex to the Hall of the Mountain King. The King sleeps, but an attempt to steal anything would wake him, and that would be unfortunate."

"I don't want them stealing anything!" Niobe protested. "They're honest girls!"

The Magician smiled tolerantly. "To be sure, Mother. But you must understand the Mountain King's definition. He will freely give the instruments to any person he deems worthy of them—but what he calls worthy, we might call theft."

"That's preposterous!"

"Not so, Mother," he informed her patiently. "A person who can take the instrument deserves it; the one who cannot, but who tries to, is a thief."

"There are standards—an examination?"

"A series of three challenges to gain entry," he said. "Then a demonstration of proficiency for the specific instrument."

"Challenges?" She wasn't sure she liked the sound of it. Not for twelve-year-old girls.

"The Annex is deep in the mountain, of course. There are cliffs, pitfalls, monsters—that sort of thing. Routine."

"Routine! I'm not sending my child or yours into that! Those girls are only—"

"Twelve years old," he finished for her. "Mother, the challenges are only illusions. No danger—as long as the unworthy person does not attempt to steal an instrument."

Now it was coming clear. "They run the course—and if they get through without making an error, then they can try for the prizes?"

"Precisely. And if they do make an error, they have simply to depart immediately, without waking the King. He gets angry when awoken."

"And proceeding on, after an error, wakes him?"

"Yes. It really isn't wise to do that."

She pondered. "Exactly what would happen if he wakes?"

"He would turn the challenges real."

"Real pitfalls, instead of illusory ones?"

"That's it, Mother," he said with the calmness that a person of normal intelligence assumes when dealing with one of limited intellect. "And if that person attempts to steal—"

"Then—not that our girls would, but—?"

"Then the Mountain King would personally intervene. I could not protect them in the King's hall; he is omnipotent there. The moonstones protect them from evil, but the Mountain King is not evil, just tough. But it should never come to that."

"I wouldn't let them take the risk!"

He shrugged. "Why don't you go along to chaperone them? Then you can be sure they don't do anything foolish. The Mountain King is a fair man; he will not bother anyone who honors his rules."

"I can do that? Run the challenges with them?"

"Of course you can, Mother!" he said, as if her intellect had turned out to be below his already-modest expectations. "The King is not fussy about details. I would take the girls in myself, but he wouldn't tolerate my presence. Rival magic, you know."

"The instruments are good ones?"

"The best that exist, Mother," he assured her patiently. "State of the art."

She sighed. "Then I'll do it."

She took them in, parking the car beside the huge sign: MOUNTAIN KING—ANNEX. They entered the marked aperture, which resembled a jewel-encrusted cave. The girls were thrilled and nervous. They had heard stories about the nefarious halls of the Mountain King, but had never hoped to visit them personally. They had wanted to dress prettily, but Niobe had insisted on jeans and sneakers. "This isn't a fashion show!" she snorted.

Inside were signs with arrows: TOURISTS—CHALLENGES. They took the latter direction.

The passage opened into a large cave with a rocky floor. A painted yellow line wound around between the rocks to the far side. Several motorcycles were parked at the near side. A big sign said INSTRUCTIONS.

Niobe moved over to read the sign. Smaller print on it clarified the conditions of the challenge. She read and whistled. "This really *is* a challenge!"

The girls read the sign. "Mother, we can't do that!" Orb protested.

"I confess I don't like it," Niobe agreed. "But remember: the hazards are not real. They're illusions."

The challenge was to ride a motorcycle along the line, which was the only safe route across the minefield. Because this was the first, one error was permitted. Because the mines were illusions, they would merely flash brightly when set off, rather than blow the transgressor apart. "How sweet of the Mountain King," Niobe murmured with a certain irony.

"But if we set off two," Luna said, "we can't get our instruments?"

"That's right, dear. Because if we took anything after failing the challenge of passage, those mines would become real." It was, she had to admit, a nice device of selection. Those who could handle the challenges would have no problem; those who could not would be absolute fools to trigger the non-illusory threats. The Mountain King played a hard but fair game.

"Ooo," Orb murmured softly. She was the more reactive of the two, quicker to turn on or off, quicker to anger or to forgiveness. "But if we play the game honestly, we have nothing to fear."

"That's right. That's a good rule for life." Niobe looked at the motorcycles, and at the minefield, and the meandering line. How much clearance was there on either side of it? And the girls—neither had ridden more than a bicycle before. One would be sure to waver too far. This was too much of a challenge!

"I'd better take you across, one at a time," Niobe decided. "The largest cycle will handle two."

She wheeled out the large motorcycle, started it—trusting that the cave was large enough to handle the fumes of the exhaust—and rode it up and down the side, making sure she had the hang of it. Obviously the Mountain King had expected a man to challenge, rather than a woman and girls. When she was satisfied, she put Orb on it behind her, the girl clasping her about the middle, and rode up to the side again. "Now lean with me when I make the turn," she said. "The balance has to be just so, as with a bicycle."

"Yes, Mother."

"Luna, you have the eye for depth. You watch us, and cry warning if I seem to be misjudging a curve."

"Yes, Grandma." The girls enjoyed their real relationships in private; in public they preferred to consider themselves cousins.

Niobe nerved herself and started along the line. The first curve went well, but when she hit the reverse curve, Orb got confused and started to lean the wrong way. She corrected herself in a moment, but it was enough to nudge the cycle off the mark. A mine was touched, and a brilliant flash blinded her.

"I can't see!" Niobe cried.

"Neither can I!" Orb screamed.

The motorcycle wavered as she tried to guide it along the course by memory. But she knew it was hopeless; by the time her vision recovered, she would be in the middle of the mines, and thoroughly disqualified. Unless—

"Luna!" she called. "Can you see?"

"Yes," Luna replied. "You're drifting right."

"Direct me!"

Luna was a smart and levelheaded girl. She understood immediately. "Bear left."

Niobe obeyed, maintaining a velocity so the cycle would not waver out of control.

"Now turn right, slowly," Luna called. "A little more—yes. And straight. Coming up is an acute left turn—make it sharp on the mark. Ready—mark!"

Niobe and Orb leaned left, and they made a sharp left turn.

"Now go straight—nudge right—yes—now an S-turn, right then left, not too sharp—more right—now edge left—more—that's it— and right again. Now straight; you're almost there."

Thus did they navigate the field without setting off another mine. Niobe parked the motorcycle, waited a few minutes for her vision to clear, then rode back alone to fetch Luna. "You did a good job there," she told the girl. "Your judgment has preserved our chance to win through." The girl flushed prettily with pleasure.

The second trip across was less eventful; sight and experience made all the difference. They parked the motorcycle and walked down the passage to the next challenge.

This turned out to be a subterranean river, broad and deep, with a wire mesh fence bisecting it lengthwise, barring passage across it. But there was another explanatory plaque. "This is a section of the River Lethe," Niobe read aloud. "One drop in the mouth will cause a person to forget for a moment; one swallow will cause forgetfulness for an hour. Water in eyes will cause the forgetting of the ability to see. Beware lethal monster who patrols at irregular intervals."

"That's funny!" Orb exclaimed. "The lethal monster swims in Lethe!"

"Not funny if it catches you," Luna reminded her.

"We shall have to swim across," Niobe said. "The problem is the barrier in the center—we'll have to dive under it. That means closing the eyes tightly. We'd better do it singly, with the others watching while one dives."

"But—our clothing!" Orb protested.

"You're right. We'll have to leave it here. We don't want to carry the water of Lethe around with us! Also, wet clothing is no fun."

"But we have no bathing suits!" Luna said.

Niobe looked at her. "Dear, soon enough you will be proud to stand nude for self-portraits. There are occasions when modesty is dispensable. This is one such. We are all family and female, and the Mountain King is asleep. No one will see. I daresay this is part of his challenge: have we the courage to go naked to his lair? Remember, the danger is only illusion; if we gulp the water we will not actually forget, we'll merely disqualify ourselves and have to give up the quest. The real test is modesty." She proceeded to undress, carefully folding her clothing and setting it well clear of the water.

Luna shrugged and followed her example, not unduly sensitive about the matter. After a pause, Orb followed suit, obviously less at ease. They were, at this age, in the process of developing, neither women nor children, and were understandably somewhat reticent about exposure. The Mountain King was giving this party a greater variety of challenge than anticipated.

"Now we can dog-paddle to the barrier," Niobe said. "Right after the monster passes. Who's first?"

Orb shrugged. "I'll try it. Someone yell if the monster turns back." They waited, watching for the lethal monster. In a moment it appeared—a globular mass of jelly that seemed to have forgotten its original form. "Ooh, ugh!" Orb exclaimed.

"It's only illusion," Niobe reminded her firmly. "But don't let it catch you. Now scoot!" She slapped the girl on her bare bottom.

Startled, Orb stepped into the water and dog-paddled across, glancing nervously after the monster. "Remember—no peeking!" Niobe called. "Keep your eyes closed after you come up on the other side, until you're sure the water's clear."

Orb nodded, then took half a breath, squinched her eyes shut, and dived. Her legs went up, then slid under. Both girls were good swimmers; it was only the special nature of this challenge that made the swimming awkward. In a moment she came up on the far side, eyes and mouth still firmly closed, and resumed her dog-paddling—in the wrong direction. She was swimming downstream instead of across.

"You're going wrong!" Niobe called. "Turn about!"

The girl, still sightless, didn't understand. She reversed course, now swimming upstream, making little headway.

"The monster's coming back!" Luna whispered.

"She'll never avoid it!" Niobe said tersely. "I'll go get her clear!" She waded in and stroked as swiftly as she could without splashing. Fortunately the monster was slow; she outdistanced it. She closed her mouth and eyes and dived, finding the bottom of the barrier and hauling herself under. Then she angled for the surface in the direction she hoped Orb was. Her head broke water, dripping—and she didn't dare open her eyes.

"To your left!" Luna called.

Niobe lunged left, and encountered one of Orb's arms.

"But the monster's between you and the shore!" Luna called. "You can't get by it! It's turning toward you!"

"This way!" Niobe ordered Orb. "To the barrier!" She side-stroked back, half-hauling the girl along with her other hand. She found the wire. "Climb up it; you don't need to look!"

Wordlessly, the girl obeyed. Niobe made sure Orb had hold of the wire, then let go of her and used hands and feet to climb up out of the water.

Once clear, she used the back of her hand to wipe out both eyes, then cracked one open. Orb was beside her, climbing blindly up the barrier. The monster was below, trying to find them; its limp tentacles flailed about.

"Up here, idiot!" Niobe told it.

The monster heard and tried to reach out of the water, but its substance was too flabby for support. It could not extend any part of itself beyond the river. After a while it gave up and drifted on downstream.

"Very well," Niobe said. "Orb, clear your eyes and climb down. We'll swim the rest of the way across."

They did so. Then Luna crossed and, with the help of Niobe's called instructions, managed to avoid all hazards. They had surmounted the second challenge.

Naked, they proceeded to the third. This one turned out to be awesome; it was a deep chasm, crossed by a narrow rope bridge. They would have to walk or crawl across it. There was another instruction plaque that said BEWARE OF THE VAMPIRE BAT.

That needed no clarification. Obviously a bite by that bat would disqualify them—and the bat would attack whoever was on the bridge. But the instructions advised them that one of the magic wands could be used to fend off the bat. Sure enough, there was a rack holding three wands.

One for each of them. How convenient! Or was it coincidence? Niobe didn't quite trust this, but saw no alternative to proceeding. They were two-thirds of the way through; it would be a shame to muff it now.

Orb stared down into the gulf and shuddered. "I don't think I can—"

"Nonsense," Niobe said, though she herself found the depth of the chasm awesome. "Remember—it's illusion. If you lose your balance, you won't get hurt; you'll just be disqualified."

"Oh, yes," she said, brightening. "It's just a flat floor, like the mine caves, and the bridge's a line through it."

"But we'll be careful, anyway," Niobe cautioned them.

"I'll go first," Luna volunteered. She took a wand, held it firmly in her right hand, and stepped out on the bridge. It sank beneath her weight, startling her, but she kept her balance and walked on.

"Ooo, it's swinging!" she exclaimed as she moved over the gulf. Indeed it was, swinging grandly back and forth like a pendulum.

"Compensate!" Niobe called. "You're all right!"

Luna did, and continued across. At midpoint the bat appeared.

The thing was huge and ugly. Bright red eyes stared at the prey. The black wings spread out a good yard. As it approached, the draft from those wings blew Luna's hair back and made her lose confidence.

"Fend it off with the wand!" Niobe called. "Just stand there, keep your balance, and point the wand at it."

Luna tried, but she was now quite nervous. The bat flew at her; she lunged with the wand. The bat sheered away. She lost her balance and started to fall.

"Grab the bridge!" Niobe cried.

The girl dropped the wand and grabbed the bridge with both hands, hugging it. The wand plunged into the chasm, slowing turning in the air, taking a long time to fall. Some illusion!

The bat, seeing the girl helpless, banked and came back.

Niobe charged out onto the bridge. Her long experience with the threads of Fate made her competent; she wasn't worried about missing a step or falling. She almost dived at the bat as it came down, jamming the end of the wand into its furry body. There was no resistance; the wand passed through. The bat shrieked almost audibly and lurched away, seemingly hurt.

"Get up, girl," Niobe snapped. "Go on across."

"I can't!" Luna cried. Indeed, she was in tears. She was a sensible girl, but she was, after all, only twelve.

"Then crawl across! I'll protect you."

This the girl could do. She scrambled on hands and knees, while Niobe followed her and watched the bat. The creature tried to come in for another pass, looked at Niobe's militant stance, and stayed clear.

On the far side, Luna was able to stand again. She was all right.

"Your turn, Orb," Niobe called. "Can you make it yourself, or shall I come to help you?"

Orb looked at the swinging bridge, and at the hovering bat. "I— you'd better come."

Niobe walked back, holding off the bat with a mere glance. It had come to know the difference between a frightened girl and an embattled woman. "All right—walk ahead of me. I'll protect your rear. Just focus on Luna over there and keep your balance. It's not hard."

"How can you be so brave?" the girl asked, awed.

"I'm a mother. It comes with the office."

It was an offhand quip, but Orb took it seriously. "Having a child makes you brave?"

"When you have something you would die to protect, it ceases to be a matter of courage," Niobe explained. "You just know what you have to do and you can't afford fear."

They moved on across. The bat came at them, and Orb cowered. "Get away!" Niobe screamed at the bat. "Or I'll ram this down your throat, batbrain!"

It spun in the air and fled. Even illusions could be cowed!

"Why is it afraid of you?" Orb asked, amazed.

"Because I wasn't bluffing," Niobe answered. "I would wring its neck if it touched you, and it knows it."

"Oh, Mother!"

"Any parent would do the same. You will, when you are one."

They made it across. Luna shook her head. "You've had to save us each time, Grandma. We'd never have made it alone."

"It's a cooperative effort. But I think you'll have to win your instruments for yourselves."

They walked to the next chapter. There were two cabinets. In one was a paintbrush with a silver handle; in the other was a miniature golden harp.

"This is it," Niobe said. "There are your instruments."

"But—" Luna said. "How do we—?"

Niobe looked around. She saw no instruction plaque. "I think you have to figure that out for yourselves."

Luna shrugged. She stepped up, opened the cabinet doors, and took the brush. She made a pass in the air—and the brush left a smear of yellow hanging there, unsupported.

Surprised, she moved the brush again, marking an X across the smear. Black appeared, a big X in air.

"It makes color from thought!" Luna exclaimed, pleased.

She went to work seriously, erasing the smear and X with deft strokes, then painting a picture of Niobe. Luna, young as she was, was good; it was a remarkably accurate rendition. Niobe had never seen the girl paint so fast and well before. Of course, she wasn't totally thrilled to have herself painted nude at the physical age of thirty-six; she had put on some weight and was no longer the most beautiful woman extant. The stretch marks from birthing Orb didn't help. But she wasn't in a position to protest; she wanted Luna to paint well enough to win the brush. The instrument was obviously ideal.

Then Luna added a gauzy halo of almost colorless paint. "What are you doing?" Niobe asked.

"Painting your aura," Luna replied.

"My—?"

"I can see it, so I'm painting it."

Niobe was silent. If what the girl said was true, she had more talent than anyone had judged.

Luna paused and stepped back. "There," she said. She had painted a huge seashell partly enclosing the figure. "Nude Grandmother on the half-shell."

"For pity's sake!" Niobe exclaimed with mock annoyance, and Orb giggled.

Then the picture moved in the air. It tilted, developed a frame, and moved into the cabinet. The glass doors closed.

"I think your picture has been accepted," Niobe said. "You have earned the brush."

"Oh, goody!" Luna exclaimed. "Thank you, Mountain King! I'll use it always! It's the best brush I ever dreamed of!"

Now it was Orb's turn. She opened the cabinet and lifted out the golden harp. It was small, but exquisitely crafted, surely the finest instrument of its kind. She seated herself cross-legged on the floor, set the base of the harp within the circle of her legs so she could hold it steady, and touched the strings with her fingers. A fine chord sounded. "Ooo, it's truly magic!" she exclaimed. "I can really play this!"

Orb paused a moment, mentally selecting a song. Then she began singing, accompanying herself on the harp.

"I want to waltz in the wetlands . . . "

Niobe was astonished. She hadn't known that Orb knew that song; she must have learned it at school. She was doing it very well, and the magic harp amplified both the sound and the natural magic she had, so that the background orchestra sounded loud and clear and stereophonic.

Twelve years old! How well would Orb sing and play and project when she achieved her full proficiency? Probably well enough to turn professional, if she chose.

"Yes I—will cry—I'll cry when the wetlands are dry," Orb finished and bowed her head. There were tears on her cheeks, and on Luna's and Niobe's too; it had been truly beautiful.

Then the song sounded again—but Orb wasn't singing or playing. The cabinet was doing it. The song had been recorded, magic orchestra and all!

The replay ended, and the cabinet doors closed. This, too, had been accepted. Orb had won her harp.

"It's done," Niobe said, relieved. "Now we can go home."

They started back. The bat cave had been turned off, and was now apparent as a concavely curving floor eighteen inches below the swinging bridge; the bat was a transparent light projection. The wand Luna had dropped lay on the stone; its long fall had been illusion. There had, indeed, been no danger.

"To think I crawled on hands and knees!" Luna said ruefully.

"As a challenge, it was valid," Niobe said, picking up the wand to replace it in the wand-holder. "Even illusions can hurt, as when we were blinded. Life is like that too; the unreal can be as important as the real, and sometimes it becomes real." She was consciously lecturing the girls, knowing that all too soon they would enter the arena of social and sexual awareness, where the pitfalls were indeed of perception.

They crossed, not bothering to use the bridge, and took the tunnel to the next chamber. This was unchanged; there really was a river and a barrier.

"That's a relief," Luna said. "I'd hate to think I went naked to swim through water that didn't exist!"

"But now it's just water," Orb said, scooping up a handful and sipping it. "And no blubber monster."

They waded in, the girls holding their instruments clear of the water as long as they could. There was a momentary flicker of light. Then Orb dived under the barrier and came up on the other side. She took a breath as she broke the surface—and screamed.

Niobe halted at the barrier. "What is it, dear?" she called, alarmed.

"I can't see!" Orb cried. "I'm blind! I'm blind!" She flailed about, dropping the harp, which sank to the bottom.

"Wait, dear!" Niobe cried. "Relax! It can't be—"

"Where am I?" Orb cried, still flailing. "How did I get here? Why can't I see?"

Niobe exchanged glances with Luna, whose mouth opened in an appalled O. "The Lethe!" the girl whispered. "It's on again!"

"And this time it's real!" Niobe exclaimed. "Something's wrong!"

The lethal monster appeared, moving slowly toward Orb.

"Get back out of the water!" Niobe cried to Luna. "I'll rescue her!" She took a breath, closed her eyes, and dived under the barrier. She was able to spot Orb by the noise of her splashing. She took hold of the girl and used the life-saving technique to haul her along. Niobe had to trust that her sense of direction was true and that she was swimming for the opposite bank. She did not dare open her eyes, or try to speak to her daughter; some water would be sure to splash in. She had no notion how close the monster was; she just had to keep them moving.

She made it. She found the bank and hauled Orb out. She cleared her eyes, then shook the girl by the shoulders to get her attention. "Be still, Orb! You've been dosed with the water of Lethe, so you can't see or remember, but the effect is temporary. Soon you will see and remember. Just relax. Relax!"

Slowly the girl calmed. "Oh, Mother," she cried, and hugged Niobe. "I'm so scared!"

So she remembered the basic relationship. Probably it was only the most recent events that were gone. "It will pass," Niobe reassured her. "You're not hurt, just inconvenienced for a few minutes. Just sit here and don't move." Then she looked across the river. Luna was standing on the far side. "Are you all right, Luna?"

"I'm all right," the girl called. "Should I cross?"

Niobe considered momentarily. "No. Go to the other cave and see whether it too has been reactivated. Don't try to cross it, though!"

"I wouldn't dare!" Luna said seriously. She disappeared into the tunnel.

Orb's tears seemed to help clear the spell from her eyes. "Mother! I can see a little!"

"Yes, of course, dear," Niobe said, expressing more confidence than she had felt. "Just have patience, and you will soon be back to normal."

After a while that seemed longer than it was, Luna returned. "It's back," she reported. "I knelt at the edge and reached down, and I couldn't feel the floor at all. Then the bat came, and I ran."

How did the illusion of a chasm become real, Niobe wondered. An eighteen-inch fall could not duplicate the effect of a hundred-foot fall. But she was sure that chasm was now there. The Mountain King's magic was no illusion!

"You'd better come across, then," Niobe decided. "It's easier for you than it would be for Orb, and I think we can handle the mine-chamber better."

"What happened?" Orb asked as Luna crossed. Evidently her memory had not caught up to the last few minutes.

"We were crossing the river—and the magic came on," Niobe said. "I don't know why. It's as if we were suddenly considered thieves instead of worthy winners."

"But we're *not* thieves!" Orb protested.

"Of course we're not!" Then something occurred to her. "But maybe there *is* a thief, somewhere in here, and he activated the magic—and we got caught."

"But we saw no one else!"

"True." Niobe sighed; it had been such a good explanation. Then she thought of an answer. "One could have tried the first challenge, and set off more than one mine, and not retreated. That might account for it."

Luna emerged from the water. "I got it!" she exclaimed, brandishing the harp. "I felt for it on the bottom, and there it was!"

"Oh, thank you, Moth!" Orb exclaimed.

"That's okay, Eyeball," Luna replied, smiling as she handed it to her.

Niobe was startled in a minor way; she had not heard these particular nicknames before. She wondered how much of children's activities inattentive adults missed.

They dressed and proceeded cautiously to the mine-cave, half expecting to encounter the thief, but there was none. The cave was empty. They tested it by tossing a stone into the center and hiding their eyes.

The explosion was horrendous. It shook the whole cave, and several more rocks dropped from the ceiling. The hazard was certainly back—and now the mines were truly destructive.

Niobe looked at the one motorcycle on this side, the one they had ridden across on. Her mouth went dry. She had crossed this cave three times, once while blind—but she was supremely reluctant to do so again. This time the hazard was real. She and the girls could be blown up! The very knowledge of that could cause her to waver on the cycle and go astray. Already her hands were shaking.

"Where's the thief?" Luna asked.

Where, indeed! If the thief had done this by pushing on regardless, he should be here—either alive or dead. The motorcycle he had used should be visible, either whole or wrecked. But there was none—and all the other cycles were still parked in their places. There seemed to be no thief.

Well, maybe the Mountain King was cheating. He might have had no intention of giving away his precious magical instruments, so he arranged to balk the girls' escape as if by accident.

That angered Niobe. "Two can play at that!" she muttered. She picked up another fallen rock. "Watch yourselves!" she warned, and heaved it.

There was another detonation. Again the cave shook, and more rocks dropped. As soon as the cave was quiet, Niobe picked up another rock and heaved it.

"What are you doing, Mother?" Orb asked after the third explosion.

"I am clearing a path through this trap!" Niobe said grimly. "A mine can't explode when it has already been exploded." She heaved again.

"Oh!" Orb exclaimed, smiling. "How smart of you, Mother! Can I do it too?"

Why not? "Yes you may—but shield your eyes."

The girl picked up a rock and heaved, then turned away. She clapped her hands with delight as the mine went off. Children of either sex seemed to have a certain muted passion for violence, Niobe reflected.

Before long they had cleared a broad channel across the cave. They tossed in a few more rocks, just to be sure there were no live mines left. Then Niobe ferried them across as before. She wasn't sure what would happen if they simply walked across and didn't trust it; the motorcycle was easy enough to use, now. Safely across, she parked it, and the three of them turned to the entrance/exit passage.

But as they approached, a man came through it from the other direction. He was huge and hairy and ferocious, he carried a giant sledgehammer, and his eyes fairly sparked so that they threatened to set fire to his beard. "Thieves!" he roared. "You would rob the museum of the Vanir? I will destroy you!" He lifted the sledgehammer.

"The Mountain King!" Luna squeaked, falling back.

Something akin to a berserker rage flooded through Niobe. She stepped forward, sidestepped the swinging sledge, and slapped the man resoundingly on his hairy cheek. "Leave that girl alone!" she snapped. "She's no thief! *You* are!"

The man could hardly have been hurt by the slap, but he paused, astonished, as he stared at her. "Clotho!"

"Not anymore!" Niobe said curtly. Then she, too, paused. "How did you know me?"

He set his sledgehammer down and leaned on the handle. "How could any man forget the face of the loveliest creature to grace the pagan realm? What do ye here, O divine one?"

Niobe stifled a flush of pleasure. "Um, how long have you been asleep this time?"

The Mountain King ticked off numbers on his fingers. "Twenty-five years or so. Why?"

That explained it. He had been asleep all the time she had been mortal. "I returned to ordinary life thirteen years ago," Niobe said. "I'm here with my daughter and granddaughter. We did not come here to steal from you."

The man glanced at the instruments the girls held. "If you speak for these, Clotho, I'll not challenge them. Indeed, methought in my dream I heard the music of my harp, played in a manner it was crafted to be." Then he did a double take. "A granddaughter—in thirteen years? Your body would madden any man's mind, but—"

"By my prior mortality," Niobe said quickly. She gestured to Luna. "Your cabinet accepted the picture she painted, so—"

"True. Then why the alarm?"

"That's what I want to know! We were halfway out when—"

"'Tis not of my doing," the giant said. "I will have the truth of this. Follow me, Clotho." He strode into the cave, and his footprints glowed in his wake. He was angry.

They followed, not bothering with the motorcycle this time; the glowing prints were their guarantee of safety.

When the Mountain King came to the middle cave, he stepped into the water—and it evaporated instantly, leaving the floor dry. When he reached the barrier, a gate in it swung open to let him pass without pause. There was no doubt he was the master of this place. They continued to follow, awed.

The chasm was there in the third cave, and the vampire bat alert. The King strode into it, and the illusion or reality vanished, leaving the cave empty. The tremulous light-pattern that was all that remained of the vampire bat fled.

They came into the display room. There was a demon with its finger in the harp-cabinet. Evidently that evil influence was what was triggering the thief-alarm; as long as that demon remained, no one could pass.

"Ho! Loki's work!" the Mountain King exclaimed, and hurled his massive sledge as if it were a toy.

The hammer struck the demon. The creature puffed into smoke. The cabinet exploded.

The Mountain King retrieved his sledgehammer. The far-flung fragments of the cabinet imploded, re-forming their original shape, with a hint of the music Orb had made.

"Go in peace, Clotho," the giant rumbled. "You and yours. My apology for this nuisance."

"Quite all right, sir," Niobe said, somewhat taken aback. She hustled the girls out again. This time there was no problem in any of the caves.

The instruments were wonderful, and both girls continued to prosper in their talents. By the time they completed school, each was as skilled as any Niobe knew. She was sure both would prosper in life, if Fate permitted. But there was the matter of the tangled skein that had not yet materialized.

After Blenda died, the Magician Kaftan moved to America with Luna, apparently unable to face the old country in her absence. Niobe was saddened more by Luna's departure than by her son's, for she had actually been closer to her granddaughter. But she could not protest. Luna was a fine, levelheaded young woman, and she would take good care of her father.

Then, after twenty-two years of their marriage, Pacian died. He was seventy-four, by no means young, but it came as a shock; somehow she had always thought of him as eleven years younger than herself, and she was only forty-six, physically. She had lived twenty-three years in her first mortality, and the same number in her second. It was as if she had finally completed the term set for her original love of Cedric. She still loved Pacian, but the intensity of it had eased over the years. Now she had raised her family, and was satisfied to meet the necessary severance of threads. She had seen Pace ailing, and had done what she could for him, never thinking he could actually die. Satan seemed to have no hand in this; the cause had been natural.

After the funeral, she tended to retreat from participation in worldly matters. Orb went away on tour as a singer; indeed, she had been traveling about the world from the time she turned eighteen. There just wasn't much left for Niobe in the mortal realm.

Then she received news that her son, the Magician, had also died. This was entirely unexpected; he was only sixty-three. Luna wrote to report that she now lived alone in the Magician's house, carrying on his business, and that she was dating the new Thanatos, exactly as the prophecy had foretold. Niobe had no stomach for that business. She kept her letters polite and left the girl alone. What, after all, had she expected of mortality—perpetual youth, bliss, and innocence? She was in as good a position as any woman to know better.

She was chronologically eighty-six years old; she had outlived her time. Her comfortable, placid world had been replaced by the modern high-tech, high-magic world. She was prepared to depart it with a minimum of fuss.

But the following year, things changed.

– 10 –

LACHESIS

The spider descended before her on a thread of silk, then transformed into a comely young woman with hair so light it was almost white. "We must talk with you," the woman said. "Do not utter the name of him who must not know." She had an accent, but was intelligible.

"Clotho!" Niobe said, suddenly remembering that moment a quarter-century before when she had drawn a refugee girl from a line in Budapest. "Lisa!"

The woman smiled. "You have changed; I have not." Then she patted her hair. "Except cosmetically. I am eternally grateful for what you did, rescuing me from that city. It gave me a new existence, and I was able to help my troubled friends. They never knew I had—changed."

"I understand," Niobe said. "It is nice of you to let me know."

"But this is not a social call," Lisa said quickly. "We—have something very important to ask of you."

Niobe smiled. Privately she was dismayed by the contrast between them. When she had selected Lisa to be her replacement, Niobe herself had been a slender beauty, while Lisa had been attractive but less stunning. Now, a quarter-century later, Niobe knew herself to be lined and dumpy; she hadn't seen any reason to maintain herself, the last two years especially. Lisa had remained exactly as she had been. What a terrible scourge mortal aging was!

"If your question is whether the—unnamed one—has been interfering in my life since I turned mortal, I'm not sure. I can think of only one instance, when I took my girls to—"

"No, no," Lisa said quickly. "Not a question. I—I have been selected to ask you this, because I am the only one of us who has met you. Lachesis and Atropos have changed—"

"Terms are getting shorter these days!" Niobe remarked. "I was an Aspect for thirty-eight years!"

"Yes, you were one of the great ones, and you dealt well with— the anonymous. I—we—had a difficult time. He twisted the threads without license, he confused us—"

"He does that," Niobe agreed. "If I was proof against him later, it was because I had some hard lessons early! I'm sure I was no better than—"

"Yes, you have had much experience. More than any other mortal. That is why we must ask this thing of you."

This sounded serious! "Exactly what is this thing?"

"You must come back."

"What?"

"To be an Aspect of Fate. We need you again."

Niobe was so surprised she stuttered. "To—to be—I, I— Lisa, I'm forty-eight years old, in mortal terms! Only a young woman can—"

Lisa shook her head. "Not to be Clotho. To be Lachesis. That is the key Aspect—the one who governs the Tapestry."

Lachesis—of course. Niobe was now middle-aged in body, and looked it. Lachesis was the middle-aged Aspect. Yet—

"Lisa, I never dreamed—it's never been done before! Once an Aspect returns to mortality—once *any* Incarnation leaves the of- fice—"

"True. That is one reason we believe it must be done this time. The unnamed will never suspect."

To fool Satan. That was one way to do it, certainly! "Lisa, I'm flattered that you should think of me for this! But I've had my turn at immortality, and don't really deserve—"

"It is much to ask of you, we know," Lisa said hurriedly. "But you are the only one who can do it. Otherwise—"

"Now wait, Lisa! New women come into the office all the time! Everyone learns on the job, and Fate is more fortunate than the other Incarnations, because there are always two experienced Aspects to guide the new one. So you certainly don't have to—"

"Please," the woman said. "Perhaps I do not make myself clear. I could speak better in my native tongue—"

"You are speaking perfectly! I'm just trying to say—"

"Please, I must explain. We—we must depart our Aspects—all together."

"All at once? That's impossible! There would be no—"

With a Tangled Skein

"Yes, we think the unnamed has arranged it. There has been much trouble, and your son's child Luna is central. All of us have had to help intervene to save her. He tried to make her die, but Thanatos would not permit it—"

Something clicked in Niobe's mind. "That period last year, when people mysteriously stopped dying—?"

"Yes. Thanatos stopped taking souls so he would not have to take hers, because he loves her. Finally he faced the unnamed down. Luna was spared, and Thanatos went back to work. We—Lachesis arranged to select him for the office, so that would happen."

"You interfered in the selection of another Incarnation?" Niobe asked, horrified.

"We—it was necessary. This is—we think it is the major battle of the war. I do not like war." Lisa paused, and Niobe knew she was remembering Budapest. "But when the tyranny of Evil advances, it must be fought by whatever means. The battles are terrible, but . . ."

Now Niobe saw the tangle of the skein. Her granddaughter was indeed standing athwart it—and the reason for her astonishing association with Thanatos was apparent. Only Thanatos could stop a person from dying, once that thread had been cut. Still—!

"How did you know about the plot against Luna?"

"The Magician, her father, he knew. He studied magic all his life and knew of a prophecy that the unnamed intended to void. The Magician planned everything and gave up his life to introduce Luna to Thanatos in a manner that would deceive the—"

"So that's why he died young! They never told me!"

"They could not, lady. No one could know until it was done. The Magician knew he had to protect his daughter beyond his own time, for the fate of mankind depends on her."

"So little I knew!" Niobe lamented. "I thought he was burying himself in magic just for—for a hobby. Or business. But he must have understood the prophecy far better than—"

"Yes. Then there was something strange. We think Chronos was involved, and that he stopped the unnamed from doing something else, but he won't say. He knows the future, but if he said, it would change, so—"

"So the Incarnations are all involved in—in a major engagement," Niobe concluded.

"A twenty-year engagement," Lisa agreed. "The unnamed means to take political power on Earth. His agents are at work in every nation, but America is difficult because its politics are so chaotic anyway. If he prevails there, the rest will fall in line, he believes, because of the economic leverage. So he must be stopped there, and Luna will cast the key vote against him—if she survives."

—150—

Piers Anthony

"And she wanted to be an artist!" Niobe exclaimed.

"Now we believe that we, the three Aspects of Fate, are at the center," Lisa continued. "The unnamed means to be rid of Luna, and we know that—"

"That I would give my life, happiness, and honor to protect her!" Niobe finished. "Of course I will do it—will become the Aspect of Lachesis—if that's what it takes! But I never performed in that Aspect before, and—what's this business about all three of you changing together? If the unnamed is pressing you as you suggest, that would be absolute folly! Three novices together—"

"Yes. Folly. That is why we come to you. *You* have experience—"

"That part I see! But you other two would have to remain, at least for a year or two—"

"We cannot," Lisa said. "We must change now—this week."

"That's preposterous, girl! You *know* what's at stake!"

"We know. But we have opportunities that come only once in a lifetime, if ever. We cannot turn those down, any more than you could have turned down your second love. The chance to have your daughter—"

Niobe held up her hand. "You make your point. We are all frail human creatures! Yet if you know, or suspect, that these opportunities have been arranged by—"

"He has, as you say, sweetened the pot to the point where we cannot desist. But it is more than that. You see, we do not know what he plans—and if we retain our Aspects, he will know we cannot be fooled, and he will do something else. Something we perhaps cannot prevent. So this trap of his—we decided it was better to fall into it—"

"With one experienced Aspect he doesn't know about!" Niobe concluded. "To spring his trap—and destroy it!"

Lisa smiled. "I knew you would understand."

Niobe mulled it over. She had sworn to have her reckoning with Satan for Cedric's death, but somehow she had never had a satisfying denouement. She had told herself that just doing her job, as an Aspect of Fate, had been sufficient, and seeing to the upbringing of Luna and Orb was sufficient, since they were integral to the foiling of the Prince of Evil. But how much better it would be to foil Satan directly, personally!

Her mortal life was over anyway. She had nothing left to live for. It was really no contest. "I'll do it."

Lisa smiled. "We're so pleased. We know you will do what has to be done. We know that our mortal situations will be protected from evil, with you in charge." She extended her hand.

—151—

Niobe was taken aback. "Wait! I didn't mean right this instant! I have to put my mortal affairs in order—"

"Lachesis will do that for you," Lisa assured her. "Before she moves on to her own situation."

Surely she could trust an Aspect of Fate to know the importance of the proper disposition of Earthly affairs! Especially when it was vital that Satan not know of the change.

Niobe took Lisa's hand. There was the odd jolt she had experienced twice before.

Then she was inside Lisa, looking out out through her eyes. A nondescript middle-aged woman stood before her: the old Lachesis.

Good-bye, mortal situation! Niobe thought with abrupt nostalgia. No life was easy to leave, even a completed one.

"Take the body," Lisa said, and turned it over to her.

Niobe stood again in her own form, in different flesh. Her original flesh had been lost when she had become Clotho, so long ago, and when she had returned to mortality she had taken Lisa's flesh. Her pattern, even to the genes of reproduction, had carried across. Now that flesh was subject to the will and image of the prior Lachesis. Surely Lisa, too, felt nostalgia, knowing that the flesh that had been hers had just passed to a third identity. It was a familiar yet strange business.

Niobe shook hands with the woman who had been Lachesis. "I think you already know anything I would say. Go to your situation and be happy."

"I can never thank you enough—Lachesis," the woman said. "Do you know what mortality offers for me now?"

"It's really not my business—"

"A title," the woman exclaimed. "I am in a position to inherit a title and a grand estate in Europe, and be a lady of quality with servants and functions and responsibilities. I always longed for this and feared it could never come about. As Lachesis I indulged my propensity for managing things—"

"That's a quality of those suitable for that Aspect," Niobe agreed.

"But now it can be real. I mean, mortal. And the estate needs me; without a person of the blood, it will fall prey to greedy distant claimants and taxes—it would be destroyed. But now it has come to me, if I claim it in time, and I know so well how to manage it! If I die of some disfiguring disease within twenty years, still I shall be well satisfied!"

Obviously so. Different folk had different dreams, and the right dream was worth one's life. "Bless you, and prosper," Niobe told her warmly.

"Bless *you*, wonderful woman!" the other responded.

Piers Anthony

Niobe returned the body to Lisa so that she and Atropos could bid farewell to their companion. It was strange, sharing Fate with the woman who had succeeded her as Clotho, but evidently she had chosen correctly, on that day a quarter-century ago. Lisa had done the job.

When the other two were done, they changed to spider form and slid up the web to Purgatory. How quickly it all came back! Niobe did not for a moment regret her second tenure as a mortal, and she felt a lingering pang for that suddenly lost life—but she also felt an abiding joy for her return as an Incarnation. To be an Immortal—there was no mortal experience to match it!

The Abode was unchanged: a cocoon, a house made of silk, the most comfortable retreat for the spinner and handler of threads. Still there was no staff, for the three women of Fate remained too independent to be waited on. There was a reasonable supply of Void-substance for Clotho. Everything was in order.

"Now it is my turn," Lisa said, and started out again.

"Already?" Niobe asked. "But we just got here!"

"Yes—to be sure you had your bearings. As you can see, I have arranged things for my replacement; it will be a fortnight before she has to visit the Void." She paused. "What an experience, that first time!"

Niobe shrugged, mentally. It was essentially the business of each Aspect to choose her successor, and the time of her own return to mortality. Niobe had become Clotho, in large part, because the prior Clotho had liked her, and now was Lachesis because the three Aspects had agreed she was needed. She would go along with what had been decided.

Clotho descended a thread toward the western coast of America. "To what situation are you going?" Niobe asked.

"True love," Lisa answered raptly. "One day last month I was hiking in the mountains when a young man floated down on a flying carpet to ask directions. He had an accent I recognized. 'You're from Hungary!' I cried. He was taken aback. 'My parents were,' he said. 'My mother was carrying me when they fled during the—' and he shrugged, for in America few understand how it was in Budapest. 'I'm from there too,' I told him, and I spoke to him in our language. 'Wait!' he cried. 'I am not good at it! All my life has been here.' But he understood enough. Now he wants to marry me. He understands about how I am, almost twice his age. We did not tell his mother about that—she would not understand—so I told her my own mother had told me how it was with her when she fled, and then I told her in our tongue my own experience as if it were my mother's—and I think it could have been my mother's, if she hadn't died in the in-

−153−

vasion of our homeland—and his mother cried with the memories, and she reminded me so much of mine, I cried too! I think she wants me to marry her son twice as much as he does! I will move in with them, and I know I will never have trouble with my in-laws!''

Niobe hated to raise the question, but felt she had to. "Yet you believe this is the work of—of the anonymous one—to get you out of the way?"

"Yes. Lachesis—the one before you—verified how that one had nudged that thread to place him flying where I was hiking, so we would meet. So little a thing—but though there was manipulation, the *person* is genuine. There is no great evil in him. The unnamed knows I would not take an evil man. An Aspect of Fate cannot be deceived by fool's gold! So the intent may be evil, but the offering is good. It is not for *me* the evil is intended, but for you."

Yes, surely so. The ways of Satan were devious but effective. But maybe this time the Father of Lies would find himself outmaneuvered, for the Incarnation of Fate was no innocent mortal to be fooled by manipulations of chance. Especially not with a former Aspect returning, with her firsthand knowledge of Satan's ways. *You have a surprise coming, O Evil One!* she thought.

They came to ground in an unsettled area. A young woman was walking at dusk toward the high cliff that descended to the crashing sea. She was Oriental and quite pretty.

Lisa intercepted her. "Where do you go, solitary maiden?"

"What does it matter? My life is over."

"But you are young and pretty and intelligent," Lisa protested. "You have much to live for!" Obviously Fate had researched this woman's thread.

"No, I have nothing to live for," the girl demurred. "My family has cast me out for not following the old ways, for being too willful and violent, and now I have no family."

Niobe knew that the Oriental cultures could be very strict about their traditions, and that there were sometimes conflicts with the ways of the Occidental world. The girl had probably refused to marry the man the family had chosen for her. Niobe could understand, even though her own arranged marriage had been a good one. She disliked admitting it, but parental judgment did seem to be as good as that of the participants. But America touted itself as the land of the free, and it had become unacceptable for girls to heed the judgment of their elders. There was more to tragedy than lost romance.

Amen! Atropos agreed.

"And now you are ready to depart this world?" Lisa asked.

The girl glanced at the cliff. A gust of sea breeze ruffled her black hair. "If I have the courage."

Piers Anthony

"I have an alternative." And Lisa explained about Fate and the role of Clotho.

It took the young woman a while to grasp it, understandably, but when she peered over the dark and savage ocean, she decided that this was a better alternative. Atropos took over the body, extended her hand, and it was done. Clotho had changed.

Lisa now stood in her physical form, just like herself; all traces of Oriental heritage had vanished. Niobe had never quite understood the magic that did this, but of course that wasn't necessary. *Welcome, Clotho,* she thought, and the process of education began.

They returned to the Abode and relaxed for a few hours. Niobe, as Lachesis, took over the body and contemplated the Tapestry, while Atropos continued to explain things internally to Clotho. The prior Lachesis had left the Tapestry in good order, considering the troubled times, so there was nothing urgent to do at the moment. Niobe had seen the job performed during her prior tenure as an Aspect, but now the responsibility was hers, and that was different. She hoped Satan would leave them alone for a few weeks while she got into it—and knew he wouldn't.

Next day it was Atropos' turn. There had been an accident, and her mortal great-grandchildren had become orphans. They would become wards of the state and be assigned to separate foster homes unless she, their only remaining blood relative, assumed control. They were eleven and nine years old; Atropos believed she had enough mortal years left in her to get the older one to the age of discretion before she died. She had to do it; they were her blood kin. Satan did not seem to have arranged this; rather, he had foreseen the opportunity and arranged for the other two Aspects to leave at the same time Atropos did. If Lachesis had not caught the hint in the Tapestry, Satan's ploy would have been effective. As it was, no easy time was coming, Niobe was sure, but at least they had a chance to win.

Atropos slid down a thread to the one she had selected. This brought her to a slum area where an old black woman sat in her rocking chair on a rickety porch, watching children play handball in the street. She looked up as Atropos appeared before her. "'Bout time you got here," she remarked.

Even Atropos was taken aback by this. "You know me?"

"I know you. I was expecting Death, though, not Fate."

"I have come to ask you to take my place. If you do, you will meet Death only as a business associate."

"I thought he already was. I've buried more kin than I can count on my hands." She held up her gnarled spread fingers.

"If you take this office, you will cut the threads on the lives of a million times that number."

—155—

"Somebody's got to do it."

Atropos turned the body over to Niobe. "Then take my hand," Niobe said. "But do not think the job is always easy."

The old woman hardly blinked. "No job worth doing is." She took the hand.

Then the old Atropos was sitting in the rocker, and the new one was with Fate.

At that point a child dashed up. "Grandma! I made a score!" Then, seeing a stranger in the chair, he skidded to a halt.

Niobe gave the body to the new Atropos. "It's okay, Jimmy," she said. "She's just visiting."

"Oh." Suddenly shy, the boy backed away.

"Jimmy, it's time for me to go away," the new Atropos said. "You do me a big favor, now, and show this lady to the bus stop. Tell the folks I'm gone."

"Gone where?"

"Just gone, Jimmy. They'll understand."

"Okay." The boy, given an important job to do, led the old Atropos away down the street.

Niobe took over the body again, changed to spider form, and mounted a thread. *Now that's some trick!* the new Atropos thought. *I always squish bugs.*

"Not anymore," Niobe said in her spider's voice. "You will master this trick too."

She brought them to the Abode and resumed her human form. "In fact, we had better practice the basic motions right now," she said. "Because things may get hectic soon."

Hectic? both others inquired.

Quickly Niobe explained how Satan had conspired to get three new Aspects of Fate together. "Now I am a retread," she concluded. "I had several decades experience as Clotho, ending twenty-five years ago. We hope Satan doesn't know that." She felt free to name the Prince of Evil, here in the Abode, because it was secure from uninvited intrusion. Each Incarnation was supreme within his or her home. "So we can afford to fumble about at first; that will reassure him, and he may be careless. But we have to take care that we don't do too much damage. These are human lives we are manipulating, remember."

They practiced using the mouth to speak, assuming the spider form, climbing the web, and using the travel-threads to move about rapidly, so that any of the three could get about well enough. Then Niobe explained the three jobs: how Clotho spun the threads of life, Lachesis measured them, and Atropos cut them to their lengths. "I hardly know my own job," she confessed. "So I really am learning too. I'm

—156—

likely to mismeasure the lengths I need for particular parts of the Tapestry, which will result in some of what the mortals take to be odd coincidences. We won't have to pretend, to make thinks look awkward.''

"But we could use a real bad blunder to start off," Atropos concluded. She seemed to have a ready grasp of the essentials; the prior Atropos had chosen well.

Clotho tried some spinning. She had no mortal experience at this, so was clumsy. She had been selected as much for availability and militant spirit as for dexterity, for the notice had been short. Niobe had to guide her carefully, and even so, the thread was somewhat loose and irregular. But she could do it, however slowly.

Now it was Atropos' turn to try some cutting. Niobe measured a thread, then turned the body over to the old woman. Atropos took the little scissors and snipped one end, then the other. "Oops," she said. "I cut it too long!" She cut a small bit off the end. "There—that's about right, now."

They prepared about twenty threads, snipping freely to trim them down to size. "When we get more experienced," Niobe said as she took them to the Tapestry for placement, "we'll do them wholesale. There are far too many lives on Earth for us to handle individually." She set the threads in—and they fell out.

That was funny. "They always seemed to grow right in place for the Lachesis I knew in the old days." She recovered a thread and set it in place again—and it fell out again. "I don't remember her having to tie them in."

"Maybe I spun them wrong," Clotho said nervously.

"I don't think so. But we can try some new ones."

Clotho spun some more, and Niobe measured, and Atropos snipped, still having trouble getting the lengths exactly right; more snippets fell to the floor. But the new threads also refused to stay in place.

They couldn't figure out what was wrong. The floor of the Abode was littered with snippets, but no threads had been successfully emplaced in the Tapestry.

There was a peremptory knock on the door. Niobe took the body and went to answer it.

Thanatos stood there, more forbidding in his hooded cloak and skull than she recalled him. The off-white bones of his fingers clenched spasmodically. Truly, he was Death Incarnate. "What are you up to?" he demanded.

Niobe was taken aback. "I'm just trying to do my job," she said.

Thanatos' square and bony eye-sockets stared darkly at her. "You have changed."

"We have all changed," Niobe said, and had Clotho and Atropos show their forms briefly. "But we're having some trouble—"

"Trouble!" Thanatos exclaimed, striding into the Abode. Beyond him, outside, Niobe saw his fine pale horse, the one she had ridden on, back at the outset. "Twenty-six babies needlessly dead!"

"Babies—dead?" Niobe asked. "I haven't emplaced any threads, let alone cut them short!"

"No? What do you think these are?" Thanatos demanded, stooping to pick up a handful of snippets. He was angry, and he frightened her even though she knew he was no threat to her.

"Just the trimmings—"

"Trimmings!" Thanatos roared. "*You don't trim lives from the front ends!*"

Niobe fell back against the silken wall, stunned. "The—the front ends?"

Thanatos held up one of the full-length threads. "Here is a Thread of Life," he said scathingly. "Here is the front, here the rear. When you cut off a segment from the rear—" he made a snipping motion with two bone-fingers—"you shorten that life by that amount. When you cut it off at the front, you shorten that life by *this* amount." And he dropped the whole thread to the floor. "Leaving only this." He held up two fingers, almost touching each other.

"Oh, no!" Niobe exclaimed with horror. "We cut them off after days—or hours!"

"And twenty-six babies died, poisoned in the hospital," Thanatos continued grimly. "Because a dietician got the wrong container and put salt in their formulas instead of sugar! The mortals think that's a tragic accident, but I knew it was your handiwork. *I had to take those babies!*" His fury fairly shook the Abode.

Niobe burst into tears. She was middle-aged, but it made no difference. She was too appalled to react any other way.

It was Atropos who took over the body and the situation. "Don't chew her out, Death," she snapped. "*I* did it, and I'm mortified. I didn't know—and I sure as hell won't do it again!"

Thanatos looked at her, their situation registering. "All three— new?" he asked. "No experience?"

"Not exactly," Atropos began.

Don't tell him! Niobe urged. *If he knows, Satan will know!*

"But all three of us have changed in the last few days," Atropos said. "And as you can plainly see, not one of us is experienced in her role."

"How could all three of you change at once?" Thanatos asked. "You lose your continuity!"

"*Now* he tells us," Atropos said. "This morning I was sitting in my rocker, waiting for you to come haul my soul away. Now I'm apologizing to you for messing up."

Thanatos relaxed. "I was new, too, last year, and your forerunners helped me greatly. I know how it is; I made mistakes too. I'm sorry I ranted at you. Let's see if we can work this out." He sat on the silk couch and drew back his hood. The face of a rather ordinary young man emerged.

Atropos did a double take. "You're a living man!"

Thanatos smiled. "They didn't tell you? I suppose they didn't think of it, with all of you changing so rapidly. Yes, all the Incarnations are living people, frozen at the ages when they assumed their offices. We are the temporary Immortals."

"You mean I won't grow older?"

"Not until you return to mortality—which you will do only by your own choice, unlike me."

"You're different?" There was a lot Niobe had not yet told the other two, owing to the press of time. She kept quiet; this was actually convenient, as she did not have to finesse any questions about herself.

"I continue until my successor kills me. Then he will assume my office."

"But then you're not immortal!"

"Oh, I am immortal—until I grow careless. No person or creature can harm me, not even Satan himself, as long as I am careful. The only one who can kill me is my successor—and even he will fail unless I let him. My cloak is invulnerable to natural attack, and my person to supernatural menace. But I cannot step down alive, unlike you."

"That must be a horror!" Atropos exclaimed.

"No, it's all right. Much better than the suicide I contemplated as a mortal." At this Clotho perked up, mentally; she knew about that sort of thing.

"But isn't your life sterile?" Atropos asked. "No hell-raising, no gambling, no women?"

He laughed. "You don't think much of young men, do you!"

"I think a lot of them! I've known a few myself, when I was young and sexy. But I know their nature. A man without a woman is hell-bent for trouble."

Thanatos smiled. "Well, I have a woman. She's mortal, but she knows my nature. Her name is Luna Kaftan. I love her and I guarantee she will not die before her time. I can't marry her, because I have no legal mortal identity; I'm listed as deceased. But I'll always be with her."

Niobe was glad she didn't have the body now; she would have given herself away. She had forgotten, in these last few hours, that

—159—

Luna had taken up with Thanatos! As a mortal, she had disapproved; now, suddenly, she approved. This seemed to be a fine young man, committed to his role. He could indeed protect Luna from death itself. That portion of the prophecy had turned out to be much more positive than anticipated.

But Atropos was learning rapidly. "Suppose I—I never would, mind you—suppose I cut your girl friend's thread short?"

Thanatos' hood was away from his head, but a shadow of the skull seemed to pass across his features, and his skin took on the hue of bone. He was, indeed, Death. "You did that once before—your prior person did. Satan had forced it. I refused to take her. You do not end the lives, you merely schedule them. Only when I take their souls do they actually die. As I took the souls of those twenty-six babies. I had to do it; their bodies were ravaged and they would have suffered had they lived, so I stood aside and let them drift to Heaven. But I *am* the one in charge of that, and by my decree a dying person can live indefinitely, regardless of his suffering. We Incarnations have to cooperate, or it becomes untenable."

Atropos nodded. "I thought it was something like that. We won't kill any more babies, that's for sure! Let's run through it now and make sure we've got it right."

Clotho took the body and spun more thread. Then Niobe measured it, and Atropos cut it carefully, only once at each end. Then Niobe took it to the Tapestry and laid it in place where she knew it belonged.

This time it took. The thread anchored, and extended into the fuzzy future portion of the Tapestry.

"That's the way," Thanatos agreed. He drew his hood back into place. "I must go; I have business elsewhere. If you have doubts about anything, check with me or another Incarnation, and we'll try to help. Chronos, especially, must work with you closely; he lives backward, so he knows the future, not the past."

Thanatos departed, riding into the sky on his pale horse. The three Aspects of Fate collapsed onto the couch. That had been some session!

But Clotho had a question: if Chronos knew the future, wouldn't he know about Niobe's prior experience in office?

"Not if we don't tell him—some time in the future," Niobe said. "I think we had better just forget about my past and carry on in the present. But about Chronos—there may be something else you should know, Clotho."

"What's that?"

"He—in the past—he has been very close to us. Especially to Clotho."

"Friendship is good, isn't it?" the girl asked, perplexed.

"Lovers."

Clotho was silent. Niobe was not sure what was going through her mind, for the three did not share their thoughts when they chose not to.

"The way I see it," Atropos said, "this isn't our mortal body anymore. This body must have been through a lot we don't know about."

"Yes," Niobe agreed.

"So maybe it doesn't matter too much what we do with it, as long as we do our jobs right."

Still Clotho didn't comment. Niobe remembered how difficult this particular aspect of being an Aspect had been for her, at first. Well, an accommodation would be achieved, in time. Time? Chronos!

They fixed themselves a meal from the available supplies and lay down for a rest. Then they worked out a regular schedule of operations—which Aspect would take what shift, which would be backup, and which would sleep. The body itself was indefatigable; it needed neither rest nor sleep, but the minds within it did.

Fate, however tenuously, was back in business.

– 11 –

TANGLE

But next day the axe, figuratively, fell. Niobe was paying a call on Chronos, because she needed his advice and assistance on the placement of specific threads. The Tapestry tended to follow its natural pattern, but left entirely alone it would soon develop rents and tangles as threads got crossed. She had to set the threads properly, and timing as well as placement was essential. For example, when a marriage occurred, the threads of the man and woman intersected—but if the intersection occurred before the mundane ceremony, a new thread could be started before the term of marriage, which could be awkward. Chronos could check such things directly; indeed, he knew the timing of every significant human interaction, though most of the routine was left to his staff. Fate, too, had a staff for the routine, but she could not afford to leave the important matters to underlings.

But first came the introductions. "I realize that you have known us for some time," Niobe said. "But from our viewpoint, this is our first encounter. We are all new in our Aspects, in the past few days, and all inexperienced in our duties. So allow us to present ourselves, and for you this will be our parting. I'm sure you will find our precedessors competent."

"Ah, is it that time already?" Chronos asked. "I have seen two of you change—"

"Please, we prefer not to know," Niobe said quickly.

"Of course. Let me only say that all three of you have been kind to me in my past, and I have a deep respect for you and shall be sorry to see you go. I hope I get along as well with your replacements."

Piers Anthony

"I'm sure you will," Niobe said, and flashed through the Clotho and Atropos Aspects for him before returning to Lachesis. "But since none of us go back to that time as Aspects, we have no firsthand information. We're all new, and we are making embarrassing mistakes."

"Yes, I know," Chronos said sympathetically.

"Those snippets of threads—twenty-six babies needlessly dead—Thanatos was in a fury!" Niobe said.

"Oh, pardon. I thought you were referring to the UN incident."

"The UN incident?" Niobe asked blankly.

"But of course that hasn't happened yet, for you, just as the dead babies haven't for me. Sorry I mentioned it."

If we're about to blunder again . . . Atropos thought.

Ask him about it, Clotho concluded. They had not yet gotten their shifts down pat, so all three were awake for this interview. They were three quite different individuals, but the disaster of the babies had unified them in their horror.

"Please don't apologize," Niobe said. "We are eager to avoid future blunders. If it is not a violation of your ethics, we would like to know more about it."

Chronos smiled. "Incarnations don't have ethics in that sense; all of us do what we have to do, or we leave our offices. We assist each other whenever asked. After all, as I believe you explained to me, Lachesis, when I first assumed my office twenty years hence, it is our common purpose to balk the machinations of Satan and promote those of God. The UN incident was very simple, but it had phenomenal consequences. It seems that someone sneaked a psychic stink bomb into the United Nations complex in New York. When it detonated, the—"

"*Psychic* stink bomb?" Niobe asked. She remembered the time Luna and Orb, as children, had obtained a physical stink bomb, one of the type called "little stinkers," and set it off in her kitchen. The stench had taken days to clear. Girls would be girls, she knew, but she had made them scrub floor, ceiling, and walls anyway. They had been less mischievous thereafter—but their reputations in school had escalated dramatically for a while.

"It generated an emotional atmosphere that no one could tolerate," Chronos said, suppressing an illicit smile. "No laughing matter, of course. The United States was expelled from the UN and the headquarters was moved to Moscow—"

"Moved to Moscow!" Niobe exclaimed indignantly.

"Well, you see, the international diplomats had some difficulty appreciating the humor of the situation," Chronos said. "Though I understand that both the Soviet leaders and the American conser-

—163—

vatives suffered some private belly laughs. It was of course impossible to conduct normal business—''

"Satan's work!" Niobe cried with dismay. But both Atropos and Clotho were stifling their own amusement.

"Naturally," Chronos agreed. "It was amazing how much profit Satan reaped from that simple incident. There was a steady attrition in world harmony and a resurgence of evil. Mars was kept quite busy managing the wars that later developed—''

"We've got to stop it!" Niobe said firmly. Atropos and Clotho settled down enough to agree; this was evidently a major ploy by Satan to generate disharmony.

"I'm sure the beginnings of the tangle are in your Tapestry," Chronos said.

"Let's take a look." Niobe had learned how to generate the image of the Tapestry, so that she could place the threads properly. She caused it to manifest now. The pattern seemed to be in order.

"If you will permit me," Chronos said. He lifted his Hourglass; the sand changed color, and the Tapestry abruptly slid forward. Niobe kept her face straight despite the amazement of the other two Aspects; she knew that Chronos had the power to affect an image she had generated. The Hourglass was truly the most marvelous of instruments. "Five days hence, your time," he explained.

Niobe looked. There was a monstrous tangle that resulted in a distortion of the entire Tapestry. Atropos and Clotho were as appalled as she was; they would never get that back in proper order once it occurred!

"We've got to stop it!" Niobe repeated. "Once it happens, it's too late; we have to see that it never happens!" Then she glanced at Chronos. "But if we prevent it, and you've already seen it happen—''

"Don't be concerned. I am immune from paradox. I change events all the time, literally, to put right what goes wrong. I had quite a campaign with Satan, let me assure you, back when I started! I had to traverse eternity itself to get my bearings back. If you change it, you change it, that's all; I will remember it merely as one of the alternate timelines."

"Then we shall," Niobe said, relieved. "If that bomb goes off in five days, it means we have four days to track down who is to do it, and cut his thread out of the Tapestry before he does, or reroute it. Then the notorious 'UN incident' will never happen!"

"It will never happen," Chronos agreed.

"And we will be spared the embarrassment of a major tangle," Niobe finished. "Obviously this is what Satan set up for us novices to struggle with. Experienced Aspects could handle it, but he doesn't think we can."

"A fair assessment," Chronos agreed. "Satan is devious in the extreme; one must always be alert for his finesses."

"We'll go home and see what we can do."

"Remember," Chronos said. "If you need the assistance of other Incarnations, simply ask. Any of us will be glad to do what we can, especially knowing that you are presently inexperienced."

"We shall," she agreed and rode her thread away.

At the Abode they held a council of war. "That tangle is impenetrable," Niobe said. "A veritable Gordian Knot. But we know that the cause is simple: someone has to plant that bomb and get away so as not to be contaminated when it goes off. The thread of life of that mortal has to be in our Tapestry, here; all we have to do is locate it and remove it."

The others gazed at the Tapestry through her eyes. "There are so many threads, so intricately meshed!" Clotho said. "We could search for months and never find the right one!"

"Needle in a haystack," Atropos agreed. "Woman, you poked me into a bigger picklement than I knew when you signed me up for Fate! I love it!"

"Too bad we don't have a computer," Clotho said.

"There's the Purgatory Computer," Niobe said. "It should store everything."

"Well, get moving, gal!" Atropos said. "I hope you know how to work it, because I sure don't!"

Niobe got moving. She entered the Purgatory front office and asked for time with the Computer. Computers had not been widely used during her term as Clotho, but Purgatory was evidently keeping up with the times. She had not had a lot of experience, but understood the general principle.

Fortunately, this one was user-friendly. GREETINGS, FATE, its screen flashed when she turned it on. HOW MAY I INFORM YOU?

She started to punch the keys, awkwardly. SIMPLY SPEAK TO ME, the screen advised.

Oh. "I need to figure out a tangle," Niobe said. "I'm new at this, and—"

IS THERE A KEY THREAD?

"Yes. But I need to locate it—and there are millions to choose from."

CONDUCT A GLOBAL SEARCH. WHAT ARE YOUR DEFINING CRITERIA?

"Well, it's some person who will visit the United Nations complex in New York, on or before a particular date."

PROVIDE THE DATE.

Niobe provided it.

The screen became a blur of lines, then cleared. THREE THOUSAND, TWO HUNDRED, FIFTY-SIX THREADS REMAIN.

Well, that was progress. "Can we get it down to a smaller number—such as half a dozen?"

PROVIDE FURTHER DEFINITION.

Niobe pondered. The other Aspects helped. *Just how big is that contraption—a psychic stink bomb?* Atropos thought.

"The person will have to carry in a psychic stink bomb potent enough to foul the entire complex," Niobe said. "If you happen to know how big such a package would be—"

The screen flickered. If Niobe hadn't known better, she would have suspected that the machine was laughing. A PSYCHIC STINK BOMB? The flickering became more pronounced.

"Yes. Someone is going to leave it to detonate in the UN complex, and America will be expelled from the UN and the headquarters will move to Moscow."

TO MOSCOW? Now jags of yellow showed at the edges of the screen, and wiggly music sounded in the background.

"Now don't shake off your stand," Niobe cautioned it, annoyed. "All I need to know is—"

With a seeming effort, the computer got itself under control. ONE THOUSAND, EIGHT HUNDRED, FOURTEEN THREADS REMAIN.

Still too many. *Maybe motive,* Clotho suggested. *Does it know who might want to humiliate the UN?*

"Can you eliminate the threads of those who might have no reason to dislike the UN?"

The screen flickered again, and the words STINK BOMB showed fleetingly, as if an illicit thought were passing through the machine's random access memory. Then it settled down again. SEVEN HUNDRED, EIGHTY-THREE THREADS REMAIN.

Still way too high! *Get practical, woman,* Atropos thought. *Ask how many have access to such a bomb. They can't be a dime a dozen.*

"Eliminate those who have no reasonable access to such a bomb," Niobe said.

FOUR THREADS REMAIN.

Jackpot! Atropos thought. *One day to a thread! Never thought all my time running down vandals would pay off like this!*

Evidently grandmothers did learn useful skills in the ghetto! Atropos had been the one to recognize opportunity as a defining characteristic.

"Please identify those four threads," Niobe said, relieved.

Four names appeared on the screen. Niobe made a note of them. "Thank you, Computer," she said.

YOU ARE WELCOME, FATE, the screen said. Then, just before it switched off, the words STINK BOMB flickered once more. The machine seemed unable to clear that concept from its banks. The devices of

Purgatory seemed to have more personality than those of the mortal realm.

You've got to admit that ol' Satan has a certain sense of humor, Atropos thought.

"Yes, I'm sure he's laughing as he humiliates us," Niobe agreed shortly. Mirth was indeed a characteristic of the Father of Lies.

Back at the Abode, they reviewed the four threads. "We may do better if we approach our own kind," Clotho suggested. "To ascertain whether they are guilty or innocent."

"We don't want to snip any innocent threads," Atropos agreed.

Niobe sighed. "True. We don't want to make a mistake. Very well, I will verify one of the white ones today." She looked at the two white threads. One was for an old man, the other for a middle-aged woman who—

"Great balls of fire!" Atropos exclaimed. "She's a Satanist!"

There was a prime suspect, certainly. "I don't want to go charging into a Satanist shrine!" Niobe said.

"Let's leave that one till last," Clotho suggested.

Niobe was glad to agree. She knew of the Satanists by reputation, but even as an immortal she did not want to get involved with them.

The other white thread was ordinary. The old man was a retired carpet salesman named Henry Clogg. That was about as much as she could get in detail. Otherwise she could have solved the riddle of the stink bomber without leaving the Abode. That, of course, was what Satan was counting on: Fate's present inability to read the threads aptly. This much of Satan's strategy was working.

She rode a thread down to the old man's home. It was midmorning here, and he was out working on his little garden.

Niobe approached. "Hello, I'm looking for Mr. Clogg."

"You got him, cutie," the man replied cheerfully.

Niobe found herself blushing. It had been years since anyone had called her that. She wished she hadn't let herself run down so much in the last few years; she was a good thirty pounds overweight and sagged in places that hadn't existed in her youth. Now, as an Incarnation, she was fixed in this form; dieting would not improve her figure. Of course she could change her appearance by means of magic or physics, as Lisa had done, but she preferred to live with herself with neither spell nor girdle. However she might conceal it, the flab was still there. Clotho had an easier time of it; all she needed was minimal magic to shift hair color and length, skin shade, and slant of eyes; she would be an attractive young woman regardless.

She focused on her mission: to discover whether this man was likely to be the bomber. "Mr. Clogg, I—"

"Call me Henry, cutie. Just plain old Henry. I'm not anyone special, you know."

Little did he know! She realized that he must call every woman cutie; it had no significance. It embarrassed her almost as much to blush for nothing as to blush for cause. "Um, Henry, I—I understand you are planning to visit the United Nations complex soon."

He plunged his trowel into the earth so that the handle was left pointing up so that it wouldn't get lost, and climbed to his feet, brushing himself off. "Oh, you heard about that! Yeah, my son's treating me to a two-day tour, and I guess that's on the list. Me, I don't know much about it, and don't much care. But he figures the old man's got to do some things before he kicks off, so that's it. Don't want no ignorant louts in Hell, I guess."

"Oh, you're not going to die soon, Henry!"

The man grinned. "*I* know that and *you* know that, but my son don't know that. I wish he'd save his money; going to need it soon enough when I get surgery."

"Surgery?"

"Got this here tumor on my butt," he confided. Like some old people, he was not at all reticent to discuss intimate details of physiology with strangers. He seemed not to question her presence at all. "It's a nuisance, but it's benign. Just a pain in the rump." He laughed. "All those years I talked about that sort of thing, and now I've really got it! Good, deep cushion takes care of it, but my son, he worries, says I got to have it out, and that means surgery and the lab and all, which is a *real* pain in the assets, just to prove what I already know. My son needs that money for his family; I don't want him throwing it away to doctors for what I don't need anyway." He squinted at her. "Do I know you?"

"No," Niobe said. "I—"

"Got an accent, don't you! You're Irish! You ever been by to kiss the Blarney Stone? Have a seat; you don't have any boil on *your* bottom, do you?"

"Uh, no," Niobe said, taking the deck chair he offered. Henry, true to his word, had a chair with a fluffy cushion on it. He eased himself onto it, wincing. Evidently the tumor was more painful than he cared to admit.

"Well, what can I do for you, cutie?" he asked.

"It's about the United Nations," she said cautiously. "There's a rumor that there's going to be trouble, and—"

"I told you, I don't care about the UN. Just a bunch of lefties soaking up our tax dollars, if you ask me. We'd be better off out of it, and tell them to get off our land and go to Russia or somewhere."

He's a candidate, all right! Atropos thought.

"But the United Nations is perhaps the major force for peace in the world," Niobe protested. "It represents a forum for dialogue between most of the nations, so that they can talk problems out instead of going to war. It would be disaster if that forum were eliminated.

Henry shrugged. "As far as I can see, they mostly talk about how terrible America is. While they take our money."

He's got a point, Atropos thought.

"That's a necessary freedom of speech," Niobe said. "Words will not hurt this country, but bombs will. It is far better to—"

He nodded. "That's right, isn't it! You know about bombs, over there! I can tell you, I wouldn't live in Ireland today if you paid me to!"

"Well, it's really not like that," Niobe said defensively. "We don't see the violence, we only read about it in the newspapers. The same as you read about crime in the big cities. The countryside is as peaceful and pretty as any in the world."

He nodded again. "You care about your land. I like that. But you know, if they have bombs going off over there, how come they aren't talking in the UN? I mean the IRS and—"

"The IRA," Niobe said.

"What's the difference? Over here they call it the IRS, and it does to your wallet what those bombers over there do to your buildings. I wish they'd all get lost!"

She saw her opportunity. "You don't like bombers?"

"I don't like bombers," he agreed emphatically. "Except for maybe the UN building. Maybe *that* could use a bomb!"

Aha! Atropos thought.

"You can't mean that, Henry!" Niobe protested. "If the UN were bombed, it could trigger another world war!"

Henry considered. "Could be. And we can't afford another war, that's for sure. Couldn't afford the last one, when it comes to that. You know why inflation's so bad? Because we're still trying to pay off the last war! But still, it's tempting. If we could have maybe a false alarm, just to make the UN move out—"

"Like a stink bomb?" Niobe asked.

He laughed so hard he winced from the motion of his posterior. "Sure! That'd be great! Make that bad smell literal!"

Niobe experienced mixed emotions. On the one hand she was relieved to have confirmation of his guilt, for it solved her problem of research. On the other, she hated to do what she knew she would have to do: have Atropos cut his thread short. Now that she had talked with Henry Clogg, she liked him; he was at least an honest man. It would be a shame to terminate his life so abruptly.

It is not certain, Clotho warned. *Many people will not do what they say.*

Niobe grasped at that straw. "Henry, if someone were to come and give you a stink bomb that you could sneak into the UN complex when you go there, so that after you leave it would mess up everything and get the United States of America expelled from—"

"Hey, wait a minute!" he said. "Why would anyone do that? A bomb that strong would cost a lot of money!"

"Yes. But let's say Satan hoped to promote discord in the world, so he brought you a—"

Henry scowled. "Satan? Listen, cutie, I'm a God-fearing man, no matter what I say about going to Hell! I wouldn't touch the Devil with a ten-foot spell!"

"Well, he wouldn't give you his identity, of course. He might come in the form of a businessman, offering to pay you enough money to cover your surgery and not be a burden to your son, if you will just take a package to the UN complex, hide it from the guards, and leave it there where it won't be noticed, in a closet or somewhere."

He stared ahead, pondering. "Satan, eh? If *he* wants to be rid of the UN, I'm not sure *I* do!"

"Well, as I said, he wouldn't *say* he was—"

"What do I want, taking money from strangers?" he demanded righteously. "Lug a big suitcase around on the tour? I don't need any part of that!"

"You mean you *wouldn't* stink-bomb the UN if you had the chance?"

"Not now that I've thought about it! When you really get down to it, stink bombs are kid stuff, not that funny. And I sure wouldn't do it for tainted money! If the Devil wants it done, let him get someone else to do his dirty work! Me, I want to go to Heaven when I kick off, even if I won't find most of my friends there."

Niobe felt mixed relief and regret again, this time reversed. Henry Clogg was not the one after all, and she was glad she had not decided to cut the thread of an innocent man. But it meant they would have to interview the others, and that the job had not yet been done.

"Say—you want some sherry?" Henry asked.

"Well, no, I—"

"I don't get much company these days," he said. "It'll be good to share it. My wife, bless her soul, she liked it. It's been three years now—" His face turned sad.

"I'll have some sherry," Niobe agreed.

He eased himself to his feet and went indoors to fetch the bottle and glasses. *He's a good ol' geezer,* Atropos thought approvingly. *Reminds me some of my old man, before he died, except mine liked moonshine.*

"I normally don't drink—" Niobe murmured.

Sherry isn't drinking, woman! Atropos thought firmly. *It's socializing.*

I don't think the other interviews will be this easy, Clotho thought. Niobe just nodded.

Henry returned with the sherry. Niobe sipped the golden wine, satisfied for the moment to relax. It *was* nice being company, however extemporaneously. This was the way she should have been with Cedric, instead of drinking too much. Alcohol was an evil only when abused—as with so many pleasures.

"My son's already bought me a ticket for the carpet to New York," Henry remarked. "That gripes me some. See, I was a carpet salesman, when I worked. We had some pretty fancy models, too. You know how those automobile companies always say a carpet's no good in the rain? Don't you believe it! We have models with canopies; no way you'd get wet on one of those. Could even close it in tight and pressurize the cabin for high flying. And magic doesn't pollute the air the way gasoline does."

She listened, and nodded agreement. She was sorry when the sherry was finished, and she had to go.

"Come again sometime!" Henry told her cheerfully.

"I will," she promised. She intended to do that, when she had time free.

They returned to the Abode and considered. "One down, three to go," Atropos said. "Who do we tackle next?"

"Well, we have a young black woman, an Oriental martial artist, and the Satanist."

"Let's take care of the easy one first," Atropos said. "That's mine—the black girl."

"But let's rest first," Clotho said. "We want to be fresh so we don't make mistakes."

The others agreed. Also, there were some routine threads to spin, place, and cut; there was no point in letting the job get behind.

They worked on the threads; then all three slept.

Next morning, New York area time, Atropos assumed the body and made her first solo trip along the thread down to the realm of the mortals. The girl was at home, flirting with two boys. She was about fifteen, the boys older.

Atropos burst in upon them like a scourge from Purgatory. "What's these boys doing here, girl?" she demanded, glaring about. The girl looked stricken, and the boys abashed. "You're not 'sposed to have company at home alone, you know that! If your grandmaw knew—"

"Grandma's dead," the girl said defensively.

"She'd roll over twice in her grave!" Atropos continued without pause. "And if your maw knew—"

The girl gave a little squeal of terror.

"She'd have your li'l black hide hung out on the line to cool!" Atropos said, fixing her with a deadly stare. "Ain't that right, girl!"

The girl nodded, unwillingly. Atropos whirled on the boys. "Now scat!" She took a menacing step toward them. The two banged into each other in their haste to exit. "And if I see you two out here again, I'll take the cane to you myself!" she called after their fleeing forms.

How did you know they weren't supposed to be here? Niobe thought. *We didn't read that in the thread!*

"I know boys," Atropos muttered. "And I know girls. Moment I saw their faces, I knew what they were up to." She smiled privately. "Same thing *I* was up to, at that age. Made me a grandma sooner than I needed."

She turned back to the girl, who was trying to recover her poise. "Who are you?" the girl demanded. "You ain't my ma! You can't tell me what to do!"

"I'm a friend of your grandmaw, girl," Atropos said. "She can't rest easy till she knows you're going straight, so I'm checking you now. I can tell you, I don't much like what I'm seeing! You going hog-wild here—why aren't you in school?"

"I'm in second shift!" the girl protested. "It don't start for two hours."

Atropos rolled her eyes skyward. "Lord, I don't know if I can do the job in two hours." Then she fixed on the girl again. "You're in big trouble, child!"

"Listen, old woman, you got no business coming in here like you owned the place! I can do anything I want. Leave me alone!"

Atropos sighed. "I see we're going to have to do it the hard way. I'm going to have to enchant you."

"You don't have no magic!" the girl said. "You can't—"

Atropos caught her by the arm and flung a thread upward with her free hand. She was getting the hang of thread manipulation very quickly. "I don't like backtalk, girl!" She slid up the thread, carrying the girl with her.

The girl screamed as they passed through the wall and sailed into the sky. "Let me go! Let me go!"

Atropos glanced down. The rooftops were already receding below. "You sure, girl? If I let you go now, you'll drop like a stone."

The girl considered that and was quiet. Atropos slid on up to the cloudbank that defined Purgatory, then paused. "Now I want you to come clean with me, girl. If you lie to me, I'll drop you right out of this cloud!"

The girl was daunted. "What are you?" she demanded.

"Just someone interested in what's right. Now talk, or I'll turn into a big spider and eat you."

Still the girl resisted. "You can't!"

Atropos assumed the arachnid form, man-sized.

The girl screamed and tried to scramble through the cloud substance. Atropos changed back, "Change your mind, girl?"

"I din't mean nothing wrong!" the girl babbled. "I din't even know what it was! This guy tells me here, just sniff this, it'll make you feel good, so I sniffed it, and in a little bit I felt like I was floating right off the floor!" She looked down nervously. "Only not like this!"

"Don't sniff anything like that again!" Atropos told her sternly. "That stuff'll be the death of you!"

"I won't!" the girl promised. The vision of the huge spider had finally convinced her that Atropos meant business.

"How are you doing in school?"

"Well, you know how it is—"

"Sure I know, girl! You've got better things to do than study, right? Figure you'll just slide through, then make it in the big world on sex appeal? Girl, you'll lock yourself in the ghetto all your life, same as your maw, same as your grandmaw! Same as me! You want to be dependent on a man for everything you need? It'll cost you, girl! A man always takes his payment in kind. You want to make it on your own, then you can look about and see what you want from a man. Then you can put your own price on it, and that's not money. What're you doing in school?"

"Not enough," the girl admitted.

"They take you on any field trips?"

The girl brightened. "Sure—there's this New York trip coming up. We're going there in a bus, see the sights—"

"Something I've got to tell you about that, girl. This man may come, maybe offer you money or something to sniff, just to take something to the UN building. Know what you tell him?"

Wordlessly, the girl shook her head.

"You tell him to go to Hell!" Atropos cried. "You don't take a thing to New York! You just go and learn all you can, so you can write up a good paper on it when you get home."

"That's all? Just tell him—?"

"That's all. That, and do your homework. You haven't—?"

"Not yet," the girl agreed faintly.

"Well, we've still got an hour. I'll help you this time, but after this you do it on your own, get your grades up, you hear? No more lip to your teachers! So your grandmaw won't roll over."

Again the girl shook her head, offering no resistance.

Atropos took her back down the thread and into the house. They got out the homework and discussed it. Atropos was not conversant with the technical material, but Niobe and Clotho thought the answers at her, so she could tutor the girl competently. It was a fine collaborative effort. By the time the girl left for school, they were satisfied that not only had they eliminated her as a potential carrier for the stink bomb, they had set her on a much better course of life than she would have followed otherwise. "The world needs more aggressive grandmothers," Atropos remarked as they returned to the Abode. The other two could only agree.

– 12 –

BLOOD

As they considered the next case, they had misgivings. The thread of the Oriental man showed him to be age thirty, and a significant force within his culture. They could not simply cut his thread; that would lead to serious complications in the Tapestry, not as bad as those stemming from the stink bomb, but still well worth avoiding. They would have to talk him out of it—and Niobe was learning to read the threads well enough, now, to know that this would not be easy.

For one thing, there was a kink in the thread that indicated something of extreme significance had touched it. That was surely Satan, making his offer. If the man had accepted, how could they stop him without cutting his thread?

Clotho assumed the body. "I will try," she said simply.

She pointed the distaff, extended the thread, and slid down it to the man's location. Again, it was morning, in the state of New Jersey, and he was at his place of business. This was a *dojo*, or martial arts establishment.

We should have guessed, Niobe thought. *His name is Samurai.*

"Which means Warrior," Clotho murmured. "A pretentious title!"

She opened the door and entered. There was a desk inside with a girl in a *gi*, or martial arts uniform. "You wish to join for the course?" she inquired politely.

"No," Clotho said. "I wish to speak to Samurai."

The girl smiled. "The Master does not sign up students. But in class he will give you the same attention he does all students, and if

With a Tangled Skein

you have talent you may be able to enroll in an advanced class and receive special instruction." She eyed Clotho appraisingly. "Of course that is more expensive and requires special dedication."

"I don't wish to be a student," Clotho insisted. "I have more personal business with the man."

The girl studied her again. Suddenly Niobe was aware of the appearance of their youngest Aspect. She was well dressed—clothing in the Abode was of the highest quality, fashioned of genuine silk, and fitted with magical perfection—and was an extremely well-formed woman to begin with. She was a person to be noticed more than passingly. "I will inquire," the girl said and touched a button.

In a moment she received an answer. She glanced up. "Take the hall to the left, through the curtain. Oh—and remove your shoes before you enter the office. He's very fussy about that."

"Thank you." Clotho walked down the hall, then paused to remove her dainty shoes before pushing through the curtain of thin bamboo.

The office was like a Japanese garden, with decorative plants and Oriental statuary all around, and a broad mat covering the floor. At the far side, seated on a slightly elevated dais, was a handsome man in a resplendent *gi*, almost a robe.

Clotho stood bemused at the entrance. "Oh, it's beautiful!" she breathed. "I have never been to Japan, but—"

"Come forward," the man said. "Do not be afraid of the *tatami*."

She stepped with her stocking feet onto the mat, which was soft but firm. "Samurai, I want to talk to you about—"

"Wait," he said peremptorily, and she paused in place. "Turn about, woman."

Clotho hesitated, then turned around.

The man got up, seeming to flow effortlessly to his feet. He strode to a curtained closet in one wall, moving like a lithe panther. He brought out a folded kimono. "Don this."

"What?"

"I want you properly garbed," he said. "Go to the changing chamber there." He gestured at a door. "Put this on. Then we shall talk."

"Samurai, I don't know what you think I'm here for—"

"Not for classes," he said. "Not for business. So you mean to be a *geisha*."

"A *geisha*!" she exclaimed indignantly.

What's a geisha? Atropos asked.

A Japanese entertainment-girl, high-class, Niobe replied.

Oh, so that's what they call them, over there! We call them whores.

It's not the same—Niobe started, but then external events interrupted them.

"You had another intention?" Samurai was saying.

—176—

Clotho switched to Japanese, spewing out a minor torrent of words. Neither Niobe nor Atropos understood that language, but they got the gist from her mind; she was calling him, in eloquent idiom, a male sexist pig.

Oopsy! Niobe thought.

That girl's got a temper! Atropos thought, half admiringly.

Samurai's face turned grim. He took a step toward Clotho. She spun about and ran for the curtained door. She plunged through, paused to pick up her shoes, and froze. A man was charging down the hall toward her.

She turned again and plunged back through the curtain. Samurai was there. She flung her shoes at him. He caught one and dodged the other; he had marvelous reflexes. She dodged to the side and ran across the room.

Samurai followed. Clotho reached out, grabbed a potted cactus, whirled, and hurled it at his head. This time she scored. The clay pot shattered between his eyes, the dirt spreading across his face.

I wish she hadn't done that! Niobe thought.

She's one hair-trigger gal! Atropos responded. *Maybe we'd better just thread on out of here.*

We can't; she's got the body.

You mean we can't take over if we need to?

Not until she lets us—and she's not paying attention to us at the moment.

Atropos mentally shook her head. *Been forty years since the last time I got raped. Going to be about forty seconds till the next time!*

A mortal can't rape an Incarnation! Niobe protested.

You sure about that?

Niobe considered. *No. I know no mortal can hurt us, but I'm not sure if rape counts as hurting. It may be just—just an interaction, no blood shed.*

No blood for me, no blood for you—but what about her?

Again Niobe considered. *She's as innocent as I was when I married, the first time. Still—*

Well, if it happens, let's see if we can change to me in the middle. That'll sober him.

Niobe thought of that, and of the likely reaction of the man. She started to laugh, though she didn't want to; it really wasn't at all funny.

Clotho, meanwhile, was running down another passage. She plunged through the bamboo curtain at the far end and burst into the main work chamber. About twenty students in white *gi*'s and white belts and yellow belts were practicing throws, supervised by a man in a brown belt. They paused at the sight of her, for Clotho's summer dress was a complete contrast to their uniforms. She was in somewhat frilly blue, with a pink sash and a pink rose on the front, and her hair was bound in a western ponytail by a pink ribbon. She was the very picture of lovely young innocence.

Then Samurai burst out after her, the very picture of masculine outrage. Earth stained his pretty robe and smudged his face, and blood dripped from his nose. The students gave way as he strode forward and caught Clotho by the arm. "Woman, you have no—"

Clotho froze for an instant, then tried to tear herself away, but his grip was like iron. She spewed more Japanese at him.

Hoo! Atropos thought, mentally pursing her lips. *No girl that age should know concepts like that!*

Niobe had to agree. Liberated women evidently learned things younger than did the conventional woman of prior generations, whatever the language.

Samurai's rage turned to something like awe, then to disgust. He snapped something back in Japanese. It seemed to translate to something like Atropos' concept of the geisha girl.

Clotho swung her hand at his head. He caught it and drew her in to him. He kissed her. She struggled, but could not escape. Slowly she relaxed.

That man sure can kiss! Atropos thought.

The taming of the shrew, Niobe agreed.

Then Clotho remembered herself. She bit Samurai on the lip. Then, at last, she remembered her powers. She flung out a thread and slid along it.

The man's arms were abruptly empty, for Fate was insubstantial when sliding. Astonished, he looked about.

There was Clotho, ten feet away. Samurai started toward her—and she slid through him to the other side. The watching students gaped. When he turned and started for her again, she slid to him, ducked down, and materialized at his legs, causing him to stumble over her. Then she slid another foot, passed through him, materialized again, and kicked him in the rear.

Samurai took a forward rolling breakfall and came smoothly back to his feet. "Magic!" he cried. "My sword!"

The brown-belt hurried out, to return in a moment with a sheathed katana. Samurai took it and drew the gleaming blade. "I know how to deal with a witch!"

Get out of here, girl! Atropos thought at Clotho.

This time the girl heard. She sailed up a thread, out of the building.

Then, in air, she paused. "But this isn't accomplishing my mission!" she exclaimed.

"Welcome to reality, girl!" Atropos muttered, using the mouth now that they were alone. "If that man wasn't set to do Satan's business before, he sure is now!"

"But what can I do? I've cost him face!"

"What?"

"Face. I've embarrassed him in public, caused him to lose status."

"You mean he won't be reasonable now?" Atropos inquired dryly.

"He's not a bad man, just arrogant! I shouldn't have humiliated him!"

"Didn't he call you a whore?" Atropos asked, and Niobe realized that the wise old woman was leading the foolish young one to a reconsideration.

"He thought I was a geisha. That's—I'm sure he didn't intend it as an insult. It is an honored profession."

"Entertainer," Niobe put in. "Companion."

"Well, then, girl, go back and apologize!" Atropos snapped, sounding much the way she had when addressing the black teenager.

"It's not that simple," Clotho said, torn. "I'm a liberated woman. I don't hold with—with—"

"You'd rather tell him to go to Hell?" Atropos demanded.

"No! When it's a matter of face—I didn't mean to do that!"

"Didn't mean to jump to a conclusion and bawl him out in gutter-Japanese?" Atropos asked.

"I—the old ways—all my life I've opposed—"

"Girl, you think your new ways look any better?"

"No," Clotho whispered. "I—overreacted."

"Well, we'd better go back and try to explain," Niobe said, "or we'll have to cut his thread."

"No!" Clotho cried in anguish.

"She's not *that* liberated," Atropos said.

"Well, he *is* quite a man," Niobe said.

"Quite a man," Clotho echoed ruefully.

"Look, girl, you go on back there," Atropos directed Clotho. "But this time listen to us. We'll help you, same's you helped me with that homework. Ain't none of us knows it all, if you want it in *my* dialect. We'll get that man re-faced, somehow."

Clotho laughed, somewhat hysterically. "It won't work! It doesn't work that way!"

"Let's try it anyway," Atropos said. "He's a man, and you're one good-looking young woman. He'll listen. What've we got to lose?"

Clotho shrugged fatalistically, then slid back down the thread.

The class was already back in session, but the brown-belt cried out the moment Clotho materialized. She walked by him and into the hall to the office.

Samurai was there, sponging off his face. He froze as he saw Clotho in the mirror.

Apologize, Atropos ordered.

"I—I came to apologize," Clotho said.

Samurai turned. "Only blood will make this right," he said grimly.

"I—I can't give you that."

"Who are you?"

Clotho hesitated. *I don't think it would be smart to tell him our nature*, Niobe thought. *It would seem like a threat.*

"I—I am a supernatural creature," Clotho said. "That is why I could not—"

"A witch!" he exclaimed.

"No. A woman. But not—like others."

Almost, he smiled. "Not like others," he agreed.

"Samurai, how can I make it right?" Clotho asked. "I did not mean to—you made me angry—"

"Because I thought you a geisha?"

"This is America! Women are independent, not the playthings of men!"

He nodded. "I mistook you for Japanese."

That stung. "I *am* Japanese—but liberated. I—I left my family because I—would not follow the medieval ways."

"Those ways are good ways!" he said.

"Will you accept my apology?"

"No. Only blood will scour that humiliation clean."

She spread her hands pleadingly. "Samurai, I am immortal. I cannot give you blood. But if we cannot work this out, I will have to take yours."

He touched his nose. "You have already done that."

"*All* yours," she said.

"Then take it!" he exclaimed. "Bring your champion to meet my *katana*! Then will the debt be settled."

Accept! Niobe thought.

"But—"

"Today," he said. "Here in my *dojo*. Before my students, where the insult occurred."

Accept! Niobe repeatedly urgently.

"All right," Clotho said faintly. "This—this afternoon."

Samura seemed surprised. "You accept?"

Now tell him our business, Niobe thought.

"Yes. I will—bring my champion here. To meet you. Now may I tell you why I came here?"

Samurai inclined his head. "You do intrigue me, woman."

"Someone will come to offer you something, for a service—"

Piers Anthony

"He already has."
Clotho paused. *We're closer to the deadline,* Niobe thought.
"You must not do it!" Clotho said.
"Why not?"
"It is Satan making the offer. He means to bomb the United Nations—"
"What do I care about the United Nations?"
"This—if this happens, there will be discord among the nations, perhaps war—"
"What's wrong with war?"
Baffled, Clotho stared at him.
He's a martial artist, Niobe thought. *A warrior. He likes combat.*
Ask him if he wants his soul to go to Hell, Atropos suggested.
"If you do this, if you serve Satan, your soul will be his."
"How can you know this?" Samurai demanded.
"I—know."
"Why should I believe you?"
Better tell him, after all, Atropos thought, and Niobe agreed.
"Because I am Fate," Clotho said.
"Now you are insulting my intelligence!"
"What proof do you require?"
"No proof, woman! I will not be mocked!"
Ask him what Satan offered, Niobe thought.
"What did Satan offer you, to deliver that package?"
"You cannot imagine the value of—" He broke off. "It wasn't Satan."
"One of his agents. It doesn't matter who came to you; it is Satan's offer."
Samurai considered. "He offered the secret of the finger death."
"The what?"
"I have searched for it for years. A blow so light it may be struck with a single finger that causes death within the hour. It causes the autonomic system to malfunction progressively until the body cannot cope."
"You want to kill someone with one finger?"
"No. Merely to have the ability to do it."
"And for this you agreed to bomb the UN?"
"No. Just to carry a package there. And I haven't agreed; I will decide tomorrow."
"You must turn it down!"
"That is not for you to say. Who is your champion?"
Mars, Niobe thought. *He will help if we ask him.*
"Mars."
"Who?"

—181—

"The Incarnation of War."

"Still you mock me!" he exclaimed. "There are no such things as Incarnations of Fate and War! I will not tolerate mockery after injury!"

"But he will come here!" Clotho said.

"I will allow no stranger here today!"

We'll bring him anyway, Niobe thought. *Samurai thinks he is being mocked, but he will believe when he sees Mars!*

"We will be here," Clotho said. Then she extended a thread and slid away, barefooted.

Back in the Abode, they reviewed what had happened. They agreed that Samurai had not intended to insult Clotho by his reference to geisha; he had honestly mistaken her purpose in approaching him. Probably he encountered a number of young women who wished to have a personal or sexual relationship with a master martial artist. So Clotho's angry reaction had been unwarranted. They also agreed that Samurai was basically a decent man whose thread should not be prematurely cut, and that his loss of face had to be compensated for. But not by blood!

Clotho promised to consult with the other Aspects before she exploded like that again. She had been ready to commit suicide after being cast out of her family, and that militancy of reaction remained. She tended to go too far. "After all," she conceded, "some male sexist pigs may be decent sorts, when allowance is made."

And here was a delicate aspect. "If you could get Samurai to turn Satan down, by being what Samurai took you for," Niobe asked, "would you do it?"

Clotho suffered a siege of sheer rage. Then she calmed, realizing that she was about to react exactly as she had promised not to. "I don't know," she whispered.

As it had been with Chronos, Niobe thought. When she herself had been Clotho. The role of Fate required its sacrifices, not so much of conscience as of image. The current Clotho thought of herself as liberated, but she was bound.

"Now we must recruit Mars," Niobe said. "I know him of old; he will help. But I do not know this particular office-holder, and it is better that he not know my past; that is one secret we must keep from all until we deal with Satan. So Clotho should approach him her way, and put the matter into his hands."

Clotho sighed. "This office and Aspect have many burdens!"

Niobe laughed. "What else is new? Would you trade it?"

"No."

Atropos smiled. "I think we're getting it together."

Clotho rode the thread to Mars. He was near the Iran-Iraq border, supervising a locally savage skirmish. "These folk of Babylon and

Piers Anthony

Persia are really dedicated to my purpose,'' he remarked with satisfaction as Clotho approached. Then he took a second look at her. "Well, Clotho, you have changed! Did that sweet Hungarian girl get tired?"

"She fell in love," Clotho said, as if Lisa had died.

Mars laughed. "That's a liability of your type! You're all right until you get mushy about a man, then you sag into—"

Clotho's temper flared again. She spoke a few sharp words in Japanese.

Mars smiled. "And you are the mother of a sickly dog," he responded in the same language. Niobe and Atropos picked up the meaning from Clotho's mind.

Clotho was aghast. "You understood!"

"Sweet stuff, War knows every language of mankind! If you wish to quarrel, you have come to the right party."

Now she was embarrassed. "I came here to ask your help."

"And right prettily you asked for it, Flower of the Orient! What can I do for you?"

Clotho explained how all three Aspects were new in their roles, so were having trouble handling Satan's machinations. "Now I have insulted this martial artist called Samurai, and must give him satisfaction before I can persuade him to—"

"Samurai! I know of him! He's a fine warrior, though perhaps not the match of those whose reputation he borrows. A man of the old school, with that old-fashioned pride. So he took you for a geisha!"

"Yes," Clotho agreed, embarrassed.

"And you kicked him in the butt before his class."

"Yes," she agreed faintly.

"You will have to give him blood."

"No! No killing!"

Mars made a gesture with his sword, and the fighting in the region ceased. The guns fell silent, and even the moans of the wounded faded out. "Woman, you have cost him face. You know what that means?"

"Yes," she said grimly.

"He is inflexible on matters of honor. Few like him exist today; he is steel in an age of rust and plastic—a genuine man. I can satisfy him on the martial level, but only you can abate his inner pain, and until you do, he will not do as you request. Nor should he. Death before dishonor, according to the great tradition."

"But we're trying to avoid death, to prevent war—" She faltered, staring at him.

"And I am War," Mars finished. "Woman, your dainty foot has a predilection for your mouth. But I understand. I am an Incarnation,

—183—

and you are another. I will do what I can for you today, and some other time you will do what you can for me."

Clotho sighed. "So all males want only one thing!"

"You will adjust your threads to simplify my situation, when I get in a bind," Mars clarified. "This is the manner Incarnations cooperate."

"Oh." Clotho was flushing as well as she was able.

"The reason women suppose that men want only one thing," Mars continued blithely, "is that that is all women are capable of perceiving in men. Women do not properly comprehend matters like, for example, honor."

"That's not true!" Clotho exclaimed.

"Ah, so? Then let's discuss honor. You have impaired Samurai's honor; if you want to deal with him, you must yield him yours. You are of course a virgin—"

"How can you know that?" she demanded.

"It is one of the things we male sexists relate to," Mars said. "Now do you understand the blood you must offer to Samurai?"

Clotho hesitated, appalled.

He's right, Niobe thought.

It's the way men are, Atropos agreed.

"You like him, don't you?" Mars inquired cruelly.

Clotho launched herself at him, clawing at his face.

There goes that temper again, Niobe thought.

Girl's got spunk, Atropos agreed.

Mars caught her effortlessly. "I can see we're going to get along just fine," he said. "I love to have pretty girls leap into my arms. Well, I'll be there, and I'll set it up for you. But at the finish, it must be you and Samurai. You'll just have to decide how bad you want to square things. He's one fine man." He set her down and turned away, and the battle resumed.

Clotho stood, angry tears on her face, unable to counter Mars' insolence.

Let's get out of here, girl, Atropos thought.

Numbly, Clotho extended a thread and slid back up toward Purgatory. Niobe sympathized with her. The girl had fought all her life for independence and equality, and now she was being thrust into the old sexist role. She was not the same person Niobe had been in her youth, yet she was close enough so that Niobe knew better than to interfere.

They had lunch and adjusted a few threads, preoccupied. Then Clotho donned slacks, low-heeled shoes, and a businesslike shirt, and rode a thread back down to the *dojo.*

Mars appeared as she landed before it. He was garbed in a white *gi.* Niobe had never been certain how Mars traveled, but it seemed to be related to his sword. Each Incarnation had a symbol of office that was imbued with much of the magic, and the red sword was obviously Mars' symbol.

"Follow me," Mars said, handing her his sword.

Clotho looked at it. The thing was unsheathed—a massive instrument, with a handle almost too big for her small hand to hold, and a gleaming double-edged blade that glowed red from some deep layer. The whole thing had a magical aura of menace; it made her nervous. She held it awkwardly by two hands, the blade pointing straight down.

Even Niobe was astonished. *What's he up to? He never sets aside his red sword!*

We'll find out soon enough, Atropos thought.

The girl at the desk recognized Clotho. "Please leave," she said. "You are not welcome here."

Mars leaned over the desk. "I am her champion. Signal your hirelings."

Two men appeared at the inner doorway. Both were in *gi*'s and wore black belts. "The lady has asked you to leave, mister," one said, stepping forward.

I think we're going to see some man-style foolishness, Atropos thought with a certain relish. *When they don't have sex on their minds, they do like to fight.*

"I have an appointment," Mars said. He stepped into the man, caught his outstretched arm, spun about, and sent him rolling across the floor.

The other man turned—and Mars' leg shot out and swept the other man's foot from under him, so that he landed on the floor with a resounding slap.

"Now go in and announce me," Mars said. "I expect a full turnout, and the courtesy of the *dojo.*"

Without further word, the two men hurried away.

"But you could have hurt them!" Clotho protested.

Mars walked back to Clotho and proffered his arm. "Not with a simple hand throw and a foot-sweep; they know how to take falls. I merely showed them a hint of my competence."

She held his sword out to him, but he demurred. "I shall not be using that here, but cannot trust it to the hand of a mortal. Hold it until we are done."

Clotho managed to hold the dread sword by one hand, and took his arm with the other. She walked with him through the bamboo curtain and down the hall toward the main chamber of the *dojo.* "Are you planning to fight all of them?"

"Certainly," Mars replied.

"But—"

"I will run the line. Then it will be your turn."

"But—"

"Do not be concerned, cutes. It will be all right."

I hope so, Clotho thought nervously.

He knows what he's doing, Niobe thought reassuringly. *The three of us may not know what he's doing, but he knows.*

They reached the second curtain. "Take off your shoes," Mars told her. He was already barefoot.

She took them off. They stepped through.

About forty students were lined along the far wall, standing barefooted on the edge of the big mat. They seemed to be arranged roughly in order of rank, with the white-belts at one end and the black-belts at the other. There were, she noted, several women among them.

In the center of the mat stood Samurai. He turned to face them.

Mars stretched out his right arm. A red cloth appeared in his hand. Slowly, deliberately, he wound this belt about his middle and tied it in place with the odd knot that martial artists used. There was a murmur of amazement from the line of students. It was as if they had never seen a red belt before.

Is something significant happening? Niobe thought.

Mars stepped up to the mat, and halted, and bent forward at the waist. *He's bowing to the mat!* Atropos thought, finding it funny.

But Clotho had heard of this. "It's the ritual," she murmured. "Always bow when joining or leaving the *tatami,* the mat, for it breaks your fall and spares your bones. Always step on it barefooted."

Now Mars stepped onto the mat. "You assume the belt of a Master Dan," Samurai said, as if in challenge.

"You are observant," Mars replied.

Samurai turned and walked to the black end of the line of students. He dropped into a cross-legged seated position.

Mars faced the class, and bowed to the line. The line bowed back.

Then Mars strode forward and took hold of the student at the white end of the line. This was a young woman, so small and light that her bare feet left the mat when he brought her forward. *He can't attack her!* Niobe thought with horror.

Yet no one else protested, or even seemed dismayed. They merely watched.

Mars brought her to the center of the mat and held her by the right lapel and left sleeve of her *gi.* "Try a throw," he told her.

The girl turned and hauled on his jacket. She got nowhere. Then Mars stepped back, drawing her along with him so that she had to step quickly forward to avoid losing her balance. At the moment her right foot touched the mat, his left foot swept against it. Her foot went up and she fell backward. She landed on the mat, her left arm outstretched, slapping the mat resoundingly, her right arm captive to his grip.

"*De-ashi harai*," Mars said. "The Advanced-Foot Sweep. Remember it." Then he let her go, and she scrambled up, bowed hastily, and returned to the line.

Mars nodded to the next student, a boy in white belt. The boy came out, took hold, and tried a throw of his own. It also got nowhere.

Mars drew him forward, as before, but this time set his left foot against the boy's kneecap and hauled him into a tumble on the mat. "*Hiza-guruma*," Mars said. "The Knee-Wheel. Practice your falls, son, or you'll get hurt."

"Yessir!" the boy exclaimed, scrambling up, bowing, and running back to his place in the line.

Mars nodded to the third student, another woman in a white belt. Again he gave her the chance to try to throw him, and she failed; then he threw her spinning to the mat with a hand-and-foot motion that seemed to be in between that of the prior two throws. "*Sasae-tsurikomi-ashi*," he said. "The Propping-Drawing-Ankle Throw."

There was a murmur along the line. "He's doing the First Course of Instruction!" someone said behind Clotho. She turned to look. A brown-belt had come in behind her, off the mat. It was the instructor of the morning beginners' class; evidently he had returned too late to join this one, so was watching from the side.

"Is that significant?" Clotho asked.

Now he recognized her. "You're the—"

"The same," she agreed. "I brought my champion to meet Samurai."

"In a red belt!" he murmured, amazed. "That's ninth or tenth Dan!"

"Is that good?"

"Oh—you don't know judo?"

"Nothing," she confessed. "I just came to talk to Samurai, and then things went wrong."

He pursed his lips thoughtfully. "Just so," he said after a moment. "Very well, I'll be glad to explain. The master grades of judo are the *Dan*, as opposed to the student grades, the *kyu*. The *Dan* are black belt. But the very highest grades may wear the red belt. Normally such grades are only achieved as honors for service to the art, by masters who no longer compete. A *competitor* with a red belt should be the finest judoka in the world."

"Oh, that explains why the class was so surprised."

"It certainly does. As far as I know, there is no living, competing red belt today. So this man is bound to be an impostor."

With a Tangled Skein

"He is Mars, the Incarnation of War."

"Oh? Then maybe he—" The brown-belt shrugged. He returned to her prior question. "There's nothing wrong with the First Course," he explained. "They're all good throws. But once people catch on to the order, they'll know exactly which throw he's going to do next. That makes it much harder. It doesn't matter for the white-belts, but he'd have trouble throwing *me* with a throw I expected, and it would probably be impossible with a black-belt."

Mars threw the next student over his right hip. "There's the fourth—*Uki-goshi*, the Floating Hip Throw," the brown-belt said. "I've never seen it done better. But I wonder where he could have gotten his training?"

Mars threw the next backward. "*O-soto-gari*," the brown-belt murmured. "He certainly knows the basics."

The next student fell. "And *O-goshi*," the brown-belt said.

"Didn't he just do that one?"

"No, that was *Uki-goshi,* a different throw. It looks similar and the footwork is similar, but the feel is quite different. *Uke* takes a much harder fall."

"But I thought *Uki* was the throw, not the faller."

The brown-belt smiled. "You really don't know, do you? The one who does the throwing is always called *Tori,* the taker, and the one who gets thrown is *Uke*, the receiver. Anyway, the *Uki-goshi* is done stiff-kneed, while *O-goshi* flexes the knees, and—oh, there's *O-uchi-gari,* the Major Inner Reaping! Beautiful!"

Clotho—and Niobe—were having trouble distinguishing the throws. They were ready to take the brown-belt's word that they were being properly done. Clotho took advantage of his presence to ask another question. "What is this—this running the line?"

"Well, a challenger shows his superiority by defeating a number of others in rapid order," the brown-belt said. "For example, a black-belt should be able to run a line of five brown-belts and throw them all, because his skill is greater. When the line is mixed, they do the lowest grades first, the *Kyus,* and work up to the *Dans.* Of course, by the time someone has thrown twenty or thirty people, he's apt to be getting tired, so it gets harder both ways. No one has ever run our full line victoriously; if your friend makes it, he will have proved his rank. Some of ours are *Sandans*, and one's a *Yodan,* and of course Samurai is *Rokudan,* the sixth level, and the champion of the eastern states. He'll be world champion one day, if he decides to go for it."

"He might not go for it?"

"Well, he's getting old for competition, and judo is only part of his interest. He's a master in karate, too, and aikido, and his specialty is the sword; no one can touch him there. He's been searching for

—188—

this mythical finger-strike, too— Say! Look at that *Tsuri-komi-goshi!*
I've never seen a prettier throw! Did you see how he got full extension? I've never been able to do that on an *Uke* my own weight!''

The throw had looked just like all the others to Clotho and the
other Aspects, but evidently there was a difference.

"But now he's into the yellow-belts, and when he hits the green-
belts he'll have to work a little for it. Oh, nice *Okuri-ashi-harai!*
That's not as easy as it looks."

Clotho was willing to take his word for it.

"God, I wish I was in that line!" the brown-belt said after the next
throw. "It's a privilege to be thrown by a master like that! Is he really
the Incarnation of War?"

"Yes, he—"

"Oh, there's the *Uchi-mata!* Samurai himself couldn't have done
it better!"

They watched while Mars moved into the green-belts. They were
trying to throw him and failing as dismally as the white-belts had,
and had no better success in resisting the return throws.

"That's amazing!" the brown-belt commented. "I've never seen
someone give them a chance like that; usually they put them away
as fast as they can. He's got a lot of confidence."

"He should," Clotho said, though she was amazed herself.

Then she saw Mars drop down. Someone had thrown him! But
immediately the brown-belt opponent fell too. Both of them were
lying on the mat.

"*Yoko-otoshi!* The Side Drop!" the brown-belt exclaimed. "Beautiful!"

"You mean it's supposed to look like that?" Clotho asked.

"Of course. It's a sacrifice throw."

"Oh."

They watched several more standing throws. Then Mars went
down again. He had his foot in the other's belly, and lifted him over
so that he did a roll and landed on his back. "*Tomoe-nage*, the Stomach Throw," the brown-belt said.

The throws continued as Mars progressed three-quarters of the way
down the line. There seemed to be no end to them. But obviously
the class was highly impressed.

"*Soto-makikomi*," the brown-belt remarked as both men went
down again. "I hate to take falls on that one! Of course it's a power-
throw; there's not much stopping it once it starts. If he can do the
next one, the *Uki-otoshi*—"

It seemed to Niobe that the brown-belt who was *Uke* at the moment
simply threw himself on the mat, but the one beside her whistled
softly. "Perfect!"

With a Tangled Skein

A black-belt came out of the line. Mars waited while the man tried a foot-sweep without success, then said, "Try another." There was a chuckle along the line.

"What's so funny?" Clotho asked.

"The situation. He's up to the thirty-seventh throw in the Basic Forty. That's *Ushiro-goshi*, the Rear Loin. It's a counterthrow following an attempted hip-throw. Clyde didn't try a hip-throw."

Clyde tried a sacrifice throw, without effect; it was as if Mars were an immovable wall. There was another chuckle.

Then, moving like lightning, Clyde tried a hip-throw—and Mars picked him up and threw him to the mat. Clyde had gambled and lost. He got up, bowed, and smiled; he didn't mind losing to an artist of that skill. "And he did it left-side," the brown-belt murmured in awe. "Clyde tried to fool him, left-side, and he was ready."

"Left-side is different?"

"And how! I really sweat on them!"

The last man in the line approached and took hold, but declined to try a throw. "*Randori*," he said.

"What does that mean?" Clotho asked.

"That's our *Yodan*," the brown-belt said. "He's a top competitor; he doesn't like to do stationary throws. He prefers to counter, or to seize his opportunity. He knows your man will try the *Yoko-gake*, the Side Body Drop; he wants to make him do it in a moving situation."

"Interesting," Clotho said, unenlightened.

The two men moved about the mat, almost as if dancing together. Suddenly the black-belt screamed piercingly, his foot moving like lightning. But Mars' foot moved too, just as fast—and they both fell to the mat.

The brown-belt shook his head. "Beautiful! He did it!"

"But how do you know who threw whom? And why the scream?"

The brown-belt smiled. "The scream was a *kiai* yell, to facilitate the throw. Didn't work, this time. And sometimes it can be hard to tell, on a throw. I saw a match once where the award was given to the wrong judoka, before the judges corrected it. But this one was a perfect *Yoko-gake*, no question."

Indeed, the class seemed to know it. Mars returned to the center of the mat, and exchanged bows with the class. It seemed he had successfully run the line.

"And he's not even tired!" the brown-belt murmured.

Then Mars walked to the edge of the mat, stepped off, turned about, and bowed to it. "All right, girl," he said gruffly. "He has to meet you now."

"He what?"

"As your champion I conquered his class. I did not challenge Samurai himself. It is you who must meet him." He took her by the elbow, urging her forward. "Honor the *tatami*."

Bemused, Clotho bowed and stepped onto the mat. "But I've still got your sword!"

"Precisely. It's an outrage. Get out there."

Like a zombie, Clotho walked across the mat. The class watched, unmoving.

Is he crazy? Atropos thought. *This girl doesn't know anything about swords, and she doesn't want to shed blood.*

It's probably an insult to the dojo *to carry a weapon onto the mat, too,* Niobe thought. *But Mars must have a reason.*

Samurai bounded to his feet. In a moment his own sword was in his hand. "For this you must die!" he cried, striding forward.

Are you sure we're immortal? Atropos thought nervously.

Well . . . Niobe thought, abruptly uncertain. When she had been Clotho, she had never faced a test like this.

But abruptly the red sword lifted in Clotho's hand. It was a heavy monster, but now it was featherlight. It assumed a guard position.

"Get out of here!" Samurai cried, making a threatening gesture.

The red sword moved to intercept his weapon. Metal clanged on metal.

The enchanted sword has made us expert, Niobe thought, amazed.

Goaded beyond reason by that gesture of defiance, Samurai attacked in earnest. *He's as hot-tempered as she is!* Atropos thought.

Two of a kind, Niobe agreed.

The red sword moved rapidly to counter the strike against it. Samurai struck again, and again the red sword blocked. He could not get through that guard.

"But this is not what I want!" Clotho whispered. "This will never bring him to reason!"

Indeed, the longer it continued, the more plain it was becoming that Samurai, for all his dazzling skill, could not penetrate the guard of Mars' sword. Samurai would very shortly look like a colossal fool.

You've got two choices, girl, Atropos thought. *Either attack, which means you'll probably kill him at one stroke, or—*

"No!" Clotho cried. She flung away the red sword and sank to her knees before Samurai. "Take my blood!"

If he strikes, Niobe thought, alarmed, *either we'll be dead, or he'll be ultimately humiliated.*

Samurai paused, as surprised as anyone. "You yield?"

"Everything!" Clotho cried, the tears streaming down her face.

Samurai paused. His fighting rage drained out of him almost visibly. Indeed, Clotho was a piteous figure of a woman.

He held his sword to the side. A student hastily came to take it away. "Then I am satisfied," Samurai said, extending his hand.

Clotho took it in both her own and kissed it.

The harder they fall . . . Atropos throught wryly.

"That isn't necessary," Samurai said, embarrassed. "Do not humiliate yourself more than is required." He drew her back to her feet, then turned and nodded to the class. Immediately they filed out of the room, each bowing as he or she stepped off the mat.

Clotho found a hanky and dabbed at her face. "I'm sorry I—"

"Accepted," Samurai said gently.

"I wanted to be liberated, but—"

"Liberation has its appeal, when understood," he said. "This is, after all, America. I would not have you other than you are. Will you join me for dinner this evening?"

She smiled. "I will."

They walked to the edge of the mat, bowed as they stepped off, and smiled at each other.

Samurai glanced at the brown-belt, who remained in the room, standing beside Mars. "Convey his sword to the Incarnation of War," Samurai said. "It is a remarkable weapon."

The brown-belt bowed himself onto the mat and hurried to pick up the fallen sword. But he was unable to; the thing seemed anchored in place. He strained to lift it, and could not.

"Permit me," Mars murmured. He raised his right hand—and the red sword floated up and across the mat, dipped momentarily at its edge as if bowing, and moved to his hand. Mars gravely sheathed it.

"And a remarkable man," Samurai said, exchanging bows with Mars. Then Mars turned and walked out of the *dojo*.

Samurai turned to Clotho. "I regret that I mistook you. Yet is it acceptable for Fate to—"

Clotho touched his lips with a finger. "I am just a woman—now."

He nodded. "Tonight, then."

"Tonight."

Clotho walked out of the *dojo*. Outside, she extended a thread and ascended.

"But we never got his commitment on the bomb," Atropos remembered.

"We shall have it—tonight," Niobe replied. "And, unless I mistake Mars, he will give Samurai the secret of the finger-strike. As a token of esteem, not as a bribe."

"I've got a lot to learn," Clotho said.

And it was so—on all counts.

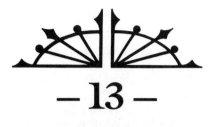

– 13 –

COUNTERPLOY

"We needed help on the last one," Niobe said. "Surely we'll need it on this one too!"

"Who can help us with a Satanist?" Atropos asked.

"My guess would be Gaea. She's generally considered to be the strongest of the Earthly Incarnations."

"Nature? I thought Time was."

"Chronos has the most potent single instrument, the Hourglass. But Gaea—" Niobe shrugged. "Let's ask her, anyway."

Niobe took the body and slid the thread across to Gaea's vegetable mansion. They landed at the door. Sometimes it was difficult to reach the Green Mother, but that depended on the situation. Niobe remembered her journey with Pacian; Ge had known what she was doing that time!

That's one fancy treehouse! Atropos thought.

The leafy door opened, and Gaea stood there.

Niobe froze. It was the same Green Mother she had known a quarter-century ago!

"Why, it's Fate!" Gaea exclaimed. Then she squinted. "But a new Lachesis!"

Gaea didn't recognize her! Of course Niobe knew she had changed considerably in the intervening period of mortality, and not for the better; why should anyone recognize in this dowdy woman the beauty that once had been? "And a new Clotho," she said. "And Atropos, too." She changed briefly to the other forms.

Gaea shook her head. "All three at once? Unusual!"

Quickly Niobe explained the circumstances. "Now we have one more mortal thread to modify," she concluded. "Because of our inexperience—"

"You seek help," Gaea said. "Very sensible of you. Come inside a moment while I change."

Inside, Niobe watched while Gaea changed. She did not do it by removing her leafy green dress; instead she stood still, and the dress turned yellow with some red; then the leaves fell off, revealing brown bark beneath. Her hair turned white. She had progressed seasonally from summer through fall to winter, complete with snow.

She moved—and the brown corrugations shaped themselves into the creases and pockets of a long jacket. The snow became a white hat; her hair was not, after all, that far changed.

Gaea brought out a small pair of spectacles, mounted on a rod at one side. "You will want these, Lachesis."

"A lorgnette? Those haven't been used for a generation!" Niobe protested. "Anyway, I don't need glasses!"

"Humor me, Lachesis," Gaea said gently.

Niobe shrugged and accepted them. "Then you will help?"

"Of course, dear. We matrons must support each other. We can't depend on foundation garments."

Niobe smiled dutifully. Gaea needed no support from clothing; she could assume any form she chose, young or old, beautiful or hideous, animal, vegetable or mineral. Seldom did she display her power in an obvious manner, but it was as deep and versatile as that of any Incarnation. Many mortals thought they could balk her in the short term, but in the long term she always had her way.

"I am ready," Gaea said. "Take me there, Lachesis."

Niobe took her hand, extended a thread, and slid them both along it. They arrived at an industrialized section of Connecticut, near a large mall. They entered and walked to a small booth set between an ice cream parlor and a mini-dozen movie theater.

Above the booth was a banner saying TO HELL WITH YOU! Inside it was a bored-looking woman of about Niobe's own physical age. "That's the one," Niobe murmured. "Elsa Mira, Satanist recruiter."

"Well, we shall allow her to recruit us," Gaea agreed. "Call me Ge; I'll call you Lack." She smiled faintly, as if the sun were masked by haze, and suddenly Niobe suspected that Gaea did indeed recognize her. But the Green Mother could keep a secret as well as any creature of the world.

They approached the booth. "We really aren't interested in going to Hell," Niobe said. "But in fairness we thought we'd look at your literature."

"Why, certainly," the woman said, coming alive. "Hell has had a very bad press, but we are working to alleviate that." She brought out a colorful brochure.

Niobe looked at the cover. Two cute baby devils were on it: the Hellfire trademarks, Dee and Dee. One was male, the other female. As she looked, the male Dee lifted one little red hand and solemnly beckoned. She was startled, though she knew she shouldn't have been; naturally the minions of Hell had magic to splurge.

"Perhaps you can read the print more clearly with your glasses, Lack," Gaea murmured.

"Oh, thank you, Ge," Niobe said. "I keep forgetting." She raised the lorgnette and peered through the lenses.

She stiffened. Instead of the cute picture, she saw a lens. She was being recorded on video!

She moved the lorgnette aside. The little devil was beckoning her again.

Now she realized why Gaea had asked her to use the glasses. They were enchanted to penetrate illusion! Already she knew that the Satanists were not merely showing their literature, they were getting a direct line on anyone who inquired. They were a good deal more professional than they cared to seem. That lens could be making a record of the complete encounter, and storing her picture in a computer file, complete with the retinal prints. Hell intended to have her number, all the way!

Fortunately, she had never had her retinal prints taken. She had existed, as a mortal, in the country, where such things were not common. Hell would not be able to trace down her true identity by this device.

Gaea opened the brochure. Niobe glanced through the glasses again, and saw that the pages were mere frames; the sinister lens remained. But without the glasses, she saw the inner material: scenes of happy, healthy people swimming, playing tennis, skiing, and watching the sunset. GO TO HELL, the print proclaimed, AND LIVE YOUR AFTERLIFE TO THE FULLEST!

"Is there skiing in Hell?" Niobe asked doubtfully. "I thought it was hot."

"Indeed there is skiing!" the recruiter said encouragingly. "Hell is large; it has climates exactly as the mortal realm does. Some regions are in perpetual snow."

Actually, Niobe had known that, because of her prior experience as an Incarnation. She also knew that poor sinful souls were frozen as solid as spirits could be, in that snow, and that the only skiers were demons who delighted in skidding over perpetually horrified frozen faces. As with many of Hell's claims, the snow was a half-truth: it existed, but was not used as represented. The whole of Hell's recruitment campaign was spurious, and only sadly deluded people could fall for it. Unfortunately, it was evident that many did.

But she was not here to show off her information about Hell. She was here to talk Mira out of delivering the bomb to the UN complex, thus eliminating the last of the potential couriers. She had to act like an ignorant skeptic until she had a better notion how to achieve her design.

"I don't know," she said. "Skiing, swimming—I thought Hell was a place of punishment."

"Oh, that's not so!" Mira exclaimed. "Hell is a place of rehabilitation! The evil-soiled souls are reprocessed to be good again. There are many incentives for a positive attitude."

And many tortures for the damned, Atropos thought sourly.

"But if people aren't good in life, why should they be good in the Afterlife?" Niobe asked. She knew the answer, but had to play the part.

"Many people don't really think about it," Mira said. "They just go their way until it's too late. Those are the ones we are catering to—the ordinary, mixed people who are too busy to be absolutely good all the time. I mean, it's a lot of work to be good *all* the time, and frankly pretty dull, and probably unnecessary, too. We feel that most people would really be better off worrying less about the Afterlife and just getting their mortal lives in shape. Then, in Hell, they can sort it all out at leisure."

Leisure? Eternity! Atropos snorted mentally. *What a crock!*

"But *shouldn't* they be good in life?" Niobe asked.

"Well, yes, of course. But it can be very difficult. Take the man whose wife is ignoring him and won't let him touch her. But she won't give him a divorce, either. Now if he finds an attractive young woman who likes him, is it really wrong for him to have an affair? His soul may suffer an accumulation of evil, *but is it wrong?* We Satanists think we should do what is natural and atone later."

Niobe hadn't heard this one before. "Are you married?" she asked.

Mira laughed. "Me? Of course not! Not anymore! I wouldn't put up with that sort of—that is, all the ridiculous things men demand. But the principle remains—"

"Pleasure first, mortality last," Niobe finished.

"Anyway," Mira said quickly. "We want you to see for yourself what kind of place Hell is. Why don't you come to our demonstration complex?"

"Your what?"

"We have set up a working mini-model of Hell, so that folk like you can tour it or sample it and see for yourselves what it offers. We Satanists want to spread the truth about Hell."

"Well," Niobe said, glancing at Gaea. "I suppose we might just look—to be fair."

Mira jumped up. "Right this way! I'll guide you on the tour myself!"

This was exactly what they wanted: a long enough association with the woman to talk her out of what she was otherwise apt to do.

I bet they get bonuses for each recruit they sign, Atropos thought cynically.

Such as a trip to the United Nations building? Clotho thought. She had been fairly quiet, recovering from her experience of the prior evening; she was in the first flush of something like love, and the warmth of it tended to spill over and buoy the other two Aspects. But she had not forgotten their mission.

"Keep your glasses handy, dear," Gaea murmured like a fussy old lady as they followed Mira through the door in back of the booth.

They found themselves in an elevator. There was a wrench. Then the door slid open, and they stepped out into an amusement park. Obviously magic had been used to transport them to the model Hell; there was no telling where on Earth it had been constructed.

Niobe stared. Directly ahead was a towering Ferris wheel, grandly rotating. To one side was a bump-car enclosure, with children squealing happily as the little vehicles crashed harmlessly into each other. Elsewhere were miniature choo-choo trains, zoom-rides, and toy airplanes whirling about a pole. "This is Hell?" Niobe asked, raising an eyebrow.

"Well, the top level," Mira said. "Very mild entertainments, for those who are just waiting for friends, or for the children of those on tour. The ones who really don't have much sin to indulge."

"What's it like for those who *do* have significant sin on their souls?" Gaea asked.

"I'll show you," Mira said eagerly, leading the way to stairs descending below the pavement. These led to a large hall, well-lighted, filled with tables. People were clustered around the tables, intent on what was there.

They approached the nearest. On it was a giant roulette wheel. "Oh—gambling," Niobe said disapprovingly.

"You don't understand," Mira said. "Watch for a moment."

They watched. The wheels turned; the ball rolled and landed in a numbered pocket. A man made an exclamation of joy. "I won! I won!"

There was a smattering of applause from the other gamblers. The man collected his winnings and bet them on the next spin. And won again.

"What?" Niobe asked. "Twice in succession? The odds against that—"

—197—

"People can be very fortunate here," Mira said. "They usually do win."

Gaea nudged her. Niobe lifted the lorgnette and peered at the scene.

The roulette table was genuine—but little else was. Most of the players were bored park employees in grubby uniforms, not the well-dressed visitors they had appeared to be. There was a control panel at the croupier's place. When the spin commenced, the croupier's fingers touched buttons. This time the gambler bet on number 19, and that was the number the croupier punched. Sure enough, the ball rolled into that slot. The game was rigged.

Now Niobe looked at the chips the gambler had piled before him. They were genuine. Where, then, was the catch? Surely the Satanists were not really going to let a mark walk out wealthy!

Well, she could inquire, without giving anything away. "How can you stay in business, if you let people win too much money?"

"Oh, the chips don't stand for money," Mira said as they moved on to another table. "They stand for points. One thousand points entitles the player to enter the next level, where the real action is."

"But it seems guaranteed he'll make it."

"No, it's not guaranteed. Only those people we feel are suitable prospects are admitted."

"Then you admit it's fixed!"

Mira turned a surprised gaze on her. "My dear, what do you expect of Hell? Of course it's fixed!"

"Ask a silly question," Gaea murmured.

"But you're giving us a tour, and we're not gambling," Niobe persisted.

"Precisely. If you don't gamble, you can't win. That's the fundamental principle. You are merely looking—but I'm sure that after you've seen what we have to offer, you'll be eager to participate."

"But isn't there an admittance price?"

"I am glad you asked that question," Mira said. "Now we are very candid about this. Everything is quite clear. To participate in our entertainments you must sign a standard contract—"

"In blood?"

"It's only a pinprick. You'll hardly feel it."

"A contract saying what?"

"Well, everyone knows what Hell requires. It isn't as if we're concealing anything."

"You're after my soul!"

"Merely a portion of it, since this is only a model of Hell. Technically, all we require is a nominal attribution of evil. Only one percent, actually. If you are seventy percent good, our contract would cause you to be sixty-nine percent good. That's hardly enough to cost you anything in the Afterlife, or to change your designation. Considering what we offer, it's a bargain.''

They were at the next table. This one was for blackjack. Again, the mark was winning; again, the enchanted lenses showed that the game was rigged. Hell wanted the marks to win.

All of the tables were like that. The methods of gambling differed, but the system was the same.

"Well, I never did like to gamble," Niobe said.

"But all of life is a gamble," Mira said enthusiastically. "Still, there are other routes to Hell. Let me show you the next level." She led the way to another set of stairs.

Niobe paused. "I see the others use the elevator."

"Well, yes, but they have to sign for it."

"Sign for it?"

"Another contract," Gaea said.

"Merely an amendment," Mira put in quickly.

"Another one percent of their souls?" Niobe asked. "I thought that was a general admittance fee. What's the point in gambling for points, if you still have to pay to reach the next stage?"

"Well, the general admittance fee gets a person into the park, and then he plays to determine his eligibility to advance to other levels, but that's a matter of qualification, not payment. If there weren't qualification, some unsuitable people would get into inappropriate levels, and if there weren't payment, we would not, as you pointed out a moment ago, be able to stay in business very long. It's a dual system, perfectly straightforward. Naturally the deeper levels have to be financed, too."

"Just how many levels are there?"

"Well, I really don't know the exact number. But no one goes to them *all*."

Because, Niobe realized, at one percent per level, that person would lose more than half his soul before he completed the experience, tipping him into Hell for real.

What a system! Atropos thought.

What a Hellish system, indeed! Only a fool would fall into that trap—but there were plenty of fools in the process.

The next level seemed to be a monstrous warehouse for money. Tables were piled with currency of many nations, with ingots of gold and silver and platinum, and with bins of precious stones. Wealth galore!

Drawn as by a magnet, Niobe went to a vat of sparkling rubies. "May I?" she asked.

"By all means examine the merchandise," Mira said generously. "Of course you can't keep any of it, as a tourist, but if you decide to join as a participant—"

For one or two percent of the goodness in her soul! Niobe grimaced. Still, the gems were lovely!

She picked up a ruby. It was a faceted stone, a deep and glorious red, just about the most beautiful thing she had seen in her life. She turned it between her fingers, half-entranced by its luster. She began to understand the nature of the temptation. Such a fine gem, for so little soul!

"Perhaps if you examined it more closely," Gaea remarked.

Oh. Niobe lifted the lorgnette and looked again.

The ruby was nothing more than a cherry pit.

Niobe made her face a mask, lest she give herself away. All the rubies were cherrystones! The diamonds of the next table were rough lumps of quartz.

Morbidly curious, she verified one of the stacks of gold coins. It was made of round slices of carrot.

Now Clotho had to laugh. *Carrots—instead of carats! That Satan had a devilish sense of humor!*

"Devilish," Niobe agreed.

"What's that?" Mira asked.

"Devilishly tempting," Niobe said. She moved on to a table of green bills.

They were leaves of lettuce.

Lettuce! Atropos thought, mentally doubling over with mirth. *Literal lettuce! That Satan's a card!*

"Yes, anyone would be tempted by that," Mira said, mistaking the nature of Niobe's smile. "It was this room that convinced me to join. When I saw all the jewelry—" She gestured to a table strung with elaborate and precious necklaces.

"But you're not a player, are you?" Niobe asked.

"No, I'm Staff. But I started as a player. Then, when I wanted too much—" She bit her lip. "That is—"

So she had been seduced into giving up too much of her goodness! The operation of the system was becoming clearer. Just as a drug-user became an addict, and the addict had to become a dealer to support his habit, so those who flirted with the trinkets of Hell got drawn ever more deeply in. It was, as Mira said, all perfectly open— except that the actual goods were fakes. Anyone who believed the Father of Lies deserved what he got!

That brought her up short. If the marks deserved to go to Hell for their greed—wasn't Satan actually performing a service to the Cosmos in ridding the world of them?

But she knew the answer. Satan did *not* rid the world of them; he used his converts to facilitate his further dirty work. All the shills at the gaming tables upstairs—all overextended gamblers who now had to work for the house. How much joy did they have here, today?

And this is only a prettified model of Hell, Atropos thought. *Think what the real thing must be like!*

It was indeed a sobering thought.

"I—know that jewelry will not cure what's wrong with me," Niobe said, letting her tummy sag. "I have eaten too much, for too many years."

"Then you will love the feasting level!" Mira exclaimed. "Right this way!"

The next level down was indeed a temptation to a woman who liked to eat. It was an enormous self-service restaurant. The tables were piled with pastries and cakes and fancy desserts. Many women were here, and not a few men and children. All were seated at tables, stuffing themselves with their favorite repasts.

Niobe paused near a fat man who was cramming cake into his face. "But this is horribly fattening!" she protested.

"No it isn't" Mira said, pleased. "Our food is absolutely nonfattening and nonfilling. The taste and texture are there, but all the calories are empty—I mean there *are* no calories. You can eat all you want and never be satiated."

Now that's a kind of Hell in itself, if the fools only realized, Atropos thought.

Endless stuffing without consequence. Niobe could appreciate the temptation, but knew that a person did not have to flirt with Hell for it; regular food companies were advertising ONE CALORIE PER BOTTLE, making a seeming virtue of both gluttony and vacuous food—while elsewhere in the world, people were starving. A little self-discipline would be better.

Then she lifted the lorgnette. And made a stifled squeak of revulsion.

It wasn't cake the man was eating. It was moldy garbage—literally. Most of it managed to shunt itself down his face and front instead of going into his mouth, which explained why he wasn't getting full, but still it was an appalling mess.

Mira caught her reaction. "What's the matter?"

Niobe pondered momentarily, then handed the glasses to her.

The woman looked through them—and gagged.

"You didn't know?" Niobe asked.

"I—this can't be—it's horrible!" Mira exclaimed. She walked to the next table, where a child was swilling ice cream sodas, and looked through the glasses. Her face turned greenish.

Gaea took the lorgnette from her hand before her slackening grip let the glasses drop to the floor. She returned the magical instrument to Niobe.

Niobe looked at the boy's drink. It was a swirling concoction of sewage. As with the man, most of the stuff dribbled down the lad's chin instead of being swallowed, but some did get in. Probably just enough to feed him.

"It's a lie!" Mira gasped. "Magic lenses that distort—"

"No lie," Gaea said. "I am able to see the truth without glasses. The food is garbage. The jewelry on the other floor was junk."

"But I've got a pass to eat all I want—it's one of the benefits of being Staff—" Mira turned and vomited on the floor beside the boy. It hardly mattered, for the area was already littered with garbage.

Niobe wrenched the lorgnette away from her eyes. She saw Mira standing by the table, eyes downcast as if glancing approvingly at the boy. There was no sign of vomit. Still, she did not look well.

After a moment the woman recovered herself somewhat. "Where did you get these glasses?"

Again, Niobe considered rapidly. "From—Nature."

"The—the Incarnation of Nature?"

"Yes. She thought I would need them, here."

"I—may I borrow them a moment more?"

Niobe gave her the glasses. "When you're satisfied, I would like to talk to you."

Mira hurried to another stairway. "There's one level I've never indulged myself in, but I just want to see—"

They followed her down the stairs, almost running. Niobe was surprised to learn that the woman really had not known about the deceit, but realized it made sense. Satan could accomplish much more evil, much more efficiently, if his own helpers were deluded. How many would consider an all-you-can-eat pass to be an inducement, if they knew the food was garbage?

That Satan, he's one sharp liar, Atropos agreed.

The new level appeared to be an elaborate brothel. Extraordinarily voluptuous young women in scanty clothing danced slowly on a stage at one side, their breasts and hips moving suggestively. This did not do anything special for Niobe, other than cause her a gentle wash of jealousy and regret for her own beauty lost, but she saw the effect it had on two men just emerging from the elevator. Both charged forward, their mouths literally drooling.

What pigs men are! Clotho thought. Then she reconsidered. *Except for Samurai . . .*

Mira was peering through the magic lenses. "No," she said unbelievingly. "They wouldn't!"

One man dashed up to the stage. "Hey, honey, you for sale?" he demanded, groping for her. The woman gazed down at him, a languorous smile crossing her bright lips. Then she jumped down to the floor, her anatomy bobbing in several places as she landed. She took the man's hand and led him to a curtained alcove. Evidently she was not for sale; she was free.

Now Niobe could hear urgent grunting from other alcoves. It seemed there were a number of clients busy.

Mira shook her head. "They are—they really are!" she exclaimed. Then she started laughing. "And to think my ex-husband, the pig, sold his soul for a permanent pass to this level!" Her laughter became so violent that Gaea had to take the lorgnette from her again.

Niobe, perplexed, took the glasses. She could understand how plain or even homely women could be recruited, just as Mira had been, to be enhanced by illusion to serve the passions of potential recruits—but what was so funny about that? It was, at best, sad.

She lifted the lorgnette. And gasped.

There were no young women dancing on the stage. It was a corral of pigs. Genuine swine, rooting about in the muck.

And Mira's ex-husband had a permanent pass.

Who says there's no justice in Hell? Atropos thought. *I know some men I'd send here!*

Mira sobered enough to recover her bearings. "You're no ordinary prospects!" she said accusingly. "You *knew* what this was like—better than I did. Who are you?"

It was time for truth. They sat down on one of the few clean places on the fence of the sty, and talked. "I am Fate," Niobe said. "I came here to talk to you, and to persuade you—"

"Fate! An Incarnation!"

"And this is Gaea, who lent me the lorgnette."

"Nature! No wonder she doesn't need glasses to see the truth!"

"We want to persuade you not to do an errand for Satan."

Mira laughed again, this time mirthlessly. "If Satan wants an errand, I'll do the errand. My soul is already lost!"

"It's not lost," Gaea said.

"Don't you understand? I became Staff because I had no soul left to give! They were going to cut me off the food—"

She put her hand to her mouth, realizing. "Oh!"

Gaea gazed intently at her. "Your soul has been corrupted, Elsa Mira, but not that far; there is twenty-four percent good remaining."

"No! There is none! I used it all up, and—you don't know how addictive unmitigated pleasure is! I just couldn't stop! I—"

"I do know," Gaea said. "It is my business to know."

Mira stared at her. "Are you really Nature?"

"I really am. And my companion really is Fate. We can redirect your thread, if you will cooperate to this extent."

"I don't believe it! I kept count of every percentage point!"

Gaea frowned. "You doubt the power of Nature at your peril, woman." She made a gesture—and abruptly the room darkened. Wind swirled. Rain came down, first lightly, then in a pelting torrent.

The pigs squealed, enjoying it. In a moment the three of them were soaked.

Gaea gestured again. The chamber shook. Now the pigs squealed in fright.

"An earthquake!" Mira screamed. "Let me out of here!"

Gaea held up her hand. The quaking stopped and the rain vanished. Sunlight streamed warmly down.

"But we're underground!" Mira protested. "The sun can't shine here!"

"Your fear is gone." Gaea told her. "You are happy."

Mira smiled. "I'm happy!" she agreed.

"Angry," Gaea said.

Sudden rage twisted the woman's face. "When I think what Satan told me—"

"Calm."

And the woman was calm. "I believe you now, Nature. I am amazed at your power, right here in an annex of Hell! Do I really have a quarter of my goodness left?"

"You really do. You have seen how Satan deceives both the clients and the staff members here. Why shouldn't he also deceive you about the percentage of evil charged to your soul? This is much more efficient for him; he caused you to become a creature of his directives when you did not need to be. You can still go to Heaven, Elsa Mira."

"No," the woman said sadly. "I'm still seventy-six percent evil, and I have no way to recover my goodness. I'm still addicted to foolish pleasure."

Again Gaea gestured. "Not any more."

Mira touched her stomach. "The hunger is gone! I'm not famished!"

"You will still have to earn your way by proper living and good deeds," Niobe told her. Niobe herself was impressed by the demonstration of Nature's power she had just witnessed; Gaea was indeed the strongest of the Earthly Incarnations. "But that is the only way *any* person gets to Heaven. God does not grant free passes. You do have time, if you start now."

"But I'm a Satanist! I signed in blood! Many times! I don't belong to any decent church."

"The contract is meaningless," Gaea said. "It is only a device to convince you that you are committed." She glanced up as another man came for another pig. The pig snorted and led him to an alcove. "It is your deeds that define you, and your thoughts, and your intentions, nothing else."

It was like dawn breaking. "You mean—?"

"Give your heart to God," Niobe said. "Your soul will follow."

Piers Anthony

"Oh, I will, I will! I don't want to go to Hell! It's much worse there than it is here! Only I never dared admit the truth—"

They got up and walked toward the stairs. "Satan will ask you to take a package to—"

"Oh, the psychic stink bomb to the United Nations," Mira agreed. "Tomorrow. I already have the bomb in my cell. I agreed to do that days ago."

"You must not do it!" Niobe said.

"Of course I won't do it, now!" Mira agreed. "I know it's an evil deed!"

They reached the stairs. "I will show you how to correct your course with minimum complication," Gaea said. "First we must establish you away from this complex—" They moved up the stairs.

Niobe lingered for a moment more. Now that the job was done, she found herself morbidly intrigued by the variety of illusion. It wasn't merely deception, it was utter degradation. Any man who later found out what he had done here would be too embarrassed to file a complaint. Thus Satan's corrupting operation continued. Truly, the ways of Evil were intricate!

She turned again to mount the stairs. Satan stood there. "So the prying Incarnation is here," he said, sneering smoke from his nostrils. "Corrupting My employees."

"You told me I had zero goodness left!" Mira cried accusingly from above.

"Don't believe everything the Father of Lies tells you, you credulous slut," Satan said.

"I resign from this institution! I'll do your bidding no more!"

"It is academic. You are fired. You never were much use anyway."

"Oh!" Mira exclaimed. She wheeled about and proceeded on up the stairs with Gaea.

Satan contemplated Niobe. His eyes were like small red fires and his horns steamed. "So now you have nullified the last of the four, you meddling frump," he said. "You think you have won."

"Evil is never truly defeated," Niobe said grimly.

"This time you haven't even started!" he said, his body smoking. Niobe raised the lorgnette, but Satan was unchanged. He was appearing in his true form. "You haven't saved your precious United Nations."

"Out with it, you old rascal," Niobe said. "You set this up."

"I set up four threads for Fate to unravel," Satan said. "Now you have used up your time on them, and cannot stop the delivery of the bomb tomorrow."

"But who's going to carry it?" Niobe asked.

"I have a hundred other carriers. Did you think only four could do it?"

"But the Purgatory Computer—"

"Listed hundreds for you."

"It listed only four!"

"What you perceived was only four, old canine," Satan said. He gestured, and the image of a computer screen appeared in the air beside him. On it were the four names. "You supposed that was the real presentation."

Niobe struck her forehead with the heel of her hand. "Illusion! In Purgatory!" Of course it was in Satan's power to distort the spoken and printed material the computer worked with; an illusion was a form of lie, and the lie was his specialty.

Gaea would have known, Atropos thought. *But she wasn't there.*

Satan's illusions are everywhere, Clotho agreed.

"The penalty of being a novice," Niobe muttered.

"Had you realized how many there were," Satan said, "you would have known that individual effort would never work. You would have found a more general way, such as alerting the UN security police, who would have set up psychic sensors to prevent any such thing from getting through."

"I feel very stupid," Niobe said ruefully.

"You're not stupid, merely inexperienced," Satan said. "The stupidity was in your predecessor trio, who allowed a change of all Three Aspects in the same week. I had really expected better from them."

The pig! Clotho thought vehemently. *He set it up!*

Niobe sighed. "It's not too late. We can still alert the UN."

"Maybe," Satan said. "It's a chance. But why take it? I can offer you a better deal."

"You're not to be trusted!" Niobe said.

"Don't depend on trust," Satan said. "Depend on common sense. If I bomb the UN, there will be a very pretty tangle of Fate's threads, leading to much disruption in the world. But no one can know exactly where that disruption will lead. Sometimes what seems good turns out evil in the long run, like the Catholic Inquisition or the Nazi SS cadre. Sometimes what seems evil turns out good, like the Black Plague."

"The Black Plague!" Niobe exclaimed. "What good did that do?"

"It alleviated the European population pressure, decimated the labor force, and so paved the way for the end of the feudal system," Satan said. "You can't keep workers in peonage when there are so few that their value is great."

Niobe suspected that Gaea's predecessors had had their own reasons for spawning the Black Plague. But it was an interesting notion. "What's your point?"

"The point is that this whole UN business is a gamble," Satan said. "It might cost Me more than it is worth. Only a fool gambles when he doesn't have to."

"Many people are gambling on your gaming floor!"

"I rest My case. You do not see Me at the tables."

"What's your pitch, Satan?" she asked gruffly.

"You want to avoid a big stink. I want merely a small, harmless shift in one of Fate's threads. It seems to Me that we might reasonably deal."

"I won't deal with Evil!" Niobe cried.

"Suit yourself," Satan said. "Be sure to hold your nose as you pass the UN complex tomorrow—not that it will do much good."

He had her there. "What deal are you proffering?"

"I will cancel the stink in exchange for a simple shift in employment in one person. No harm done to her, no evil on her soul, just an inconsequential change."

"If it's inconsequential, why do you want it?" Niobe demanded.

"Inconsequential to *you;* important to *Me.* This woman is to go into politics soon. I would prefer to have one of My own in the office she seeks. Most politicians are corrupt anyway, so it hardly matters to you. I promised this minion—well, never mind. The point is, it's something I'm willing to trade for. Are you interested?"

"I don't trust this," Niobe said.

Still, let's see how it looks, Atropos thought. *We don't want to hit the UN tangle if we can avoid it.*

"Who is this person?"

"A young woman, hardly more than a girl, of no consequence, really."

"So you say. Name the woman."

"Oh, she's named Moon, or some such," Satan said carelessly. "It hardly matters."

"How do you expect me to adjust her thread if you don't tell me exactly who she is?" Niobe demanded, aware that she was sliding toward agreement.

He's up to something, Atropos thought. *I wish Gaea had stayed; she's one savvy lady!*

Satan paused, touching his beard as he concentrated. "She's actually the child of a former Incarnation, so maybe she had delusions of grandeur. Name's—let me see—Kaftan."

Niobe stiffened. It was Luna he was trying to eliminate—the one the prophecy said was destined to be the savior of man! Now it was clear that this whole UN tangle was merely a false issue, intended to make his supposedly offhand compromise seem worthwhile. In fact, the manner he had arranged to have all three Aspects of Fate change together now made sense. All three of the prior Aspects would have known about Luna, so they had had to be eliminated. Satan was playing a very long-range game!

But she would play along, just to get a better picture of his intent before she balked it. The three prior Aspects had chosen her to return because they had known Satan was plotting something devious; they had chosen better than they knew! But she wanted to be certain she knew the whole plot.

"There must be several women with that surname," Niobe said, feigning perplexity. "What's her lineage?"

"Oh, not much. One of My minions spotted her some time back. Two girls who look like twins, but a generation apart. I want the one who's descended from the former Incarnation. The one with the darker hair."

Again Niobe stiffened. Had Satan made a mistake? Her granddaughter Luna was destined to save man; Niobe's daughter Orb was destined to become an Incarnation, if the prophecy was correct. Of course Satan was a busy entity; he probably hadn't paid much attention to Niobe's mortal affairs. Obviously he did not recognize her now. For the first time she blessed the loss of her youthful beauty! Perhaps the demon who had sneaked into the Hall of the Mountain King and activated the thief defense had confused the two girls— easy enough to do!—and reported Luna as the buckwheat-honey girl, and Satan had never thought to verify the identification. Luna was in fact the clover-honey girl, slightly lighter in hair hue.

"You find this unreasonable?" Satan asked, noting her silence.

Niobe sighed. "Gaea told me not to trust you. You're up to something."

"My dear associate, there is no call to trust Me! You can handle it yourself! Simply give Me your word that if no bomb goes off at the UN, you will modify the girl's thread to shunt her away from politics."

Niobe tried to decide whether Satan was confused, or had some double devious plot in mind. "No harm will come to the girl?"

"I promise never to harm the girl whose thread you change," Satan said magnanimously.

"But your promise is worthless!"

"That is true. I am the Father of Lies," he agreed with pride. "But My word is sacred when properly given."

"How is it properly given?"

"In blood, of course."

"You have blood?"

He laughed. "Of course I have blood! I'm an Incarnation, like you!"

Niobe remembered. In her prior Incarnation she had learned things about the other Incarnations, and one of them was this: that Satan's blood did bind him, and that the word of one Incarnation to another was inviolate. In this particular case, she could trust even the Father of Lies.

"Then we shall swear on blood," she decided.

Are you crazy, woman? Atropos demanded, like a conscience. *That's your flesh and blood you're sacrificing in that girl!*

And the salvation of man, Clotho added. The two of them had picked up the information from Niobe's strong conscious thoughts.

"Excellent," Satan said. He held up his hand, and Niobe drew a needle from a reserve in her clothing and pricked his thumb so that a drop of blood welled out. Then she did the same for her own hand. The blood of Incarnations could not be shed by anyone, mortal or immortal, without consent, except perhaps in the case of Thanatos' change of office. Satan had agreed to have his blood shed, and so had she—for this occasion only.

"An oath between Incarnations," Niobe said. "Sealed in blood. You will spare the UN and respect the life of that woman, and I will adjust the thread of the life of the darker-haired descendent of Niobe Kaftan so that she never enters politics."

"An oath, agreed," Satan said. They shook their bloodied hands.

"I hope it's worth it," Niobe muttered, worrying what mischief Satan might try to do to Orb, despite his oath. There were ways to make a person miserable without doing actual harm. Yet the language was broad and the term "respect" covered a lot—especially considering the relevance of the prophecy. This oath was merely a step in the implementation of that prophecy. She was not completely easy about it, but thought she had done right in a difficult situation.

"It is for Me," Satan said. "Considering that the matter is academic anyway."

"Academic?"

"Chronos, curse his backward hide, acted on his own, and warned the UN security police about the bomb. They are installing psychic shields already."

"You knew that?" she demanded, outraged. "You cheated!"

"Hardly. I agreed to spare the UN, and Niobe's non-political offspring. They will be spared." Then Satan did a double-take. "How did you know that name 'Niobe'? I never uttered it."

"Satan, it is my business to know. The threads—"

But he was already making the connection. "You—I thought you looked faintly familiar! You are Niobe—once Clotho!"

Niobe shrugged. "Now I am Lachesis. But I will see that my mortal daughter Orb never enters politics. An oath is an oath."

"Orb? I meant Luna!"

"Oh, is the matter academic?" she asked sweetly. "I swore to keep my darker-haired descendent free of politics."

Satan considered. "You came back—to deceive Me!"

"Close enough." Niobe shrugged. "Had you specified that it was Luna whom you—"

She expected an explosion, but Satan only nodded. "Sometimes the Father of Deceit is hoist with his own petard. I congratulate you, Niobe, on an excellent counterploy."

"That is a compliment indeed, coming from you."

"But now I know you, and I shall not be deceived again. There are other ways." He vanished.

Niobe was not reassured. That had been too easy. Yet how else could she have played it? She extended a thread and slid toward home.

– 14 –

BRIBE

Back in the Abode, they rested, then returned to the routine. They had indeed foiled Satan, for the UN was not bombed. Perhaps, as Satan had claimed, the matter was academic—but only because Chronos had been alerted by their reaction and joined in himself. Since he lived backward, his subsequent action would have occurred before their conversation, but—well, that problem had been dealt with. Niobe's daughter and granddaughter would continue their lives unobstructed; the existing course of their threads was unchanged.

What a stroke of luck it had been that Niobe had returned as Lachesis to deal with this particular matter! No one else would have known about the two fair moons, and been able to divert Satan's thrust into a harmless channel.

Yet was it coincidence—or was there a deeper current of Fate that transcended the efforts even of the Incarnations? If so, what was the origin of that current?

"God," Atropos said.

There it was. God honored the Covenant by not interfering in the affairs of mortals, while Satan chronically cheated. Evidently Satan had not signed that one in blood. But if God guided the larger pattern, all of Satan's machinations would became—academic.

Was her return merely part of God's will—or was it true coincidence?

"We'll never know, for sure," Clotho said.

With that, Niobe had to be satisfied.

Niobe now worked with Chronos more than she had as Clotho. True, she had had a long-term backward affair with the earlier

Chronos, but that had been on a different level. She suspected, by the way this Chronos glanced at this Clotho, that there would be something of the sort again, but not for some time, and perhaps not with this particular Clotho. The youngest Aspect of Fate seemed to be a magnet for male attentions, whoever and whenever. But the main business was between Chronos and Lachesis. Only he could locate the specific chronology for the complex interactions of the threads. His staff and Fate's staff coordinated the great majority of events competently enough, but there was a constant development of situations that required the attention of the Incarnations themselves.

It was during one such session that Chronos mentioned another thing that alerted her. "Periodically Satan has opportunity to free a few demons from Hell," he remarked. "I don't know what governs this, and it happens infrequently, but when a demon is freed, there is always mischief in the mortal realm."

"Even the spirit of a demon is bad," Niobe agreed.

"Ah, then you know the nature of the problem! I remember when I had to run the world backward to eliminate—but of course that hasn't happened yet, for you. But it seems that such an occasion is about to happen again—has already happened, in your frame. I suspect it behooves us to verify exactly what mischief is being done, this time."

"Can't you tell, from your past?"

"That's the odd thing. There doesn't seem to be any effect. Yet Satan never lets such an opportunity pass unfulfilled."

"No mischief?" she asked. "That *is* suspicious! What mischief could Satan do that you would not be aware of?"

"Something of limited scope," he said. "Or something subtle."

"If it's too limited or subtle to affect the balance of good and evil in the world, it's too limited to be worth his while," Niobe said. "I'm sure he wouldn't waste a valuable demon on anything genuinely minor." She remembered the various demonic attacks on her own family. "There has to be something."

"Perhaps something that manifests after my term began," Chronos said. "That way I would not know of it. Satan is adept at sleepers."

"Yes! Luna is supposed to be the salvation of man some time in the future, perhaps twenty years hence. Satan has enormous cunning and patience; he can afford to wait, to nullify your perception. There must be something the demon does now that will show up then."

"He has done that sort of thing," Chronos agreed. "Never that long-term, in my experience, but of course I foiled the shorter-term efforts. With difficulty, I confess. It was quite wearing; if it hadn't been for your support and Clotho's—I mean this one's successor—I might have given up."

Niobe chose to ignore the remark about Clotho's successor, and hoped Clotho had not picked it up; none of them wanted to know the times of their departures from office, voluntary as they might be. "That must be it. What could a demon do today, that wouldn't take effect for twenty years? A time bomb?"

"Such devices are notoriously unreliable. More likely it would be some kind of change in personnel somewhere, so that someone would not be available to do something to oppose Satan in that time."

"We have pretty well safeguarded Luna," Niobe said. "So I don't think the demon can touch her. She's the only truly critical person I know of."

"At one point, Satan sent a demon to nullify the accidental poisoning of the senator she replaced, so that—"

"Wait, wait, Chronos! You're talking of the future! I wish you wouldn't do that. Just speak in generalities, if you please."

"Sorry. My point is that if Satan can affect people Luna interacts with, he can affect her indirectly. If she is to be pivotal in a political sense, the change of other personnel might transfer the pivot to another person."

"Now I understand. You say she's to become a senator?"

"Yes, if you don't mind that information. A good one."

"So the Senate is the likely arena for—whatever it is?"

"I would say so."

"Then I'd better check potential changes in the makeup of the Senate. I'm learning how to read the threads better, so I should be able to do this more efficiently than I did for the stink-bomb carriers. Did I thank you for your effort there?"

"Stink bomb? Oh, there was something in an alternate reality. The UN?"

"That's right—if I thanked you last month, you wouldn't know it now!"

"I'm sure you did what was proper—and I will too."

"Well, thank you anyway—for that and this."

She left the mansion and, as usual, took time out before returning to her Abode, so as not to meet her self of the immediate past; that was always unsettling. She had done it on occasion by prearrangement during the time of the child-Chronos, and that had been interesting, but she was too busy for that sort of thing now. She slid her thread down to pay a brief call on Luna, just to advise her of the current situation. She hadn't seen the young woman since assuming the Aspect of Lachesis, so it really was time.

She landed at the door of what turned out to be a rather elegant fenced estate guarded by two fierce griffins. When they menaced her, she slid through them on a thread, showing them what they were dealing with.

The door opened, and there stood Luna. "My dear!" Niobe exclaimed. "What have you done with your hair?"

"Grandma!" Luna exclaimed. "Come in!"

They had a nice visit, in the course of which Niobe learned that Luna had used a spell when she moved to America to darken her hair to chestnut brown. "My father insisted," she said. "I really don't know why."

Niobe remembered Satan's confusion, supposing Luna was the one with the darker hair. Satan had seen her more recently than Niobe had! "I believe I understand why," she murmured. Her son the Magician had really been on the job!

In due course she kissed her granddaughter adieu and slid home. She had serious business to attend to.

She checked the skein, searching out the threads of current senators. Of course there would be many changes in twenty years, so nothing much should show. But—

She was disappointed. She started with the youngest, who would be most likely to remain for another twenty years or more, therefore the most likely targets for Satan's effort. After all, what use to corrupt a senator who would not be there for the payoff? But one after the other, the threads were normal. None of them had been touched by the distinctive stigmatum of Satan's influence.

"Well, it was worth checking," she said. "It was just a wild guess anyway."

"Why not check the old ones?" Atropos asked.

"They'd be replaced anyway, by then."

"Check them anyway. I've got a hunch."

Niobe shrugged and checked the thread of the oldest senator. She stared. There was the kink of Satan!

She checked another old one. There was another stigmatum. Satan had definitely influenced these men!

"But it doesn't make sense!" Niobe protested. "One of these men is seventy-six years old now, and in failing health; there's no way he's going to make it another twenty years!"

"Unless he gets a youth potion," Atropos replied.

"A youth potion!" Suddenly it made sense! Trust an old woman to think of that! An old, corrupt man would gladly give his soul for that, figuring he was going to Hell anyway. Satan, in effect, could be offering these men twenty more years of life, in exchange for their support at the critical moment. Since they would otherwise be replaced by younger and perhaps more God-fearing men, it was to Satan's interest to do this.

Luna was being bypassed. That could not be allowed.

She checked more threads. The four oldest senators were kinked; the fifth and sixth weren't. "The demon hasn't finished making the bribes!" she said. "We're not too late to cut short its activity!"

"I don't know about tangling with a demon," Clotho said. "Samurai's teaching me self-defense, but he says it won't work against magic, and a demon can't be killed by mortal means."

"Of course it can!" Atropos said. "Just sprinkle some holy water on it."

Niobe agreed. "And of course we are invulnerable to injury, as an Incarnation. Neither mortal nor demon can shed our blood unless we concur."

They fetched a vial of holy water, then slid down to the senator's residence. As seemed to be customary, the senator had feathered his own nest considerably; it was an elegant estate, with a broad expanse of green lawn, sculptured bushes, and assorted outbuildings surrounding the central mansion.

There was no physical barrier to admission, but a yellow line had been painted around the senator's property. *Magic,* Atropos thought darkly.

Niobe walked on along the walk, knowing that no magic could harm an Incarnation. This was one of the greatest advantages of her prior experience: she could proceed with confidence because she knew her powers. Had there been three new Aspects of Fate, Satan would surely have convinced them that they were physically and magically vulnerable, and gained considerable advantage. Thanatos had mentioned being worked over that way by the Father of Lies, until at last he had realized the truth. Niobe remembered how close Satan had come to convincing her to resign her office, the first time in the Void. There were so many forms a lie could take, and Satan practiced them all!

As she crossed the yellow line, there was an alarm. A cloud of birds took off from the roof of the house and came toward her. They seemed to recognize her as an intruder, for they didn't hesitate; they folded their wings and dived like little hunting-hawks.

Ooo! Clotho thought, mentally ducking. But Niobe merely flung out a loop of thread, and another intersecting it at right angles, defining a sphere about her body. The birds darted into this sphere and abruptly slowed. They lost strength, being unable to penetrate to her body, no matter how hard they flew.

Like the tatami! Clotho thought. She had been picking up martial-arts terms during her association with Samurai. *The mat is soft, but it breaks the fall without injury.*

"Exactly," Niobe murmured. "There is nothing more subtle but certain than the web of Fate. No mortal creature can avoid it or nullify it.'' She walked on, and after a while the birds gave up and returned to their roosts on the roof.

Nice estate, Atropos thought. *I wouldn't mind working in a place like this.*

You're no servant! Clotho thought angrily. *You're a free woman!*

Of course I am, girl—in my mind, Atropos agreed. *But in the real world, I always did have to earn my living and I never was ashamed of that.*

Niobe smiled ruefully. She had been neither liberated nor servant, but had partaken somewhat of both. Unlike Clotho, she had married the man her father chose for her; unlike Atropos, she had never had to go to work for another person. Yet had she rebelled a little more, initially, she might readily have gone Clotho's route—and then would have had to follow Atropos' route. It was still basically a man's world.

But we still spin the threads of life! Clotho put in.

And we still cut them! Atropos added.

''Well, we are Woman,'' Niobe said, smiling. ''We possess the sort of power no man can deny.''

As she approached the house, there was a scream from a tree. It was partly like that of a great bird, partly like that of a shrewish woman, and wholly horrible. Then a great, dark shape rose from the tree, flapping ponderous wings.

That's a damned harpy! Atropos thought.

''Oops,'' Niobe murmured. ''The magic threads won't stop that; it's immortal.''

Maybe I can use self-defense, Clotho thought.

''No good. You could strike it or throw it aside, but its filth would still get on you. It can't actually hurt us, even if we do nothing, but it could make us sickeningly unclean.''

The ugly creature lumbered toward them through the air. It had the face and dugs of an old woman, and the body of a vulture. The close-set, wrinkle-shrouded eyes peered out at Niobe. For a moment the harpy hovered, surprised, a perfumed stench washing down from the wingbeats.

''What are you doing here, Lachesis?'' it demanded. The teeth were long and yellow. ''This is none of your affair, you meddlesome ilk!''

''It *is* my affair, you putrid hen!'' Niobe retorted. ''Now give way, or I'll lasso you with a thread.'' It was a bluff, but she hoped the harpy wouldn't know that.

''No thread of yours will hold me, spider-face!'' the harpy screeched. ''Turn aside, or I'll poop on you!''

It was no empty threat! But Niobe knew she had to reach the senator before the demon from Hell did. She couldn't afford delay.

Give me the body! Atropos thought. *I know how to handle that sort!*

Niobe turned it over. Atropos took form. She strode from the walk, across the lawn to a nearby garden shed.

"Oh, so it's Atropos now!" the harpy screeched, following. "Whatcha think you're doing, you old black slave?"

"I'm going to clear out some trash," Atropos said. She reached the shed and took hold of a weathered broom inside it.

"Go sweep it out, like the stupid stoop-labor hag you are!" the harpy screeched, its stringy hair flinging out as it whirled to fly above Atropos' head. "Here, I'll make you feel right at home by emptying the pot on you!"

"The white folks used to set the dogs on us when we came to clean their houses," Atropos said, hefting the broom. In her competent hands the broom moved almost like a weapon. "Know what we did then?"

"You got chewed up?" the harpy asked with a raucous cackle, following it with the kind of racial epithet no one but a harpy would use.

"We let those bitches have it in the tail!" Atropos said. She swung the broom in a mighty and accurate arc. The bristles caught the harpy in the tail just as it was letting go its poop, and knocked it spinning.

The creature landed claws-up on the ground, screeching piercingly. Atropos, undaunted, strode toward it, broom aloft. The harpy scrambled to its feet and pumped its wings furiously, launching clumsily into the air. It fled, wanting no more of this.

Atropos returned the broom to the shed. "A woman does learn a thing or two in the course of a working life," she muttered with satisfaction.

She certainly did! Niobe resumed the body and proceeded the rest of the way to the house.

As she came to the door, it burst open and the demon itself charged out. It was about seven feet tall, had a hairy body, a long and tufted tail, horns, and a prominent masculine appendage. It pounced on Niobe, wrapping its long arms about her and opening its mouth so wide that the remaining features were squeezed back into oblivion. The huge pointed teeth descended toward her face.

"Oh, come off it!" Niobe snapped, disgusted. "You can't bite me!"

Indeed, the demon's teeth came down to touch her forehead, and stopped. Her flesh was invulnerable.

The demon growled and squeezed her, trying to crush in her ribcage, but the compression had no effect. She was proof against that, too.

Then the demon thought of something else. It brought up its clawed hind feet and raked along the front of her body. Her clothing ripped asunder, but her flesh was unscathed. "You can't even scratch me, you fool. I am proof from physical injury by any creature your infernal master can send."

The demon brought its foot up again, ripping her clothing the rest of the way. Now it hung on her by the sleeves, leaving her front exposed. The demon did not release her, but loosened its grip enough to enable it to glance down at her body. It snorted steam.

Then she realized what it was up to. It intended to rape her!

The thing could probably do it. She was secure from physical injury, but not from emotional injury. As experience had long ago shown her, she could participate in sexual congress; it represented no physical abuse of her body. The demon was stronger than she was; it could hold her for this act.

Now she struggled, but her arms remained captive at her sides. She tried to run, but the demon lifted her off the ground. Its member was growing; in a moment it would do what it intended. At the least, she would be utterly humiliated.

Maybe I can fight it! Clotho thought.

How? Atropos responded. *It's immune to our attack, too; we can't even bite it.*

At least let me try!

Niobe, as desperate as any of them, gave her the body. The demon paused, startled at this change, but did not let her go. Then, perceiving that the captive had grown more attractive, it renewed its effort.

Clotho twisted desperately, managing to swing her body away a little. Then she brought up her right knee in a savage strike at the demon's groin. She scored—but the creature did not even gasp. It was, as Niobe had warned, invulnerable.

My turn! Atropos thought.

Clotho turned the body over to her. Again the demon paused, noting the change, but again it resumed its design after a moment. It changed its grip, to force the body closer, and used its nether claws to grasp the legs and wedge them apart.

"Damn!" Atropos swore. "I thought I could slide away on the thread—but I can't fling out any strand while my arms are pinned!"

The demon grinned. It had known this.

Suddenly Niobe knew what was required. *We're all fools!* she thought. *Give me back the body!*

Atropos gave it to her. Niobe assumed control just as the demon's hot flesh nudged hers.

She shifted to spider form. Suddenly she had eight limbs and was much smaller. Fate could be any size arachnid she wished. She slipped out of the surprised demon's grasp and dropped to the ground.

The demon tried to stomp her. Niobe simply stood there and let the clawed foot come down on her body. When the foot rose again, she remained unhurt. The spider was as impervious as any of the human forms.

She reverted to her natural form. The demon grabbed for her again, but this time she had the vial of holy water out. As the demon's arms clasped her, she put the vial to her own lips and sipped the fluid. "Kiss me, demon," she murmured, putting her face forward.

The demon's head jerked back as it smelled the water, but she pursued it. Her arms now clasped its body, preventing its escape exactly as it had prevented hers before. She jammed her mouth against its mouth and spat out the water.

Kiss of death! Clotho thought.

It was indeed. The demon's flesh melted where the water touched. The lips dissolved and dribbled down the chin, which was rapidly eroded by that fluid. The flesh of the cheeks and tongue puddled, leaving the teeth bare, like those of Thanatos. Then the gums faded away, and the jaw fragmented, and one by one the teeth fell out. The destruction proceeded up the face, eating away the nose and then the eyeballs. Now the thing's brain came into view, smoking at the outer surface as the effect touched it. The whole brain blackened, then went up in smoke.

Now THAT is the way to deal with a rapist! Atropos thought.

After that, the rest of the body went more quickly, dissolving into vapor from top to bottom, like a gross cigar burning. At last all that remained was the noxious cloud of smoke.

But as the smoke dissipated, something moved. The demon's right foot remained; it hadn't dissolved, and had been hidden by the swirling vapors. Her kiss of death had reached its limit.

Niobe reached for her vial again. *What harm can one foot do?* Clotho thought.

"Any part of a demon is bad news," Niobe said tersely. She put some holy water on her fingers and reached for the foot.

The thing scrambled across the step, using its claws to hitch itself forward. It was trying to escape. Niobe sprinkled it by snapping her wet fingers outward, and puffs of smoke erupted where the drops struck. The foot fell off the edge of the step, into the grass. She pursued it, sprinkling more water, but the fragment disappeared.

"I hope I got it all," she muttered.

Can't be more than a toe left, Atropos thought.

"Demons aren't like mortal folk," Niobe said darkly. "Pieces of them can survive."

Can one toe hurt us? Atropos thought. *How?*

Niobe shrugged. "I don't know. But I hope that thing is all gone, now."

With a Tangled Skein

Well, let's see what's inside, Clotho thought. Like Atropos, she did not take the toe of one demon seriously, and Niobe had to admit she was probably a bit paranoid about demons. One had killed Cedric, another had killed Blanche, another had tried to eliminate Luna and Orb, and now one had tried to rape her. She had reason—but what, indeed, could one demon toe do?

Niobe pinned her torn dress together as well as she could, and strengthened it with strategically placed strands of thread. Then she walked on into the senator's house.

A young man stood in the hall. His clothing hung on him, enormously baggy. He seemed oblivious to his surroundings. He was staring at himself in the full-length hall mirror.

She was too late!

She sighed. "Senator?"

He answered without looking at her. "Yes, of course I'll have to resign my office. There would be talk, gossip, perhaps an investigation. I couldn't afford that! I might even have difficulty proving my identity. After all, I've just lost forty years!"

"You're—not staying on?" This surprised her.

"Of course not. It just isn't feasible. I'll have to make a new life. But it's worth it! Forty more years, starting with everything I already know!"

"But don't you owe Satan?"

"He asked no price. It's a gift, no strings."

"But the burden of evil on your soul—"

"No evil attaches to the acceptance of a gift freely proffered, when I provide no political favor in return. And I won't; I'm dropping out of politics."

This amazed her. If the senators weren't staying in office, how could they do Satan's bidding, twenty years hence? It didn't make sense!

At least she had destroyed the demon. There would be no more bribes of restored youth. She extended a thread and slid up it to Purgatory.

They discussed it at the Abode as they rechecked the threads. As they fathomed the changing pattern, the situation came clear. The senators had been bribed indirectly—by being freely given what they most desired. In order to enjoy it, they had to vacate their offices. That meant there would be appointees to complete the terms—and Satan surely controlled those appointments. The new senators would all be young and competent and would give no sign of their true loyalty—until that day, some twenty or so years hence, when Satan required it, to negate Luna's position and give the final victory to Satan. A long-term plan, a real sleeper—but it seemed it was already in place. In a vote as close that one was destined to be, four changed votes would be more than enough. Five, counting the senator who had just been eliminated here.

The new threads were not yet in place, however, for the appointees had not yet been appointed; that process would take a few days. But, search the Tapestry as she might, Niobe could find no way to nullify it. Satan had made his play, and could readily defend it against any effort she might take. The five old senators had already been bribed to vacate and could not be unbribed; youth was already theirs.

"There has to be a way!" Niobe exclaimed. "We can't just give up the world to Satan, even if it *is* twenty years away."

She checked quickly with the other Incarnations, but none of them had an answer. At last she went to the person most concerned: her granddaughter Luna.

Luna took it in stride. She was a truly beautiful woman now, despite the distortion of her hair color. "My father told me that something like this might come up," she said. "He left a message for that occasion."

"My son anticipated this?" Niobe demanded, surprised.

"He was a most accomplished Magician," Luna reminded her. "Perhaps the best of his generation—and he spent the last thirty years of his life researching this very problem. He used to apologize to me for his neglect—but he really didn't neglect me. We were very close."

As Niobe and her son had not been. But that was ancient history. "What is the message?"

Luna fetched a small blue topaz, a pretty but not truly precious stone. She set in on a small shelf before a white screen and turned on a special light. The stone fluoresced, sending a pattern of blue shadows across the screen.

"It's a magic stress on the molecules of the topaz," Luna explained. "I just need to get it in focus and find the right angle; most of the facets are nonsense, but the right one will display the message. The Magician set it up that way so that no one would accidentally read the message before it was time. Premature divulgence would alert Satan, you see." She turned the stone, and the pattern on the screen changed.

She turned it again, and suddenly several lines of fuzzy print appeared on the screen. "Ah—there it is! Now for the focus." She moved the light, and gradually the print clarified; in a moment it would become legible. Then something rolled across the shelf and collided with the topaz. The stone slid out of position, and the image was lost.

"The demon's toe!" Niobe exclaimed. She brought out the vial and dumped the remaining holy water on it. The thing vanished in a puff of smoke.

Luna recovered the stone. "Good thing the creature didn't hurt it," she said. She set it in place, and refocused the beam of light.

Only blank blue showed on the screen. Surprised, Luna turned it to a new facet, but no pattern showed. "It's been erased!" she exclaimed in dismay. "The magic is gone!"

"The demon did it!" Niobe cried. "Its mere evil touch canceled the good magic!"

And we wondered what one toe could do! Atropos thought, chagrined.

Niobe exchanged a stricken glance with her granddaughter. Now they had lost the vital message!

"Is there any backup stone?" Niobe asked after a moment.

"No. None for this occasion. The Magician didn't want it to be obvious—"

"That's what I thought," Niobe said heavily. "Satan must have known or suspected about the stone and given his demon a secondary instruction to erase it when it had the chance. Now it has done so."

"Now it has done so," Luna agreed.

"So now only the Magician knows the message."

"And he is dead."

Niobe embraced the young woman, and they both cried the tears of hopelessness.

Then Niobe straightened, lifting her chin. "But I am an Incarnation! I can go to my son in Purgatory and ask him directly!"

"Yes!' Luna cried, her gray eyes lighting. "My father did not know you would become Fate again! He focused on me."

They embraced and cried again, this time with renewed hope. Then Niobe rode a thread back to Purgatory to seek her son.

But when she checked the computer for the specific location of his soul, she received another shock.

MAGICIAN KAFTAN'S SOUL IS NO LONGER IN PURGATORY, the screen said.

"You mean his penance is finished? He has gone on to Heaven already?"

NO. AN ERROR IN HIS CLASSIFICATION WAS DISCOVERED. HIS DAUGHTER HAD BORROWED SOME OF HIS BURDEN OF EVIL. SHE IS DESTINED FOR HEAVEN, BUT HIS TRUE BALANCE WAS NEGATIVE.

Why would Luna have done a thing like that? Niobe wondered. But she had a more immediate problem. "Negative? Then—"

YOUR SON IS NOW IN HELL.

Niobe stared at the screen in horror. She was sure this was the real information, as she had taken steps to see that none of Satan's illusions interfered this time.

The only person who knew how to nullify Satan's victory—was in Satan's power.

– 15 –

MAZE SQUARED

Back at the Abode, they hashed it over. "We know there is a solution," Niobe said. "We just don't know what it is."

"And chances are, we won't find it on our own," Atropos said. "Maybe, if we were all experienced, we'd know it, but by the time we get experienced enough to know, it'll be too late."

"We're still in Satan's trap," Clotho agreed.

"Not entirely," Niobe said. "If all three of us were new, that might be true; but I did have thirty-eight prior years of experience. I know Satan's power is not complete. There has to be something he's hiding from us."

"The solution!" Clotho exclaimed wryly.

"Too bad we can't go to Hell and ask the Magician what his message was," Atropos said.

Niobe pounced on that. "Maybe we can! Incarnations have special powers!"

They checked with Thanatos, who confirmed it. "I have been there," he said. "But only in spirit. The physical body has to be left behind. All the things there are spirits, but they seem solid, as they do in Purgatory. But Satan wouldn't let you visit anyone there."

"But then how did you go there?"

"I was invited on a tour."

Oh. She knew about that sort of thing. Still—

"Can he stop a mother from visiting her son?" she asked.

All three of them paused at that. *Who would know?* Clotho thought.

"Gaea," Niobe said. "The Green Mother understands everything about human nature and then some."

With a Tangled Skein

They went to Gaea. "Satan cannot stop you, in this instance," she said. "But he will not help you. This represents a conflict between Incarnations, and your chance of success would be half."

"But I *can* do it?" Niobe asked.

"You can cut off your foot, too, but you might not want to." Gaea smiled coldly.

"If I do this—if I go to Hell—I stand to win the salvation of man—or at least enable my granddaughter to. What do I stand to lose?"

"Your soul," Gaea said grimly.

"But I'm an Incarnation! Satan can't touch my soul!"

Gaea shook her head. "You must put your soul on the line to gain entry to Hell. If you win your objective, you keep your soul. But if you fail, your soul is forfeit. Hell is not child's play, Lachesis!"

Niobe sighed. "It certainly isn't!"

Well, that lets that out, Atropos thought. *A good soul locked in Hell—*

"How do I set it up?" Niobe asked.

Don't do it, Lachesis! Clotho thought.

What shall it profit a woman to win the whole world, if she lose her own soul? Atropos thought.

"That's figurative; this is literal," Niobe said. "The whole world *is* on the line, this time."

"You must choose a referee," Gaea said. "To ensure fairness in the proceedings. Otherwise Satan will cheat."

Niobe considered. "How about Mars? He knows how to supervise war—and this is really a battle in the war between Good and Evil."

Gaea nodded. "Excellent choice. Go to him and ask."

"Thank you, Ge."

"Every Incarnation must sooner or later confront Satan," Gaea said. "You did it long ago, in the Void. Now you are doing it again—but the locale is not neutral and the stakes are higher. We shall be watching—but none of us will be able to assist you, once you enter Hell."

"I know." This was, among other things, confirmation that Gaea *had* recognized her, the day of the excursion into the model Hell, and had kept her secret.

"You will leave your body and your two other Aspects behind. If you fail, they will have to choose your replacement—with no soul to exchange. That body will die."

A heavy penalty indeed! Yet, added to the loss of the world, did it matter? She had to make the effort!

"Farewell," Gaea said. "You are a fine woman, Lachesis."

Niobe slid her thread to Mars' castle. This time he was at home. Quickly she explained the situation. "You have courage," Mars said gruffly. "I trust you know that Hell is no picnic."

"I know, but I must go. Will you serve?"

"I will serve. But I can guarantee only that the terms are honored. I cannot help you or advise you in any way. Once you enter Hell, you are on your own."

"But—I have no idea what to expect there!"

"As referee, it is my job to help arrange what to expect," Mars said. He raised his red sword, and it flashed. "Satan!"

Satan appeared. "What the Hell do you want, Mars? A war?"

"Both," Mars agreed, unperturbed. "Lachesis wishes to visit her son, the Magician Kaftan. You may not deny her that."

Satan turned on Niobe. "So you learned of that, you meddling female! But it will cost you your soul."

"The one offer you cannot turn down," Niobe agreed.

"No," Mars said. "She is not buying the visit with her soul. She is putting up her soul as the stake for the game. That is a different matter."

"A different matter," Satan agreed reluctantly. "A technicality."

Already the referee was functioning. That was some technicality!

"We must select the format," Mars said.

"Aerial combat while mounted on firedrakes," Satan said.

"Competitive tapestry weaving," Niobe retorted.

Atropos laughed in her mind.

"Perhaps a compromise," Mars said, smiling grimly. "An event that combines elements of both monsters and threads, illusion and reality. A demon-infested maze."

Satan considered. "Could be. Those are fun."

Niobe also considered. A maze was a bit like a tapestry, with passages instead of threads. Demons were monsters—but should not be able to hurt her. If, as it seemed, she had to navigate some sort of challenge course in Hell to reach her son, this might be the best type for her. But—"Threads? Illusion?"

"An illusion-maze is less challenging, physically," Mars said. "But more challenging, intellectually."

Niobe knew herself to be no genius, but she did have a flair with the weaving of intricate threads. "That sounds good," she agreed tentatively.

"No way," Satan said.

"Superimposed on a physical maze," Mars said. "Shall we say, one hundred illusions of your choice—and one hundred reality-threads for her? With some of the properties of her normal threads, so she can travel expeditiously—"

"Limited," Satan said. "I don't want her traveling all over Hell."

"Limited," Mars agreed. "The maze so constituted that the best course can be traversed by fewer than fifty threads, the worst by more than one hundred fifty threads, but centered on one hundred?"

"A fifty-fifty chance," Satan agreed. "But *I* set up the maze, and choose all the configurations."

"And I verify the balance and call the fouls," Mars said. "I will inspect the maze before she enters, and there will be no changes after she enters."

"Done," Satan said.

They looked at Niobe. She wasn't sure she trusted what those two males might agree was fair. But she knew Mars would not betray her, and it seemed to be the best compromise she could get. "Very well."

They cleared the remaining details. Then Niobe sat back in a chair, waited a moment, and stood—and left her body behind. She was in spirit form!

She turned and reached out to touch her physical hand. As she did so, she felt the other two Aspects. *Give 'em Hell, girl!* Atropos thought. *Find your son!* Clotho thought. Both sent the emotion of support and best wishes.

I shall! she replied.

She turned again. Satan stood directly before her, while Mars watched from the side. "Come to Me, fool!" Satan said, and laughed.

She stepped into him—and discovered he was a kind of door. She passed through it and found herself in Hell.

Hell was a crystalline place. Bright hexagonal facets surrounded her, red and green and blue—all colors, each facet her own height. She stood on another, the same size.

She turned to look back the way she had come. There was only another facet there, highly polished, so that she saw her own reflection clearly.

She looked exactly as she had in life, in her physical body: a nondescript, middle-aged woman whose once-flowing buckwheat-honey hair was now cut to a less-flattering length, and the honey seemed soiled. Her dress was a drab gray, and not well-fitted. That last wasn't really carelessness; if the dress fitted better, it would show up the inadequacies of her present figure all too clearly. Ah, for the flesh of youth! She could understand how the old senators had found the lure of renewed youth to be irresistible.

The irony was, she had kept her youthful appearance for an extra thirty-eight years, and then given it up. And would do so again, for Pacian. And would have given everything up, for Cedric. She had understood Clotho exactly, when the girl had yielded "everything!" to Samurai. When a woman loved a man—

But now she had to find her son. She checked her left hand: it clasped a handful of measured threads. She was not Lachesis any more; she could not travel to the ends of the world. She was merely

—226—

Niobe, and every thread she used would be one thread lost. She had to use them well; though the worst-case route through the maze would require over 150 threads, she had only 100. Her mission and her soul would be forfeit if she used them all without finding her son.

Well, this was a puzzle, certainly. She reached out to rap a knuckle on a blue facet. The sound rang, setting up a sympathetic tintinnabulation throughout the region. It was a rather pretty sound, but it didn't get her through the maze.

She saw that one hexagon was not a facet, but an open space. She stepped through it, onto the golden floor tile there—

Her foot passed right through the floor. There was nothing there. With a scream she fell down past several hexagonal levels, until she fetched up against another golden tile. She was unhurt—but in a hole, literally.

There was a puff of vapor at her hand. She looked—and saw the remains of one of her threads curling as it dissolved into smoke. That fall had not hurt her physically, for a spirit could not be injured that way, but it had cost her a thread. That was one of the details of this game. Now she had ninety-nine threads left, and she had exposed the first illusion.

She tapped the surfaces about her. All were solid. She was in a nether chamber with no ready exit. The slick facets offered no purchase for her fingers; she could not climb out.

She sighed. She tucked her threads carefully into a pocket, saving out one. She flung that upward.

Now she sailed up, following the thread's course, much as she did as an Aspect of Fate. In a moment she was back at her original level, facing the golden floor panel. An illusion—but she had expended two of her precious threads in making the discovery and recovery. Two for one; Satan had gained one on her.

She looked at the golden tile. It still looked real. She would not be fooled again by it, of course, so in that sense it had been expended—but how much better it would have been to identify it without falling through it! Then she would have been one ahead, having expended no threads to identify one of the hundred illusions.

She felt at the edge of the illusion. She found a small ledge; part of the golden tile was real. She could walk on that to get through. There had to be a way through the maze; that was part of the deal. She had only to move carefully, to avoid falling for any more tricks.

But she could not get through without using close to fifty of her threads. That meant that she couldn't simply close her eyes and feel her way the full length of it. There would be illusions she had to penetrate before trusting her body to them, and climbs she had to make regardless of illusion. She could not hoard her threads; she would not get through that way.

With a Tangled Skein

She completed her circuit of the golden illusion and entered a new chamber. This one had a solid floor—but no other exit. She looked up and saw a high green ledge, out of reach. Evidently that was the route. Not an illusion, just one of the thread-requiring avenues.

She brought out another thread and flung it at the ledge. In a moment she slid up it, landing neatly on the green. Good enough.

Except that it turned out to be a dead end.

She sighed again. She had been suckered into using another thread, unnecessarily.

She squatted, touching the edge of the ledge. It was glassy smooth. She stood and scraped the sole of one shoe across it. Then she tested it with her finger again.

Yes—there was faint scratching. The material was not super-hard. It could be abraded.

She scuffed it some more, then lay down. She nudged her legs over the edge, sidewise. She spread her fingers against the roughened surface. The slope beyond the edge was not vertical; there were no perfect right angles in this place, just the obtuse angles of the hexagons. Her body was sliding down at about a forty-five-degree angle—she wasn't sure what it was for a hexagon, but that was what it felt like. Maybe fifty degrees. Her fingers had some purchase on the roughened level face.

When enough of her body was on the sloping face, it swung down. Her fingers were unable to hold; she slid off the surface and dropped to the floor beneath. But it was not as long a fall as the one she had suffered before, and she was better prepared for it. She landed neatly on her feet.

She watched the threads in her pocket, but there was no puff of smoke-vapor. She had made it down without sacrificing another thread! She had not "killed" herself this time.

But it was a minor victory, for she had now expended three threads and discovered only one illusion. She would have to do better than that.

She checked the golden floor panel again. The ledge continued around the other side—and there was another open panel. Had she skirted it the other way, she would have found it, and saved herself the dead end.

Well, the bad break had taught her a lesson or two; not to assume a given route was the only one, and not to expend a thread on a route just because the route was there.

She got into the new chamber. This one had two other exits; which should she take? Both went far enough so that she could not tell which was a dead end.

She shrugged and took the one to the left. It looped around to the right, over and under crystalline formations of differing sizes—it seemed there was nothing sacred—sacred, here in Hell?—about the full-size ones. In due course it debouched back into the chamber she had left.

She went around again, verifying every surface. No way out. She had walked into another dead end, in effect.

She went back to the golden tile, and the rest of the way around it. Now she was back to her starting point, three threads gone—and she had made no progress through the maze!

Then she had a bright thought. She returned to the golden tile, got down on her belly, and put her right arm through it. She felt for the surfaces below.

All in reach were solid. She got up, walked to the far side, and lay down again. She reached—and discovered that there was an open panel directly beneath her.

She braced her feet as well as she could against the edge-surfaces and hunched her body forward over the golden panel until she could put her head through the illusion. She peered under.

Sure enough: there was an opening. There was her true exit! The illusion covered a dead-end hole—*and* the way through. She had fallen right by it, and passed it again on the way back up. Satan was certainly a cunning devil!

She crawled around, letting her body down. Here she was able to get a better grip on the edge of the panel—but she didn't trust it. She was no muscular man, she was a weak-fleshed woman.

She sighed a third time. Then she brought out another thread and flung it toward the hole.

Her body followed. Now she was perched at the edge of a hexagonal tunnel. It sloped sharply down—and she could not hold her position. She felt herself sliding. She tried to spread her legs and brace her feet against the sides, but this was ineffective. She was bound for the end of this tunnel—wherever it might lead—unless she expended yet another thread. She decided to risk the slide.

She slid into a new aspect of the maze. She landed in a chamber with transparent walls, and behind those walls were demons in horrendous shapes. There were five exits from the chamber—but each was guarded by a monster. How could she get through?

Obviously at least one of the monsters was illusion, so she could pass through it without getting "killed." Because there had to be a route through, and she couldn't pass a real monster.

She approached the tiger-headed man at the nearest exit and flung a thread at him. He disappeared. Victory—she had found the route on the first try!

She walked into the passage. It turned at right angles, then turned again, in the manner of the kind of maze that was printed on paper.

She moved along it cautiously, so as not to fall through an illusion-section of floor, but the floor was opaque and solid.

She came to a division. Which should she take, the left or the right? It didn't seem to matter, as neither would cost her a thread. She took the left.

That led to a small chamber containing a man-headed tiger—the reverse of the prior monster. She tossed a thread at it.

The thread shriveled and puffed into vapor—but the monster remained. This one was real!

"Come here, morsel!" the tigerman cried. "You look good enough to chomp!"

She backed away and retreated to the other part of the fork. That one led her to a man-headed wolf. It paced restlessly, watching her.

She flung a thread—and the monster evaporated with the thread. Another illusion. The way was clear.

But she paused. She had just expended two threads to uncover one illusion. At that rate, she would use up all her threads before the illusions gave out. Satan was winning!

But she knew that if she walked blithely into a monster and it was real, it would chomp her. That should not hurt her physically, as she was here only in spirit, but by the laws of the maze it would cost her double: two threads. Being "killed" by a monster was like taking a fall, then having to thread out of the hole. So it paid her to verify a monster before stepping within its range.

Or did it? If she had an even chance that a given monster was real, then she could assume that half of them would tag her. Double the threads—and she lost the same number as if she had checked all the monsters. No loss—but no gain. She might as well use the threads.

This bothered her. There seemed to be no way other than sheer chance to beat Satan, and the chances were against her. She had—she checked the count—used up four threads and exposed one illusion in the crystal section of the maze; she had used three more threads and exposed two more illusions here. That was a cumulative score of seven threads and three illusions. Yet her chances of getting through the maze were supposed to be even. She was definitely falling behind.

Well, she had been checking every monster. The problem was that there could be ten times as many real ones as illusory ones. She could use up all her threads without getting anywhere, that way! There had to be a better way—but what was it?

She set her jaw. Obviously, checking every monster was a losing strategy. So she would check none of them. Had she followed that course so far, she would have been chomped by the tigerman, and lost two threads—but that was less than the three she had used checking every monster.

She proceeded on down the passage. She came to a huge human head from which five human legs sprouted. No torso. A monster indeed! She walked right into it.

The thing rolled at her, each foot touching the floor in turn—and kicking her when it arrived. "Ooo!" she howled as she got kicked in the knee. Then the next foot caught her in the face. Her nose exploded in pain, and she fell down. Then the monster was all over, tromping her to death.

It wasn't death, of course. But it felt like it. In due course, satisfied, the foot-face withdrew, and she dragged herself back to her feet. The pain abated, and she discovered that neither her nose nor her limbs were broken. She was uninjured, physically. The blows had hurt terribly, but caused no lasting damage. She had been wrong about the discomfort of getting chomped!

Two more threads were gone. Score: nine to three, in favor of Satan.

And she couldn't pass this alcove. In fact, this whole passage had been a mistake. It was a dead end, blocked by monsters.

So much for her new strategy. She could have saved herself one thread and some pain by testing the monster for illusion.

She made her way back to the original chamber of this section. There were the four other exits with their guardians.

She eyed the monsters. One was a bird with the head of a fox; another was a woman-headed snake; another was a man's head with two muscular arms growing where the ears should be; the last was a pig-headed dog. This was Hell, all right! The demons hewed to no normal Earthly shapes.

Four chances. She could either use four more of her precious threads to verify them, or chance walking through them—with the odds even that it would cost her four threads anyway to find the true passage. If it *was* the true passage; the first had not been.

This just wouldn't do! She needed a strategy of approach, not only to make her way through, but to do it economically enough to get ahead on threads. She needed to expunge two illusions for every thread, instead of the other way around. Blundering through by blind chance simply wasn't going to accomplish that.

Well, she did have time. There was no time limit on the maze; she was to continue until she either won through to her son or lost her soul. If she hesitated forever, she would never escape Hell—or save Luna's position. Her timing was her own.

There had to be some key she had overlooked. How she wished she had Cedric's ready intelligence, or her son's! Obviously sheer chance was not going to get her through; only an appropriate strategy would do that. But *what* strategy?

She played her mind over it, knowing there had to be something. Satan might have deceived her about the odds, but Mars would not have. She had at least an even chance—if she could only figure it out.

Slowly it came to her. She had to ration her threads—but Satan had to do the same for his illusions. Each was limited to one hundred. If she didn't want to throw away threads, he didn't want to throw away illusions. Each of them had to calculate a strategy to make the assets count most. But while she could change a nonproductive course, Satan could not; he had set up the maze at the outset, and could not change it. It stood to reason that wherever Satan didn't *need* an illusion, he wouldn't use it. He had to use some in key places, because otherwise she would be able to thread the maze simply by avoiding visible monsters. An illusion-monster could seem to block off the one route through, shunting her into real monsters and trouble.

Here were five exits. It would make no sense to have several illusions down one passage—if the start of it was blocked by a real monster. She couldn't pass the monster, so would never have a chance to be fooled by the illusions. The illusions had to come early— or along the real path.

All five of the monsters at this junction had to be illusions. That was the only pattern that made sense. No wonder she had verified the first illusion she had challenged, here! She could have saved the thread.

Furthermore, since Satan's illusions were limited, there were only so many he could spare for any one segment of the maze. She had discovered only one in the crystal section, strategically situated; that might be all there was there. Perhaps nine of ten monsters would be real, because here in Hell monsters were relatively cheap. In the mortal world, illusions were cheaper than demons, but here in Hell it was the other way around. So the chances were that after the beginning of any passage, most of the monsters would be real. If a passage divided into ten alternate routes, nine of them would be blocked by real monsters, with only the one that actually led somewhere having an illusion. That would give her nine chances to lose threads, regardless whether she gambled or tested. That was why she had been falling behind; she had not perceived the strategy of Satan.

That being the case, what she needed to do was figure out the pattern of the overall maze, and select the route that was *most likely* to have illusions. The wrong routes would be blocked mostly by real monsters.

But how could she analyze the maze when she couldn't see it as a whole? The walls might be of glass, but that gave her no notion of the overall layout. She could see many monsters, but could not make out the convoluted channels of the maze.

She looked up, and saw that one tower rose above the rest. Most of the maze seemed to be open, and the tops of the walls, in addition to being too high for her to reach, looked knife-sharp; she could not climb them. The tower sported a short diving board. Into what was she expected to dive, from there? The illusion of a lake? She knew she couldn't risk that; it would cost her at least two threads.

But the tower was high. From it, she might be able to see the layout of the puzzle as a whole. If so, that would be a useful spot to reach, even if it was not the correct route.

She selected the passage she deemed most likely to lead to the tower and walked through the monster that guarded it, the woman-headed snake. The monster hissed at her, but could not touch her; it was, as she had surmised, illusion. She had saved herself a thread; in fact, she had saved four, for all these monsters had to be illusion. Just by pausing for thought, she had brought the running score up to nine to seven, for once she had identified an illusion she didn't have to waste a thread on it. These illusions were fixed in place; they could not follow her about. She could check off any she was sure of, and the more she could discover by deduction, the better off she was. She found herself shivering with release of tension; by bracing the monster "blind" she had not only saved her threads but also had confirmed her analysis. Had she been wrong . . .

Now there was a snake-headed woman, the inverse of the prior monster, blocking the passage. Since there was no alternate route, she knew this was illusion. Satan wanted her to be able to navigate this route, after wasting a thread, perhaps hoping she would indeed dive off the tower. She braced herself again and marched through the monster: illusion number eight.

She came to a coiled staircase. That fitted in with the serpentine theme. She had to admit that Satan had a certain artistic sense. But of course all art could be considered a form of lie, because it differed from reality; that was certainly in the bailiwick of the Father of Lies.

She mounted the stair, testing each step for illusion so as not to fall through; that required no threads. Soon she emerged at the top of the tower. It was enclosed by glass that distorted the view of the surroundings; she had to go out onto the diving board to see clearly.

She went out—and was attacked by a siege of acrophobia. The board was about fifteen feet above the top of the walls of the maze, and twenty-five feet above the ground. It gave slightly under her weight and she shivered. She had never been a confident diver and was less so now. She remembered that she had been bolder when crossing the seeming chasm in the Hall of the Mountain King, so maybe her courage had eroded with age. She got down on her hands and knees and crawled to the end and peered over.

There was a clearing below. Five giant cushions sat in it, each one so fluffy that it was obvious that she could jump down on it, even from this height, and not get hurt. But some might be illusion, so she couldn't risk it without using at least one thread.

Also, she realized, it could be a trap; she might locate a good cushion, land safely on it, and go on—only to discover this was a dead-end path. Then how could she return to the starting point? She could see that there was no access to the base of the tower from that yard. The jump was one-way.

She could use a thread to rise back to the diving board, of course—but that would put her further behind. Every thread she used that didn't dispel an illusion was a loss for her.

However, she had not come to jump, only to look. She had expended no threads on this path, so was gaining. She decided to assume that two of the five cushions were illusions, the two closest; if she had used her threads to verify her landing, it would have cost her several more to explore this dead end. She was learning to figure the odds.

Now she concentrated on the rest of the maze. It was not as large as it had seemed from below; the convolutions made the distance seem greater. She traced the path of the first passage she had tried, to make sure she knew what she was doing; then she traced the route to the tower. Good enough; she was able to see them clearly from here.

She traced the other three routes very carefully. All of them had several splits, but most of the splits dead-ended immediately after passing monsters. Obviously they were intended to seem to go on, so she would challenge the monster—and waste either one or two threads. One route looped back into the other, so that she might win through it—and find herself back at the starting point, perhaps several threads poorer. But one route wound its tortuous way all around the maze, with three separate splits and rejoinings, and finally exited to a hole in an opaque wall. That was evidently the one. There were a total of thirteen monsters along it. She concluded that all but three were illusions, the three being used to block one arm of each split. There was no way to tell which of each pair of monsters was real—but it didn't matter. The ratio now favored her. She needed to test only in the splits, using three threads, and she would pass ten illusions. Assuming she had correctly analyzed the two cushion illusions, that would put her running score at twelve to twenty. Twelve threads for twenty illusions—and perhaps other illusions bypassed in the other passages. *That* was the kind of ratio she liked!

She memorized the route, then backed off the board. She got to her feet in the tower and descended, pleased with herself. If she had calculated correctly, she was now winning the game.

The passage she wanted was guarded by the head with the muscular arms. Was that symbolic? A muscular head, meaning good thinking. Symbols were a form of art, and Satan had an insidious sense of humor; it was possible.

She walked through the illusion and into the passage. The next monster was a cat with chicken's legs; she walked through it too. She reached the first split, took the left fork, and threw a thread at the hawk-headed dog that guarded it. The creature screeched and charged her; it was real. She retreated, took the other fork, and marched through the headless man whose face was on his belly.

On the next split she caught the illusion the first time. It really didn't matter; one thread got her through regardless, now that she knew how to play it. She completed the course without difficulty and came at last to the opaque wall. She had done it! Her mind had enabled her to prevail.

She walked through the doorway in the wall. In a moment she came to a blank barrier—but it was an illusion. She stepped through it—

First one foot, then the other landed on something that rose up to fasten about her ankle. Startled, she looked down and discovered she was on skis. They started to move. She had skied as a child, so knew how to keep her balance and guide herself down a snowy slope—but that had been seventy-five years ago. The last thing she had expected to encounter in Hell was skiing! Still, she *had* known it was possible.

She was picking up speed. She saw two ski poles standing upright on either side of the track. She reached out and grabbed them. Evidently Mars had ensured fair play for this aspect of the challenge; she had the necessary equipment.

She shot out of the chamber. She was on a high mountain, on a steep slope, accelerating. Below her were diverging tracks in the snow, marked by thin columns of fire. One track led to a towering ski jump, another to a broad and ice-covered lake.

She skewed into the third track, which seemed to be a slalom: a twisting path between the firepoles. She was no slalom expert, but this seemed a better bet than the others.

She passed the first pole and made a wide turn around it, almost losing her balance. She was way out of form and she lacked the lithe muscles of youth. Who ever heard of a middle-aged woman doing the slalom?

She overcorrected and brushed by the second pole, touching it. There was a sizzle as it burned her elbow; her clothing caught fire, and the pain was sharp. She brought her other hand about to slap out the flame—and the ski pole whirled around, upsetting her balance, and she spun out of control on the skis. She went right through a firepole; this time her face smarted from the burn, and her hair caught fire.

She flung aside the ski poles and dived into the snow, trying to douse her blazing head. The skis twisted sidewise, and her dive became a preposterous belly flop. The snow was hard, almost like ice dusted by a powdery layer. Now she was sliding on her stomach down the slope, completely out of control. One leg was twisted; she felt the pain shooting along it.

Then she was rolling, her skis tearing free along with one shoe, leaving the foot bare. The slope steepened, then became a dropoff. She fell—

Into the lake. The ice cracked, and she plunged under it, immersed in the shockingly cold water. She tried to swim up to the surface, but she had drifted under the unbroken section of the ice and banged her head on it from below. She inhaled to scream—and sucked in water.

Her consciousness was fading, but she focused on one thing: the threads. She clutched out a thread and flung it as well as she could.

Suddenly she was moving upward. She passed through the ice without breaking it and landed on her feet on the surface. She had managed to avoid drowning, thanks to the magic.

She looked about her. The ice supported her weight, in this region. To the side was a single ski that had followed her down; the other seemed to be lost in the snow of the slope. One ski pole floated in the open water where she had broken through. Her bare foot was freezing. She was here in spirit only, but only her intellect knew the difference; she felt every bit of it. Now she had the proof that those who suffered in Hell really did suffer!

She looked at her collection of threads. It had shrunk significantly. She had destroyed herself several times over, in the course of that spill! She was well behind on the running score now.

She limped across the ice, coughing out what remained of the water she had tried to breathe. She picked up the lone ski and found it was the wrong one; it was for the left foot, while her right foot needed the shoe. Of course her right foot was the wrenched one, so skiing on it might be awkward anyway. But she used the ski as a clumsy pole to brace against, and started dragging herself up the nearest slope that could be navigated. She would have to go the long way around, to get above the dropoff and find the other ski with her shoe, and it wasn't going to be pleasant, but she had no choice.

She slogged up. Her bare foot hurt in the snow, but soon it became numb—which was no good sign. She tried to hurry, but her left leg also had been wrenched, it was now apparent, and haste was impossible. To make things worse, a wind was coming up, cutting cruelly through her inadequate clothing.

She was never going to make it this way! She sighed, and fumbled out another thread. She flung it up at the top of the dropoff, and followed it up. She had just saved herself perhaps half an hour of slogging—but lost yet another thread.

A white figure loomed before her. It was a snowman!

"Damn it!" she swore. She swung the ski at the monster.

It passed right through without resistance. Niobe spun around and fell to the ground, a victim of her own inertia. An illusion!

She picked herself up and plowed on until she came to the slide-marks of her own descent. These she followed up until she spied the other ski, with her shoe attached. She hurried toward it—and dropped into an illusion-covered hole.

It was only an ice-pocket, but it cost her two threads. She got out and proceeded on to the ski, where she detached her shoe, dumped out the snow, and put it on. The stocking was gone. It hardly mattered; her whole leg now felt like a dead stick.

Where to, now? She had to find her way out of this frozen mess!

She decided that the slalom remained her best chance. She tracked over to it and tramped down its slope. She no longer had any trouble keeping the course; what were impossibly tight turns at speed on skis were quite simple on foot. If she had been smart, she would have gotten off the skis at the outset and walked down. She was not on show for skiing here; she just wanted to cover the course. The whole ski-setup was probably a diversion; she had allowed Satan to dictate the mode of play, and naturally this had led to disaster.

She paused to warm herself at a firepole, but it was an illusion. How fiendishly clever: the early poles were real, so that they had burned her, while some key later ones were illusion; probably she could have skied down the course successfully if she had known which firepoles to ignore. This one blocked the direct course, so that the skier had to make a wide and dangerous turn to avoid it.

She went to the next pole, which was real, and came close to it. But it wasn't effective as a heater; the fire was too hot up close, and inadequate at a distance. She needed a warm ambience, not a sharply defined line-source. She dragged herself on along the track.

There was a termination station at the foot of the mountain. A ski lift was there, but it didn't go up the slope she had descended. Evidently it led to the next aspect of the maze.

She was too cold and tired to debate the merits properly. She climbed into the seat. It was comfortable; it was a blessing to get off her feet. She buckled the safety harness. Imagine that: a concern for safety in Hell!

The thing began to move. It hoisted itself into the air, hanging below its line, and proceeded slowly across the terrain.

Now she counted her remaining threads. There were just twenty. Sixty-eight threads she had lost in that fiasco! That seemed an impossible number—but Mars would not have let her be cheated. Probably some had fallen out of her pocket during her slide down the mountain, and some had been washed away by the water. How would she ever catch up now?

But she reminded herself that she didn't have to catch up; she just had to make it through the maze. If she used her mind henceforth, she could still do it. She had to believe that.

How much more of the maze remained? She didn't know. But whatever it was, she would negotiate it.

She reached down to chafe her cold leg. Some sensation was returning. That was good and bad; good because it indicated recovery, bad because it hurt. But that would pass; she had been tromped to death, as it were, by the headfoot monster, but had recovered immediately. It seemed it took longer to recover from sixty-eight threads worth of mischief than from two threads worth. But she *would* recover.

The lift entered a tunnel. Light flared—and she saw she was in a kind of factory. The chairs of the lift moved among robots that used tools to adjust things. Obviously if she were in the correct spot, she would get adjusted—and that would not be at all comfortable. She had to find a clear route through.

The line overhead divided. She shifted her weight to the right, and the seat took the right line. She could control her travel, to some extent.

What she evidently could not do was pause in her progress. The seat kept moving forward at its measured pace. That provided her inadequate time to decide. The thing would not go backward, which meant she was committed to whatever decision she made. She could not change her mind and withdraw. She might already have made the wrong choice!

A robot loomed ahead. It had a roughly humanoid head-box and a pair of articulated metal arms. One terminated in a giant pincers, the other in a sharp knife. Evidently the robot was intended to hold and slice, trimming off excess material from the subject. If she was the subject, she could lose some flesh. Unless the robot was illusion.

She flung a thread at it. The thread struck the robot and vaporized. The robot remained. So much for that faint hope.

Niobe hastily unbuckled her belt and jumped out of the chair. She fell to the floor of the foot-pedestal of the robot. Vapor wafted up; that fall had cost her another thread. This was an ongoing disaster! She was sure she couldn't proceed through the maze unless she rode the lift—and this was the wrong line.

But she didn't want to depend on chance at all. She had to figure out the pattern, as she had in the maze-and-monster section. Then she could get through with minimal losses.

She stood and looked at the towering robot. How could she analyze *this* pattern? She couldn't even *see* it from below—and she perceived no way to get above it. Not for a weak middle-aged woman.

She had to use her mind, because her body was inadequate. She sat at the base of the robot and pondered, while the seats of the lift trundled on over her head. Assume that she had to ride the lift to get through and that her options were limited once she was on her way. She could not fathom the overall pattern, so would have to guess. Could she win through? She had lost what little faith she had in luck, here in Hell.

What about guile? Satan was the master of guile; could he fall victim to his own technique? He had done so in the Luna-Orb matter, yet—

Then she had it. If this failed—well, she probably would have lost anyway. If this succeeded, she might win through.

She tossed a thread toward the robot's shoulder, and in a moment she was there, clinging to her precarious perch. She took hold of the robot's head and yanked. The covering came off; it was a cup-shaped cap with apertures for the eye lenses. Underneath were the gears used to rotate the head on the neck. She didn't bother with them; all she needed was the helmet. And maybe an arm.

She set the helmet-cap on her own head. It reeked of oil and fit quite loosely, but she was able to see out of the lens apertures. She grabbed for an arm.

The robot felt the contact, or perhaps the pressure on the extremity. The gears spun in the head, and the lenses swiveled to cover the arm. Then the hinge-elbow flexed, and the arm folded back on itself.

She grabbed it and pulled. It froze in place, and did not move. All of her strength could not budge it.

So much for that. She would have to settle for the helmet. She hoped it would suffice.

She watched the seats of the lift as they passed. When a suitable one approached, she threw a thread at it and followed the thread onto the seat. Quickly she settled herself and fastened the belt.

The robot reached for her. "Uh-uh!" she exclaimed, facing it with her eye-slits. Her voice reverberated in her helmet. "I'm a testing robot. Clank-clank!"

The robot hesitated, its head-gears spinning as its gaze followed the motion of her seat, almost as if the gears were brains in operation. By the time the machine made up its mind, she was beyond it.

The line diverged again. She picked her course, and moved on to the next robot. "Clank! Clank!" she cried again in the helmet. Again the robot hesitated, its program not quite covering this, and again she got through. It was working!

Unfortunately for her, this line was not the correct one; it dead-ended. It terminated in a station that went nowhere. The seats turned over, folded up, and followed in a line leading back to the other side of the factory; no way to ride farther. But nearby a line seemed to be going somewhere. She used a thread to reach it—and passed through it, crashing on the floor. It was an illusion!

She had to use yet another thread to reach another line. This one was real—but it too dead-ended.

She kept trying. At last she made it to a line that went somewhere. A robot reached for her; she warned it off—and it kept coming. It had not been deceived by the helmet, and she had no time to scramble free! She screamed as the pincers took hold of her—and passed through her body harmlessly. It was another illusion!

That meant she was back on track. She rode this line to the true terminus: a walk that led out of the factory. She removed her helmet and surveyed her situation. Her frozen leg had thawed and was serviceable, but she had only five threads left. She didn't know how far she still had to go, or how many illusions remained. But she was sure that, one way or another, she was near the end.

– 16 –

ANSWERS

Outside the factory was another hall. She walked cautiously along it, alert for tricks. There seemed to be none. Soon she came to an intersection with a hall at right angles. In the center, mounted on a base, was a fancy plaque. She approached this and looked at it. It said: WELCOME TO THE FINAL SERIES OF CHALLENGES. THREADS REMAINING: 5. ILLUSIONS REMAINING: 10.

She considered this. Was it genuine, or a trick by Satan? Certainly it had her threads correctly listed; if the illusions were also correct, then she was much closer than she had supposed. She could still win this contest!

But it could be a plant, intended to deceive her. Should she use a thread on it to verify its accuracy? No, that would be foolish. If it was a lie, it should be a complete lie—and obviously it wasn't. Better just to assume it was correct and make sure she wasted no more threads. She would count off the remaining illusions, because, once that total reached zero, she would know she had won. But she would not trust it too far, because, if the plaque were a lie, it could cause her to think she had eliminated the last illusion when she had not—and that last illusion could wipe her out. But probably Mars would not have allowed Satan to volunteer false information, because there should, after all, be a distinction between illusion and outright lying.

She pondered, then turned right—and discovered a dead end. She felt along the walls, floor and ceiling, but all were solid. No exit here.

She tried the left hall, but this, too, was a dead end. So she went straight ahead—and found a third dead end. None of the passages went anywhere.

She stood by the plaque and pondered. Could the message be a fake, not in its accounting of threads and illusions, but in its implication that the route was here when it was not? So that she would waste her few remaining threads looking for what did not exist? What a fiendish trap!

She walked around the plaque—and saw that there were words printed on its back. DO YOU YIELD?

Satan's humor, all right! "No, I don't!" she exclaimed.

That plaque could be here to make her think it was a lie, so that she would write off this annex—when it was the correct route. She had to make absolutely sure it was not, before she gave up on it.

She explored the halls again. It occurred to her that an illusion did not have to be merely sight; it could be sound or touch too. Some of the illusion-monsters had roared. There might be an exit she couldn't find because her hands missed it as readily as her eye did. In that case she would have to use a thread—which would leave it at four threads, nine illusions. She couldn't afford to trade off one for one. Not now.

She discovered a slanting connecting passage between the straight-ahead hall and the left hall, making the overall configuration of passages resemble the closed figure 4. Why should that extra passage exist, when it was easy enough to go from one hall to another via the center? About all it did was make it possible to walk down every hall without having to double back.

Something nagged at her. Some figures had to be "solved" by tracing them without doubling back. There were some traffic patterns in large cities like that, where three right turns substituted for one illegal left turn. Could this be one such?

She returned to her starting point, at the base of the 4, then resolutely marched forward. She proceeded past the plaque to the apex, then turned sharp left. She followed the slant down, then turned sharply left again. She walked past the plaque, into the end of the 4—and now the passage opened out into a cave. She had penetrated the illusion, without using a thread. Two left turns had unraveled what one right turn could not.

Now she saw a straight path leading like a pier into a deep black pool. The path widened, forming a kind of island in the center of the pool—and on that island a dragon. The path continued on beyond the dragon, to terminate in a blank wall.

Obviously she had to pass the dragon to get through. But through to what? There was no exit there!

Ah, but there had to be! Satan had nine illusions left; he must have covered the exit through the wall with illusion, and set a genuine dragon to guard it. Most of the prior illusions had been of monsters, guarding real passages; this one was the other way around. She could probably penetrate the illusion, once she got by the dragon; she didn't need to use any thread here.

But how could she get by the dragon?

Well, the dragon could be illusion too. But if she walked into it, and it was real, she would lose two precious threads and still not be past. That was hardly worth the risk. It would be better to verify it with one thread—

No, she had a better notion. She approached as close as she dared and threw the helmet at it. The metal bounced off the dragon's scaled side and rolled into the water with a splash. The dragon snorted fire. It was certainly real.

She looked to the sides. There was a ledge just above water-level beyond the dragon; it curved around to either side, approaching the path on which she stood within eight feet before terminating.

She sighed. A man might have leaped across; she had no such hope. She had to find another way.

She saw that there were vines hanging from the ceiling, but they looked insubstantial. She took hold of one and jerked; it broke near the top and came tumbling down. There were some that looked strong enough to bear her weight, but they were dangling tantalizingly out of reach.

There seemed to be no other avenue, unless she went back to the figure-4 annex, which she would only do as a last, *last* resort. There had to be a way; she just had to find it.

She found it. She yanked down another weak vine, bunched it and tied it in a rough knot. Then she tied that knot to another hanging vine. Then she swung the knot across to one of the more substantial vines. After several tries she was able to entangle that larger vine and draw it over to her, using the weak vine. Now she had hold of the one she wanted.

She hauled at it with increasing vigor. It held; it was firmly anchored and it was strong enough to take her weight.

She held on tightly, drew back, then ran to the edge of the water. She leaped at the margin, clung for dear life, and swung across to the other path. Something flashed below her in the water as she passed, like a huge shark. She landed heavily but adequately, and the vine swung back behind. It might have been pitiful as a gymnastic feat, but she was across. She was glad she had not tried to swim.

She made her way along the narrow path, her right hand brushing along the wall. The dragon watched her, but could not reach her.

Where the straight path intersected the current one, she found the exit; it was indeed illusion-covered. She stepped through cautiously, alert for a pitfall, but there was none. She was through—and she still had five threads, with eight illusions remaining, if the plaque was to be believed. She remained behind, but her ingenuity had enabled her to gain.

She came into a broad cavern with a wide river running through, reminiscent of one she had encountered in the Hall of the Mountain King. Perhaps Satan had borrowed the concept. If so, she knew how to cross.

But it was not the same. There was— no mesh fence in this river, and no sign advertising it as Lethe. Of course it could still *be* Lethe, as that was one of the rivers of Hell, so she would treat it with caution. There were fish in it; when she dipped her finger in, three horrendously-toothed little monsters converged. One leaped as she drew her hand quickly away; the fish's teeth clacked in midair where her hand had been, before it splashed back down. There would be no swimming in this river!

There was a wide path along the bank, originating at the point she entered this section. She walked slowly along it. Obviously her challenge was to cross the river, but there were no more hanging vines; and in any event the river was about fifty feet wide. Well, she would see.

She heard something. She stopped, listening nervously. It was the even footfalls of a striding man. She shrank into an alcove to the side, not wanting to encounter the sort of man she would in Hell.

The man came into view. He was tall and blond, muscular and handsome in a boyish way.

All Niobe's reserve crumbled. "Cedric!" she cried.

Cedric turned to face her. "Niobe!" he exclaimed, spreading his arms.

Then several things caught up with her. "But you're dead!" she said, stopping before she reached him.

"Of course I am. But my love for you remains."

"But what are you doing in Hell? You were a good man in life— a wonderful man!"

He shrugged. "A glitch in the system, maybe. But if you're here, that's where I want to be. With the most beautiful woman of her generation."

"But I'm not beautiful anymore! I've gone to seed."

He shrugged again. "It doesn't matter. My love is eternal."

"You're an illusion, aren't you!" she said indignantly. "A demon in disguise! I can use a thread on you and expose you for what you are!" She was angry now that Satan should use this particular device to trick her. To taunt her with her long lost love!

Cedric just stood there, not answering. He looked just exactly the way she remembered him, and her love fought in her breast to emerge and take over. There was nothing in life as sweet as first love! That made her angrier yet. "Get out of here!" she screamed. "I'll not waste a thread on you! You're just a—a mockery!" Now the tears

Piers Anthony

were flowing. She had been caught entirely off-guard by this specter, and her emotion had to be expressed somehow. "You have no right to—to—"

"I'm sorry you feel that way," Cedric said. "But of course your love for me was never as true as mine for you."

There was just enough truth in that to sting. She rushed at him and struck him with her fist, scoring on the nose.

Blood streamed down his face, but he made no motion to strike back. "I'll always love you, Niobe," he said quietly.

Her rage was so great that she was ready to kill. Her fingers curled into claws. She started for his eyes—

And caught herself. Hate was Satan's way. She was falling into Satan's trap! If she allowed hate and rage to dominate her, she would remain in Hell forever.

This was a demon in disguise, for it was solid under the illusion. Surely the demon could wipe her out with a single blow! But it had not done so. Instead it was taunting her into rage, baiting the love she could not afford to express. She could have used one thread on it, to expose it—or it could have killed her, costing her two threads. The rules of the maze did not allow monsters to chase her down; they could only hurt her if she made contact on her own initiative. She had made contact—but the thing was trying to destroy her rationality, not her body. To ruin her objectivity about her mission here, so that she would act foolishly and waste her remaining threads. *That* was the trap she could not afford—the one that would cost her all.

She calmed herself. "I'm sorry, Cedric. I shouldn't have struck you. Of course your love is true." She brought out a hanky and dabbed at his face.

Now he became uncomfortable. "Please don't bother," he said. "I'll be all right."

"Oh, but I must help you," she said warmly. "It's so important to love you back as strongly as you love me."

He jerked away. "I really must be going."

"*Must* you—so soon, Cedric?" she asked sadly.

He hurried away without further word.

She knew why. Demons were creatures of violence and hate, and could hardly tolerate gentleness and love, whatever they might say. This demon had been besting her—until she became positive. Then it could not handle the situation. Love defeated hate—with a little management.

She walked on—and encountered another man. "Pace!"

"Niobe!" he replied.

But it had to be another demon, for Pacian, like Cedric, had been a genuinely good man, not destined for Hell.

−245−

She headed for it. "Darling, it's so good to see you again!" she exclaimed.

It hesitated. "Uh, yes, of course. And I know you aren't really to blame for my being here."

So that was its ploy! Force her into an angry denial of that outrageous implication. "Oh, but I am," she replied. "I know you wouldn't be here now, if it weren't for me."

Again it hesitated. This wasn't following the script! Then it tried again, gamely enough. "Well, actually, you know it's not exactly *me* here—"

"Let me give you a big fat kiss, dear," she said, approaching.

It lost its composure and fled. Niobe smiled. She was learning how to handle demons.

But she wondered whether she had been correct in assuming that her anger was worth more to Satan than her life. She was so low on threads that the two threads a killing would have cost her represented forty percent of her total. Either of those demons could have dropped her total to three threads, putting her critically behind in the terminal stage of the maze. Was her anger really worth more than that?

She stopped where she was, certain that she was on her way to an important realization. Satan was evil, but hardly stupid. Anything he did made sense. So why would he instruct his demons not to attack her, if their taunting was not effective? There had to be some way he expected to gain from this.

Well, suppose there was a way she could get into more than two threads worth of trouble, if not diverted from it by the demons? She had recognized the wrong courses in prior segments of the maze because they were impassable. Now she was encountering demons who could have stopped her, but did not. Did that mean she was heading into more than two threads worth of mischief? That she was in fact on the wrong route?

If so, she should reverse course and get out of here. But that would mean encountering the two demons she had passed—and they surely would not let her travel that way. She could get killed twice, costing her four threads. These were more sophisticated than the prior monsters; they hadn't had to kill her as long as she was going in the direction Satan desired. And if she managed to get back past them—where would she find the correct route? She had no idea.

She concluded that she simply had to gamble on this being the right course. It was after all possible that the demons were merely trying to make her *think* she was going wrong. Wouldn't that be an irony: for her to turn away from the correct route, simply because the demons let her pass!

Meanwhile, she had an advantage: she knew that Satan was not about to force her to lose two threads. He wanted her to lose at least three. That must be the minimum number she needed for victory. He was willing to throw away illusions; they didn't matter. It was the threads that counted.

Yet all this had been set up before she entered the maze. How could Satan have known how many threads she would have left?

She resumed her walking, ill at ease. And—another person approached.

It was Blanche, Pacian's first wife who had been killed by the demon at the wedding. Again, there was no way Blanche could have gone to Hell; she had always been a good woman. This was another demon—or demoness—clothed by illusion. She could be handled as the others had been.

"Blanche!" Niobe cried, approaching her with open arms. "I'm so glad to see you!"

Blanche did not blanch. She came right up and embraced Niobe. She felt completely human and real. "Thank you so much for taking care of my husband!"

This was a new approach! Apparently the creatures of Hell were not always repelled by affection. Maybe demonesses were more gentle, as they were commonly used to seduce men to evil—literally. If they were driven away by love, they would not be able to perform. How, then, could she get rid of this one? "You don't resent that I married him after you died?"

"Oh, no, dear!" Blanche exclaimed. "He was such a good man, he deserved the best—and you were the best. He always loved you, of course, because of your beauty; it was only right that he have opportunity to enjoy it before it faded."

The demoness was beginning to get into it! The stilettoes of women were more subtle than those of men, but no less sharp. "I'm so glad you understand," Niobe said with as much warmth as she could manage. "The prophecy said he would possess the most beautiful woman of her generation, and obviously you weren't it."

"All too true!" Blanche agreed without rancor. "I feel privileged to have shared what part of his love I could, while I could, and to have had a lovely child by him."

"Yes, my son the Magician married her," Niobe agreed. She seemed to be unable to rattle this demoness, and she was not enjoying the effort. This woman was too much like the real Blanche, always good and giving. "I'm on my way to see him now."

"Yes, I know. I'll be glad to help you find him."

What? For a moment Niobe reeled with doubt. *Could* this be the real Blanche? She could verify it with a thread . . .

No! That might be part of the trap. Use a thread on this demoness, verify what she was, and then be killed by her: three threads gone,

−247−

and Satan's victory. Or try to retreat from her, and have to run the gauntlet of two male demons behind. A losing strategy, surely.

Blanche *had* to be in Heaven. This *had* to be an illusion/demoness, playing her part the way only a female could. The males had failed, but the females were more adept.

Well, if she couldn't get rid of this one, she would have to play along. "Why, thank you, Blanche! But this is, after all, Hell. Will Satan permit it?"

"We aren't completely evil, even in Hell," Blanche reminded her. "We're just more evil than good. What good I possess is tied up with Pacian and my daughter and your son. I will help you reach him— but I am not allowed to tell you anything. You understand."

"I understand." But she did not understand. This was exactly the way the real Blanche would have acted—but what demoness would help an intruder defeat her master? There had to be a limit to the playing of a part—didn't there?

Disquieted, Niobe continued her walk, and Blanche paced her. If this was another one of Satan's traps, it was too sophisticated for her to fathom at the moment.

Unless, she realized abruptly, Satan *wanted* her to reach her son. Or to encourage her to believe she could reach him. Naturally he would provide her all needed assistance—to go the wrong way.

Well, she was stuck for it. The game was getting more devious, as Satan proceeded from straight maze-challenges to psychological ones, but it wasn't over until it was over. The outcome hadn't been decided yet, for she still had five threads.

Another person showed. The next demon—and she hadn't yet gotten rid of the last one!

It was Blenda, the Magician's wife, mother of Luna. This was getting eerie indeed!

"Mother!" Blenda cried.

"My baby!" Blanche cried.

The two swept together and hugged each other, shedding tears. Niobe watched, bemused. They had to be two demonesses—yet they acted real in all ways. Blenda was not the perfect beauty she had been in youth, but the somewhat wasted woman who had died of leukemia at age forty-seven, leaving the Magician a widower. His magic had extended her life, but had not been able to cure her. So she, too, had entered the Afterlife—but not Hell. She had at one point been a virtual twin of Niobe's, and Niobe had known her well— a woman with very little evil.

Then Blenda turned to her. "I'm so glad to see you so well, Niobe!"

Piers Anthony

So well? Hardly! But compared to Blenda, she was healthy. Niobe didn't even try to unmask her; she hugged Blenda and exchanged pleasantries.

"So now you're coming to talk with my husband," Blenda said.

"My son," Niobe agreed. "He has the answer I need."

"I will help you find him," Blenda said. "I haven't seen him since I died."

Surely not! Blenda was in Heaven, the Magician in Hell. But Niobe had to play along. "Why not? He's been here for two years."

Her mouth quirked. "We don't get visiting privileges. That's part of our punishment."

Niobe had to admit that made sense. So now she had two demonesses ready to help her find her son. Curiouser yet!

Niobe set off again, paced by a woman on either side. She had five threads, and only four unidentified illusions remained.

"How are the girls?" Blenda asked.

"Orb's on tour," Niobe answered shortly. "Luna's getting into politics."

"Oh, yes—to foil Satan!" Blenda agreed. "But you need the Magician's advice."

Another form appeared. In fact it was three forms: outright demons. Evidently Satan was not about to expend three of his four remaining illusions on these; he had to send them in undisguised. They spied the women and hurried toward them.

"Watch out for them!" Blanche cried. "I know their kind! If they get us outnumbered, they'll rape us or eat us!"

"Or both," Blenda amended.

"Or both," Blanche agreed. "We must stay together; then they won't try it. They're cowardly; they must have numerical advantage, or they won't act."

Niobe did not comment. As far as she was concerned, she was now in the company of five demons. How was she going to get out of this? Why hadn't Satan simply sent ten demons?

The demons came close. They had horns and tails and hooves and obvious masculine appendages, in the manner of their kind. They eyed the women. "You need company?" one asked.

"Oh, go away, you foul fiend!" Blenda exclaimed.

The demon considered, evidently trying to figure out how to separate the three women so that they would become vulnerable. "Maybe we help," he said. "You want cross river?"

"Yes," Niobe said. It was, after all, the truth; she could see that the path on this side came to an end a short distance ahead.

"We help. We got boat."

"Why should you help us cross?" Niobe demanded. With overt demons, at least she didn't have to pretend.

—249—

The demon looked at her. It licked its lips. It shifted its posterior. It didn't answer.

It hardly needed to. The demons would help one woman cross, so that the three would be separated. Then the three demons would converge on the one or two women, and do their dirty work.

Would one demon actually rape or eat a demoness? Apparently so, by the rules that evidently governed this strange portion of the maze. Perhaps it was just Niobe who would be attacked, once she was separated from her "friends."

Well, the answer was simple. They would all cross together. If the women intended to desert her, they would have done so already. It seemed that they would stand by her—for now.

"Show us your boat," Niobe said.

The demons showed the boat. It was a small canoe, just big enough for two. It was obvious that it would sink if any more got on it.

Niobe looked at Blanche and Blenda. They spread their hands. It was clear that it was not possible for the three of them to cross together.

But if they did not, one or two of them would be left to the appetites of the demons. Niobe might cross alone, but she realized that she could not in conscience leave the other two women to that fate, even if they were demonesses beneath. They had not betrayed her, so far; she was unwilling to be the one to initiate that sort of thing. This might be Hell, but she carried her standards with her.

Perhaps that was the real nature of this test: to ascertain whether she would desert her conscience when it seemed convenient to do so. An ethical standard that bowed to convenience was not worth much.

She considered crossing with one demon, so as to keep it even on both sides of the river. But then that demon could cross back after Niobe went on, making it three to two. Or it could return to fetch across another demon, both of which could pursue Niobe.

She had to arrange to get all three women across—without ever letting any of them be outnumbered, on either side of the river. That was the only proper course.

She pondered. She remembered something that might help: a series of intellectual riddles she and Cedric had struggled with during their first summer. He had been uncannily bright, and she knew in distant retrospect that the foundation of her love for him had been laid when the power of his mind began to show in such games. He had seemed like little more than a boy, then—but what a bonnie boy!

She felt the tears starting and shook herself out of the reverie. She was, after all, in Hell.

One of those riddles had been the story of a river crossing: three civilized hunters, with three untrustworthy natives. They had had to cross the river, using a two-man boat, without ever letting the natives outnumber the hunters. Exactly the problem she faced here! So she knew there was an answer—

But she didn't remember it.

The others stood there, looking at her—the two women and the three demons. Yes, this was definitely a test, an aspect of the maze. She had been able to unravel the confusions of passages and illusions, and to survive the rigors of the snowy slope, and to get by the robot factory, but now the maze was focusing increasingly on her weakness: intellect. She had never claimed to have more than ordinary intelligence, though she had been attracted to smart men.

If she could solve this riddle, she could proceed; if not, she would shortly commence her Afterlife in Hell with a truly Hellish experience.

Did Satan know of her prior exposure to this puzzle? Did it suit his humor to dangle the prize this close, to see whether she could come through? What an exquisite torture it would be, to know she had had victory within her reach and had been unable to grasp it! He had even sent a demon in the guise of Cedric, to remind her!

"*Damn* you, Satan!" she swore under her breath. She thought she heard a responding chuckle, though perhaps that was merely a ripple in the river.

She concentrated. How had that long-ago puzzle gone? Two women could cross first—no, that would leave the third with all three demons. Well, one woman and one demon could cross, keeping it even. Then—oops! Who would bring the boat back? The woman would have to. Then there would be three women and two demons on the near bank, and a lone demon on the far bank. Then one woman and one demon could cross—and when they got to the far bank, there would be two demons to one woman there. No good.

Well, suppose two demons crossed first? One would bring the boat back. Then two women—no, that left two demons and one woman on the near shore.

No matter how she tried it, at some point she encountered an imbalance. It seemed impossible to cross successfully—yet she *knew* there was an answer! Cedric had worked it out.

There was a key—a special way of looking at it. Something that the ordinary person, like her, did not think of. What was it?

She pictured Cedric's boyish face, the tousled hair tumbling over his forehead. He had shown her the key, such a simple, obvious thing, and she had laughed ruefully.

Cedric! she thought, her ancient love for him suffusing her. *I need you!*

And then she thought: *return.* Perhaps she had heard Cedric say it, her love bringing back the dear memory of his voice.

The key was in the boat's return trip. Something surprising, non-sensical—until understood. The return of—

Then she had it. Thanks to Cedric, Luna's grandfather, she knew how to cross the river and save Luna. Satan had gotten too cute, taunting her; she had gotten away with the bait.

"Two of you take this boat across," she directed the demons.

They didn't argue. They got into the canoe and dipped their hand-paws in to paddle, not bothering with the paddles that lay in the bottom of the craft. The carnivorous fish swarmed, biting at the hands. When a fish took hold, a demon simply drew his hand out of the water along with the attached fish, brought it to his mouth, and chomped the fish. In a moment the eater became the eaten, and the paddling resumed.

Soon they were across. "Now one of you get out; the other bring it back," Niobe called. The demons shrugged; one got out and stood on the bank, while the other dog-paddled the canoe back by sitting in the front and pulling it along. It wasn't a smooth trip, but in due course the demon got there.

"Two more of you cross," Niobe said.

Two crossed. When they arrived, all three demons were on the far bank, while all three women remained on the near one.

"Now one of you bring it back," Niobe called.

"But if one of us crosses next—" Blanche said worriedly.

"Don't worry," Niobe said.

The demon arrived back. The two on the far shore licked their gross chops, anticipating something pleasant on the next crossing.

"Now two of us will cross," Niobe said. "Come on, Blanche."

"But I—" Blenda protested.

"You will have the company of one demon," Niobe said. "No problem."

She and Blanche took up the paddles and started off. The fish swarmed in again, but found nothing tender to chomp. The journey was somewhat erratic, as neither woman was experienced, and at times Niobe feared they would tip the craft over in their effort to keep it on course, but they did eventually make it across. The fish clacked their teeth angrily.

Now there were two women and two demons on this bank, one of each on the other. Who was going back: a woman or a demon?

"One of each," Niobe said. "I'll go—and you." She picked a demon.

The demon shrugged and joined her in the boat. It didn't know what she was up to, but was sure that sooner or later it would find the women outnumbered.

It was eerie, riding with the demon. She knew it could overturn the canoe at any point, dumping her in the water and costing her a life. But she also knew the demon wouldn't do it. It would attack only when it had the advantage of numbers. She was finessing Satan, offering him the chance to penalize her two threads when he wanted three.

They reached the bank. Now there were four on this side, two on the other, still evenly divided.

"Two women," Niobe said.

Blenda joined her in the canoe, and they crossed, leaving the two demons behind. When they arrived, there were three women to one demon. "Now you can ferry your friends across," Niobe said. "We'll be moving on. Thank you for your help." She led the way on down the path, leaving the demon to scratch his horny head in perplexity. How had the three morsels managed to escape?

"That was very clever of you," Blanche said.

"It was just a fond memory," Niobe said enigmatically. She knew it had been a close call, though—and four illusions remained, with the challenges getting harder.

The path diverged from the river. It led to a large hall, a virtual cathedral.

A man sat on a throne on a dais in the center. He stood as the women entered. "So you have come!" he exclaimed, rising.

It was the Magician!

Blenda was the first to approach him. "My husband!"

"My wife!" he agreed. They embraced and kissed.

Now Niobe approached him. But she remembered those four remaining illusions. It was possible that she had bypassed them when she crossed the river, or that the count given on the plaque in the 4-hall had overstated the number, but she doubted it. It was more likely that she would have to fathom every last one of those illusions before she won through. She couldn't trust this.

But suppose it *was* her son, ready with the answer she needed—and she passed him by? That was as good a way to lose as any! Wouldn't Satan laugh if he offered her the solution on a platter—and she rejected it, for that reason. Exquisite irony.

Well, one day Satan was going to try so hard for that irony that he would lose more than an encounter.

She brought out a thread and flung it at the Magician. If this was no illusion—

The thread touched—and the Magician became a demon with three faces and six arms. Its head seemed to be mounted on ball-bearings, for it rotated without limit to aim one face at her, then another, and then the third. One face was young, one middle-aged, and one old, but each seemed uglier than the other two.

"So!" the middle face hissed. "You doubt me, bag!" the old one grated. "I will perforate you!" the young one cried. The demon stepped toward her.

Blanche and Blenda screamed. Niobe expected them to run away, as their challenge was done, but instead they closed in before her. "You shall not have her!" Blenda cried.

"This is my concern, not yours!" Niobe said. "Don't—"

The three-faced demon grabbed Blenda, using four of its arms to catch hold of her two arms and two legs. It picked her up and spun its head to view her triply. "You aren't worth bothering with, you prune!" it said, and hurled her beyond the throne.

Now Niobe saw a gulf there. The throne was not in the center of the chamber; it had only seemed to be, from a distance. It was perched on the edge of a void. Blenda screamed as she fell into this hole and disappeared.

Again the demon advanced on Niobe. This time Blanche interposed herself. "You can cross, Niobe!" she cried. "The landing is hidden by illusion—"

The demon caught her, wrapping two hands about her throat to cut off her words. With three more hands it ripped off her clothes. It growled with disgust. "Damned flesh is no good; I want the real thing. To Hell with you!" And it threw her also into the gulf.

Niobe was shocked on several levels. These were demons—sacrificing themselves to protect her. They were giving her information that she needed to defeat their master. That made little sense, unless—

Unless Blanche and Blenda were what they had seemed to be. In which case—

No! There was no way those two could really be in Hell. But they weren't necessarily demons. They could be other souls, ordered to impersonate the women Niobe had known—or maybe even caused to believe that they *were* those women. Thus they could have acted in good faith, despite being false—and had paid a terrible price for it.

Terrible price! No—they were damned souls anyway. The fall into the pit could not hurt them; it merely took them out of this context. Niobe was alone again. Still, she regretted their passing, and was sorry she had not been able to do anything for them.

Meanwhile, the three-faced demon was coming at her again—and this time there was no one to intercede. She had used a thread exposing it; if it killed her now, that would make three threads lost, and put her below the critical threshold as she understood it. She had to escape—but the void was too broad for her to slide across on a limited thread.

If she retreated, she would be trapped between this demon and the three at the river. She *had* to go forward.

There was a landing, hidden by illusion—if Blanche had been telling the truth. If that damned soul had been a true emulation of the blessed one, she would have told the truth. Blanche had been one of the finest people Niobe had known, though she had known her mainly by observation. Satan had made a mistake, using damned souls to emulate blessed ones; naturally they had longed to *be* their roles, as an actor might wish to be the hero he portrayed, and they had played them too well. It had been their closest approach to the illusion of Heaven, of escape from Hell.

Niobe ran for the void. She threw a thread ahead of her.

There, just a yard away from the edge, was a platform. It had been concealed by the illusion of the void.

She leaped across. The three-faced demon, following her, tried to stop, skidded on the smooth floor, and fell into the crevice between the edge and the platform. Screaming from all three faces, it descended.

She was across, and she had three threads left, while Satan had only two illusions. It was coming down to the wire, and for the first time she had a genuine hope of winning.

She set herself and walked on, hardly exhilarated, still regretting the fate of the two damned souls who had helped her cross.

She came to another large chamber. Here there were a dozen demons of the kind she had encountered at the river, all looking alike. They stood beside a huge set of balancing scales.

What was she to make of this? The demons made no hostile gesture; they seemed merely to be waiting. This must be the final challenge—but how could she solve it, when she couldn't even tell its nature?

Then something occurred to her. Pacian, her second husband, had had a mind very like Cedric's. Magic music and intellectual brilliance—they had been cousins, so it was not surprising that they shared traits. She had played games of riddles with Pace, too, and he had bested her readily. Now she remembered the first, at the sea of grass as they tried to approach Gaea's residence. Twelve coins, a set of scales. Eleven coins specified to be genuine, one counterfeit—but the counterfeit looked exactly like the others. Only its slight difference in weight distinguished it. The problem had been to discover which one was the counterfeit, and whether it was heavy or light.

Easy enough; it was necessary only to weigh all the coins in pairs. If two balanced, both were genuine; if the scales did not balance, then one coin was the counterfeit. Then each of these could be balanced against one of the others, and the counterfeit would be exposed.

Except that only three weighings were permitted. It was necessary to weigh them in groups—and no combination of group weighings seemed certain to isolate the lone counterfeit, let alone identify the nature of its difference.

With a Tangled Skein

Here were twelve identical demons—and she had just three threads left. Could that be it?

Satan had two illusions remaining, it seemed. Two demons could be made to resemble her son, concealing him—but that had not been done. None of these demons had been masked.

Then she caught on. "One of you is my son!"

All of them nodded affirmatively.

"Which one?"

All nodded negatively, refusing to tell.

Why didn't the Magician simply step forward so she could verify him with a thread?

She considered and realized that, just as her threads were not merely illusion-disposers but also life-restorers and flying devices, so Satan's illusions were not confined to the senses. Satan could have used one illusion to change the Magician's appearance to that of a demon—and the other to prevent him from identifying himself.

More than that, she realized. Satan could have bound the Magician so that once she identified him, he would not tell the truth. Then she would have a lie for an answer, and when she applied it, Satan would win.

Well, then, she would reverse whatever he told her, and have the truth.

But suppose it *wasn't* a lie? Then she would forfeit the game despite having the truth—another delicious irony.

She had to know whether the Magician had been enchanted to tell the truth or to lie. A thread would do it—but would she have a thread left, once she found him?

Her son was the counterfeit coin, in this Hellish inversion—and what he told her could be either true or false. He could be honest, and be slightly lighter than the demons, or dishonest, and be slightly heavier, for dishonesty was a sin and sin weighed down the soul. She had to know which.

She had three threads—and now she knew that each one entitled her to one weighing. She had to locate her son among the identical demons, and determine his relative weight.

It seemed impossible—yet Pacian had done it, and shown her how. But that had been a quarter-century ago, and she had forgotten the solution.

This was a tougher one than the river-crossing; she knew that. She had barely solved the other; how could she ever fathom this one? Her advantage in threads had been nullified by her lesser intellect and fading memory. Now she wished she had been the smartest woman of her generation, instead of the prettiest!

A fireball manifested. It expanded and became the form of Satan himself. "So it has come to this at last, sad sack!" he exclaimed.

She had been less annoyed during that confrontation in the Void, when he had called her "cutie" and other such mock endearments. But she held her peace. "I can win, Satan."

"Can you, old hen? Let's see you try!" He gestured, causing a throne of fire to appear. He ensconced himself in it and settled down to watch.

"Why not invite the whole world to watch?" Niobe asked, irritated.

Satan shrugged. "The world? I think not. But selected parties, perhaps." He clapped his hands, and a wall of the chamber vaporized. Beyond it was a segment of an amphitheater. Seated there were all manner of demons and lost souls, including the two who resembled Cedric and Pacian, and the two who resembled Blanche and Blenda. There were also the five major Incarnations.

Five? Oh, yes—she was not at the moment Fate; she was just the soul of Niobe, perched on the verge of damnation—or salvation. Clotho and Atropos had the body, and they shifted back and forth as the mood took them.

"Now perform your miracle of failure, O dismal dog!" Satan said sardonically. "Your friends will see your humiliation!"

Still she resisted the baiting. If she allowed herself to get rattled or angry, she would certainly lose. She concentrated on the immediate problem. Twelve coins, three weighings—how could it be done?

She considered balancing six against six. One group would certainly rise—but would that mean that a light counterfeit was among them, or that a heavy counterfeit was among the others? If only she knew the weight first! Then she could take the lighter six, if that happened to be it, split them into two groups of three, and weigh two of the three from the lighter group. If one was light, that was it; if they balanced, then the odd one out was it. It would work as well if the counterfeit was heavier. Such a simple process!

But without the knowledge of the relative weight, it became a complex process, a single weighing determining nothing. She would need a second thread to weigh the halves of one of the original sides; if they balanced, then the counterfeit was in the other group, and she would know its weight. From that point two more weighings would do it—four in all. No good.

But as she struggled with it, she began to remember. That odd-man-out system could be used throughout! Weigh four against four, with four out. If the eight balanced, the counterfeit was in the four remaining. Then weigh two against two—no, that wasn't it. Weigh all four against one of the other groups, now known to consist of good coins (demons); that would tell whether the counterfeit was heavy or light. Then—no, one weighing wasn't enough to finish it.

Still, she was sure she was on the right track. Weigh just three coins from the subject group against three good ones; if they balanced, it was the odd one out, and the last weighing would determine its relative weight. If the two sets did not balance, then it would be known that, say, the counterfeit was light. Then a simple weighing would identify it.

But suppose the first weighing of fours did not balance? Then she had the counterfeit somewhere amidst eight coins—too many for two weighings.

She went over and over it while the audience waited silently. By chance she might win, if the counterfeit fell in the right group. But she was sure that chance would not favor her—not here in Hell. She had to exclude chance and guarantee it in three weighings, regardless.

She was getting a concentration headache. No matter what strategy she tried, she could not be sure of the answer in just three weighings. What was she to do?

The tears started. It didn't help that Satan spotted them and smirked. He knew he was winning—and the audience knew it too. Her final humiliation was upon her.

Oh, Pace! she thought. *How did you do it?*

Then, as if it were the answer to her prayer, the solution came. Pace—or something—had responded. Her memory clarified, and she knew the key. "Exchange!" she exclaimed.

She stepped before the scales. "You four—get on this side," she ordered the nearest demons. They obeyed, tromping to the large plate. "And you four—to this side." The next four obeyed.

When the eight stood on the two plates of the scales, Niobe released the fastenings and let the plates find their levels. They were not in balance. Slowly the left plate descended. There was a trifle more evil there. This was the hardest case to fathom, of course.

Now came the key step. She gestured to the innermost demon on the left, and to the one on the right. "You and you—switch places."

The two demons shrugged at this nonsense and exchanged places. There was a murmur in the audience. Satan scowled.

"You there," she said, pointing to those remaining on the right side. "Get off." They got off.

"You three," she said, indicating three of those in the unweighed group. "Get on." And the three marched on.

Niobe saw the Incarnations shaking their heads. They thought she had lost her common sense. Blanche and Blenda were bowing their heads with regret. Nobody believed in her—but she knew what she was doing. She hoped.

The scales, when the weighing proceeded, remained unbalanced, the left side still down. That told her much of what she needed to know. Had they become balanced, she would have known that the counterfeit was among the three she had removed, and light, because she had taken them from the light plate. Had they become unbalanced the other way, she would have known it was one of the two that had exchanged places; then she could have weighed the light one against a good one and defined it, for if it remained light, it was a light counterfeit, and if it balanced, then the other one would have been the heavy counterfeit. As it was, she knew that the counterfeit was one of the three she had neither moved nor switched, and it was heavy.

"You and you," she said, pointing to two of those three. "Weigh against each other." This was her third and final thread.

The two did. They balanced.

Niobe turned to the odd one out. "Hello, Magician!"

The Incarnations, surprised, applauded. Blanche and Blenda looked up in glad surmise. Satan's scowl deepened.

But Niobe knew it wasn't over yet. She could ask her son for the answer—but what he would tell her would be a lie. She had used up all her threads getting to this point; she could not make him tell the truth.

She could get the truth by elimination. Only the truth was perfectly consistent; sooner or later, a pattern of lies would trip itself up.

"You have one question," Satan said.

"One question!" she exploded. "That isn't part of the bargain!"

"One soul is on the line; one question to be answered."

That had not been her understanding, but she realized that she hadn't made it tight. Mars, too, had overlooked this. The Father of Lies had found a loophole. She was stuck with Satan's interpretation.

One question! Had she been assured of a true answer, she could have asked, "How can I foil Satan's plot against Luna?" But his lie could be anything else—making that question an exercise in futility. She had to find the question whose lie would be instructive. That was more of a challenge than she had cared for!

Could she phrase a suitable yes-no question so that the lie would give her a direct answer? Only if she pretty well knew the answer already—and she did not.

Had Satan won after all? Not entirely, for she had gotten through to the Magician and identified him. She had threaded the maze. But until she got the answer she had come for and got out of Hell, her soul was not safe. Neither was mankind.

Her gaze passed over the audience again. There were the demons, licking their chops in anticipation of victory. There were some of the damned souls, looking soulful. There was Mars, his face set carefully neutral. He had made sure Satan didn't cheat, but he could not help her now.

With a Tangled Skein

The Incarnations—the personifications of the major factors governing the destiny of man. Thanatos, who had assumed the office and refused to take Luna's soul, because he loved her. A selfish reason, perhaps—but it had caused him to face down Satan directly, thereby preserving Luna for her eventual role in the salvation of man. *One may marry Death . . .*

Chronos, who had similarly fought Satan, in what was the future for the rest of them. She was glad, now, that she had comforted Chronos' successors in her past; they were all worthy holders of the office, even the child, and had/would do their part in securing the salvation of man.

Gaea, who had helped significantly. Niobe's daughter Orb seemed destined to assume that office, if the prophecy carried through. Surely she, too, would have to overcome Satan's evil designs, for the Prince of Evil always pounced on the newest and least experienced Incarnations. *And one may marry Evil . . .*

Surely not! That was unthinkable! Yet—she had in a sense given Orb to Satan. It had only been a commitment to keep her out of politics, capitalizing on Satan's error of identification, but *any* commitment to Satan was treacherous. What had she let her child in for? But Orb was a sensible and talented young woman, if a bit short on temper, and she well knew the treacheries of the one who had struck directly at her in the Hall of the Mountain King. Orb would never trust Evil!

Yet that prophecy kept coming true, stage by stage, in its own devious manner. Niobe hoped she was misinterpreting its import, here.

Thanatos had balked Satan's power by using an aspect of his own power over death. Chronos would do it by manipulating time. Each Incarnation fought Satan in his/her own fashion. Now she, as Fate, had to prevent Satan from distorting her threads of life. Some aspect of her power should do it.

She felt a flash of realization. Her power—because it was for her that the Magician had left his message. That limited the range of options considerably! The solution to her problem should not lie in Thanatos' province, or Chronos', or any of the other Incarnations. It had to lie with Fate. In some special power that she, as Fate, could invoke.

But *what* power? She still couldn't ask what it was!

Yet if it was a power of Fate, it had to be a power of an Aspect of Fate. There were three Aspects; in thirty-eight years she had pretty well learned the powers of Clotho, and none of them related to this situation. Her successor, Lisa, had discovered or developed a power she hadn't know about, the ability to change her appearance from

—260—

one pretty young form to another, so perhaps there were others. But Clotho spun the threads; she did not manipulate them after they were in place. So it really wasn't likely to be Clotho.

Niobe had not been Lachesis long enough to fathom all her powers, but she had made progress. There could be some major power she had not yet discovered, but she doubted it.

That left Atropos. She knew very little of Atropos' powers. The job seemed simple enough, however—merely to cut the measured threads. Not really enough to warrant a full separate Aspect, when she thought about it. Could there be something they had not realized?

This had become a three-coin problem! One coin she could set aside: Clotho. That left two to weigh. If she knew which one had the necessary power, she could focus exclusively on that, and have a much better chance to discover it. This wasn't the direct answer she had sought, but it would give her a better fighting chance.

"Magician, here is my question," she said. "Is it Atropos who has the power to defeat Satan's present scheme?"

"No," the demon-figure said.

There was a sigh of disappointment from the damned souls, and a chortle of glee from the demons. They thought she had failed; they didn't realize that the answer was a lie, or that she knew it was a lie. The Magician had just confirmed her guess, giving her the key to victory.

Satan rose from his throne of fire. "So you have failed, and you are Mine, you wretched woman!"

"Get away from me, you foul fiend!" Niobe snapped. "My threads are done, but so are your illusions. I threaded the maze."

"But you lost your answer," Satan said, walking toward her. Now flames appeared in a circle, enclosing the two of them and the twelve demon-forms.

"I *got* my answer!" she cried. "I knew from my weighings that you had enchanted my son to lie. Atropos is the one!"

"Ridiculous!" Satan said. The ring of fire closed in, burning the demons, who disappeared one by one in puffs of flame as they were ignited. "Everyone knows you lost." He reached for her, and now his hands were flaming too. "I have desired your soul for sixty years, and now it is Mine!"

"No!" Niobe cried. "I cry foul! I have the answer!"

Mars stood. "Satan, you presume," he said. His hand descended to touch the hilt of his great red sword.

Satan scowled, but he paused, and the ring of fire paused too. Four demons remained standing, including the one who was the Magician. "Your turn will come, Warmonger!" he muttered. Then, to the audience: "Then let the threadbare one present her answer, if she's got it. Here and now!"

"Agreed," Mars said. He remained standing, hand still resting at the sword.

So Mars had now acted directly to enforce the rules of the maze. She had been wise to choose him as referee.

Satan's head swiveled on around in a full circle and returned to cover Niobe. Now the flames danced within them. "Present your answer, saggy! I call your bluff!"

But Niobe had not worked it out yet; she knew only that she had the key to it. "In due course, stinkhorn."

"Now—or forfeit!" Satan said.

"There is no time limit, remember?" she insisted. "The maze is finished only when I have the answer—or do not have it. I can take twenty years, if I want to. Isn't that right, Mars?"

Mars smiled grimly. "That is right, Lachesis. Time is not specified. I lacked authority to agree to Here and Now, so I withdraw it."

"A blessed loophole!" Satan muttered. "Well, then, I'll wait—till Hell freezes over." He gestured, and the circle of flames resumed its contraction. "Which will not be soon."

Niobe knew that those flames could not hurt her—not as long as the game was unfinished. But probably they could make her quite uncomfortable. Satan was applying a hotfoot to distract her.

She concentrated as well as she could. So it *was* Atropos who had the power. Therefore it related to the cutting of threads. But Atropos could not cut a thread until it had been measured, and measuring was Lachesis' province. If the pawns of Satan on Earth could be eliminated by the action of Lachesis, why had the Magician's answer excluded her? He should have said "yes," so as to direct her toward Atropos, since he had to lie. So this should not involve measuring.

What would happen if Atropos cut an unmeasured thread? Well, if she cut the front end, it was disaster; they had discovered that the hard way. But it was too late to cut the front ends of Satan's agents in the Senate. They were already well established in the Tapestry. The other ends—if they had already been measured, cut to length and woven in, it should not be possible to cut them. Yet they *could* be cut, obviously. Atropos would never do it, because of the harm it would do to the Tapestry, but—

She was on to something here. When Lachesis measured a thread, she determined its potential. But not all threads lived up to their potential. Some broke early and were lost. The mortals thought of that as suicide—a self-arranged cutting. Normally the mortal instinct of self-preservation prevented that, but when that instinct broke down—

And there it was. Niobe faced Satan. "When Atropos cuts a thread out of turn, after it has been measured and woven into the Tapestry, that thread will end despite the destiny Lachesis has measured for

it. An unfated end is a suicide. What Atropos does, in effect, is terminate that person's impulse to exist—eliminating the instinct of self-
preservation. Without that instinct, the average person will soon get
tired of the routine frustrations of life, and decide to try the Afterlife
instead. Especially if he believes he is going to Heaven—or has a
promise of preferred treatment in Hell.''

"I don't treat suicides any better than the others!" Satan exclaimed, his flames brightening indignantly.

"But you have promised preferred treatment to those who do your
bidding on Earth," Niobe said. "Such as the ones slated to replace
the senators who have returned to enjoy their newfound youth. Well,
those folk may come to you sooner than you anticipate."

"I'll assign them double torture if they do!" Satan raged. "I need
them on Earth!"

"For twenty years or so," Niobe agreed. "But when Atropos cuts
their threads early, so that they lose their indomitable desire to live,
they won't care to waste all that time waiting for their reward."

"There *is* no reward!" Satan was almost engulfed in flames now.

"In which case, why should they agree to your bidding?" she asked
sweetly. "You will have a lot of trouble garnering the votes you want
if those folk realize that your promises are meaningless."

"You're bluffing!" Satan cried. "You wouldn't abrogate your own
threads!"

"To save mankind?" she asked. "Perhaps I would not—but I suspect practical old Atropos would."

"You bet I would!" Atropos cried from the audience.

"And without those corrupted votes, twenty years hence, the final
decision will be left to the powers that will be—and the swing vote
will remain with my granddaughter Luna!"

Satan didn't answer. He stood there, glowering, as the circle of
fire closed in on them both. It ignited the last demon—the one who
was the Magician. As the demon-semblance went up in smoke, her
son stood there in his natural form. A slow, grim smile was spreading
across his face.

Then the flame engulfed her, blotting out the rest of Hell. But Niobe
felt no heat.

In a moment the air cleared. Hell was gone, and with it the audience. She stood in Mars' castle, where she had started this strange
challenge. She was back in her physical body, her soul safe as an
Aspect of Fate. Mars was standing before her, his smile very like
that of the Magician.

You did it! Clotho cried in thought, kissing her internally.

Good job, woman! Atropos thought next.

Niobe laughed with relief and delight. "Upon my soul!" she exclaimed. She knew she had a long and satisfying role ahead of her
as Lachesis.

AUTHOR'S NOTE

In the first *Incarnations* novel, featuring Thanatos, I explored the subject of Death in a manner not commonly seen in fiction. That novel seems to be doing reasonably well, commercially and critically, and my fans have reacted favorably. But I noted in the "Author's Note" for that book that Death seemed to be lobbing shells at me while I worked on the novel. This was disquieting. Next year I wrote the sequel, featuring Chronos, and explored aspects of Time that other writers may have overlooked. I was then besieged by problems of time, and really had to struggle to complete the novel on schedule. I don't believe in the Supernatural—I regard it as fantasy—but I dreaded what I would encounter when I wrote the next, on the subject of Fate.

Well, now it is done, and this is my report on the manner Fate has affected me. I am broadening the scope here, for as I trust this novel shows, Fate is not a matter of a few months or particular episodes; it is an ongoing tapestry of interacting life, fashioned from the tangled skein of reality. So herewith my usual warning: the entertainment portion of this book is over, and this Note is of a more introspective nature. If you are not interested in the musings of anonymous writers, don't bother to read further; the novel can stand perfectly well without this.

How did I come to write *Skein*? Well, of course I went the usual route, presenting a summary of the notion to the editor, who put out a contract on it, and in the winter of 1983–84 I settled down to write the first drafts of the third *Bio* novel for Avon and the third *Incarnations* novel for Del Rey. You will remember my system: I so arrange my year so as not to have to type in my unheated study in winter, preferring to sit by the warm woodstove and pencil the first drafts of two novels, then type them in spring. This really is no answer, though, because the question is too limited. How did I, an established science fiction writer since 1963, come to be writing fantasy? How did I come to be a writer at all?

Let me start at the beginning, because the true course that took me to Niobe was more devious and difficult than most folks would care to realize. If parts of this narration seem uncomfortably personal—well, this is my nature.

There is an element in my fiction that appeals to certain readers who claim they don't find it in most other fiction, and much as I might be tempted to call it Competence or Quality or Genius, I really can't. There are other writers with these traits who are less successful than I am. I regard myself as a good writer, not a great one, and my current success has as much to do with the efforts of the publisher and its sales force as it does with my skill as an author. This isn't modesty on my part, false or otherwise; it's observation based on my desire to know the truth, whatever its nature may be.

I have what some others would call an obsession with truth, which manifests in a lively curiosity about practically everything that exists or fails to exist, a very strong desire for integrity—and contempt for its absence—and an ornery attitude about ascertaining the facts and making them known. This attitude has gotten me in a lot of trouble in the past, but is paying off now, because I am working my way closer to comprehension of the nature of ultimate reality, and it helps. Of course I have a way to go yet, before that comprehension is complete; let's give it a millennium or two and see where I stand.

Anyway, I suspect that special element in my fiction is the personal touch. I am not content to follow the standard rules of plotting, characterization, and style, though these are good rules; I want my fiction also to live. When I succeed, it does live for me, and I hope for my readers, too. I do feel what my characters feel and I can cry, literally, when they hurt. I can suffer pangs of parturition when I finish with a novel; of course the words remain, but I am no longer *in* it; it has ceased to be an ongoing aspect of my life and has become part of the record of my achievement. Its thread has been cut, and I must proceed to the spinning and measuring of the next one. But while I'm in, I am involved.

Sometimes I dream about my characters. I love Niobe, I love Cedric, I love Luna and Orb; they live in my fancy much as living people do. Is it foolish to care for nonexistent folk? Then leave me to my foolishness! There is too much insensitivity and isolation in this world; there should be no shame in caring, even if only for constructs

With a Tangled Skein

of the imagination. Indeed, in certain respects, I prefer imagination
to reality and shall explain why. But this entails some baring of the
nerves and is uncomfortable for some folk, including some writers.
I happen to be more introspective and expressive than most, so I do
get personal in these Notes. Bear with me

I was born in Oxford, England, where both my parents had their
degrees. Ours was a Quaker family, and my father worked with the
British Friends Service Committee in Spain, supervising their relief
program there during the Spanish Civil War. As I understand it, this
was largely concerned with the feeding of hungry children, who had
the worst of it during the ravages of combat. Generals like to speak
of conquering territory and reducing the enemy's combative ability,
but this is rough on the children whose territory it is; their houses
are destroyed and their families killed and their food disappears. That
is the real meaning of war, after the generals have played their games
and moved on to new challenges. I will have a good deal more to say
on the subject of the suffering of innocents in war in the next novel
in this series, *Wielding a Red Sword*; too often it is the blood of
children that accounts for the color.

This war in Spain went from 1936 to 1939 and presaged World War
II; the Nazi regime used it as a kind of testing ground for new weap-
ons, then turned that experience into something that caused the rest
of the world to take note. Many people were affected by the war in
Spain, including such literary figures as Ernest Hemingway and
George Orwell, and science fiction writer Ted Cogswell . . . and me.

My father was arrested by the victorious Franco government; he
disappeared, in the manner that has more recently been popularized
in Latin America, but was fortunate enough to manage to smuggle
out a note. It reached my mother, and, armed with that proof, she
was able to get the authorities to admit that my father was in custody;
they had, of course, denied it. Truth is the first casualty in war and
in its aftermath. They agreed to release him conditionally: that he
depart the country. That way the dictatorship did not have to admit
to making a mistake—dictatorships just don't make mistakes—and
got to take over the stores of food intended for children. I doubt that
much of it reached those children thereafter. Thus it was that we
came to America. It is entirely possible that had this false arrest and
eviction not occurred, I would be living today in Spain, perhaps trying
to write fantasy in Spanish.

I was not aware of such details at the time, but I felt their impact.
I was not in Spain during the actual war; I remained in England with
my sister, cared for by "Nana," a British girl hired for the purpose,
as has been the custom there for perhaps a longer time than America
has been colonized. Thus it is not surprising that some of my earliest

and fondest memories are of Nana, whose actual name I never knew. Even my memory may be skewed; it was probably "Nanny." Then the time came for my sister and me to go to Spain. I learned to my chagrin that Nana, who I thought was my mother or equivalent, was not going. We were to be in the charge of two other people, who were in fact my parents. They had spared me the possible anguish of separation from them, before, by distancing themselves; they overlooked the discomfort of *this* separation.

I don't want to make more of this than it was, but my awareness of that separation has remained with me throughout my life. The echo of it is apparent in the separation of Niobe from her son; the things of my life do make their way into my fiction, though not in ways that any critic comprehends. I suspect the same is true for other writers.

In Spain I adapted gradually to the culture and the language; at age five I was beginning to speak Spanish. My sister had a pretty, lacy Spanish dress. I would wake in the mornings and see the moving shadows of palm fronds cast against my wall; I viewed this as an adventure, trying to guess which frond would dive farthest in the wind. I saw my first movie there, *The Three Little Pigs*. My memories of Spain are more populous and clear than those of England, though not as fond. But then, abruptly, we left. Oh, it was an adventure; we traveled to Portugal, to Lisbon—I remember the hotel room there—to board the ship *Excalibur*. No, as far as I know, that name has no connection to my later taste in fantasy, but perhaps it was a signal. As it happened, the Duke of Windsor—the former King Edward VIII of England—was taking that same ship to the New World to be Governor of the Bahamas; I remember seeing his car hoisted out of the hold at Bermuda. The Nazis had hatched a plot to kidnap or convert them to their cause, but that had been botched and he crossed the Atlantic unmolested.

Again, my memories of the time are more personal than historic; I was seasick, vomiting over the rail into the ocean—the Atlantic remains polluted to this day—and I had my sixth birthday at sea on August 6, 1940. The chef lacked sugar, because of the War, and so I was presented with a cake made of sawdust, nicely covered with icing and candles. It was a surprise when we cut that open! I was somewhat put out at the time. Today, ironically, when I can afford a genuine cake, I can't have it, because of my mild diabetes. I think my daughters are jealous; they've had many real cakes, but never a sawdust cake. For a present I received a harmonica, which I played ceaselessly thereafter; I trust the Duke appreciated the music. I have always liked harmonica music since then; it, too, appears in my fiction, most notably in the *Adept* series.

But this was my second uprooting, though not my last, as my family slowly fragmented and my parents eventually divorced. Gardeners will tell you that root-pruning doesn't hurt; I hesitate to agree. I did not understand the problem, though in retrospect I do. I had no continuing security of situation; both the people and the places closest to me kept changing. By day I got along, but darkness brought nightmare. I would lie awake at night, staring at the wan lamp that was my only security from nocturnal monsters.

If I were to personify my closest acquaintance of these years, it would be Fear; I have known it longer and better than anyone else would believe. I began to wet my bed at night, and this persisted, despite the efforts of others to shame, cure, or punish me, until I was ten years old; living folk simply lacked the leverage my nightmares had. I remember being in boarding school in first grade, when one of the bigger boys took off the sheet to expose me in my soaking nakedness. It didn't matter; what does one humiliation matter, when one is already in Hell?

My family moved again, and again, and I attended five different schools in the course of my three years in first grade. I learned how to fight, because I had to; I just couldn't learn how to read and I wasn't strong in math, either. That may explain why I was later to be a math instructor in the U.S. Army and an English teacher and professional writer in civilian life. In the throes of this childhood I developed nervous twitches of head and hands, and I counted things compulsively. I suspect early tests showed me to be of subnormal intellect. My physical growth slowed, then stopped; I became the smallest in my class, male or female. I suffered daily stomachaches, and every few months there would be a real gut-tearer that would incapacitate me all day. Not until I had a kidney stone at the age of forty-seven did I experience worse abdominal pain.

The only thing worse than being with other people, who picked on me physically and emotionally, was being alone. I would imagine that it was all one interminable bad dream and that eventually I would wake up and be back in England, the land of happiness. But it never happened, and in time I accepted the fact that I was in America to stay. There is a direct adaptation of this in my three-volume novel *Tarot*: a day in the life of an eight-year-old boy. It is literal. I retain an interest in Hell, as is evident in this novel, *Skein*. When I was wet and shivering in my bed in New England, my feet so cold they felt hot, I decided that if Hell was hot, I had no fear of going there.

There is no need to detail all of it, though there is a great deal more. I have, I trust, presented enough to show that my early life was not perfect, and that the realm of imagination seemed to have more to offer me than did reality. In this, I believe, was the root of my later passion for writing. How much better to organize my worlds of imagination so as to make them meet my needs more completely! To come to terms with the monsters that first pursued me and discover the joys that lay beyond. A popular song played on the radio while I worked on this novel, one line going, "My dream is real; reality is wrong." Oh, *yes!*

I finally discovered reading, progressing in a bound from exclusion to complete inclusion in the world of print. Suddenly I was in *The Cloister and the Hearth* by Charles Reade, a novel of the Middle Ages written in 1869, about three hundred thousand words long. It took me months to get through it, but I read every word faithfully, and I lived in that world, and was desolate when it ended. Later I got into reading fantasy and science fiction, and there were worlds galore for me to romp in. I read slowly but deeply—to this day I am a slow reader—and tuned out all the world around me in favor of the universe perceived through the window of the printed page, some-times to the annoyance of others who thought I was being perverse. But I needed that other universe; in a certain respect I owe my sanity to it, for it helped me to survive the rigors of the real world. I had no solid emotional place to stand in reality; the fantastic genre pro-vided me with my anchorage. And so it was perhaps inevitable that I become a creature of that genre, as I am today. Piers Anthony is my strength; it is a pseudonym, but more of my reality is associated with it now than with my mundane identity. I was always a nonentity in Mundania, and remain so, but in fantasy I am a figure of conse-quence.

Perhaps ironically, my mundane existence has improved steadily since my teenage years and is a good one today by any standard. I have been married more than a quarter-century, have two bright and healthy daughters, and a pleasant lifestyle. Of course, much of this is runoff from my success in fantasy, for it is mundane money I re-ceive for my fantastic efforts. But even the course of an improving life does not necessarily flow smoothly. I have shown the foundation of my need to write; of course it also helps to have some reasonable intelligence and creativity and perseverance and luck, and these have helped me. But I feel in one major respect I came at my career via the monkey's paw.

"The Monkey's Paw" is a famous story by W. W. Jacobs in which a couple is granted three wishes on a monkey's paw, but each wish is granted in a manner that makes it horrible. They wish for money—and their son is killed, so that the benefit comes to them. They wish him alive again, and the corpse reanimates and approaches. At last they wish him dead again, and are left with nothing.

Well, the mundane world gave me a wife, but I wanted more; I wanted to be a successful writer. It was an unrealistic ambition; only one in a hundred who make the effort ever breaks into professional print. But for eight years I kept trying. Our first child miscarried at four months and was stillborn; that was not only a personal loss, it eliminated my exemption from the military draft, so that, before my first year of marriage was done, I was in the U.S. Army. Our second baby was stillborn at five months, at the time when I declined to sign up for the U.S. Savings Bond program (as I recall, they then paid 2.5 percent interest) and was therefore removed as instructor and set to weed-pulling and similar duties, as well as being denied promotion beyond PFC. It was also the time when I was naturalized as an American citizen; in the final courtroom ceremony there were forty-nine Army wives and me. That event made the local TV news in Oklahoma; you don't see too many PFCs in uniform getting naturalized. I also had my first science fiction story accepted, by a magazine edited by Damon Knight—which folded before payment or publication, washing me out.

Back in civilian life, our third baby was born prematurely at six months, lived one hour, and died the day I lost my good job at an electronics company and had a doctor advise me that the mysterious fatigue I suffered was all in my head. One day in May 1962, and much of my mundane world was lost, again. It looked as if we would never be able to have a child of our own, my ability to earn a living was shot, and I was in serious doubt about my health, for I knew that my physical condition was not imaginary. It actually was ten years before it was diagnosed as diabetes; in the interim I was ridered on insurance for all mental diseases. No joke—and it wasn't funny at the time. One company tried to jack up my premium to almost double in addition to the rider; now I once sold insurance, so I know that was blatantly unethical, if not illegal.

So we lost three babies, and each loss was associated with dramatic and generally negative changes in our married life. But after that Day in May we gradually reorganized. My wife went to work, so as to earn our living while I made a more serious effort to become a writer—by putting my full time into it, instead of writing on the side. In that year I succeeded; I sold my first two stories. I was on my way at last—but I never would have had the chance, had any of those first three babies lived. There was the monkey's paw. My wife had to be free to work, and our expenses had to be low; a child would have nullified that. I would never have sacrificed my babies, had I known, had I had any way to save them—yet their loss enabled me to achieve my ambition. Thus it was that I became a writer, by the devious and often unkind machination of Fate. Motive had at last been joined by opportunity. That sort of thing, too, is reflected in this novel.

So I had become a writer. Even then, the devious route had problems and surprises. I couldn't earn a living on stories; the word-rates were too low and editors too fickle. So I moved into novels, and it was a struggle, because short fiction was my natural length. It wasn't until I sold my fifth novel, *Macroscope*—actually the ninth I had written, and it had been rejected by five publishers, for book editors are fickle too—that I felt comfortable in that length. Then I liked it well, and I gave up on stories; today I have had more novels published than stories, which is unusual for a story writer.

But by then I had trouble in Parnassus: a publisher was taking in money for subsidiary rights but neither reporting them on the statements nor paying me my share. I protested in a private letter—and got summarily blacklisted. I protested privately to a writers' organization—which funneled my letter on to the publisher and advised me that I had acted rashly and might be guilty of libel.

There were other complications, but the upshot was that I got a lawyer, got most of my money, lost several publishers because of blacklisting, and departed in deep disgust from that writers' organization, which was evidently operating under false pretenses. I damn well did have the right of the case and detest such dishonesty. After that, times were lean for me, as a writer; my success fell behind that of others who had come into the picture when I did, and I piled up a total of eight unpublished novels even as my name was deleted from contention for awards. Parnassus is no kinder than the U.S. Army to those who stand on their rights, and Satan smiles.

But I had not lost all my publishers. I survived, though my income from writing was not great. My wife continued to work. Another writer showed me how to sell novels from summaries, rather than writing them complete; that meant that instead of selling part of what I wrote, I wrote only what sold. That one change in marketing caused my income to triple. Meanwhile editors were shifting about, publishers were buying each other out, and most of those who blacklisted me went elsewhere. Markets reopened. I can't say this was because the establishment had any change of heart; Parnassus, like dictators, doesn't admit error. Mainly it was that I never gave up and I now had an agent to help fight the war. It's harder for a publisher to blacklist an agent, because he represents a number of writers, some of whom are important enough to have clout. My leverage had improved.

Two of the editors I had worked with on stories moved into books: Lester and Judy-Lynn del Rey. They remained interested in my work. But there was a problem: I was writing my science fiction for Avon, who had always treated me well, and Avon had the option. That is, in the vernacular, they had first dibs on my next novel in the genre. So—I expanded into a "new" genre, one I had had little success with before: fantasy. It was a purely tactical move, to take advantage of

With a Tangled Skein

a new market. Avon was generous enough to agree to this, with the understanding that if Del Rey (technically that imprint didn't exist then, but let's not quibble) did not like my fantasy, Avon would have the next crack at it. But Lester did like it, and thus I came to write *A Spell for Chameleon*. It wasn't perfect, either in summary or in manuscript, but I had the fortune to encounter in Lester an editor who knew what he was doing. That, unfortunately, is rare in Parnassus. I revised the novel per his advice, and it was published.

I had the additional fortune to encounter in Judy-Lynn an executive who knew what *she* was doing; that, too, is rare, but it manifests in the type of presentation, promotion, and sales push novels get, and this can make an enormous difference. *Spell* took off like magic. It won the August Derleth Fantasy Award in England, where they evidently hadn't gotten word about my bad reputation. A leading American genre newspaper got sudden amnesia and failed to list the August Derleth awards that year, and of course *Spell* took no American awards. But it became one of my most commercial novels, and the Xanth series it commenced has about as many fans as any.

In this manner I discovered that I liked fantasy. Oh, I had always liked it as a reader; it just hadn't scored for me before as a writer. Now I found that it was easy and fun to write, and the readers liked it too. There was then developing a high tide in fantasy, fostered in significant part by Del Rey, and I just happened to get into it in time to surf my way to the top—through no initial effort of strategy or timing of my own. Chance put me into it—or, if you prefer, Fate. Once I was in, of course, I was quick enough to capitalize on my situation. Thus by this devious and seemingly coincidental route my serious career in fantasy proceeded. My income tripled again . . . and again. I now have a better career in fantasy than I had dreamed of as a writer; reality has surpassed imagination. One series led to another. And *that*, roughly, is how I came to write this present novel, *Skein*. It is not the path I would have chosen, but it got me here. For those who tell me they would like to be just like me and write fantasy the way I do, I pose this question: do you really? Then go fetch your monkey's paw.

Reality has a way of weaving itself into my fiction, whether I will or no. I had many notes for minor examples of this for this novel, but I fear they would become tedious in detail, so I'll go into detail on only one. There are several major themes that recur in my novels that critics seem to be unable to perceive, such as the value of integrity or my effort to merge the city (science fiction) with the country (fantasy). These themes have complex personal bases that I may unravel at another time; there is a good deal more on my mind than simple entertainment, though I do feel that clarity and entertainment are paramount in fiction. I normally write on more than one level. The top level is like the conscious mind, concerned with immediacies; the reader can buzz through and enjoy it without stretching his mind. The nether level gets into symbolism and feeling and meaning and theme; it puts on record my world view, for those who care to examine it. As far as I know, no critic has ever perceived this level in my fiction, but many of my readers seem to grasp it, and, of course, it is for them I write.

One of my major themes relates to music. I believe that man is most fundamentally distinguished from animal by his art, and an aspect of that art is music. I believe in the power of music, as I believe in the power of the word. At critical junctures in my novels you will find music, right back to the first one I had published, *Chthon*, which shows a quest for a broken song and the effort to make it whole again; and *Macroscope*, where music is the key to the mystery of the universe; and right on into my fantasy series, this one included. The heart of my feeling is in song. I try to name the particular song I have in mind, because I want the reader to hear the music too, and share my experience. You saw it in *Pale Horse* in the hymn scene, and the hint of it in *Hourglass* as Orlene commits suicide by her piano. (Did you note Orlene's honey-hair, the same as Niobe's? Do you really suppose that's coincidence?) You will see it in *Red Sword*, when a stutterer learns to sing, and emphatically in *Green Mother*, when Gaea sings with Satan—and falls in love.

And of course you see it here. The song that starts *Skein* is not identified in the text. It is *The Bonnie Boy*, and the recording I have of it is sung by the Irish lass Mary O'Hara. It tells the story as I have it in the first three chapters, the romance of a young woman and a bonnie boy, and its tragic end. Of course I have embellished it somewhat—but if you like my story, perhaps you will also like the song. I don't know whether that record can still be purchased. It is *Songs of Erin*, on the London label; I bought it in New York in 1959.

The Shepherd's Song, in various guises and titles, has its own story: "Come live with me and be my love . . ." In the course of Izaak Walton's *The Complete Angler* (sometimes rendered "Compleat"), which dates from 1653, there are two songs presented, and these are the two used here. Actually, the first one originated with Christopher Marlowe in the sixteenth century. As poems they may not seem like much, but with the music it is another matter. Seldom, I suspect, has a love song had a more enduring appeal—or a snappier rejoinder.

There is a more recent story on another song, *The Wetlands Waltz*. I have an interest in nature, especially the wilderness environment, as also shows throughout my work, and in this case it overlapped my interest in music. A couple of years ago one of my daughter

With a Tangled Skein

Penny's forest-camp counselors stopped by to say hello and meet Penny's horse, Blue, who also appears in various guises in my fantasy. The counselor's name was Jill Jarboe. This winter she sent Penny a cassette tape: *Songs from the Water World.*

It seems that Jill Jarboe had formed a group with four of the boys in the summer camp, called it The Ecotones, and produced this collection of ecologically oriented songs. It's an integrated group; Jill Jarboe is white, while Mike Carey, Mike Kinsey, Shaun Martinez, and Andrew Rock are black. (I support integration, as may also be evident in this novel.) This group is not a high-powered, big-promotion thing; it's just an attempt, I think, to popularize the worthy cause of ecological awareness. Penny more or less put the earphones on my head one morning as I was eating breakfast and reading the newspaper, and turned on the cassette recorder, and there it was. I was impressed; they were nice songs, not your Top-Forty-type popular stuff, but pleasant and quite to the point for those who value Nature as I do.

So I used one of those songs here in *Skein*, with permission, and anyone who is interested in obtaining the original cassette should write to Jill Jarboe at the address listed in the credit behind the title page of this novel. My reference to *The Wetlands Waltz* is actually anachronistic, as the song did not exist in 1915 where this novel places it—but of course Chronos could have heard it and carried it back. This is, after all, fantasy; we are not much concerned with anachronism.

Meanwhile, as I worked on the several stages of my writing, Fate stirred her fickle finger in the ongoing minor maelstrom of my daily existence in sundry ways. Life does, after all, go on, and mine is packed with tokens of my interests and orneriness. I bought another *Songs from the Water World* cassette and sent it to an environmental organization of which I am a life-member, suggesting that they might review it in their national publication for other members who liked a positive approach to ecological awareness. They never responded. I might as well have dropped the cassette into the Void. Then they sent me three separate form-solicitations for contributions. But I had seen how they answered *their* mail, and the Golden Rule came to my mind, and I did not respond.

I bought some of those sonic bug-repelling devices you see advertised all over, as I don't like hurting bugs if they aren't actually biting me, but don't like roaches in my food or fleas on my dogs—then had a months-long hassle to get a refund, finally involving a visit to a lawyer and a stiff note to the balky local Better Business council, because the devices simply didn't work as represented. I queried the "Troubleshooter" column of the newspaper: is there any objective evidence that any of these sonic devices work? So far, none has turned up.

Our Basenji dog, who we adopted eleven years ago after he was run over and the owner never came to claim him or pay the vet's bill for rebuilding the bone of his leg with wire, died of complications of age in the quarter-hour that I received the hardbacked poster for *Dragon on a Pedestal* used at the American Booksellers' Association convention in Dallas: an unfortunate juxtaposition. Now that poster graces the wall near the dread spot. That was not my favorite dog, but death disturbs me with an intensity that others do not seem to understand. I know that someday I will have to deal with the death of someone a lot more important to me than that dog, and I don't know how I'm going to make it.

I went out on my usual three-mile run, and returned to a different address; the Post Orifice had swallowed our science-fictiony "Star Route" and disgorged "Pineleaf Lane"—fortunately we had gotten to name our own street—sending us into a tailspin of address-change notifications, because our daily mail can amount to as much as ten pounds at a time. We received the notice in March 1984, advising us to notify all correspondents by the end of December 1983. The P.O. expects a lot of an anachronistic fantasy writer.

I got into second-draft typing of *Skein* and hit a record rate for me—65,000 words in five days, despite a cold snap into the thirties that forced me to bundle up as if in the arctic, and a jamming tab on my manual typewriter. Seems there are only about two writers in the genre who still use a manual machine, and I'm one of them—I think Harlan Ellison is the other—but they don't make manual Olympias anymore, and this one is ten years and ten million words old, so I may yet have to vault to the computer word-processing age, getting custom equipment so I can retain my special keyboard. You know, word-processing is hailed as a great boon to writers, but I do more actual writing in pencil and on the manual typewriter than anyone I know who is in word-processing; technology does not substitute for imagination and a Dvorak keyboard.

Anyway, after those five days I had to take three days off to catch up on forty more letters. Happened again next month in the final five days typing of the submission draft; in one day forty-seven items of mail arrived, ranging from packages of books to fan letters, including one from a hopeful writer asking whether I would read his 800-page novel and give advice how to get it published, one from a publisher asking for a favorable comment on its enclosed advance proof of a novel, and one from another publisher who sent complimentary copies of a novel I read and blurbed in December. It's a funny thing, seeing my name printed on the cover of someone else's novel; too bad they didn't bother to make the corrections of errors I called out.

I may have noted before the irony that when I had time to read everything in the genre, I lacked the money to buy the stuff; now that I can afford it, I lack the time even to keep up with what I am sent free. I suppose that's parallel to the cake problem I face as a diabetic. And a note from an eight-year-old girl: my youngest fan so far, the same age as Xanth. I answered that one immediately; after all, I was once that age myself. The other twenty-nine fan letters from that day I'll tackle right after I finish typing this Note and my summaries of the final two novels in this series.

I pinched the nerve in my back three times in succession, trying too hard on my exercises, and had to call a ten-day halt while the sciatica abated; now I am easing up on those exercises, and that's a significant private turning point. Every year at my birthday I note the levels I do, and at my forty-ninth birthday I broke all my birthday records, but at my fiftieth I'll break none. I'm two-thirds of the way through my life, and the tide has turned during this novel.

You know, *Skein* just might turn out to be my fiftieth book to see print. The writing of it was punctuated several times by calls from my agent, setting up the sale of eight of my back books in a package; those fans who bug me about where to find my out-of-print material may soon have an answer.

During that sciatica—that's a shooting pain in the leg where there is no injury; the pinch is actually in the spine, but the body thinks it's in the leg—I glanced at the published comment I had made a year before on Gordon Dickson's *Dorsai* series (actually it's the *Childe Cycle*, but I don't know any better), and saw my reference to "Eileen?" therein. Suddenly I had a pain in my mind to match that in my leg, for several days. In Dickson's novel *Soldier, Ask Not* we see the death of an innocent young man, drafted to fight a war he does not understand on a far planet. He revives from his lethal injury long enough to speak the name of his wife, Eileen, as if trusting her to come and make the hurt go away. That tore me up; I have a deep feeling for those who are taken far from what they have known and loved, and who plaintively wish for return that is impossible.

But on: we bought a videotape recorder, a great boon to my daughters, who have more time for TV than I do. Now they watch the weirdest stuff, some of it unsuitable for the fathers of teenaged girls. Sigh. We also got a cordless remote phone extension, so that I no longer have to dash from the study to the house just in time to catch the dial tone after the last ring; that does simplify my life. My daughter Penny finally got her driver's license; whew! One down, one to go. My other daughter Cheryl took second place in a verbal presentation of her paper on the conservation of soil and water. That was a fitting topic, during this novel; I had taken time to help drill her on it, and

Piers Anthony

suspect she really took first place but that the judges were closet sexists. Of course I may not be completely objective.

I saw a bright triangle of stars in the morning sky, so I ferreted it out in the star books and discovered it was the constellation Libra— the scales. Yes, I was writing the coin-weighing scene along about then. Libra is Penny's sign, because she reads a lot—you know, the Library. I finally got a line on a mysterious, lovely melody I'd heard in fragments for years; I think it is titled *Twin Sons of Different Mothers*. Reminds me of this novel again, with virtually twin girls, daughters of different mothers. I quest for melodies as I do for story notions; I am haunted by those that flash a few tantalizing notes and disappear, leaving me longing.

I also continued my quest for the Perfect Ping-Pong Paddle—and believe I have found it. It's made of graphite, very light and fast, and the backside has a "long pips" surface that sends the opponent's spin right back at him, messing him up instead of me. Lovely! I used it to defend the honor of Fantasy at my first SF convention, NECRONOMI-CON, in Tampa, in Oct-ogre 1983, the month that three of my novels were published. Of course I took my daughters with me; they loved it, and now they're con-crazy. One of my correspondents attended, and when she introduced herself I didn't make the connection. I wish I were better at spot memory of names!

Phone call from Bowker, publisher of *Fiction 1876–1983*, in response to my curt note about the way they listed some of my novels under Anthony and some under Piers, omitted my first *New York Times* bestseller *Ogre, Ogre*, and listed my mundane name nine times in succession. I had suggested that they hire a proofreader, since this volume costs $100 and is supposed to be comprehensive. They were apologetic, but noncommittal about the proofreader. Call from a Colorado fan who wished to visit me; he would be traveling with a school group of about twenty people and needed advice where they could stay cheaply. My wife phoned about and finally arranged free camping for them at a local park, and we went out to talk to the park people and clarify that we had the camping permit for them . . . and then the group changed its mind and went elsewhere. But the fan did come to visit me, and I chatted with him for a couple of hours. He wrote later that it was the high point of his life. He was generous; I'm a pretty ordinary character in person, really not worth that sort of effort.

My wife spied a sale on some nice enclosed bookshelves; now we are in the process of dismantling my rickety prior shelving and setting up the beautiful new ones. At last my file copies of my own books are getting proper treatment! I keep one file copy of every edition of every book I have published, hardcover, paperback, British, German,

French, Japanese and so on; at present that makes about 150 volumes, and it's growing.

In the spring came the mundane political primaries, and I had to watch the best man in the field, former Governor Reuben Askew of Florida, bite the dust in New Hampshire. Once again the political process wends its inevitable way to mediocrity. And I heard about a recent survey; 96 percent of Americans believe in God, 90 percent of those also believe in Heaven and Hell (it's hypocritical to believe in one without the other); only 4 percent expect to go to Hell. Oh, yeah? Well, I have news for someone. . . .

Thus my mundane life, proceeding in its petty pace from day to day. You can see that when the fantastic is removed from my life, not much of interest remains. If you fell asleep during the last paragraph, I understand. Now it is time to separate from this novel, too, and I do it with a certain muddled mixture of emotions. In one sense I am satisfied, for I believe *Skein* to be a decent novel. I feel nostalgia for the experience of it that is now passing behind me. I am concerned as I anticipate its coming course through the gauntlet of the publication process and the cynosure of the great readership beyond. I feel advance resentment for the scoffing some reviewers will do about its merits and demerits and the inevitable sneer at this Note. A recent survey shows that the more ignorant a reviewer is, the more critical he is; any professional writer could have told you that twenty years ago. In fact Alexander Pope told us two and a half centuries ago:

'Tis hard to say if greater want of skill
Appear in writing or in judging ill

But he had the answer:

Let such teach others who themselves excel,
And censure freely, who have written well.

I am also apprehensive about the flood of mail this Note may generate when the novel sees paperback publication. Oh, yes, I get mail on my Notes; sometimes the reader doesn't bother with the novel at all, just the Note. I had one letter from a person who fished my novel out of a trashcan, read only the Note, wrote me a fan letter, and (I suspect) threw the book back in the can. But he really liked the Note. Well, I daresay he got his money's worth.

I do try to keep up with my mail, but after doing 702 letters last year—yes, I remain a compulsive counter—I see the handwriting in the figurative bruises my head makes against the wall, and suspect that my performance in this respect will turn the tide and begin to

Piers Anthony

ebb, as with my exercises. They aren't all simple notes, either; I have to try to make meaningful responses to those who wish to become instant successful writers—if I had known how to do that, I could have saved myself eight years!—or who ply me with complex lists of questions for their research papers, or try to convert me to Jesus (I came to know Jesus when I put him in *Tarot* as a character, but I don't think that's what they mean), or who are contemplating suicide. This is no joke; there are some very real problems out there, and I do not feel competent to address them—yet I have to try, because these folk really do want my input, such as it is. I remind myself that it is much better to be relating to my readers than to be emotionally alone.

If Fate is the plot of life, then feeling must be its content. To be known, to be needed, to be loved—this may be the true problem of our society. We see people turning to alcohol, to mind- and mood-affecting drugs, to gambling, to casual sex both hetero and homo, to violence, to cults, to self-destructive behavior, when these may be but poor sublimations for the recognition, interaction, security and love they truly crave. Isn't it an awful irony that some of us must even turn to fantasy to glean some semblance of the companionship we are denied in mundane existence, and we cannot even cry "Eileen"! We suffer all manner of compulsive behavior, in futile reaction to fundamental inadequacies of emotion we do not comprehend.

As I worked on *Skein*, a woman was gang-raped on a barroom pool table; when the rapists were tried and convicted, women of that community demonstrated in favor of the rapists. Loveless sex pervades the media. Preschool children are sexually molested by the staff of the nursery—and this is said to be only a hint of the abuse and incest that is not rare but is typical today. Satan's mischief, surely.

Yet there is also joy in the world. Some find their solace in religion, in the belief that God loves them. Some find it in close family ties. I myself have gained some share of the Heaven of a close family life, after emerging from the Hell of the denial of it, but I remain scarred. I don't like to travel, for as a child I found that my travels had no returning. I don't like to leave my family, because I remember how fragile family existence can be. Some regard me as overprotective as a father, but I resolved at the outset that my children would never be exposed to what I was and, after losing three, I know that no life is guaranteed.

I turn down most invitations to be Guest of Honor at conventions, not from any dislike of people or any fear of public appearances—stage fright, like writer's block, I conquered long ago, and I am quite at ease among fans—but simply because there is nowhere I'd rather be than home. I trust that after reading this Note, those who have

With a Tangled Skein

been disappointed by my relative isolation from the public will understand that there is nothing frivolous in this. It is one of the ways I have come to terms with the problem of my own existence. I hope that what I write helps others come to terms with theirs.

ABOUT THE AUTHOR

Piers Anthony was born in August 1934, in England, spent a year in Spain, and came to America at age six. He was naturalized American while serving in the U.S. Army in 1958. He lives with his wife Carol and their daughters Penny and Cheryl in Florida. His first story was published in 1963, and his first novel, *Chthon*, in 1967. Through 1984 he has had forty-eight books published, with translations in eight languages. His first Xanth novel, *A Spell for Chameleon*, won the August Derleth Fantasy Award as the best novel for 1977. The fifth novel in that series placed on *The New York Times* bestseller list, and his five following fantasies did likewise. He is currently writing three novels a year, and answering several hundred fan letters a year. His house is hidden deep in the forest, almost impossible to find, and he does his typing in a horse pasture.